SHE
FELL
AWAY

AS LENORA BELL

How the Duke Was Won
If I Only Had a Duke
Blame It on the Duke
What a Difference a Duke Makes
For the Duke's Eyes Only
One Fine Duke
Love Is a Rogue
The Devil's Own Duke
Duke Most Wicked
You're the Duke That I Want
Can't Get Enough of the Duke

SHE FELL AWAY

A NOVEL

LENORE NASH

EMILY BESTLER BOOKS

ATRIA

New York   Amsterdam/Antwerp   London
Toronto   Sydney/Melbourne   New Delhi

ATRIA

An Imprint of Simon & Schuster, LLC
1230 Avenue of the Americas
New York, NY 10020

For more than 100 years, Simon & Schuster has championed authors and the stories they create. By respecting the copyright of an author's intellectual property, you enable Simon & Schuster and the author to continue publishing exceptional books for years to come. We thank you for supporting the author's copyright by purchasing an authorized edition of this book.

No amount of this book may be reproduced or stored in any format, nor may it be uploaded to any website, database, language-learning model, or other repository, retrieval, or artificial intelligence system without express permission. All rights reserved. Inquiries may be directed to Simon & Schuster, 1230 Avenue of the Americas, New York, NY 10020 or permissions@simonandschuster.com.

This book is a work of fiction. Any references to historical events, real people, or real places are used fictitiously. Other names, characters, places, and events are products of the author's imagination, and any resemblance to actual events or places or persons, living or dead, is entirely coincidental.

Copyright © 2026 by Lenore Nash

All rights reserved, including the right to reproduce this book or portions thereof in any form whatsoever. For information, address Atria Books Subsidiary Rights Department, 1230 Avenue of the Americas, New York, NY 10020.

First Emily Bestler Books/Atria Books hardcover edition March 2026

EMILY BESTLER BOOKS/ATRIA BOOKS and colophon are registered trademarks of Simon & Schuster, LLC

Simon & Schuster strongly believes in freedom of expression and stands against censorship in all its forms. For more information, visit BooksBelong.com.

For information about special discounts for bulk purchases, please contact Simon & Schuster Special Sales at 1-866-506-1949 or business@simonandschuster.com.

The Simon & Schuster Speakers Bureau can bring authors to your live event. For more information or to book an event, contact the Simon & Schuster Speakers Bureau at 1-866-248-3049 or visit our website at www.simonspeakers.com.

Interior design by Davina Mock-Maniscalco

Manufactured in the United States of America

1 3 5 7 9 10 8 6 4 2

Library of Congress Control Number: 2025949203

ISBN 978-1-6680-9837-0
ISBN 978-1-6680-9838-7 (ebook)

Let's stay in touch! Scan here to get book recommendations, exclusive offers, and more delivered to your inbox.

In memory of my Grandma Florence,
who caught a 130-pound halibut in a small wooden boat
by herself, then decided to stay in Alaska forever.

SHE
FELL
AWAY

PROLOGUE

Her wrists are tied behind her back with something thin and unyielding that bites into her flesh. She twists and wriggles but there's no give, only pain. Her arms are numb, her mind clumsy. Legs made of clay. Weak from hunger.

She tries calling for help but her voice is a thin croak, her throat raw, salt crust of blood on her lips. The floor beneath her is cold and damp. A garbage disposal grinds broken glass inside her chest.

A dark shape slumps in the shadows. Broken neck hanging at a tortured angle. Body split open. Her guitar. Stripped of its strings. They're tied around her wrists.

It's a message. She can be broken. She can be silenced.

Panic rises. She sees stars. The Milky Way smeared across the inside of her eyelids.

Even now, with every breath a fresh stab wound, lyrics glow in her mind. A song begging to be born. Key of D minor. The saddest key.

Star light. Star bright. Last star I see tonight.

The stars weren't nearly as beautiful in Vegas.

Elvis impersonator crooning in her ear. *You're down at the end of lonely street.*

This can't be the end.

She used to crave darkness when it was a mood to wrap herself in, dense and familiar. Now all she wants is to live, to feel the sun on her face again. She wants light like honey drizzled on a blueberry sea. Laughter tossed into the wind like a gull's cry.

A shimmering ringtone, somewhere far away. It drifts into silence.

She's drifting, too.

The room spins. The world fades away.

1
LAKE

Dead bodies in lonely rooms are the worst part of my job.
This one's splayed on the beige bathroom tiles, limbs frozen in a sprinting position, as if he tried to outrun death. He has the soulless features of an Oscar statue—pronounced brow, straight nose, blunt jaw, linebacker shoulders.

Bloody fingerprints stain the front of his white performance hoodie. Designer Swiss watch. Flashy sneakers. He looks like he lives in a lakefront mansion with a double-wide boathouse.

A snail trail of vomit the mottled color of bruised bananas winds from his open mouth along the tiles, up the side of the toilet, and into the bowl.

A tall police officer in the Wellington uniform of dark blue vest over a light blue polo shirt approaches me as I stand just outside the door of the bathroom. "You must be Lake Harlowe?"

I nod. "I'm the American Citizen Services officer."

"Sergeant Mason Yates. Have you had any luck locating the deceased's next of kin?"

"Not yet. I've left several messages." I'd done a quick Lexis-Nexis search on my cell phone after I received the death notification call from the New Zealand police, but the contact number listed rang through to voicemail.

"Sad business. Such a young lad. The Airbnb has an optional daily cleaning service, and the housekeeper discovered him. Do we have a cause of death yet?" he asks Dr. Charlotte Grayson, the soft-spoken forensic medical examiner. She's bending over the body, not much of her visible beneath a white protective suit, coverall with hood, face mask, and safety glasses.

"Pulmonary aspiration, inhalation of vomit into the lungs causing asphyxiation. Could have been caused by mixing pills and alcohol. He has a prescription for hydrocodone—the pills are on the shelf there." She clicks her tongue. "Americans and their painkillers." She glances at me. "No offense, Ms. Harlowe."

"None taken. Why is there blood on his shirt?"

Dr. Grayson nods at a razor sitting on the edge of the sink. "He might have decided to shave while intoxicated. There are nicks on his jawline here"—she points—"and blood on his fingertips. We won't know for certain until after the postmortem."

The three of us share a disturbing secret. We know what this person looks like freshly dead. He's not a person anymore—he's a specimen to be examined, a case to solve, paperwork to file.

I reverse the footage of his last moments in my mind. Vomit flows backward from the toilet into his throat, down his esophagus, and back into his roiling stomach. He takes a gasping breath. Sits up. Walks backward to whatever Wellington harbor tourist bar he was drinking at last night. He orders one less Jägerbomb. Never knows how close he came to this.

We roll out of bed in the morning and move through our day making choices as if we're in control. We notice the invisible spider's web connecting survival and tragedy only after it's too late, after beads of blood paint the threads crimson.

I've witnessed death too often to walk through life easily. I've had to be wary. To tread softly, keep my eyes open. If I sinned, I was punished.

When I was a child, I imagined that hell was a root cellar lined with jars containing all my sins. Rows and rows of pickled sins. Falsehoods. Rebelliousness. Envy. Preserved in vinegar, coated with dust and mouse droppings. In hell I only had my sins to eat. Every bite corrosive.

"You all right, love?" Sergeant Yates asks, turning to look at me.

It throws me for a moment, this casual endearment, though it's normal. Even the grocery store clerks call me lovely, or love.

"I'm fine."

"Not your first death case, I hope?"

"No." I've seen death before. I close my eyes and corpses wash across the darkness like nightmare northern lights.

Blood soaks the sweat-stained shirt of an expat sex offender in a shoddy hotel room in Phnom Penh. A young flight attendant in Lisbon wears a necklace of purple and yellow bruises, her wrists tied to the bedposts.

The reel spins faster, back to Alaska. A hazy memory—ink dropped into water, a cloud spreading through my mind. Smell of chanterelle mushrooms, of moss, a wet growing odor that feeds on decay. Gnarled tree roots. No, not tree roots . . . fingers, cramped into a claw, nails black and rotting. Holes where eyes should be.

Don't think—breathe. That was a mistake. The room is saturated with the scent of bile and booze. My stomach heaves.

"Steady on." Sergeant Yates crosses the room in two long strides and takes hold of my arm. "You need some air."

My face heats up, and I'm sure my cheeks are as red as my lipstick. I'm not some easily spooked newbie. He tightens his grip when I attempt to pull away, leading me into the large bedroom with floor-to-ceiling windows and an expansive view of Wellington harbor.

He's around six feet three, thickly muscled, with a rugby player neck. His nose is barroom-brawl crooked, and his knuckles show faint bruising. He's rough enough to give me splinters. The intensity in his brown eyes is as bone-crushing as his grip.

There's the urge to lean against the solid wall of his chest, to catch my breath, but I stiffen and put distance between us instead.

I know danger when I see it.

"I'm fine, really."

"You almost fainted back there."

"Low blood sugar. Where's the passport?"

"On top of the valise there."

"Do you know why he was in Wellington?"

"Not a clue. We can't find his mobile phone."

October is spring in New Zealand. The weather is still chilly, but the kōwhai trees are blooming, their vibrant golden blooms attracting tūī and bellbird.

I open the passport. I already know his name: Bruce Bartholomew Walter II. Twenty-one years old. Born in Las Vegas. His passport photo is better than most. He has a confident, almost aggressive stare. He traveled light. One silver hard-sided carry-on spinner. The police have been through it, but his clothes are still folded. Everything is designer. The Cartier sunglasses alone probably cost more than I make in a paycheck.

It always feels wrong sifting through a stranger's luggage while they lie dead nearby. The secrets I've found have sometimes been difficult to forget. There's nothing out of the ordinary here, though: clothes, noise-canceling headphones, high-end deodorant, swim trunks with a shark print.

"There's nothing here to indicate why he's in Wellington," I agree. "But he's no ordinary tourist. Did you do a search on him?"

"He's an American football player, right?"

"A quarterback. I did some research. He was selected tenth overall in the draft this year by the Jacksonville Jaguars, but he tore the meniscus in his left knee during a preseason game. He was going to miss his entire rookie season. Now he'll never have a career. He's the son of Glen Walter, son of Bruce Walter the first. They're a famous American football dynasty. The grandfather opened The Trophy sports-themed casino in Las Vegas in the 1970s. They're seriously wealthy. This is going to be big—it'll make national news in the States."

"Damn," he mumbles under his breath. "Just what I need. A rabid pack of American reporters in Wellington. I've had a run-in or two with your journalists. Inventive bunch. They don't let the truth get in the way of a sensational story."

"The Public Affairs section at the embassy will help you. They'll want to know about this ASAP. I'd better contact his parents soon because it will be difficult to keep a lid on this."

Making death notifications is the second worst part of my job.

"What's happened to the other ACS officer—Jordan Singer?" Mason asks. "Thought he had a year left in Welly."

"He curtailed abruptly and unexpectedly." My colleague, Sara, told me that Jordan supposedly curtailed for family reasons, but she thinks he might have had a falling out with U.S. Ambassador Lyndon Hunt, a Texas billionaire political appointee who wears cowboy boots to work and hangs antique pistols over his desk. Whatever the reason, the position was an urgent vacancy, so I applied to leave my grueling job in Phnom Penh early and fill the position on a temporary basis.

"Did you work with Jordan often?"

"We covered a domestic violence case involving an American citizen. Surprised to hear he left. He was keen on dirt biking and was always going on about how epic the trails were here. How are you finding our Aotearoa so far?"

"It's incredibly beautiful here."

My plane landed in Wellington next to a crescent of yellow sand hugging turbulent blue water. I walked through the small airport, between red carved pillars with iridescent abalone shell eyes, and under a giant sculpture of Gandalf riding an eagle. Outside the air was crystalline with a salt tang, so pure it tasted as though they should be charging Swiss Alps bottled water prices to breathe it.

It was as though the sea and the jagged rocks, the dense green beyond the shore, had accidentally grown an airport that could be reclaimed at any time, returned to wilderness. I'd had the thought that here was a country that could steal my heart and never let it go.

"Done much exploring yet? Made it to the South Island?"

"Not yet. I've only been here a few weeks. I hear Milford Sound will remind me of the fjords in Alaska."

"You're from Alaska?" His gaze roams my body. "You don't look like you'd last long on those reality TV shows."

He's judging my petite stature, my nipped-waist vintage tweed blazer and matte-red lips. He thinks I look like a hothouse flower, a woman who requires silk scarves and rose petal moisturizer to survive. He doesn't know my past. The rough spun wool. Homegrown vegetables for breakfast, lunch, dinner. Hauling firewood until my back ached.

I judge him right back. He's a medieval fortress. Built to withstand battles. Massive arms folded and lips quirked dismissively. He looks like the quintessential tough guy. But I could be wrong. Maybe he cries during animal shelter commercials. Maybe he memorizes Emily Dickinson poetry.

He doesn't know me. I throw my shoulders back. "Looks can be deceiving. I've made my own crossbow and shot a moose with it. Field dressed it with my own hunting knife, too." Why would I tell him that? He's put me on the defensive. I need to prove myself.

His lip quirks higher. "Did you now? I'd pay good money to see that. I'm imagining you wielding a big sharp knife. Maybe we'll go hunting for wild boar sometime. I'll take you for protection."

The glint in his eyes says he's laughing at me.

"I don't hunt anymore." Although I do still carry my hunting knife. It's a reminder of my past. I left Alaska when I was eighteen, and I've never been back.

Alaska is the hoarse voice of a raven, a frozen crust of snow crunching under my boots, the sweet-tart scent of boiling strawberry-rhubarb jam, snowy mountain ranges bathed in rosy alpenglow.

Alaska is darkness. Fear. Rules that had to be followed. Lies that had to be told.

"So where were you posted before this?" he asks.

"Phnom Penh."

He smirks. "Now that must have been a rough tour. I'd imagine Americans get up to all sorts of mischief in Cambodia, eh?"

"Regrettably. I was hoping this would be a quieter tour. At least this isn't a crime scene?"

"No signs of foul play."

"I should be getting back to the embassy. When you're finished with the luggage I'll take it for his family."

He pulls a card out of his vest pocket. "We'll try to keep it quiet for now, keep it out of the press until you notify the parents and we know more details. Call me if your team has any questions."

"I will. Nice to meet you, Sergeant Yates."

"Wish it had been better circumstances. And call me Mason? We don't take ourselves too seriously around here, if you haven't noticed."

"Thanks, Mason. And I'm Lake."

"My pleasure, Lake."

I'm halfway out the door when I overhear Dr. Grayson teasing him.

"*Call me Mason. My pleasure, Lake.* Fancy her, do we?"

"I like gingers. And I didn't see a wedding band."

Interesting. Not that I'll do anything about it. He's attractive, but I'm not in the market for a lover. It's only been six months since Lucas cheated and tried to blame me for being emotionally unavailable. *You're a closed book. You never let me in. I don't think you're capable of love.*

The accusatory refrain rings through my mind as I walk up the steep hill to the embassy. My shoulders hunch against a rising wind. They don't call it Windy Welly for nothing. This gale holds a grudge. It scours my cheeks, stings my eyes, deliberately messes my hair like a schoolyard bully.

I wish it could scrub my mind clean of the last hour. I can't stop seeing Bruce being zipped into a body bag, darkness closing over him forever.

And now it's time to call his family and ruin their lives.

2
LAKE

Wellington feels like a small town after Phnom Penh. No one's in much of a hurry. Even the business district is sleepy, not too posh. For the most part, women wear sensible shoes: Allbirds trainers, Birkenstocks, or Docs for the teenagers.

There must be an ordinance against skyscrapers, a policy staving off urban density. There's no litter, very few billboards, and only a brief afterthought of neon. Children walk themselves home from school.

I stop to watch a sleek blue and bronze feathered tūī fly overhead, the white feathers at its throat ruffled by the wind. There's not enough traffic noise to drown out the chorus of birdsong.

The U.S. Embassy is the only building in the charming, historic neighborhood of Thorndon that is surrounded by high metal and concrete walls topped by barbed wire. Seems like overkill in New Zealand, but the department follows the same security protocols whether we're in Moscow or Montreal.

The Marine at Post One could still be in high school. He has close-cropped blond hair and acne across his forehead. He unlocks the door for me. It's so heavy I'm forced to use both hands to pull it open.

The spiked gates, the metal detectors, the Marine with his

rifle—it's all to keep me safe in the unlikely event of an attack, but sometimes it feels claustrophobic, like a prison to keep me inside, instead of to keep others out.

Everything looks slightly off today. A crumpled tissue on the gray carpet. A fluorescent light flickering and buzzing overhead. I'm in a sci-fi movie and I've entered another multiverse without realizing it. Brushing up against death will do that, push you off your axis, make familiar sights look sinister, leave a taste in your mouth like burning plastic.

A colleague avoids my eyes in the elevator. I imagine that death hangs over my head, a cartoon thundercloud, and no one else wants to get rained on.

I send a brief report about the case to Washington and make notes in ACS-Plus, the antiquated database used to store information on Amcit special citizen services cases. It's one p.m. in Wellington and six p.m. in Las Vegas. I open a notebook and line up a pen, and Bruce Walter's passport, beside it. I close my office door, take a few deep breaths before calling the contact number for his mother again.

It rings to voicemail. The embassy number usually shows up as spam. I'll have to call back until his mother realizes this could be an urgent call. I call again. And again.

This conversation will remain carved in Nadia Walter's memory forever. What I say and how I say it. Every word, every nuance. I'll be a recording she plays again and again, desperately searching for a different outcome.

She answers on the fourth call. "Hello? Who is this?"

"Hello, is this Nadia Walter?"

"Yes, who's this?" She speaks with a slight accent. I know from my research that she's an ex-Vegas showgirl from Slovenia.

"My name is Lake Harlowe. I'm a consular officer with the U.S. Embassy in Wellington, New Zealand. Are you driving right now?"

"No. I'm at home."

"Are you alone?"

"My husband is here with me. What's this about?"

"I have some very bad news to tell you. You may want to take a seat."

I hear what sounds like the scrape of a chair across a floor. "Who is it?" a gruff voice asks in the background.

"It's the U.S. Embassy in Wellington. You take it. I can't." Her voice falters. She already senses the landslide that's about to reduce her life to rubble.

"Who is this?" Glen Walter asks in clipped, combative tones.

"My name is Lake Harlowe, Mr. Walter. I'm a consular officer at the U.S. Embassy in Wellington, New Zealand," I repeat. "I have some very bad news to tell you." I wait a beat, giving him a moment to prepare for the shock. "I'm very sorry to tell you that your son, Bruce, died this morning in his Airbnb in Wellington." I wait. There's no response. "Mr. Walter?"

People have unpredictable reactions to tragic news. He may have hung up on me. One parent threw their phone into the toilet. I'd heard the whooshing sound of water and then silence.

"Bullshit!" I hold my phone away from my ear. "Bruce is in Jacksonville."

"I'm truly sorry, Mr. Walter, but that's not true. Your son is here in New Zealand. And he is deceased."

I hear harsh breathing. He speaks, low and lethal, "What do you want, money? How much?"

"Mr. Walter, I don't want money. I'm calling from the embassy. I identified your son this morning at the—"

"No you fucking didn't. This is a sick prank. How did you get my wife's number? You're going to burn in hell, you piece-of-shit scammer."

He thinks that if he yells loud enough, bullies me into submission, I'll back down and admit defeat, tell him it's a prank.

"I'm going to trace this call. You're going to wish you'd never been born. You—"

"Mr. Walter," I break in, raising my voice to be heard. "This isn't a prank call or a scam. If you would prefer to have a video call I can arrange that. I'll show you my government I.D. and Bruce's passport. I have it right here."

"You're lying. My son isn't dead. What do you want from us? Tell me what you want, damn it!"

His fury hits me in waves of nausea, breaking hot, then cold, cramping my stomach. His voice like the one from my childhood.

Jezebel. Wicked sinner. You've fallen away from the path of righteousness.

Two angry men shouting at me. One from my past, one in this moment, thundering in my ears, making my heart pound and my throat close. I drill the sharp point of the pen into my notebook hard enough to rip the page.

"Glen," I hear his wife pleading in the background. "Glen, stop yelling at the poor woman. Give me my phone."

A moment of silence and then a soft, trembling voice. "I'm sorry, what did you say your name was?"

"Lake Harlowe. I'm an American Citizen Services officer. Your son was found this morning by a housekeeper. He'd been drinking. He choked on vomit. He was alone."

"No," she says vehemently. "That's not right, Lake. It must be someone else. Bruce isn't in New Zealand. How could he be there? He only had surgery a few months ago. He's still in rehab. He attends every football practice and game, even if he can't play." She laughs softly, nervously. "You've got the wrong person."

She's still clinging to hope. He's still alive in her mind. She didn't see what I saw on the bathroom floor. Those sightless eyes. The gaping mouth crusted with vomit.

"I'm so very sorry. It was Bruce, Mrs. Walter. I looked through his luggage and checked his passport. He has a tattoo in Roman numerals of the year his grandfather won MVP on the inside of his left wrist. He was wearing a Rolex Day-Date watch with diamond hour markers."

"No." A strangled moan. "No. It can't be true."

"I'm so sorry." Those words painfully inadequate. I want to

soften the blow somehow, but there's nothing I can do. I can't take away her agony or shoulder her burden. My gut clenches, and I feel nauseated again.

There's a seasickness in these turbulent, irreversible moments that change the course of lives. Nadia Walter is reeling, capsized. The wave of shock will be replaced by grief soon, heavy and earthen, like clay soil tossed over a grave.

She begins to sob. Her next words are barely audible. "My Bruce. My beautiful boy. He's gone."

"Bullshit!" Glen yells in the background. "Fucking bullshit."

"She saw his tattoo. She has his passport. His Rolex."

"She could have seen those online. Or stolen them!"

"Mrs. Walter? I'm going to send you my official report. There will be details of the next steps. I'll be your liaison if you come to Wellington. Or I can make the arrangements for repatriation on your behalf. Please give me the best email to use."

There's the sound of a scuffle, and suddenly Glen's furious voice pierces my ear. "She's not telling you anything, you fucking bitch. Who put you up to this? I'm going to track you down. You're going to be sorry you messed with me."

Said as though there's a long list of people who might want to mess with him.

"I'll send my report to your wife."

"Fuck you!" There's a loud bang and the line goes dead.

I lean my head on my desk for a moment, shaking and drained.

There's a knock on my office door. Robin Garcia, the Information Management officer, pokes her head through my door. "Hey, Lake."

"Hey, Robin."

She walks into my office. "Are you okay?"

"Just had to make a death notification. He was only twenty-one. The mother was sobbing and the father called me a fucking bitch."

"Shoot. That sounds ugly."

"It was."

She perches on the edge of my desk, concern filling her brown eyes. "Want to talk about it?"

"I'm okay. But it never gets easier making these calls." Consular officers don't usually have a background in social work or counseling. I always try to be as sympathetic as possible, but Glen Walter's angry reaction was a first for me. "It's hard not to take things personally. I don't want to be the bearer of such bad news."

"Sounds like you need a drink and some company. Close up shop and come for cocktails with me and Ashley. It's Friday. Live a little."

Ashley is Robin's Kiwi girlfriend. They seem really happy together, always calling each other babe and sweetie and taking romantic weekend trips.

"Thanks, but I have a backlog of cases to close out and report since the last ACS officer left so suddenly."

"Yeah, that was weird. Jordan didn't even tell any of us he was leaving. He was just gone from one day to the next. It sucks that he left you a backlog."

I shrug. "ACS never sleeps. I have the duty phone this weekend. And here I thought Wellington would be peaceful after Phnom Penh."

"Seems pretty darn peaceful to me, being from New York City. If you change your mind, we'll be at Wayfarer drinking some of that tasty Kiwi microbrew."

"Tell Ashley next happy hour drinks are on me."

Robin grins at me, eyes twinkling. "Our next happy hour will be an overnight trip to Martinborough. There's this amazing winery called Devotus that only grows old varietals of pinot noir. It's crazy good. It sells out super fast but we reserved some bottles. Guess one of them will be on you!"

"It sounds like a lot of fun."

"You should come with us. Experience more of this amazing country," she says on her way out.

It's refreshing to see a powerful woman running the IT department at an embassy, a job usually occupied by men. If I was going to confide in anyone at work, it would be Robin. But confiding isn't in my nature. I learned very early to sweep the darkness under the rug, jam all the bad things into the back of my mind.

Open the door even a crack, and all the secrets might come tumbling out.

Embassies are like tiny rural towns. Everyone knows everyone, and the gossip flies thick and fast. The instructors at orientation in D.C. are always talking about your corridor reputation—how it starts on day one and sticks to you like flypaper. Are you difficult to work with? A team player? Do you have leadership potential? Are you resilient enough?

They love the word *resilience*. Can you bounce back after an embassy bombing? Maintain calm after months of protests outside the gate?

Some Foreign Service employees create their own little America at every post. They host potlucks and chili cook-offs and organize group activities with the Community Liaison officer.

They get drunk and tell stories about their tangential brushes with history—the one degree of separation from important people and important events: *I was the control officer when X visited for the peace summit. I wrote the cable summarizing the coup.*

Many of my colleagues are ambitious. They want to rise to the top. Political officers are the ones who have the best shot of becoming ambassadors. They foster connections with people in high places and play the promotion game.

I'm surviving. I'm a green screen. Cities, countries, lovers, friends flicker across me, but I remain the same. I can't put down roots, or get too close to anyone, because underneath, in the deep, is where the memories with claws live.

3
LAKE

My cat, Edgar, greets me at the door of my apartment with an indignant yowl that says it's well past feeding time.

He's always miffed about something. He still hasn't forgiven me for being quarantined upon arrival. They sent me photos of him in his cage, his black fur matted into disgruntled tufts. New Zealand is serious about keeping rabies out of their small island nation.

He camps out next to his food dish and fixes me with an impatient glare. In his mind my only reason for existing is to feed him.

"Your mom had to work late," I tell him. "I have to make money to keep you in crunchies and catnip." I swear he knows how to roll his eyes. "Don't give me that. I rescued your flea-bitten ass, remember?"

He was so tiny. A puff of black fur and big yellow eyes. Starving, injured, and covered in fleas on the side of the road in Phnom Penh. His left back leg had to be amputated. I nursed him back to health with milk from an eyedropper and named him Edgar Allan Three Paws. I was going to find a home for him, but he dug his little claws into my heart. He has a dark turn of mind. He's always startling, his ears twitching, listening for some distant threat. He's a lost soul. Prickly and mistrustful. We understand each other.

In Phnom Penh he had a three-bedroom town house and a walled patio to patrol, where he sometimes caught and tortured grasshoppers. Now all he has is this small, boxy apartment. I imagine that when he's not sleeping, he's hatching elaborate plots to escape and hunt down more hoppy, wriggly things to kill.

"Oh, all right." I give him a heaping portion of food.

"Mommy's turn." I fill my wineglass to the brim with pinot noir and collapse on the couch.

You fucking bitch. I'm going to track you down.

I gulp half the glass, trying to drown out Glen Walter's voice, but the ugly words keep echoing. I walk to the window and open the curtains. Wellington is quiet, even on a Friday night. My apartment is on the top floor of a modern building near the waterfront in the central business district. It has the white walls and clean lines of most government housing, with the same boxy, menacing Drexel Heritage furniture the department ships around the world.

The only decorations I brought are books and maps from the countries where I've served. I have new maps of New Zealand and Wellington, with pins marking the places I want to visit. I don't know how long I'll be here on temporary duty, so my household goods are in storage for now.

I never stay in one place for too long. It's a roulette wheel: Where will I bounce and land next? I've served in Shanghai, Lisbon, Phnom Penh, and now Wellington.

It sounds like a glamorous career to my friends back in the U.S., but I'm not hosting galas or brokering peace treaties. I'm the one you call when you're traveling and things go sideways. Go missing. Turn deadly. Your passport is stolen. You drive on the wrong side of the road and hit someone.

A stag night becomes a nightmare when the groom's brother gets a little too drunk and decides to go swimming in a riptide. Or a hiking trip ends at the bottom of a ravine.

I'm the one you'll talk to if your loved one books a tour to visit a volcano, and it suddenly decides to belch an active lava flow. Or I visit you in a foreign prison if you get caught for drug smuggling.

When you call, panic stretches your voice taut as a sheep-gut guitar string. Sometimes you're sobbing. You want me to fix everything, put your life back the way it was, but I'm only a resource, a guide. I have a script to follow. What I do is triage, with no long-term involvement.

My job is measured in passports, visas, birth certificates, death certificates, body bags. The repatriation of remains.

I still wonder sometimes how I made it into the Foreign Service. My security clearance investigator looked like he was an actor playing an FBI agent. Hulking frame encased in a black trench coat that looked like it was grafted to his skin. He interviewed my friends and neighbors in Portland, Oregon, where I moved after attending Evergreen State College in Washington State.

My friend Amber told me she leaned closer to him. "You want to know Lake's deep, dark secret?"

The investigator nodded, betraying no emotion behind those mirrored sunglasses.

"She buys way too many vintage handbags," Amber whispered.

It's good to have friends you can count on. But even my best friends don't know my worst secrets.

I was sweating as he interviewed me. A standard questionnaire about finances, drug use, potential links to terrorists or anyone else who could blackmail me to obtain state secrets. His gaze flicked over my overstuffed bookshelves and then he focused on me, taking in my demure cream-colored turtleneck, pleated skirt, and ballet flats.

He nodded, a clipped movement. "You're a good girl, aren't you, Lake?"

And I answered, "Yes, sir, that's right, sir."

And that was that. I widened my eyes, confirmed that I was a good girl, and my murky past disappeared. I was issued a clean slate:

> *This message is to notify you that you have been successfully granted access to classified information up to and including the TOP SECRET level based upon a Single Scope Background Investigation.*

They didn't dig too deeply into my childhood. They interviewed my mom, but only briefly. She's good at lying. We both are. We had to lie, to tell them what they wanted to hear.

If they'd dug deeper, I wouldn't be here today. I have to be careful what I say. I can't trust anyone. Or let anyone get too close to me.

I'm pouring another glass of wine when my personal cell rings. Think of my mom and she calls. We haven't spoken in months, not since I told her I wasn't coming home for my brother's wedding next year.

"Hi, Ruth."

"Lake. Have you changed your mind yet?"

"I want to come to the wedding but I'm only here on temporary duty and I'm not sure where I'll go next, so—"

"You only have one little brother." Her voice rises, fills with helium-frustration. "You can't miss his wedding."

"I told him it might be bad timing for me."

"This isn't about you, Lake. It's about Heron. You haven't been back to Alaska in far too long."

"You know why."

"It's been so many years. It's safe for you to come back. It's all forgotten."

My mother might be able to pretend Alaska is safe and our past is buried and forgotten, but I can't.

"It's not like we're asking you to come back in winter. July is always beautiful. Ray wants to pay for your ticket. Sockeye prices were good this year and he has extra."

Ray is my stepfather. He married my mom a few years after I left. He's a silent man with a long brown beard and kind blue eyes, a fisherman. Always mending nets or working on his boat and gone fishing for months at a time. A good, steady man. The washtub bass to Ruth's high-strung fiddle.

"That's nice of him but I can afford to buy my own ticket. I'll try to come."

"No, you won't. You're only saying that so I'll leave you alone. You don't care about us at all."

"I really will try. So, how's winter going?"

"Oh, you know. Ten feet of snow. Ray had to shovel the roof again. It rained and the streets are glare ice."

I remember winters. The darkness that shuts down your brain. People are grouchy, on edge. Petty political feuds intensify. The false spring when it warms to forty degrees and everyone peels off their parkas. Then it goes back down to minus two.

"It would really give me and Ray something to look forward to if you were coming home."

"I . . . I'm busy. I'm working ten-hour days. I had a death notification today. An American football player. High profile. You'll hear about it on the news soon."

"And that's why you need a partner. To help you shoulder the emotional burden of your stressful job."

Here we go. "I'm too busy to date."

"And too busy for your brother's wedding. Your priorities are screwed up."

"My job is demanding. You know that."

"Always some excuse. I liked Lucas—I don't know why you let him get away."

Like he was a salmon that had wriggled off my hook. I should have held on tight. Reeled him in. Changed myself to fit him. Forgiven him for cheating on me multiple times.

I'd met Lucas during my tour in Portugal. He was a chef at a café I liked. I resisted his wooing, but he kept plying me with home-cured ham and crisp vinho verde, and I let my guard down.

There'd been a sharp, clear joy to that first year, like fresh snowfall sparkling in a streetlamp. When it melted away, I discovered what was buried beneath all that giddy happiness. Resentment. Accusations. Lies.

"I don't want to talk about it."

"You never want to talk about it and that's not healthy. You have to talk about it someday or you'll get an ulcer."

"He cheated on me. End of story."

"Most men will if given the chance. Or a reason."

"Are you saying it's my fault that he cheated?"

"Of course not."

"Not all men cheat. Ray would never do something like that."

"Ray is . . . simpler. He's down-to-earth. You should find someone else before you turn forty."

"That's ten years away."

"Ten fertile years. At least freeze your eggs. I want to be a grandmother."

"I'm well aware of that." Heron told me that she's been collecting baby clothes in a trunk she hides under her bed. Tiny booties and pastel crocheted sweaters. "Heron is your best hope for grandkids."

The slow-leak sound of her sigh. "Life will pass you by if you're not careful. You're too focused on your work. It's the weekend. You should be out having fun. Being young."

"I have the duty phone. I can't go out."

"Bring it with you. Lake, don't waste your life. One day you'll wake up with creaky joints and realize that you're fifty. You won't even know how it happened."

"Mom, it's late and I haven't had dinner yet."

"Seriously? Isn't it ten p.m. there? I'm worried about you, Lake."

"I'm okay."

"Don't think I won't stop pestering you. It would mean so much to Heron if you came."

"I'll do what I can to be there." I love my brother. I don't want to let him down.

And she's gone, swallowed by the snow and ice, a world away. She always sets me on edge, my mind resonating with wariness like I'm a tuning fork that only she knows how to strike.

"Moms are kind of a pain, aren't they, Edgar?"

He licks his paw and wipes it over his whiskers haughtily, which means he heartily agrees.

Instead of dinner I drink more wine on the couch. I haven't even bothered to change out of my work clothes. Life is like that sometimes. The smallest tasks become insurmountable when they mean taking care of yourself, instead of someone else.

Edgar manages an awkward hop and lands on my lap. His purr rumbles straight to my heart. I'm alone in a mostly empty apartment in a strange city where I'm friendless by choice.

I could die tonight, and the embassy security detail would find me in a few days, when I didn't show up for work. They have a set of keys. I'd become just another Amcit dead in a foreign country. One of my colleagues would have to call Ruth and deliver the news.

I'm very sorry to inform you that your daughter passed away in her apartment in Wellington. She'd been drinking wine. She slipped getting out of the shower and hit her head at precisely the right angle on the edge of the bathtub and bled out on the white tiles.

Wine mixed with blood seeping into the grout between the tiles.

Edgar's had enough. He jumps down from my lap and settles into a ball on the floor, licking the fur I touched as if to wash away any traces of me.

4

LAKE

I'm jarred out of a cramped, wine-blurred sleep by a harsh, piercing ringtone.

"U.S. Embassy New Zealand duty phone." I struggle upright on the couch. There's a shooting pain along my right collarbone, an old injury that never healed properly. "What's your emergency?"

"It's my daughter. She's missing." The caller's voice is high-pitched, agitated, chain-smoker raspy. "We always talk or message every day. I've sent her so many texts and she hasn't responded to any of them."

I stagger to my feet, fumble for the light switch. Find the pen and logbook, the splintered laminate on one corner of the coffee table clawing at my sleeve. Edgar rolls over and goes back to sleep on his side of the couch.

"Is she an American citizen?"

"Yes. She's an exchange student living in Wellington. I can't reach her host parents, either."

The lurid red of my clock screams five a.m. My head throbs. I crave coffee. And painkillers for this wine headache.

"What's your name?"

"Suzie Bishop. Suzie with a Z-I-E."

"And your daughter's name?"

"Bowie. B-O-W-I-E. Like David Bowie."

I ask for Suzie's and Bowie's full names and dates of birth. That's the best way to verify their citizenship in the passport database after the call. Suzie is forty-six and Bowie is eighteen.

"When was the last time you had contact with Bowie?"

"She called me on Tuesday, late evening Las Vegas time. Wednesday evening in Wellington."

My still-foggy mind manages the time calculation. "Only a little more than forty-eight hours."

"Don't make it sound like I'm being paranoid. She's my only child. She never goes this long without contacting me. *Never*."

A sound like ice hitting the side of a glass. It's morning in Las Vegas. Let's hope that's ice water and not a cocktail, although I wouldn't be surprised. People who call the embassy duty phone are either in trouble . . . or they *are* trouble.

"I'm only trying to determine the facts, Ms. Bishop. Did Bowie say anything about her plans when you spoke with her last?"

"We only talked for a little while. She was really excited about performing at the Cat's Meow tonight with a local band."

The drinking age is eighteen in New Zealand. Bowie would be legal to perform in bars without a parent. "Have you spoken with the band or with the club?"

"I called the bar and they think she's coming tonight. But why hasn't she called me back?"

"Hopefully there's a simple explanation. Maybe she lost her cell phone or something."

"Maybe. But she'd find another way to let me know she was okay. We always video call before shows to go over her set list. I'm her manager. She's going to be a star. When her exchange program is over, we're going into the studio to record demos for Stratus Records. They're very interested in Bowie. It helps that I know the music biz from the inside. I was in the band Bitter Pill. I'm sure you've heard of it."

"Um . . . sure." My mind feels fuzzy. I really should have eaten some dinner to soak up some of the wine.

"I'm constantly worrying about her, wondering where she is, who she's talking to, if she's safe." The words tumble out, sloshing together like raindrops hitting a moving windshield. "I work in a casino. I know the world is a dangerous place for young girls. Why did I let her leave me? What if she has a stalker? What if something horrible has happened to her?"

She's probably better off in Wellington than Las Vegas, I think, but don't say. New Zealand consistently ranks second only to Iceland as the safest and most peaceable country on Earth. The police don't routinely carry firearms unless the situation is expected to merit them.

"You said she's an exchange student. Who are her host parents?"

"Stuart and Myra Shepherd. Stuart's a big-deal politician. Old money. Ancestral estate, all of that. He paid for me to visit Bowie in New Zealand and took us to lunch at his exclusive club. It was all steak and kidney pudding and portraits of his ancestors in the billiards room. I thought she'd be safe with them."

A sob cresting, ready to break. More ice clinking. The glug of liquid being poured into a glass.

"Do you have any reason to believe that Bowie might be in immediate danger?"

"No . . . but what if something's happened to her and they don't want to tell me? What if there's been an accident and they're all dead at the bottom of a ravine?"

"Let's not jump to conclusions."

Probably Bowie's out having fun with her friends and forgot to call her mom. Or maybe she's taking some breathing space. Suzie's definitely giving me intense stage-mom vibes.

"You said you tried to contact the Shepherd family?"

"They're not answering their phones. It's so strange. And I messaged Bowie's host sister and friends and no one has responded yet."

"I could do a welfare and whereabouts check on Bowie for you."

"Would you? Oh my God, that would be such a relief. You're there in Wellington, right? You can visit the Shepherds' house, find out what's going on. I'll give you their address."

I record contact information for Bowie and her host family.

"What's your name?" Suzie asks.

"I'm the duty officer on call."

"I know that," she says impatiently. "I want to know your name."

I hesitate. Even something as small as a name can be a land mine. But Suzie is a worried mother, not someone I need to hide from.

In Phnom Penh I'd had a caller who invented a long, convoluted tale about having his wallet stolen and being left with no money to return to the U.S. and then—out of nowhere—his voice changed, lowered to a snarl, and he detailed precisely how he was going to torture and kill me. And then he gave me the address of my apartment.

That's when I started carrying my old hunting knife again. I changed apartments, but it wasn't enough. I still heard his voice in my head.

They always find me. At bars, at work, sometimes on the street. The ones with grievances to air, conspiracy theories to spin, filthy fantasies to spew. I work so hard to project a tough shell, but I must give off some kind of invisible signal. I show up as a target on their tracking system.

"My name is Lake."

"Do you have any children, Lake?"

Not something she needs to know. "I'll check on Bowie for you, Ms. Bishop. If I can't reach the Shepherds by phone, I'll visit their house."

"And then you'll call me immediately?"

"I will."

"Oh, thank you. Thank you so much. Lake, you're a lifesaver. If something bad has happened to Bowie, I don't know what I'd do. Call me soon, okay? Maybe it's all a mix-up. I hope so. Bowie lives her life online. Her fans will want to know where she is, why she hasn't posted any new content in a few days."

"I'll call you."

"Just the other day, I had a message from the record scout at Stratus and he said—"

"Sorry, Ms. Bishop, I should sign off now. This line is supposed to be kept open for emergencies."

"Oh. Of course. Yes. I'm babbling. I do that. Especially when I . . . well I had a long night at the casino, so I'm having a little after-work drink, you know?"

"Goodbye, Ms. Bishop."

"Goodbye, Lake."

Suzie would stay on the phone with me all morning telling me about Bowie if she could. And she probably wouldn't even remember the conversation the next day, depending on how strong those drinks were.

Edgar jumps down from the couch, righting himself adroitly. He nudges my knee with his head.

"Oh you think it's crunchie time? It's not."

His eyes close as I scratch between his ears. Sometimes he decides to be sweet for about ten minutes, the bare minimum to keep me hooked.

I plug the duty phone back into the charger and switch to my personal phone. It's easy to find Bowie Bishop. She has quite a following. She's tall, or maybe just thin—model thin—long limbs and a rust-colored miniskirt. Shoulder-length dark brown hair. A wide smile. Dark shadows like smudged fingerprints under wide-set gray eyes. In every photo she's wearing what looks like a crystal pendant suspended from a silver chain around her neck.

She's been in New Zealand for ten months of a twelve-month exchange program with ILA, Intercultural Learning Abroad. She hasn't posted any updates on her social media since Wednesday afternoon when she posted a wide-eyed selfie with the caption: Can't wait to play Cat's Meow again with the ridiculously talented @DeanHira. See you there! It's going to be . . . 🔥🔥🔥🔥

More posts. A dead bird. Orange flower petals strewn in spirals. She used a filter to make her photos look like old Polaroids. Her combat boot, laces undone. Her hand, black nail polish chipped, holding a mug that says *sweet as*, the ubiquitous response to so many things in New Zealand. Bowie in her Wellington school uniform, making an oversized red-and-blue-striped blazer look like runway fashion.

Selfies of her at Wellington tourist sites. She's wearing all black and standing in front of one of the Writers Walk quotations overlooking Wellington harbor. She points to one line of the Lauris Edmond poem etched into the concrete slab: *You have to do and be, not simply watch.*

I scroll deeper. The same smudges under her eyes. Red lipstick in such a deep shade that it looks like congealed blood. Videos of her playing a black acoustic guitar with star-shaped inlays on the headstock and neck.

A bedroom selfie in a red camisole, one thin arm crooked behind her head, silk riding up and exposing a flat abdomen with a belly button piercing. She stares directly into the camera, her gaze sultry. She's younger in this one, maybe fifteen. I wince, knowing that what we post online never really goes away. Only the wealthy can scrub the internet and erase their past.

There are photos of her with her host sister, Isla, a tall athletic blonde, and two younger host brothers who look like twins.

There's a series of Bowie in Nevada with a much taller and earthily gorgeous girl posing for a Halloween photo shoot in an old amusement park. The caption: **Abandoned amusement parks are the CREEPIEST. BoLo Forever!**

Then there's Bowie and Suzie with arms intertwined. Suzie is peak Vegas and peak aging rock star. Black leather skinny pants and cheeks plump with fillers, her bee-stung lips taking up most of the screen.

I visited Vegas with some girlfriends during college. It was the anti-Alaska. Everything fake. Flashy. Artificial. Water pumped in to make flowers bloom in the desert. Phallic monuments to mob money. Does Bowie think New Zealand is too quiet, or has its beauty stolen her heart, as it threatens to steal mine?

I tell myself that Bowie Bishop is a routine case of a teenager forgetting to call her mom. I don't want to imagine the alternatives. The wrong man seeing that bedroom selfie. Stalking her. Watching her flick that long mane of brown hair over a thin shoulder. Following her, forcing her into his car, raping and murdering her. They won't find her bones until they bulldoze a field for a new housing development.

Don't go down that path. Everything will be fine.

And then I see it. In the background of the mother-daughter selfie. The Trophy casino in grandiose gold lettering over their heads.

What the hell? Suzie said she works at a casino. Glen Walter owns The Trophy. His son, Bruce, is dead in Wellington. Bowie Bishop might be missing. There must be a connection. Hopefully I'll be able to ask Bowie about it when I find her, safe and sound today. If she doesn't answer her phone, I'll go and visit her host family.

I try calling but it rings directly to voicemail. *This is Bowie, leave a message.*

"Hi, Bowie, it's Lake Harlowe from the U.S. Embassy in Wellington. I need to speak with you urgently. Please call me back, any time of the day or night."

The same thing happens with both Stuart and Myra Shepherd's numbers.

I play some of Bowie's videos. She sings a lilting, sad song sitting on the steps of a crumbling mausoleum between two marble columns covered in twining vines. A weathered stone angel with the tip of one wing broken off stands watch overhead against a turquoise sky. A tree with waxy green leaves and strange bristling red blooms watches her performance.

Let me sing you the ballad of Graveyard Rose
And the fate she could not cheat

SHE FELL AWAY

It starts beyond the heavy gate
And ends beneath my feet

My angel with one broken wing
Who used to soar so high
You'll never leave the ground again
No matter how hard you try

If stone could learn to become flesh
If sightless eyes could see
If I could bring you back to life
I'd keep you safe with me

I'd do anything
To feel your satin petal skin
I'd give anything
To see you bloom again
My graveyard rose

Her guitar playing is confident, her voice arresting, soaring between an earthy growl and ethereal shimmering high notes. It reminds me of a Neko Case concert I saw in Portland. Her voice was a burned-out cathedral, a place for the broken to worship. Ruby light pouring through my stained-glass heart.

It's the same with the selfies Bowie posts. Not much text. No hashtags. Instead of airbrushed glamour, carefully staged meditations with a clear sense of artistry. Not simply *Look at me. I exist. Aren't I gorgeous,* but *This is the way I see the world. I see beauty in loneliness, in dark things. I'm sweet . . . with a serrated edge.*

Suzie was right. The world is a dangerous place for young girls. But hopefully not for Bowie.

5

BOWIE

"Give us a song, Bowie."

Her stomach clenches and her hands ball into fists. Relax. It's not Suzie wanting her to entertain her drunk party friends. She's in New Zealand. She's been here almost one month.

Her host mum, Myra, pats the camping chair next to her. "Come on, love, you brought your guitar, may as well use it."

"Be right there."

Bowie's been standing under the enormous tree ferns that border the campsite, feeling like Alice in Wonderland. A plant she'd known only as delicately scrolled leaves curling in a clay pot now towers over her head, casting striped shadows across her arms. Disjointed song lyrics flicker through her mind like fireflies.

Cradling raindrops on my tongue like secrets. Ancient forests know how to grow. Wash me clean. Make me whole. These trees will outlive me . . . I'm only a brief downpour . . . I'm only here to feed their souls.

If she slept overnight beneath the giant silvery ferns, the frond patterns might imprint her soul. She might wake up a completely different person. She could have a fresh start.

Her hand moves to the small glass vial she wears on a silver chain around her neck.

She can never be washed clean. She doesn't deserve a fresh start.

The Shepherds sit in a contented ring around the campfire, teasing one another softly under a blanket of stars. They're like the description on a box of cereal—packed full of wholesome goodness and nutrition.

Myra is a grief counselor and sometimes asks difficult questions because she wants everyone to be happy. Isla, Bowie's host sister, has an inner glow from being loved, being safe. She's a champion swimmer and all-around athlete who's always bringing home medals and trophies. She has swim practice this summer, and she comes home all shiny and flushed and eats more than everyone else at dinner.

The seven-year-old twins, Byron and Oliver, fight sometimes and it ends in tears, but they're always back to being best friends the next day.

Stuart works a lot, but when he's home he reads books to the boys and makes complicated gourmet vegetarian meals from Ottolenghi cookbooks.

At night they sometimes make popcorn and watch a slideshow with actual old slides of their family history. Faded images of Shepherd ancestors blowing out candles at birthday parties, visiting tourist sites, holding wrinkled newborn babies.

She's fascinated by the slides of Myra's mother, Ellen, on a trip to Italy in the early seventies. She's wearing bell-bottoms, an orange and green print blouse, and brown leather clogs. She has the same bright smile as Myra as she stands in front of the Colosseum.

Bowie loves the sound of the carousel whirring, the way the screen goes blindingly white for a few seconds before the new image materializes. Anything is possible in that blank space. The next slide might reveal Bowie's grandma, the one she's never met, the one she can't find on the internet.

Bowie has no siblings. It's just her and Suzie in a run-down apartment in the concrete wasteland of suburban Las Vegas.

She's never even met any relatives. Suzie says they're all trailer trash living in Ohio and they're jealous of her rock-star past and Vegas life. When Bowie was old enough to wonder about her father, Suzie said he could be any number of men from her party days and it's better not to know because they were all deadbeats.

Bowie grabs her guitar from the back of the camper van. The silky finish beneath her fingers always calms her. She loves the glowing mother-of-pearl star inlays and the way the strings press back reassuringly. The wood is worn down in the places where her fingers touch the neck, where her forearm rests on the body.

She doesn't feel separate from her guitar. It's like another limb, something that was attached when she was born. Amputated at birth and found again when Suzie gave her that first mini guitar at age five.

Ah, there you are, she remembers thinking, stroking the smooth wood of the guitar, twanging the strings and hearing her voice, her true voice, for the first time.

She experiences the world through music. She sees motion, the limbs of a tree moving in the wind, a bike whirring by, a bird in flight, and she hears music. A constant symphony. Lyrics swirling like autumn leaves.

"What would you like to hear?" she asks, joining them by the campfire.

"Ed Sheeran," Byron shouts, bouncing up and down on his camp chair.

"Justin Bieber," Oliver counters.

"Sorry, don't know any of their songs."

"Know any Radiohead?" Stuart asks. "They're my favorite."

"Really?" Isla rolls her eyes. "She doesn't know your ancient music. Do that Taylor Swift I love."

Stuart reaches over and pokes Isla in the ribs. "Someday Taylor Swift will be ancient music to know-it-all teenagers everywhere."

Bowie's tired of people asking her to play Swift songs. "I should do something everyone can sing along to."

"Creep!" says Stuart. Isla throws a twig at him.

Her fingers find the arpeggio riff from "Creep."

"See?" Stuart crows. "She does know Radiohead."

"That song's not appropriate for the boys," Myra interrupts with a frown, smoothing Byron's hair out of his eyes. "How about something from a musical?" She loves everything Broadway or Disney. She likes a happy ending. You can tell by the way she smiles so much, and so brightly. Although Bowie sees shadows in her eyes. "How about one of your originals, Bowie? We want to listen to you. We don't have to sing along."

"Nope. We're on a camping trip. We're supposed to sing around the campfire." She tunes to open G. "My mom used to play these for me when I was little." She starts with "Hey Jude," moves to "I'm Looking Through You," and ends with "All You Need Is Love." Myra and Stuart join in on the choruses and, by the end, Isla and the boys are singing along as well. It's this nearly perfect moment. Music bringing them together. Making her feel like she's truly part of their family.

"That was lovely, Bowie," Myra says. "Thank you. Right, then, sleepyheads. Off to bed."

Stuart rounds up the boys and takes them to their sleeping bags in the back of the camper van.

Isla yawns and stretches her toned arms over her head. "Think I'll turn in. Going to swim across the lake tomorrow morning before we go tramping. Care to join me, Bowie?"

"I couldn't make it even halfway. You know that."

Isla's laughter has an edge. "You should get more exercise. You're too thin. Survival of the fittest, and all that." She unzips the tent she's sharing with Bowie and climbs inside.

Now Bowie and Myra are the only ones left. Time for the difficult questions. To head her off, Bowie sings and plays softly—a medley of ABBA songs from *Mamma Mia*. Myra hums along and even jumps up and does some dance moves. She flops back down on her chair.

"You know 'Dancing Queen' is supposed to be a happy song, right? You managed to make it sound sad."

"Probably the tuning I'm in."

"No, it's more than that. I've noticed the bleak spin you put on everything."

"It's the only way I know how to play." Jangly pop songs make her head hurt. Suzie used to try to make her play bubble-gum pop-princess songs, and then, when she grew older, sexy dance anthems, but lately she's rebelled. She's always listening for the bass notes instead of the melody. The descending steps leading her down into the dark cellar of a song. Down to the underside of life, all the dirt hiding under there.

"You'd tell me if you were feeling too homesick, wouldn't you?" Myra asks.

"Sure." She strums her guitar. "I mean, I've only been here a month."

"School's starting soon. That will be a good distraction. You'll make lots of friends. You're going to be a dancing queen . . ." Myra pulls Bowie up out of her chair, and Bowie can't help but smile, set down her guitar, and join in the dance.

"You're mine now." Myra holds both of Bowie's hands. "At least for the next year. I'm going to find a way past those thick walls you've built to protect yourself." She kisses Bowie's cheek. "Don't stay up too late. We're going tramping tomorrow, and it will be rough and steep terrain. You'll need your strength."

After Myra's gone to bed, Bowie bites her lip to keep from crying. She'd considered telling Myra the truth. She's the opposite of homesick. What would that be? Home-weary. Home-wary.

She's already thinking that eleven more months won't be enough. She doesn't want to go back to Vegas. Back to the casino and the jagged, painful memories.

Back to Suzie.

Her mom's the one who craves fame. Suzie was in this band

Bitter Pill that had one medium-big hit, "Hurt So Happy," in the nineties but then faded into obscurity. She was so pretty when she was Bowie's age. Wide eyes and long, messy, bleached-blond hair. She wore platform Mary Janes and thrifted lacy baby doll dresses.

The video for "Hurt So Happy" was shot in an abandoned Nevada hotel already half consumed by desert. There she is in torn fishnets and smeared black eyeliner, swaggering around the graffitied rubble, a metal toilet prominent behind her.

Hurt so happy when you hold my hand
You're my dirty little secret
Forget your wedding band

The song was a hit and she was about to go on tour with Bitter Pill when she got pregnant. There were complications. The doctor wouldn't let her tour. She lost the baby at five months. Bowie's ghost big sister.

The band replaced Suzie with another lead singer, and the tour crashed and burned. Now Suzie is a bar manager at The Trophy casino and sometimes the owner, Glen Walter, lets her sing in one of the second-rate lounges. She's bitter because she wrote the lyrics and music for "Hurt So Happy," but she signed a shit contract and doesn't see any royalties even though the song is still in heavy rotation. She spent everything she had on lawsuits, and now she lives paycheck to paycheck.

Bowie stares at the charred remains of the fire. It's funny. Suzie always says she works so hard so that Bowie will never have to serve drinks to men who think they can grab her ass because she's wearing a short skirt. But slinking around onstage in a miniskirt for record executives and music industry gatekeepers doesn't feel that different.

Stratus Records is interested, but Suzie warns her that they won't wait forever. She's supposed to be developing an album concept, working on her first singles.

During the meeting at Stratus, Suzie kicked Bowie's foot under the table to catch her attention. "Smile," she whispered out of the side of her mouth.

Bowie smiled.

The men stared. At her face, her lips, her body, their eyes skittering like the cockroaches in their kitchen when Bowie turns on the light at night to make a snack.

Everyone always wants her to smile. She'd be so much prettier if she smiled.

Suzie hired a photographer to do promotional headshots when Bowie was fourteen. Bowie wanted to wear jeans and a mock turtleneck, but Suzie picked out a plaid schoolgirl miniskirt and a tight white crop top.

When the glossy headshots arrived, Suzie gushed over them, and Bowie thought they were hideous. She didn't even recognize herself. She tore up the photos into tiny pieces, as if that would make them disappear. Those photos were out there forever.

Suzie had been furious. "I paid good money for those. Can you maybe put in a little more effort? This is your future. This is your shot."

Bowie wonders why the language of making it big is always so harsh and bleak. It's your shot. We'll break you out. You'll go viral.

"Maybe I don't want to go viral," she'd said.

"Not this again. You're too talented to be a nobody. Look, honey, I know this would be easier if I was a stockbroker or a rich housewife, but I'm doing my best, okay? People like us have to work even harder. No one's going to hand you fame on a silver platter. But I'll be damned if you make the same mistakes I did. You have me in your corner, and that's all you require."

When Isla and her best friend, Daphne, tell Bowie that they wish they could go to Las Vegas parties and get discovered, Bowie tells them that being discovered isn't always a good thing. She tells them to scroll through the nausea-inducing comments she gets on her videos.

You're a beautiful young girl. I want to fuck you so hard. I want to be your first. I want to take your virginity.

And those were the innocent comments. Predators have been telling her their sick fantasies since she was a little girl.

"That's the price of fame," Suzie says. Her fifteen minutes of fame gnawed a hole through her heart that can never be crammed full enough. Bowie is supposed to bring back the spotlight. Reclaim the glory. Rescue Suzie from the one-hit-wonder garbage dump.

Bowie is a star. That's the message carved into her skull since birth. And when you're a star, you're also a product. Her name was a brand chosen for her while she was still coiled in Suzie's womb.

Bowie does miss her mom. The constant snarky commentary. Sharing clothes and makeup. She doesn't miss being her art project. Or the feeling that if she's not talented or famous enough, her mom might crumple her up and throw her away.

No one's trying to make her a star in New Zealand. They don't like show-offs. If you stand out too much, if you think you're something special, they call you a tall poppy.

And tall poppies get cut down.

She can't imagine Suzie here. She'd be complaining about the lack of Wi-Fi and having to use the communal toilets. It's so quiet. Instead of horns honking and drunk tourists shouting, there're birds. Even in Wellington when she video chats with her friends, they ask what's the noise in the background, and it's the birds—the tūī and fantails and bellbirds—singing in a choir.

There's no smog. It's never too hot. The stars make her heart hurt, they're so beautiful. It makes her wonder who she might be without this constant guilt. This feeling that she's not good enough. Not famous enough.

Sometimes she feels like two different people. Wellington Bowie and Vegas Bowie. Vegas Bowie is a swimming pool at night surrounded by palm trees fed by water pumped into a desert, a slick, glassy surface, a darkness to plunge into. She can never drain the darkness completely. It's always there. Even when birdsong fills her ears.

When she first arrived in New Zealand, she had her guard up. She was wary of every glance, every hello, every smile. She's started to relax now, to believe that not everyone here is a potential predator.

There's nothing to be frightened of on this camping trip, like coyotes or bears. Not even any snakes and hardly any spiders.

If Myra could read Bowie's mind, maybe she wouldn't want her living in their home. Maybe Bowie is the predator here.

She attracts the darkness.

Because of what she's seen. Because of what she did.

6

LAKE

It's raining softly as I pull into the Shepherds' driveway. I'm stopped by a high wooden gate. It's a sprawling Victorian painted white with black trim set on a hillside bordering a large cemetery. There's no response when I ring the buzzer mounted on the gate. It looks like a house that's been closed for the weekend, holding its breath until the family returns.

Some of the neighboring homes have children playing in the yards. I approach a woman wearing yoga leggings and a striped T-shirt as she's herding two young children into a station wagon a few doors down.

"Excuse me, do you know if the Shepherds are gone for the weekend?"

"Jackson, don't hit your sister!" She fastens a toddler into a car seat and straightens. "I'm sorry?"

"I'm trying to find Stuart or Myra Shepherd. Do you know if they'll be back any time soon?"

"No idea. Sorry. I've got my hands full with these ones. Jackson! Stop, please!"

"Do you know the American exchange student living with them, Bowie Bishop?"

"We just moved to the neighborhood. The Shepherds keep

to themselves. Sorry, I really must go." Children secure, she hops into the driver's seat and leaves.

I scan the street. There's no other adult to talk to—I'd have to start knocking on doors. I look down over Karori Cemetery. I've been meaning to visit. I've pinned it on my map of Wellington. It's the second largest cemetery in New Zealand, the final resting place for more than eighty thousand souls. This must be where Bowie records her videos.

The rain has stopped. My boots squelch into the soil between the rows of graves. The cemetery has gone feral in places, with trees growing in front of gravestones, obscuring them from view. I walk around the back of the Shepherds' house.

The small mausoleum where Bowie recorded the video I watched is almost directly behind their house. It's not visible from the road and is bordered by a steep, overgrown hillside. Stone steps lead up to a wooden door with faded green paint and a rusted padlock. The steps are inset, forming benches on either side bordered by columns. I read one of the family inscriptions:

DULCIE MORRIS.
DIED 26TH JUNE 1921
AGED 17 YEARS
Dearest daughter, how we miss you, none but God himself can tell,
but in heaven we will meet you, until then, farewell.

Poor Dulcie, only seventeen when she died. She must have inspired Bowie's eerie song.

There she is, framed by the vine-covered columns, brown hair curtaining her face, bending over her guitar.

Let me sing you the ballad of Graveyard Rose

Trees stretching above her with crimson blossoms hanging down. Like blood dripping over the graves.

It's the video I watched, not a real memory, but it's so vivid.

Dense trees cover the back of the building, and dried old vines snake over the walls. I place my palm against cool marble. The damp, mossy smell beckons the same half memory I had yesterday. Fingers like gnarled tree roots. Sightless eyes. Pine needles under my fingernails. I'm digging frantically with my hands into wet soil.

I walk quickly away from the mausoleum, following a different path back toward the street. A woman with long white hair is tending one of the gravestones, scraping lichen from the lettering.

"Excuse me, do you work here?"

"Unofficially," she says with a smile, the wind whipping strands of white hair against her cheeks. "I clean the graves that have no one to care for them. The cemetery staff only maintain accessways, but the plots themselves are the responsibility of the families. Some, like Ida Greenaway here, have no family left to visit anymore."

"That's kind of you. Do you live nearby?"

"I'm over there." She gestures toward a house a few doors down from the Shepherds. "I'm a retired teacher. It's been my hobby for decades now to come here and restore the lonely graves." She continues working as she talks. "I always start with some water and a brush with soft bristles. Where I go from there depends on the lettering type. If it's lead, like this one, I'm very careful because if the letters fall out they're costly to replace."

"Do you know Stuart and Myra Shepherd?"

She glances up from the grave. "Myra's a good friend, why?"

I'm in luck. "I'm searching for Bowie Bishop, the American exchange student who lives with them."

"Such a talented young lady." She resumes brushing the lettering.

"I watched a video of her performing a song here."

"Oh yes, she likes to use the graves as backdrops. She's always filming herself out here. Very American, isn't it? The urge to document one's life every second of every day. But then you're American, aren't you? Or perhaps Canadian?"

"American. My name's Lake. I work for the U.S. Embassy in Wellington."

"Martha Tilbury. I believe Bowie is on a trip with the Shepherds. Stuart loves tramping and camping and everything outdoors. Myra goes along with it, for his sake."

"They're camping this weekend? Is Bowie with them?"

"I think so." Her brow furrows. "Though I can't be sure. They all piled into the camper van so quickly. It's always chaotic with the young twins. Such spirited lads."

"Do you happen to know where they were headed?"

"They usually go to Tōtaranui this time of year during the spring school holidays. It's a lovely site in Golden Bay, on the South Island. You should visit it if you have time."

"Is it possible they don't have cell reception at the campground?"

"Quite possible."

My spirits lift. Finally, an explanation that makes sense. Suzie will be so relieved. Bowie's camping with her host family, and they're out of cell range. But why would she go camping without telling her mother, especially when she has a gig tonight?

"I do hope nothing's wrong?" Martha asks.

"Bowie's mother hasn't heard from her in a few days and is trying to reach her."

She wrinkles her nose. "Ah. The mother."

"Did you meet Suzie Bishop when she visited Wellington?"

"I only saw her from a distance. She's like one of those Real Housewives, isn't she? Tottering around on spiked heels, with lips like pillows and puffed-out cheekbones. They all start to look the same, don't they?" She gives me a sharp look. "At least you've left your face natural. But you're still young. You can't be more than thirty?"

Nosy, opinionated neighbors. Every town has them. And they always know everyone's secrets.

"Thirty it is."

"Don't have any work done, dearie. It never fools anyone."

"I'll take that under advisement."

"I've heard that even young girls are having cosmetic surgery in the States. I don't think Bowie's had any done. A pretty girl, but too thin, really. She must eat like a bird. But that's the fashion these days, more's the pity. Isla's far more attractive, to my mind, so glowingly robust, but the lads do seem to prefer Bowie."

"What do you mean?"

"Well." She tilts her head toward me. "I did overhear Isla and Bowie having a bit of a row one night. They were whispering outside my window at an ungodly hour of the night. I sleep lightly at this age."

"What were they arguing about?"

"Isla was upset because Bowie had performed at a club and stolen everyone's attention. She said, *You can't have Dean. He's mine.* She sounded very distraught, poor dear."

They must have been fighting about Dean Hira—the musician Bowie is supposed to perform with tonight.

Martha sets down her brush and runs a forefinger over the restored name. "There, now isn't that better?"

"I'm sure Ida's ancestors would appreciate your work. Thanks for letting me know about the camping trip. Bowie's mother will be relieved."

"You're very welcome. Why don't you come and take one of our tours? I'm a member of the Friends of Karori Cemetery. I lead the Murder and Mayhem tour sometimes. It's quite fascinating the number of drownings, murders, and accidental deaths represented here."

"Thanks. I will."

She nods, gathers her cleaning supplies, and walks back toward her house.

I have what I came for. A plausible explanation for Bowie's silence.

Back in my car, I find a number for Tōtaranui campground in Golden Bay, but it's only a recorded message giving hours and driving instructions. I send a message to the email address listed for the campground administration.

When I call Mason, I get his voicemail and ask him to call me back. Then I call Suzie.

"Hello? Lake? Have you found her?"

"The Shepherds aren't at home, but I spoke with a neighbor who says the family is camping on the South Island. Apparently, it's a remote location with spotty cell reception."

"But Bowie would have told me she was going camping. She would have posted about it—told her fans she'd be going off the grid for a few days. Plus, she has the show at the Cat's Meow tonight. It doesn't make sense that she'd miss it."

"Or maybe she forgot. It was a spur-of-the-moment decision and she joined them not knowing that she wouldn't have cell service and wouldn't be able to contact you."

"We don't know for sure that Bowie's on that camping trip."

"We don't. I've called and emailed the campground administration but I haven't heard back yet."

"There must be some way of contacting them."

"I'll ask a contact in the New Zealand police force to reach the campground and find you a definitive answer."

"Yes, yes, of course. Call me back."

"Wait, Suzie, I have a question. Does Bowie know a Bruce Walter?"

There's silence for a few seconds. "Why would you ask me that?"

"I can't really say—it's about something that will be public knowledge soon but isn't yet."

"She knows Bruce because he's the son of my employer, Glen Walter."

"Did they date?"

"Never. What's this about? Why can't you tell me?"

"I'm sorry, I shouldn't have brought it up. I really can't say anything until the news is made public."

"What news? Has something happened to Bruce?"

"I'll call you back soon, Suzie."

I glance back at the Shepherds' house as I drive away. The

wind has ripped most of the petals from the crimson roses climbing the trellises on either side of the gate, leaving some plastered against the white walls of the house, like splotches of blood.

I know that the most tranquil of neighborhoods in even the most idyllic of towns can harbor evil. In the small Alaska town where I grew up everyone knew everyone. People left their keys in the ignition when they visited the grocery story. Most people didn't lock their doors at night.

But everyone had secrets to hide.

7
LAKE

Later that afternoon I'm showering when my phone rings. I shut the water off, grab a towel and reach for my phone, slipping on the wet tiles and righting myself against the wall.

"Mason, thanks for calling me back."

I hear background chatter, a bass thumping.

"What's going on?"

"I received a call early this morning from a mother in the U.S. who thinks her daughter is missing. Her name's Bowie Bishop. She's an exchange student living with Stuart and Myra Shepherd."

"Stuart Shepherd, the MP?"

"Yes. I went around to check on her a few hours ago and they weren't home, but I spoke with a neighbor who said they're at Tōtaranui campground in Golden Bay for a long weekend. Which explains why they haven't been answering their phones since it's a remote location with limited cell service. The neighbor assumes Bowie is with them."

"Right then. Case solved."

"Not quite. Here's the weird part. Bowie's mother, Suzie Bishop, works for Glen Walter, the father of—"

"Bruce Walter. Our body from yesterday." He gives a low whistle. "That is odd."

"Too odd to be a coincidence, maybe? I asked Suzie if Bowie knew Bruce, or maybe even dated him, and she said no. Seems like there must be a connection, though."

"Right. I'll investigate it."

"I was going to ask if you could find a way to contact the campground. I tried to reach them but I had to leave a voicemail."

"Will do."

"Bowie's mom swears that she wouldn't have gone camping without telling her or posting about it on social media. And here's another strange thing. She's supposed to play a show tonight with a local band at the Cat's Meow bar. Her mother thinks she really wanted to perform and wouldn't miss it."

"She probably decided to skip it and go camping. Teenagers are unpredictable. I have several teenaged nieces, and I never know what they're going to say or do next."

"I don't know . . . I'm just thinking out loud here, but maybe Bruce was stalking her? She rejected him, went on the camping trip, and then he got drunk to drown his broken heart."

"That's one theory. Anything to base it on?"

"Not really," I admit. "I can't even find a photo of them together online. I'm trying to make sense of it. Maybe she really is missing, and crucial seconds are ticking by."

"The most likely explanation is that she's with the Shepherds. I'll find a way to reach the campground, then I'll ring you again."

"Suzie will appreciate that. She's going out of her mind."

"Don't worry before there's something to worry about, I always say, Lake, my love."

"I hope you're right."

"In the meantime, you should try to enjoy your Saturday evening. It's called having fun."

"How do you know I'm not having fun tonight?"

"I'm training to become a detective. I detect a distinct note of non-fun in your voice." There's mumbling in the background, silvery laughter. "Have to run, Lake. You'll hear from me soon."

"Thanks, Mason." For a moment there I'd thought he was

leading up to asking me out. My heart had gone a little fluttery. Unreliable heart.

I finish dressing and settle on the couch with Edgar. He purrs as I scratch behind his ears. "You think I'm fun, don't you?"

Yes, I'm home by myself on Saturday evening, talking to my cat. I hear my mom's exasperated voice. *Life will pass you by if you're not careful.* Life isn't passing me by. I'm hiding from it on purpose.

I hear back from Nadia Walter via email. They're flying to Wellington on a private jet. They don't need a pickup at the airport. They'll meet me at Wellington Hospital mortuary tomorrow afternoon. The message is very businesslike and filled with times and details and formalities. She's still in shock. The emotion will come when she sees her son's body.

Is there a connection between Bruce Walter's visit to Wellington and Bowie's disappearance? She's eighteen years old. Maybe there's some drama between them. She was flirting with him online, and he showed up suddenly and she backed out.

Or maybe Bowie had a falling-out with Dean Hira and decided to ditch the show and go camping instead. Martha Tilbury mentioned that Bowie and Isla were arguing about Dean. I click on the link Bowie posted. There's a video of him playing a song with Bowie on a dimly lit stage. Even though the sound quality isn't great, they sound fantastic.

They're singing a mid-nineties Nick Cave and Kylie Minogue duet, "Where the Wild Roses Grow," but they've reversed it—Dean's singing Kylie and Bowie's doing Nick. They make a striking pair. Both dark-haired and slender, soulful eyes, and heart-stopping voices. Hers has a touch of gravel, and his is smooth as honey. They stare at each other longingly and sing of sweet scarlet roses. I don't see the twist coming.

Bowie smiles wolfishly as she sings about bludgeoning her lover to death with a stone. This isn't a love song—it's a murder ballad.

My phone buzzes. "Mason. Any news?"

"I reached the campground administrator. She said the Shepherds were on a long trek today and probably wouldn't be back until just before nightfall."

"Okay. Did she know whether Bowie was with them?"

"Her name wasn't registered, but the person I talked to wasn't personally there when the Shepherds arrived, so there's still a possibility she could be with them."

"Shit. Nothing conclusive."

"I told her we're attempting to locate Bowie, and she promised to contact me immediately when they arrive back at the campground."

"Keep me posted."

"Absolutely." He goes back to whoever has the silvery laugh, and I go back to researching Bowie online. Still nothing new posted on her social media. I text Suzie the news from the campground and promise to call her when I know more.

Waiting for answers is making me restless. As an ACS officer, I take this duty personally. There's a distraught mother in Las Vegas desperately hoping for news about her daughter. I want to help. I want to be able to call Suzie and let her know her prayers have been answered.

Dean's performing tonight. If Bowie's somewhere in Wellington, and not on that camping trip, she'll show up at the Cat's Meow.

I can't just sit here. I need to know if Bowie is safe.

8
LAKE

The decor at the Cat's Meow is steampunk meets 1920s speakeasy. Lots of riveted iron and royal blue velvet. There's a small stage and a dance floor surrounded by cozy booths filled with the tattooed nighttime crowd.

The band hasn't started yet, but several guys in skinny jeans with messy hair are setting up mic stands and testing sound levels.

My hair glows red-gold like a lit jack-o-lantern in the gilt-framed mirrors mounted behind the bar. I catch the eye of a bartender with dyed black hair, blunt bangs, black eyeliner, and a tight black rocker T-shirt.

"What'll you have?"

"A whiskey sour, please. With Maker's."

"Haven't seen you here before."

"I'm new in town."

"Canadian?"

"American."

"Here on holiday?"

"Work."

"I'm Tasha, by the way."

"Lake."

She drizzles an extra Angostura Bitters heart on top of my

drink before sliding it to me across the scarred wooden bar. She glances at the wildflowers and vines twining around both of my forearms. "Sweet ink."

I have a tattoo for each country where I've lived. Wild Alaskan roses and purple fireweed; blue lotuses from China; lavender and other herbs from Portugal; a spray of white and yellow Romduol flowers from Cambodia. Memories forged from pain have a way of sinking deeper beneath our skin than any others. This is my way of transforming pain to beauty.

"Thanks. Yours are stunning." She has full-color sleeves with a mix of flowers and pin-up art. "Are those from a local artist?"

"Yeah, she's a legend. Name's Aria. I can give you her contact info, if you'd like?"

"That'd be fantastic."

Tasha moves away to serve another customer.

The lemon hits first, bright on my tongue. Then the whiskey warms my belly. It feels good to be out of my apartment. The duty phone is set to both ring and vibrate. I'm waiting for Mason's call and I have to be available for other callers, though I'm hoping a death case and a missing girl is as busy as Wellington gets.

Tasha glances back at me and winks. The night we'd have unspools in my mind, the buzz saw of attraction; whiskey-soaked kisses; and tangled, sweaty sheets. I think about my apartment, the mess of laundry I haven't done, the cat litter that needs cleaning. I think about getting so drunk that I don't care. Yeah, right. I have the duty phone. And then there'd be the morning after. Awkward chitchat. She'd leave early. Sometimes it feels like my life is all morning after. The aftermath and none of the pleasure.

My heart is a used-car lot with some guy in a polyester suit strutting up and down the rows. *Come on down to Lake's Lot, where you'll find only the finest in preowned hearts.* But the new paint jobs hide rust tumors and the speedometers all tell lies.

I swallow the rest of my drink. I'm not here for casual hookups. I'm here for Bowie. I will her to walk through the door, guitar slung across her back, long hair ink-black in the dim bar light.

Dean Hira takes the stage, and there's an energy about him, an intensity that commands every gaze in the room. He moves with grace and self-possession. When he steps up to the mic, the room hushes. I see the looks on peoples' faces, the adulation.

His face is long, and he has a wide, expressive mouth. He's tall and much thinner than he looked in the video. So thin that I wonder briefly if he's doing heroin, until I remember that this is New Zealand and the hard drugs are more difficult to come by in this isolated location. Which makes my job easier. I won't have to visit dozens of Amcits jailed for drug use or drug smuggling, like I had to in Cambodia.

"Hullo, friends, thanks for coming out tonight. We're Dean Hira and the Lopsided Hearts."

Cheers, catcalls.

"Here's a song by a talented American singer-songwriter named Bowie Bishop."

I sit up straighter. Does he know where she is?

"She was supposed to join us tonight, but something must have come up. Here's her 'Graveyard Rose.'"

His version is even slower than Bowie's, his voice crooning low, the texture of rose petals falling on rain-soaked graves.

A voice that swoops between octaves, growls and shimmers. A soaring, gravity-defying voice that shifts effortlessly between low-plucked bass notes and a crystalline falsetto. It's a voice to make you weep. Or fall in love.

Between songs I listen to the conversations around me.

"You're better off without that asshole. Don't waste another second on him." A woman comforting her sad-eyed friend.

It's such a soothing sound, the conversation of women helping each other to understand life. Even women I don't know.

I have a sudden wave of longing for my two best friends in Portland. The sound of their voices, familiar as my own, the ache in my belly from laughing so hard. I'm disconnected from them now. I missed the birth of Caroline's baby, and Amber's promotion to tenure track. It's not the same when we can't meet up in person. When I first joined the Foreign Service, we mailed a journal back and forth between us, adding entries and photos and bucket lists. I still have the journal, though Amber and Caroline had a falling-out, and now when I visit Portland I have to meet with them separately, like they're my divorced parents.

"Another?" Tasha asks, appearing in front of me.

"Sure." She's all slink and poetry as she expertly mixes a new drink. Her black T-shirt has a red hand holding a skull-topped silver dagger. The blood spatter beneath the tip of the dagger spells out the words *Earth Tongue*.

"Is that a local band?" I ask.

"Yeah, they're fucking brilliant. Heavy fuzz psych-rock duo. Ezra's on drums and Gussie shreds. She's a phenomenal guitarist. They both sing. They're on a European tour right now."

"Hope I can catch them when they come home." I find and follow them on Instagram.

"How long are you here for?"

"I'm not really sure." Dean's singing a rockabilly song, channeling Roy Orbison. "Dean's great."

"Isn't he? New Zealand's indie darling. He could make it big in the States, but he doesn't want to leave."

"I don't blame him."

"You like it here, then?"

"It's fucking brilliant."

Her grin makes my knees a little weak. "He said Bowie Bishop was supposed to perform tonight but she's a no-show?"

Tasha shrugs. "Too bad because she and Dean sound dreamy together."

"I've been trying to reach Bowie but she's not answering her phone."

"Are you a friend of hers?"

There's no reason not to tell her. If Bowie's truly missing, the police will be all over this bar.

"I work for the U.S. embassy. Bowie's mother hasn't heard from her in a few days and I'm trying to locate her."

"Ah." She takes a step backward. "You don't look like you work for an embassy." Her gaze lingers on my arms. "Cover those tats up at work, do you?"

"Yep." My standard work uniform always includes long sleeves and a high-necked blouse or a vintage silk scarf. I try to blend in. I don't want anyone playing the one-of-these-diplomats-is-not-like-the-others game.

"I haven't seen Bowie in weeks, not since her last show with Dean. But you might want to talk to Dean later. They're good mates."

"How good?"

"I don't think they're an item, if that's what you're asking. He's with a tall blonde."

"Isla Shepherd."

"Could be. I never caught her name."

"Have you talked to Bowie much?"

She scans the bar, but everyone's focused on the music right now. "The first night I met Bowie, she was sitting right where you are. She asked me for a pen. She did a shot of Patrón and then scribbled on the back of one of our coasters for several minutes. Then she joined Dean onstage, without so much as a by-your-leave, and performed the song she'd just written. It was furious, sad . . . beautiful. She has this old-soul energy."

She takes a small frame down from behind the bar and hands it to me. "When I tried to give this back, she told me to keep it. Said she had the song memorized. I reckon when she's famous I'll sell this and retire early."

Tiny, cramped block letters slant across the white cardboard coaster. The blue ink is blurry in places. She signed her initials at the bottom, the twin B's bleeding into the edge of the coaster.

SHE FELL AWAY

Make me your trophy
Hang me on your wall
Tell me I shine brightly
Tell me I'll never fall

Every time a star is born
Another star must die
Every time a star is born
You tell them the same lie

Crowded bar at midnight
Thick with silent screams
Night sky is a graveyard
Filled with buried dreams

When I write my future
You will not be there
When I rip the suture
You will feel the tear

The next time a star is born
She won't believe your lies
The next time a star is born
You're the one who dies

That reference to making her a trophy. Was that about The Trophy casino? The line about writing her own future could be a reference to Suzie—the micromanaging stage mom. "Dark stuff," I comment.

"She's eighteen. She likes to dabble with darkness. Didn't we all at that age?"

"Has she ever been a no-show before?"

"She's only played here a handful of times when I've been working. I don't recall her being late or not coming."

Tasha moves away to serve someone else a cocktail. No more winks since she learned I work for the government.

I study the lyrics. *The next time a star is born, you're the one who dies.*

If Bowie's missing, the police will want to see this. I'm taking a photo of the framed coaster when a call comes through. It's Mason. I give a silent prayer that it's the news I'm hoping for. Bowie, safe and sound on the camping trip.

I hurry outside of the club before answering. "Mason?"

"Lake." His deep voice is somber. There's no music in the background this time. "I'm afraid I have some troubling news."

9
BOWIE

"Here comes lover boy," Isla's friend Daphne says with a giggle and a toss of her light brown curls. Isla fluffs her hair around her bare shoulders and freshens her pink lip stain. People keep stopping Dean, wanting to talk, to sun themselves in his glow.

Bowie and Isla snuck out of the house tonight to meet Daphne at the Cat's Meow. Isla's boyfriend, Dean, is playing a show. It's the first time in the three months she's been here that Bowie has broken any of her host parents' rules, but she really wanted to see the show.

Stuart and Myra don't approve of Isla dating Dean because he's a few years older and he's a musician. They told Isla to focus on athletic scholarships and university entrance exams, not dating wannabe rock stars.

Not that there's anything wannabe about Dean. He's the real deal. He has star power in spades, as Suzie would say. He's gorgeous, with that Elvis profile and that slouchy, long-limbed grace. His voice during the first set gave her shivers. One minute he was a rockabilly crooner, the next an indie balladeer, then a glittery glam rocker.

"Hey there, sunshine." He slides into the booth next to Isla and pulls her into a kiss.

Several people in the room give Isla dirty looks, clearly wishing Dean was single and they could take him home.

"Heya, Daphne," Dean says.

"Dean. Great set."

"Ta. And who's this?" He looks at Bowie expectantly.

"This is my . . . this is our exchange student, Bowie," says Isla, stumbling over the words a little. Had she started to say that Bowie was her sister?

"Oh, the one you told me about. Bowie, how're you going?"

Bowie loves the way people here ask how you're going, instead of how you're doing. It implies a forward motion, a friendly destination that's missing in the American greeting. And she's noticed that they're genuinely interested in her answer. They listen intently and expect real details, not throwaway half-truths.

"Right now I'm a little starstruck, to tell you the truth. Isla told me you were talented but you know, she's your girlfriend, so she kind of has to say that, right? But you're freaking amazing. That madrigal at the end would have made Jeff Buckley weep."

His brows raise. "Aren't you a little young to know Jeff Buckley?"

"I listen to all kinds of music from all eras. I'm loving the scene here."

"Who are your faves?"

"Too many to name. Marlon Williams and Lorde, of course."

"I hear you're a musician, too?"

"She's a singer-songwriter. She has like a million followers," Daphne chimes in.

"Hardly," Bowie mutters.

"Does she now?"

The way Dean says it makes it sound like she's sold out. Like having tons of followers is something to be ashamed of, and, yeah, sometimes it does make her uncomfortable. Half of her followers are lechy old men who are there only for the crop tops.

Dean takes a swig from his beer. "Maybe you can sit in with us one of these nights. Send me one of your songs."

Isla frowns. "We had to sneak out tonight. You know my mum and dad don't want me coming here. They're hardly going to allow Bowie up onstage."

"What do I have to do to convince them that my intentions are honorable?" He grins and lifts Isla's hand, kissing her knuckles and staring into her eyes.

Isla visibly melts, and Bowie can't blame her. He's insanely charming. Which makes her mistrust him more. She knows the cruelty that lurks behind handsome faces. She'd wanted to hear him play live, and she'd also wanted to check him out, to make sure he was worthy of Isla.

She hasn't made up her mind yet.

"You two are disgusting." Daphne swats Dean's arm. "Get a room already."

Dean drapes an arm around Isla's shoulders. "Wish you could stay later. Your parents won't have to know if you're back in your bed by morning."

"It's a school night," Isla replies, but she doesn't sound convinced. She'd rather stay here with Dean. Go a little wild.

Can Isla trust him? In Bowie's experience, male rockers have massive egos and wandering eyes. Or maybe he's as nice as he is talented. Maybe he's one of the good ones. She'd like to give him the benefit of the doubt.

The way he'd looked at Bowie when they'd been introduced had been admiring but not sleazy. On a scale from unwanted-eye-fucking to goddess-on-a-pedestal, he'd been somewhere in the middle.

"Great set, Dean." An older man with tousled hair and a still-boyish face claps Dean on the shoulder.

"Thanks. Hey, man, I want you to meet my girlfriend, Isla."

"Isla. Nice to meet you. I'm Mark Edison."

"He's the American music producer I was telling you about. He's making the new album sound phenomenal. And this is Daphne and Bowie."

Mark studies Bowie for a moment. "Unusual name. You look familiar. Have we met?"

"No. Maybe I remind you of my mom, Suzie Bishop? She was in Bitter Pill."

Mark's eyebrows raise. "Bitter Pill. Now that's a trip down memory lane. Yeah . . ." He smiles, his gaze distant. "I met your mom once briefly at a club in L.A. Her makeup was all smeared and she was rocking this leather flight-attendant uniform—equal parts terrifying and gorgeous."

"That's my mom."

"You look a lot like her. Only less terrifying."

"Thanks, I guess."

"Gotta get back onstage," says Dean. "Invitation stands, Bowie. Sit in with us anytime you like." He kisses Isla on the lips and lopes back to the stage.

Mark lingers, still staring at Bowie. "You're a singer like your mom?"

"I dabble."

"Don't be modest." Daphne's about to launch into her million-follower nonsense again. Bowie cuts her off.

"I'm an exchange student. I'm not here to perform."

"Ah. Well, if you change your mind, I'd love to hear you sing. Your mom was legendary in her day. Be it ever so brief."

He returns to his table in front of the stage. Dean and his band play a sexy anthem with a disco beat. He prowls the stage, singing about private parties, about bodies pressed up against walls. No one can look away. He's mesmerizing.

"Oh my God, Isla," Daphne says with awe and envy in her voice. "You scored the hottest bloke in Welly."

"I don't even know how I did it," Isla says wonderingly, her pale green eyes shining as she watches Dean tune his guitar. "Why does he even like me?"

"Because you're stunning and talented." Bowie means it. Isla lives and breathes swimming, lacrosse, and all things athletic in the same way that Bowie lives and breathes music. It's amazing to watch her—sleek and powerful—slice through the pool with the precision of an X-Acto blade cutting paper.

"I've never been that popular. I think it's because I usually prefer sports to real life."

"Popularity doesn't mean everything," Bowie says.

Daphne rolls her eyes. "Says the girl with legions of followers."

"My mom runs my social media. It's not like I'm desperate for more followers. She's the one who wants me to be famous."

"Whatever, Miss 'I hung out backstage with Billie Eilish.'"

"That was only because my mom knew one of the roadies."

Daphne obviously thinks Bowie's a fame whore, and really, who can blame her? Anyone who follows Bowie and Suzie thinks they're dripping with rock-star glamour. You can make anything look glamorous if you try hard enough. And Suzie tries so hard. She stages most of their photos at the casino.

In real life they rent a tiny apartment in an ancient building that was probably listed as having "vintage charm," which just means the plasterwork is chipped and the windows rattle with every step taken on the scarred floors. The water comes out tinged the color of blood. The back of the toilet is cracked and held together by duct tape.

Isla and Daphne sit arm in arm, watching the show and sharing private jokes. The way they tease each other brings a searing ache of longing for her best friend, Florica Baciu.

Bowie and Florica had met the first day of public high school. Bowie immediately nicknamed her "Lo," and Florica called her "Bo," and from that day forward they were the inseparable duo known to their classmates as BoLo.

Lo was Romanian; she'd moved to the U.S. with her parents

when she was fourteen. She still spoke with a strong accent when Bowie met her. She'd been her best friend. The one who knew all her secrets and who had her back, no matter what.

Bowie can't stop the memories from burning through her, leaving charred tracks across her heart.

"Platforms or thigh highs?" Lo had asked her that night—the night everything became a nightmare—holding out the shoe choices.

Bowie had pointed to the gold platform Mary Janes. "You wore those to my open mic last week. That was a good night."

"Tonight's gonna be a good night," Lo had said, buckling the shoes. "You're going to slay."

"You totally are, baby." Suzie adjusted Bowie's leather mini-skirt higher on her thighs and Bowie tugged it back down. She wished she could wear her original outfit choice of black tank top and baggy jeans, but she'd been overruled by her mom and her best friend.

"Remember when you meet the record scout, don't forget to—"

"Smile," Bowie finished. "I know, I know. Smile, and the world smiles with me."

Suzie gave Bowie one more critical once-over. "What do you think, Florica?"

"She's perfect. Except maybe a little more contouring?" Lo approached with a glittery gold brush and Bowie held up her fingers in the sign of the cross.

"Stay back, foul creature."

"Do it, Florica," Suzie urged. "Hold her down and contour the heck out of her. She has to be perfect. Glen says if the scout likes you, you'll have a chance to hand a demo directly to Stratus Records. Fuck, baby!" Suzie gripped Bowie's shoulders tightly. "That's the big leagues. This is the night we've been waiting for. Believe it with all your heart and it will come true. Do you believe?"

She shook Bowie's shoulders and stared into her eyes. "I asked, do you believe? Do you believe you can do this?"

"Yes." Bowie pulled away. "I believe I can do this."

"Good. That's my shining star." She blew them both air kisses. "See you in the VIP room in a half hour!" She left the room humming.

Lo laughed, shaking her head. "Your mom is super intense."

"I hate it so much."

"But it's not all bad, right? I mean, she really loves you. She's obsessed with you."

"She needs to get her own life."

"At least she knows you exist. That's better than being forgotten." Lo started tidying up her makeup case.

"I'm sorry." Bowie hugged her friend from behind and laid her chin on her shoulder, looking at their reflection in the mirror. "Did something happen with your dad?"

"He's not even coming home for the holidays this year. He's basically never coming back again. He has his new family in Auckland, and he says it's too far to travel back to Vegas. I wish I could go visit him there, but my mother says we don't have the money. Or there could be something wrong with our immigration paperwork."

Suzie had found Lo's mom, Livia, a job as a housekeeper at The Trophy. Even if her immigration paperwork was in question, the casino management tended to turn a blind eye if an employee worked hard enough.

"I don't want you to leave. Stay here with me. We'll have so much fun being sarcastic about the slot machine zombies spending Christmas in the casino."

"Yeah." Lo shut her makeup case. "You're right. He doesn't want me there, anyway. He's forgotten all about me."

"That's not true. You're unforgettable, Lo." Bowie kissed her cheek and she ducked away.

"Hey, watch it. My makeup's on point tonight, unlike someone else's."

"Fine. You win." She turned Lo to face her. "Do your worst."

Lo smiled and opened her makeup case again, searching for the right bronzer in her box of mysterious potions and palettes.

Bowie would do anything to make her friend smile. It didn't happen often enough. Lo was the perfect nickname for her. She had a core of sadness that Bowie recognized because she had the same one. They understood each other.

As they walked through the casino floor, hungry gazes followed Lo, drawn to her long bare legs, high cheekbones, impossibly large doe eyes, and the sway of the dyed pink hair tumbling down her back.

It was almost impossible to make the zombies look up from the slots, but Lo was wearing a shimmering gold bodycon dress that hugged every ample curve. Her cheekbones looked like they'd been dusted with pollen.

"Everyone's staring at you, Lo."

"See what a contour brush can do?"

"That's not it and you know it. You're so beautiful. You're a shooting star and they all want a little stardust."

"They're staring at the girl carrying the badass guitar. Wondering if you're famous. Don't forget about me after you score that record deal, okay?"

Bowie bumped her friend's shoulder. "Never. It's BoLo forever."

Her friend was so sweet, genuinely sweet, and she could have been so full of herself because that kind of beauty couldn't be purchased, injected, or carved into existence.

Bowie knocked on the VIP suite door, and Glen's chief of security, Ryan Colgan, opened it and led them inside. Colgan was always so brooding and silent, a hulking presence with a beard that hid his face and an obvious gun-shaped bulge under his suit jacket.

Glen's gaze always made her skin crawl, but Colgan looked right through her, as if she were too small and insignificant to mean anything to him. She didn't know which one was worse.

"You're late." Glen lounged against the bar, glass of whiskey in one hand.

Her mom's boss, owner of The Trophy, was rude, sexist, and never sugar-coated anything, but Bowie would rather deal with a man who didn't hide his sins under a layer of false kindness.

"All this," Bowie waved a hand over her made-up face and skintight clothes, "doesn't simply appear by itself."

"I like that skirt," Glen said, his gaze crawling along her thighs.

Of course he liked the skirt. It barely covered her butt.

Then he noticed Lo. Normally, Bowie enjoyed watching people meet her friend for the first time, the way they were caught and trapped by her beauty, how they always looked a little flustered, as if they were in the presence of royalty and should maybe bow or curtsy or something, but she didn't like the calculating way Glen eyed her.

He set his drink down and came toward them. "Hello there. Have we met?"

"I'm Florica."

Glen took her hand. "Are you a singer, too, Florica?"

"Can't hold a tune."

"A dancer? You could definitely be a showgirl." He stroked the top of her hand. "Do you want me to make some calls?"

"Jesus, Glen, she's the same age as me," Bowie said, pulling Lo's hand free from his grip. "As soon as we finish high school, Lo is attending Stanford. She's going to be a lawyer."

"I haven't been accepted yet."

"But your test scores are good enough."

"Actually, I've been thinking about applying to be an exchange student to New Zealand next year."

Bowie stared at her friend. "You never told me that. You mean you want to go for a whole year?"

"Sounds like someone would miss you too much if you left," Glen said. "And I'm sure your family would miss you, too."

"My dad moved to Auckland with his new wife and kids. And my mom's never home anyway." Lo caught his gaze and held it steadily. "Her name's Livia. She's one of your housekeepers. She's too busy working her fingers to the bone."

Glen looked away. "I'll make sure she gets more vacation time," he muttered.

The room was empty except for the three of them and Colgan. "Where is everyone?" Bowie asked.

Colgan flipped a switch on the wall, and suddenly the large mirror became transparent and they could see into an adjoining room.

"Travis McCray is the one I want you to meet," Glen says, pointing him out. "He's a scout for Stratus. He's wearing the Pixies T-shirt. And there's my son, Bruce."

"Bruce is here?" Lo asked, her eyes widening. "I didn't know he'd be here. I used to go to all the games to watch him. I was there when he threw for two hundred eighty-one yards and three freaking touchdowns!"

"Uh-oh, we have a football groupie here." Glen's smile didn't reach his eyes.

Lo hadn't stopped staring at Bruce.

Bowie poked her. "You're drooling."

"You didn't tell me Bruce Walter would be here."

"I didn't know. He's never around anymore. Where's my mom?" Bowie asked Glen.

"There was an emergency on the floor. One of the cocktail waitresses is in the hospital. Suzie's filling in for a half hour until the replacement arrives. She's such a trooper, your mom."

"Do you really think Travis wants to hear these old covers you chose?"

Glen wanted her to sing an old song called "Hot Child in the City." She'd done her homework. It had been a hit in 1978 for Canadian singer Nick Gilder, who said he wrote it after watching teen prostitutes work Hollywood Boulevard. It did have a banging bass line and a good hook but . . . teen prostitutes?

"Sing the songs I chose. I know what I'm doing," Glen said curtly. "Once you land the audition, then you hit the label with your originals, the songs you want on your first album."

Glen's nose and cheeks were red in the dim lighting. He had that sweet-rot smell to his breath that meant he'd been drinking since lunch. The same smell as on Suzie's breath after a long shift at the casino.

Could she trust him to know what was right for her career? He'd arranged this meeting, and Stratus was a big deal, so she had to play by his rules. At least for tonight.

"Come on, Florica," Glen said, taking her arm. "Let's introduce you to my son. And Bowie, you're gonna knock him dead. I know you will."

"Right? She's so amazingly talented. Don't be nervous, Bo."

"I'm not," Bowie lied. She always got nervous before performing. Like her stomach was an elevator with faulty cables, plummeting into an abyss.

Lo squeezed her hand and leaned in to kiss Bowie's cheek. Her orchid perfume lingered, caressing Bowie's senses as Lo left the room with Glen.

Bowie tuned her guitar and watched through the mirror-window as Glen introduced Lo to Bruce. Of course Bruce fell immediately under her spell, ditching the blonde he'd been talking to. Lo drank up his attention, laughing and flirting, happier than Bowie had seen her in a long time. It put a smile on Bowie's face to see her friend smile.

Glen nodded at Bowie, eerily finding her eyes through the glass. That was her signal. Suzie still wasn't here, but Bowie knew exactly what she would have said: The show must go on.

Bowie slung her guitar across her back and followed Colgan into the neighboring VIP suite. She tapped on the mic and did a few vocal tests. No one paid her any attention. They were too busy laughing and drinking, Lo included. She was practically sitting on Bruce's lap.

Travis was talking to a stunning brunette, but he kept checking his phone, so he couldn't be that into her. He was actually kind of hot. Bowie had expected an old balding guy, but Travis was young and fit, with chiseled cheekbones and collar-length black hair. He reminded her a little bit of Keanu Reeves.

Bowie was supposed to sit on a high leather stool, but her skirt was too short. She perched awkwardly on the edge of the stool and lifted her guitar.

Lo caught her eye and lifted her glass. *You got this*, she mouthed.

Glen tapped on the side of his cocktail glass with a metal swizzle stick. He nodded at Colgan, who pressed a button and stopped the piped-in house music.

"Hey everyone, we have a treat tonight. Some live music from a very talented young lady named Bowie Bishop. She's going to blow your minds, guaranteed."

One of the VIPs, an old dude with feathered gray hair wearing a white fringed cowboy shirt, mumbled something dirty about blowing, looking directly at Lo, but Bowie didn't let it bother her. She was focused now. The elevator had landed. She knew exactly where she was.

Inside the music.

She'd changed the "Hot Child" song. Twisted it until she was singing from the perspective of the girl, not the male observer. She'd hoped it would be enough to make it interesting, but halfway through the song she knew it had been the wrong choice. Travis looked bored. His eyes roamed his cell phone, then the room, finding the door. He shifted in his chair. She had to do something fast. She sang the chorus one more time, then paused to retune her guitar.

Lo's eyes held a question, and Glen frowned.

She strummed the opening chords of the song she'd written for Lo last New Year's Eve, when her father had told her about his new family and she'd sobbed all night.

Really don't take much to fall apart
Just a little push to help it start

SHE FELL AWAY

Pick up the pieces in the dark
Pull out the arrows that hit their mark

A slow tempo. Key of D minor. The only key a Lo song could be.

Travis stopped fidgeting. Turned to face her. He was listening now.

You find your balance when you're standing still
Sometimes it feels like you're a spinning wheel
Close your eyes and count to ten
Find a place to hide again

Between your future and your past
You find your balance when you're running fast
Feels like nothing good will ever stay
Find a place for you to hide away

You find your balance when you're dreaming far
Sometimes it feels like you're a shooting star

She was dimly aware that, one by one, each person in the room had fallen silent.

When she performed on a stage, it was impossible to command the attention of every single person in the room, but here in this room she could reach everyone. She could show the record scout that she had something to say. Show Glen that he didn't control her. She chose her own songs. Her own words.

And mostly she could tell Lo that she was strong. She was beautiful. She could write her own story.

It feels like you can taste the color blue
Sometimes it feels like you can hear it too
Between the flower and the drop of dew
Just tell a story and then make it true

As she sang, her voice grew more powerful. Most of the men in this room saw her and Lo as jailbait pieces of ass, objects they'd like to own briefly and then throw away. But Bowie owned these men tonight. Bowie and Lo were the VIPs, and everyone else was there to clap.

When she stopped singing, the last note shimmered in the air for a moment and it felt like the whole room was holding its breath . . . and then the applause started.

Lo's eyes were shining with tears, but she was smiling. Travis stood up, clapping loudly, and walked toward her.

"Bowie." Daphne waves her hand in front of Bowie's face.

"What?" Bowie's disoriented for a moment, lost in the memory, the nightmare.

"Are you here with us?"

"I was remembering this time I sang for a record scout in Las Vegas."

"Well, la-di-da," Isla says.

"It was a bad night. The worst night of my life."

"What happened?"

"My best friend, Lo . . ." She can't say the words. She'll start crying. Lose her shit in front of Isla and her friend. "I need a drink."

Isla cocks her head. "I thought your exchange program had a zero-alcohol policy if you're under twenty-one."

"I don't care." Bowie gets up from the table on unsteady feet. All she can see is Lo. The last time she'd seen her. The glowing smile on her face. The tears shining in her eyes.

"Patrón. Make it a double," she tells the rocker-chick bartender. The tequila sears her throat, but she welcomes the cleansing fire. She wants to burn away her memories.

"Do you have a pen?" Bowie asks the bartender, who hands her the pen that had been tucked behind her ear.

Bowie grabs a bar coaster, flips it over, and begins to write.

10

LAKE

"I spoke to Stuart Shepherd, and Bowie's not on the camping trip with them," Mason says. "They'll come home first thing tomorrow."

"Shit," I mutter, pacing the sidewalk outside the club. I shiver in the stinging wind. I left my leather jacket on the barstool.

"Bowie told Stuart and Myra that she wanted to stay in Welly to play the show at the Cat's Meow. She'd played there a few times before, and her mum was all for it. She personally called the Shepherds to give her permission for Bowie to perform there any time. Bowie arranged to stay with a friend, Daphne Anderson."

"I'm at the Cat's Meow right now. Bowie's not here."

"That's what the bar manager told me when I called earlier. Bowie was supposed to take the bus to Daphne's house on Thursday but she never showed up. Instead, she called Daphne and told her that she'd decided to go on the camping trip after all. Daphne had no reason not to believe her."

"She lied about going on the camping trip."

"Someone's lying, that's certain. I'm at the Shepherds' house right now with a team, searching for any clues as to Bowie's whereabouts. Her passport is still in her bedroom. But Lake, here's the truly ominous part: Her room has been torn apart, as if someone was desperately searching for something."

"Whoa. Any valuables missing in the house?"

"Nothing missing from Mrs. Shepherd's jewelry box, or the safe in the study. All the antiques still here. The only missing items of value we've been able to identify are Bowie's guitar and her laptop."

"I researched her guitar when I saw it online. It's a vintage Gibson Everly Brothers J-180 with an ebony finish. Worth a lot of money."

"Mrs. Shepherd says it's her most treasured possession. If the guitar and the laptop are missing, it could mean that she's a runaway."

"She could have searched her own room. Maybe she was missing something?"

"Maybe."

"Or someone else could have been in the house."

"We'll be reviewing the security camera footage. Mrs. Shepherd is beside herself. She's a mental health counselor. She says Bowie has depressive tendencies."

"Along those lines, I'll send you a photo I took tonight of some lyrics that Bowie wrote on a bar coaster. The bartender kept it framed behind the bar. They're fairly bleak."

"Ta. We're escalating this to a missing persons case. I know you wanted to be the one to break any news to the mother, Suzie Bishop, but my superior, Detective Senior Sergeant Jill Sutherland, is the lead on this now, and she wanted to speak with Ms. Bishop, ask her some questions."

My jaw clenches. "She already contacted Suzie?"

"They're having a brief conversation right now. I wanted to give you a heads-up before you talk to Ms. Bishop. Please keep us informed of any information she gives you."

"I will. What about Bruce Walter? I keep thinking there must be a connection between his death and Bowie's disappearance."

"DSS Sutherland is going to request a full postmortem to see if there's any physical evidence connecting them."

"Bruce's parents, Glen and Nadia Walter, are arriving tomorrow morning by private jet. They insist they have no idea why their son was in Wellington. Maybe they'll have more information when they arrive. I'll have Rob Smith, our Regional Security officer, contact you immediately. He'll be the one working with you on the investigation, law enforcement to law enforcement."

"This is priority number one for my unit now. A famous dead American athlete with ties to a missing teenager who is housed with a high-profile MP. Let the media feeding frenzy commence."

"We have to find her, Mason."

"We do," he says grimly. "And here you were hoping for peace and quiet after Cambodia."

"No chance of that now." People start to spill out of the club doors. The show can't be over already; maybe the band is taking a set break. Dean Hira emerges with a bandmate, cigarette in hand.

"Mason, I have to go. I see someone who knows Bowie."

"Right. Call me if you hear anything important."

I slip my phone into my pocket and approach Dean, where he's leaning against a wall, smoking. "Excuse me, Dean Hira? Can I talk to you for a minute?"

His bandmate gives me the once-over, then grins lazily. "I'll leave you two alone, shall I?" He slouches away. He thinks I'm a groupie.

I'm taken off guard by how tall Dean is even offstage, how long-limbed and graceful.

"I'm Lake Harlowe." I hold out my hand.

He glances down, flicks cigarette ash onto the sidewalk. "Are you a reporter?"

"No. But I do want to ask you some questions."

"Yeah, naw." He shakes his head, hair flopping over one eye. "I'm in the middle of a show."

"This is important. It's about Bowie Bishop."

He glances up, more interested now. "What about her?"

"I caught your show because I was hoping Bowie might be here."

"So was I."

"You had no idea she wouldn't be here?"

"None. It's kind of annoying, to tell you the truth. A real diva move."

"I'm a consular officer with the U.S. embassy. Her mother hasn't heard from her in a few days. I'm trying to find her."

"You mean, like, she's missing?"

"Maybe. The police will most likely be contacting you. I thought I'd ask a few questions since I'm already here and it's my job to do a whereabouts check for her mother. When was the last time you saw her?"

He takes a deep drag on his cigarette, brow wrinkling as he thinks. "I honestly haven't seen her in weeks. I have some texts from her on my phone from Thursday morning."

During my consular training I took a workshop on micro expressions. Those tiny, involuntary facial movements that sometimes contradict the words we speak. The instructor showed video clips of press conferences and slowed the footage down. There was that split second where an eyebrow arched, or eyes widened, betraying the true emotion before the lie was told. I worked the insanely busy visa line in Shanghai. I developed a sixth sense about when applicants were lying.

Ask him a few things that I know the answers to, to gauge the truth of his responses, whether he has any tells when he's lying, and then the real question. The one I don't know the answer to.

"Did Bowie ever perform with you before?"

"Yeah, the first night I met her she jumped up onstage and sang a song she wrote a few minutes before. It was impressive."

"What was the song about?"

"Not sure really. Something about not becoming anyone's trophy. She's a fiery one. We invited her back a few more times."

SHE FELL AWAY

"I saw the video of you and Bowie singing that Nick Cave and Kylie Minogue duet. Whose idea was it to switch the roles?"

"That was Bowie's idea. She always wants to switch things up, twist old classics in new ways. D'you think I make a good Kylie?" He sticks one hip out and blows a smoke ring, vamping for me.

"I think you two were gazing soulfully into each other's eyes."

"All for the camera, luv." He laughs softly. Takes another drag from his cigarette.

"Do you admire her?"

"Of course. She's brilliant. Talented. A bright light. All of that. I'm not obsessed with her or anything, like the blokes in her DMs."

"Does she like New Zealand?"

"She loves it. Started using Kiwi slang, everything was *sweet as*, and *no worries*." His expression softens. His lips curve up. "She even learned some basic te reo Māori."

His answers are made confidently, with no hesitation, full eye contact. His hands never shake. Feet don't jitter.

"Was Isla Shepherd jealous of Bowie? Did they have a fight about you?"

He pauses with the short stub of his cigarette halfway to his lips. "Who told you that?"

"I'm asking you."

"Not that I know of. Isla and I dated briefly, but her parents shut it down."

One more question.

"Do you know where Bowie might be?"

He blinks. This could be a lie.

"I have no idea." He stubs his cigarette out on the brick wall. "Gotta go, Lake. Fame and fortune await."

I watch him walk away and disappear into the club. I hug my arms around my ribs, shivering. I turn to follow him back in when the duty phone buzzes in my pocket.

I don't even manage a hello before Suzie starts in with her usual galloping pace and raspy voice. "She's missing, Lake, just like I feared." She blows her nose loudly. "I know something bad has happened. I talked to a detective named Jill. I wasn't there to watch over her and something bad has happened. The detective told me Bruce Walter choked to death in Wellington. What was he doing there?"

"I was hoping you could answer that question."

"I have no idea. Bowie didn't like Bruce. She always called him a nepo baby because he was the heir to the Walter football dynasty and fortune."

"Do you think he could have something to do with Bowie going missing?"

"Bruce is focused on his football career. He wouldn't do anything to jeopardize his future. You know who gave me a strange vibe when I visited Wellington, though? Stuart Shepherd. He was so obsessed with his reelection campaign. So concerned about his reputation, and not having anything negative said about him in the press. He had all these rules for Isla and Bowie to follow."

"What are you saying? You don't think Bowie was safe with her host family?"

"I'm just saying that rich men can't be trusted. I should know." She laughs bitterly. "All they've ever done is screw me over. You think the wealthy ones can save you, but it's the opposite. They come with far too high a price."

"Glen Walter is your employer, right?"

"Speaking of rich, untrustworthy dudes. Glen and Nadia must be devastated about Bruce. He was their pride and joy and now he's dead. What if . . . what if . . ." Her voice trails off.

I know what she means. *What if Bowie's dead, too?*

"Lake. You have to find her. Find my baby. I put a plane ticket on a credit card. I leave early tomorrow morning."

"Rob Smith, the Regional Security officer from the embassy, will take over now. He'll coordinate with local law enforcement.

You can expect the same quality of service from law enforcement here in New Zealand that you would in the U.S."

"I want you to be my liaison, not some guy with a badge who thinks he knows everything."

"I'm here to help and support you however I'm able, but I'm not a trained law enforcement professional."

Diplomats aren't law enforcement. Although there have been a handful of high-profile cases where we've been instrumental in bringing criminals to justice, like the Dutch diplomat whose meticulous documentation of missing tourists helped track down the serial killer known as The Serpent in Thailand.

"You must have had some training, right? They wouldn't throw you out there blind. Have you had a missing persons case before?"

"I've done welfare and whereabouts checks but the person has always been found." I won't tell her about the two times when they were found dead. "Do you think Bowie could be a runaway?"

"Absolutely not. She didn't run away. She wouldn't. She was coming home to Vegas in two months. She has an album to record. She's finally going to break through. And I don't care that you're not a police officer, Lake. Personally, I think that's better. I have a feeling about you. You're Bowie's guardian angel. You're only thirty. You were eighteen not so long ago."

My breath catches. "How do you know how old I am?"

"I'm a social media manager. I have my ways. I saw your photo on the embassy website. You're very pretty. You don't look like a government drone. You could be an actress from the 1930s." Her words are beginning to slur together, as though she's taken a sleeping pill or a few shots of whiskey. "Lake Harlowe, with red-gold hair and fine features. I see sadness in your eyes. Like Bowie. You'll understand her. You'll get inside her skin . . . think like her."

"Suzie," I say gently, "maybe you should get some sleep." It's early morning in Las Vegas.

"Don't leave me! Please stay on the phone with me. It's the

not knowing that's the worst. The imagining. I see her lying somewhere, blood spreading around her. Or she's been kidnapped and she's being held captive. Frightened and alone. It's like I can't stop my thoughts from going there."

"Do you have someone who can stay with you tonight?"

"I'm all alone." Her raspy voice is pumped full of pain, bloated and shiny with it. I know this brand of pain. It cauterizes your heart. Stains everything gray.

I can't end the call when she sounds so fragile and lost. I talked to Dean. I'll report what he said to Mason later, but the police will interview him more thoroughly if Bowie's still missing. I can do this small service for Suzie.

"Lake? Are you still there?"

"I'm here. Let me switch to earbuds. You can talk to me while I settle my tab."

"Bowie is special, Lake. You'll know that after you find her. She's born to be a star. She learned how to sing before she could talk. She'd sing along with me while I played Beatles tunes. I knew she was going to be famous the first time I heard her baby voice singing 'Let It Be.' She had a way of interpreting songs, making them her own, even at five years old."

She keeps talking about Bowie as I settle my tab and call a ride back to my apartment. Nothing is required from me except the occasional murmur of acknowledgment. Her voice is growing hoarser. She's had several cigarettes while we've been on the phone. I arrive home and throw on sweats, wipe off my lipstick, and collapse on the couch with a bottle of pinot noir, some Australian cheddar, and rosemary crackers.

Edgar hops up and licks my sweater sleeve when I spill some cheese crumbs. His rough little tongue gets stuck, and he wiggles his head awkwardly.

"Are you close with your mom, Lake?" The question catches me off guard.

"It's complicated," I say carefully.

"You should call her tonight. You never know what's going

to happen. I wish Bowie had called me before she disappeared. Maybe she would have said something to me. Some clue about the person who's responsible. Maybe I could have stopped this from happening."

"We don't know what's happened, Suzie. There's no use thinking you could have prevented it, whatever it is. We'll do everything in our power to find her."

Her words come slower now. She's stopped crying. I think she's falling asleep.

"Suzie?" I whisper. There's no response. I can hear her even breathing. She's asleep.

I end the call and settle back against the couch cushions.

You should call her.

I shouldn't. Calling my mom is like picking a scab that hasn't fully healed yet. I know it will end with fresh bleeding.

I severed that connection on purpose. There's a layer I keep between me and my past. The outer skin of an onion. Thin yet tough. I left Alaska when I was eighteen, running away from unsettling childhood memories, from my mother. Has Bowie done something similar? Myra Shepherd said she could be depressed, and the song lyrics Bowie wrote weren't exactly sunny.

When I was eighteen, I thought in absolutes. You were for me or against me. Good or bad. My mother or me. This small town or me.

At thirty, I know that the margins of life are cloudy like a cancer that's metastasized. The decisions we make in our present are tied to the umbilical cord of our past.

I feel tied to Bowie.

I pull up her Instagram, scroll deeper and deeper, looking for something that could tell me why she's missing.

Where are you, Bowie?

She stares back at me, this lost girl, with not even the ghost of a smile, her face the only light in my room.

11

BOWIE

Isla has been silent the whole ride back from the Cat's Meow. Daphne drops them off a few blocks away, and the two girls walk down the moonlit, quiet street. They keep to the shadows, hoping to escape notice from nosy neighbors.

"Is something wrong?" Bowie whispers.

"You couldn't help yourself, could you?" Bowie can't see Isla's face clearly, but she sounds furious. "You had to go onstage and steal the attention for yourself."

"Dean said I should sit in with them."

"He didn't mean tonight. You did it to impress him and to show off for that record producer, Edison, or whatever his name was."

"I wasn't thinking about anything except the song I'd written. I had to let it out. I wasn't trying to steal the attention from you. And I certainly wasn't hitting on Dean."

Even as she says it, Bowie knows that Isla isn't going to understand. The song she'd shared with Dean tonight was almost more intimate than if she'd slept with him. Music was a world that Isla could never be a part of.

"Isla. Do you believe me? I swear it's true. You have nothing to be afraid of."

SHE FELL AWAY

"Shhh. Be quiet." They're nearly to the house now.

"Wait." Bowie tugs on Isla's arm to stop her. "Let's talk about this. I don't want you to be mad at me."

Isla jerks away. "All right. Let's talk. You think everyone should be obsessed with you. Well, I have news for you. The world doesn't revolve around you. You're not the sun, the moon, and all the shiny stars. I'm sick of you swanning around like it's your universe and we're all just the warm-up act."

"Is that really how you see me?"

"That's the way everyone sees you. You're larger than life. You walk into a room and I don't even exist."

"That's not true and you know it. You're so amazing. I'm just the new girl in town. The allure will wear off."

"Trust me, it has."

"This isn't only about Dean, is it?"

"It's about everything. You can't borrow my life like you'd borrow a jumper. My parents aren't yours, and neither is Dean. He's mine. You can't have him."

"I don't want him. Isla, you have to believe me, I honestly don't."

"Yeah, but that won't make any difference if he decides that he wants you, now will it? I saw the way he looked at you onstage. He couldn't stop staring."

"It was only the music. He liked the song."

"It was more than that. How can I compete? When you're onstage, it's like a lightning bolt crackles down from the heavens and strikes you. You're brighter than anything else."

Bowie tries to catch her eye, but Isla stares at the ground. "I'm sorry you feel that way. I honestly wasn't trying to upstage you."

"Whatever. I'm tired. I want to go to bed." Isla stalks away, and Bowie has to run to keep up with her long-legged stride.

They make it inside and are tiptoeing up the stairs when a voice sounds from Stuart's study. "Girls? Is that you?"

"Fucking great." Isla grabs Bowie's arm, her nails sharp

against her skin. "We're in trouble now. It's all because you had to bask in the spotlight and we stayed too long."

"I'm sorry."

"Just don't say anything about Dean," Isla whispers urgently.

Stuart stays seated behind his desk in the study while they stand in front of him. Bowie's never seen him look so serious. "Where were you?"

"We went for a walk to the—" Bowie begins, but Stuart cuts her off.

"Don't lie to me. I know you've been out to a club. I can smell alcohol on you. Which club, Isla?"

"The Cat's Meow."

"To see Dean's band," Stuart says.

"No."

He stares at her.

"Yes," she mumbles, hanging her head.

"It was my idea," Bowie jumps in quickly. "I asked Isla to take me because I wanted to see some Wellington nightlife. It's much tamer than Las Vegas, believe me."

"I don't care how bohemian your life was in Las Vegas, Bowie. You can't act like that here. You're under my roof now. I won't have you leading Isla astray."

"It's not even midnight," Isla says with a toss of her hair. "It's not like we've been out tarting around."

"You didn't answer any of my calls. Another quarter hour and I would have been forced to wake your mother and maybe even call the police. Do you think that would have been good for my reelection campaign?"

"I'm so sick of your bloody campaign. It's all anyone ever talks about in this house. What about my life? I didn't ask to be born the daughter of a politician in a long illustrious line of bloody politicians."

"Don't speak to me that way, young lady."

"I should be allowed to see a show if I want to."

"I forbid you to date Dean Hira, do you understand?"

"Why?"

"Because he's too old for you and he's a party boy. He's obviously a bad influence on you, luring you out to nightclubs on a school night. Bad boys only want one thing. Your mother and I are trying to protect you from—"

"Teenage pregnancy? Scandal? Your reelection campaign in the toilet?"

Stuart sighs heavily. "I don't know what's gotten into you. Go to your room."

"With pleasure." Isla storms off, slamming the door on the way out.

When she's gone, Stuart turns to Bowie, shaking his head. "What am I going to do with you? Isla never acted out this way before you came."

Hardly fair. But Bowie was willing to take the blame, for Isla's sake. "It was my idea." She feels like she should be calling him "sir." Like she's in a BBC period drama, and she's been called in for punishment by the headmaster of a boarding school.

Watery lamplight washes over Stuart's face. His eyes are flat, expression stern. No laugh lines, no boyish grin. "Was it really your idea to sneak out, Bowie, or are you trying to protect Isla?"

"Does it matter?"

"Spoken like a politician. Answer a question with a question. Bowie, I know your mum was much more lenient than we are. I know that you were often in a more permissive environment."

"You mean the casino?"

"Well, yes. It's not exactly the best environment for children. All that noise and greed. No windows or clocks because they don't want you to know how long you've been trapped there."

Even though she agrees with him, she doesn't like his pointing it out. "Suzie does the best she can. She's a single mom. We don't have inherited wealth."

"I'm not casting aspersions on your mother. We expect you to follow our rules while you're living in our home. We're only trying to protect you. To keep you safe. Was Isla with Dean?"

"You'll have to ask her about that."

"He's inappropriate for her. Myra says he's too old but I object more to his rock-'n'-roll lifestyle."

"If you forbid her from seeing him, she'll only want it more."

"Wise words for a young person."

Bowie doesn't feel young. She's seen too much of the world.

"We have rules for a reason, Bowie. Myra has a . . . troubled past. She's strict with you and Isla because she's trying to keep you safer than she was at your age. We expect you to follow our rules. Promise me that you won't sneak out again."

"Your house, your rules."

"I need your promise," he says sternly.

"I promise. Sir." She adds the title ironically, but he seems to accept it as his rightful due.

He nods briskly. "Very good. It's a clear rules violation and there should be some consequences, but I don't want to tell Myra about this little incident. It would only worry her. She took a sleeping pill tonight because she's been on edge lately. Let's keep this our little secret, shall we?"

"Fine. May I go now?"

"Yes." He turns back to the papers on his desk. She's been dismissed. It's the first time she's felt like an interloper, an unwelcome stranger in their home.

The door to Isla's room is cracked open. Bowie tiptoes past, but Isla is waiting for her, the hall light giving her a halo of fire. "What did he say?"

"I told him it was my idea. He asked about Dean and I evaded the question. Why didn't you answer his calls? It would have been worse if he'd called the police."

"I didn't have my phone with me. At least not the one he has a number for."

"You have two phones?"

"Don't you?"

"I used to, but it was too much hassle keeping track of them. He said we should keep this a secret from your mother."

"Really? That's odd but . . . good, I guess."

"So are *we* good?"

Isla gives her a scornful look. "No, we're not. My life was perfect before you came. I thought I'd always wanted a sister, but I don't want one who constantly outshines me. It's exhausting. You're exhausting, Bowie."

Her harsh words find their mark. She's accusing Bowie of being too much, of taking up too much space. It's the same accusation Bowie makes about her mother. Could she really be acting like Suzie?

"You don't even know what it means to have friends. What you have is an orbit, and you draw everybody into it, and then it's the Bowie show and there's no room for anybody else there."

"That's not fair, Isla. I do know what it means to have friends. I lost my best friend in Las Vegas." Tears threaten to spill. "My best friend Lo died. She was the one who wanted to be an exchange student to New Zealand. I'm here because of her. For her."

Isla tilts her head. "You never told me that. How did she die?"

Bowie clenches her fists, digs her nails into the flesh of her palms. "It's a long story."

"Girls?" The door to Myra's bedroom opens, and she enters the hallway wearing a long white robe, her silver-streaked hair tumbling about her shoulders. "Is something wrong?" Her speech is slightly slurred. Stuart had said she'd taken a sleeping pill.

"Nothing's wrong. Go back to bed, Mum." Isla retreats into her room and closes her door.

Myra captures Bowie's forearm as she attempts to walk past her to her room. Her green eyes are glassy, like moss at the bottom of a shallow lake. "Sometimes secrets corrode us, Bowie. Consume our souls. They're like corpses slowly rotting beneath the soil of our minds. Fading to brittle bones." She lays her palms on Bowie's shoulders, pulls her closer. "Spit them out, Bowie."

Bowie's heart speeds. All she wants is to crawl into bed, and now Myra is clenching her by the shoulders and whispering creepy shit. "Um . . . I should go to bed."

"Spit them out," Myra repeats, her eyes dull, shaking Bowie by the shoulders.

"Spit what out?"

"Your secrets."

"Um . . ." Bowie tries to remove her hands.

As if a switch has been flipped, the clouds in Myra's eyes clear and she smiles. "Good night, dear." She kisses Bowie's forehead and lets her go.

Bowie flops on her bed fully clothed, her mind whirring. The hatred she'd seen in Isla's eyes. The jealousy. The shadowy stripes across Stuart's face as he told her he'd keep tonight a secret.

Myra shaking her by the shoulders. Her chilling words.

Life was filled with illusions. The illusion of being in control. The illusion of belonging. If she doesn't belong here, then where? Not Las Vegas. Not anymore.

What if she's just like Suzie? Taking up all the air, all the space in a room.

She feels cursed. Destined to hurt everyone she cares about.

Nobody told her that the relationship between her and her host sibling could be so complicated. She calls her sister, but they're not related by blood or adoption, even though they're living together in the same house for a year.

Bowie had been thinking that a year wasn't enough, that she wanted to stay in New Zealand forever. No one here knows her past. What she did. What she can never undo.

She's begun planning her transformation. She'll become someone her mom won't even recognize.

Most of the other exchange students double down on their cultural identity like *I'm so American I eat apple pie for breakfast and laugh so loud it makes people turn their heads on the street.* Not Bowie. She wants Aotearoa New Zealand to claim her as its own. She wants to be consumed by this lush green paradise, where the colors are more saturated, and the people seem so much more real. She's been learning basic phrases in te reo Māori. She wants to learn more. She holds her fork with her left hand now, tines down. It feels more natural. She feels more natural. More free.

Or maybe it's all been an illusion. A lie.

She'll always be an outsider. She's not one of the Shepherds. She's a shadow passing across their lives. A temporary disruption.

She'll be gone in nine months. They'll repair the Bowie-sized crack in their lives with mud and tape and go on with their idyllic, peaceful existence as if she never even existed.

12

LAKE

The snowy path has a thick rind of ice that makes every step treacherous. It's dark. My flashlight beam is weak and flickering; the battery is about to die.

"Where are we going?"

Ruth doesn't answer, her face a pale blur under a bulky red knit cap.

Is this a new duty we've been assigned? Gathering firewood. Snow removal. But why is it so early in the morning? And Ruth isn't carrying an axe or a shovel, she's carrying Heron, who somehow manages to stay asleep, his head bouncing against her shoulder with every step.

We're almost out of the woods now. My heart thumps painfully, and there's a queasy feeling in the pit of my stomach. *We can't leave the woods. It's forbidden.*

Ruth's face is grim, her lips tinged with blue. Cold shakes me by the shoulders, numbs my cheeks and freezes my snot, turns my fingers to icy lumps. My injured shoulder aches from the cold. My long skirt gets tangled between my legs, and I almost fall.

"Hurry up." Her voice is hushed and ragged. She keeps glancing back over her shoulder, as if someone might be following us.

We break free of the woods and walk along the wider road

leading to the bridge. It's so quiet and still. The dense woods crouch behind us. The bridge hulks ahead, stark steel against a weak, struggling dawn.

I follow Ruth across the bridge and to the side of the road that leads to Canada if you go left, and into town if you go right. I think a long time ago we used to live in town. The memories are wrinkled and faded. A run-down house painted moss green. My face swollen and itchy from mosquito bites.

"She said she'd be here," Ruth mutters. "Where is she?"

"Who?"

"Aunt Jenny."

Aunt Jenny belongs to those faded memories. Red hair streaked with gray. A wide smile.

"Is she joining The Fold?" I ask, heart surging with hope.

"She's taking us away from here."

"No." I shake my head wildly, braids whipping my cheeks. "No, we can't leave. We'll be cast out. Damned forever."

"We have to leave." She stares straight ahead, scanning the road. She won't look at me. "I never should have brought you here. I'm sorry. So sorry."

She's crying. My stomach cramps.

Heron wakes up and sniffles. "I'm hungry."

Ruth reaches into her pocket with one hand and pulls out a box of raisins.

Headlights appear in the distance. A forest-green station wagon pulls to the side of the road.

"I'm not leaving. You can't make me." I start to run back toward the woods, but I slip on a patch of ice and fall, skinning my knee on the frozen, jagged ground. Blood seeps into my gray woolen tights.

Ruth hauls me up by my coat collar. "I know you don't understand but we can't go back there. Do you hear me? We have to leave."

She shakes me by the collar, and Heron starts crying, clinging onto her neck.

A dog barks in the distance, and Ruth spins around. I follow.

Two huge silvery-white huskies with glowing eyes emerge from the woods. Behind them a tall dark figure holding a flashlight.

"He's coming," Ruth shouts. She rushes to the car and yanks the back door open. "Get in the car!"

"No," I say, confused, hurt. My heart skinned as raw as my knee.

Ruth shoves Heron into the car, and she's back, dragging me with her. I fight her, but she's too strong. I've been unwell since my accident. I have blank patches in my mind. Whole days lost.

She pushes me into the car. Slams the door. The dogs are barking louder; they're almost upon us now.

"Drive, Jenny. Go!" Ruth shouts, jumping into the passenger seat.

I lie on the back seat, holding Heron, as the car wheels spin and careen on the ice.

Headlights in the distance, from the other direction, coming from The Fold. Shouting and dogs barking.

I can't breathe. Heron is a deadweight on my chest, pressing me down. I'm scared. We're going to be punished. I pray silently. *Whatever is happening, please make it right. Don't let my mother sin. Guide her back to the Way.*

"I have a rifle in the trunk," Aunt Jenny says grimly. "I won't let him take you. Not again. I'm not losing you again." The car leaps forward, and I'm thrown against the seat back. Heron wails and burrows his head into my shoulder.

Him. She must mean Father Kincaid. He's the leader of The Fold. He's father to every member of his flock, but I'm special to him. He told me that I was.

"I want to go back," I whimper. "I can't leave Charity." My best friend is Sister Charity. We steal books from the elders' rooms when they're out and hide them under our mattresses. We took a blood oath. I pricked her thumb with a sewing needle, and she pricked mine, and we pressed our fingers together until we couldn't tell whose blood was whose. We're sworn to secrecy. About the books. About what happened that night.

The car goes faster, flying over the road. Wind whistling in my ears. Sound of metal slicing through snow. It's not a car, it's a sled. Charity and I are flying down the big sledding hill, faster and faster, shrieking with laughter and fear. We dared each other to keep our boots and hands tucked in to go as fast as possible, but one of us is going to have to do something. We've veered off course. We're heading straight for the cliff's edge and the frozen lake below.

My lips are numb with cold. I press them into her neck, holding to her waist tighter and tighter, my legs tangled with hers.

"We're heading for the cliff," I cry.

The blades slice, slice, slice through the snow. Charity's the one who usually sticks her boots out and slows us down until we stop, but tonight it's like she's frozen. I'm scared now. We'll crash through the ice and drown in the lake.

Desperate, I try to disentangle my legs from hers, but she's immobile, unyielding. I push against her back.

"Jump, Charity! We have to jump off the sled." The wind whistling past and stinging my cheeks takes my words and twists them into gabbled nonsense.

I wrestle with her. At the last possible moment, I heave both of us off the sled and into a snowbank. I rest, panting, as the sled careens over the cliff and falls, soars toward the frozen lake. There's a splintering crash as the sled hits the lake.

My breath comes in gasps; my lungs are filled with shards of ice. "That was too close."

She doesn't answer. I push against her shoulder, and she flops toward me.

I scream.

It's not Charity. It's Bowie.

Her mouth gapes open.

Her eyes are as blank and soulless as plastic bottle caps washed up on a beach.

I wake up gasping for air and drenched with sweat. My heart beats wildly. My throat feels like someone attacked it with a loofah. I must have been really screaming. Hopefully my neighbors didn't hear.

The nightmare had begun the same way it always did, and then at the end . . . Bowie. Dead in my arms.

I'd been fourteen when we left the rural Alaskan farm community known as The Fold. The years after we escaped were agonizing. I'd been taught that the end times were nigh, and only the true believers of The Fold would be saved. I was lost. Caught between two worlds. Expected to attend high school with normal kids when I was still reeling from the realization that it had all been lies. That I'd been manipulated. Brainwashed.

I believed Father Kincaid's lies. I hated my mom for taking me away from him, from the only life I knew. And then when I realized the truth, I hated her for exposing me to him, for bringing us to live there. She told me that she'd been devastated when my father was diagnosed and died of cancer within a matter of weeks. She needed hope and purpose and she thought she'd found it in the community of The Fold. She didn't mean to hurt me.

After we moved back to town, she sank into a depression, sometimes not leaving her room for days. Sometimes she was fine. She started dating Ray.

One morning when she refused to leave her bed, Ray took Heron and me for a ride to the mudflats.

"It's one of the lowest tides of the year," he'd said after we finished eating the pancakes he made us. "Let's go check it out."

Usually I would have said no, I'd have stayed in to do my homework. At that point I didn't trust Ray yet because I knew that men could seem friendly, kind, and then turn cruel behind closed doors. But I hadn't wanted to be left alone in the house with Ruth. All she did was lie on her bed and stare at the ceiling.

Ray drove us to the beach in his old jeep with the duct-taped windows. Heron bounced in his car seat, talking a mile a minute about a Lego spaceship he was building. The sun touched my cheek through the window. A young eagle, dappled with brown and white, stood on a stump and watched us as we passed.

Ripe salmonberries glowed with orange flame.

This new life had fewer rules and more open spaces. Sometimes I felt so lost without someone telling me what to do, what to think, every minute of the day.

Ray pulled over at a viewpoint and held Heron's hand as we climbed down a steep slope to the beach. The mudflats stretched so far we could almost walk to the other side of the bay.

Heron ran around the mudflats, searching for treasures. "I found a jellyfish!" He danced around the shriveled, translucent jellyfish.

So many secret things revealed by the retreat of the tide. I noticed a barnacle-crusted piece of metal sticking out of the sand. "What's that?"

We all dug together in the wet sand and mud until Ray wrenched an anchor from some ancient vessel out of the muck. He pulled it up the flats and leaned it against a rock.

"We'll clean it up and put it somewhere in the yard. Maybe it's even from a shipwreck. We'll try to find out which boat it came from."

"I'm going to start cleaning it right now." Heron used a stick to scrape at the barnacles.

I hugged my arms around my chest. Something about the barnacles made me feel sick. I had this nightmare sometimes that I thought might be a real memory. It terrified me.

Open eyes. Gaping mouth like a fish. A smell like rotting leaves.

"Are you okay, Lake?" Ray asked.

I swallowed. "I'm worried about my mom."

Ray nodded. "That's understandable."

"Is she broken? I mean, will she ever stop having these bad spells?"

"I don't know the answer to that. I haven't known your mom for very long."

"Why are you staying? Don't you want to run away?"

Ray stared across the flats. "This is how I see it. Your mom's mind is kind of like these mudflats. There are things buried that she doesn't want to see again. And then some days, when she's feeling low, the bad stuff sticks out of the mud and she can't ignore it like she usually does."

That's my mind, too. When bad things shift beneath the surface, I shove them back down. My anger and pain are hard and crusted over with barnacles. They cling to my heart and can't be pried loose. Anger like cold metal in my mouth, rust in my lungs.

Thinking about Bowie out there somewhere, possibly alone and afraid, tugs at my mind like a receding tide, revealing all the things I've buried, forcing me to confront my past.

I have to find her before too many secrets come to light.

13
LAKE

"Mr. and Mrs. Walter, I'm Lake Harlowe."

"I expected to be met by someone more senior." Glen Walter eyes me coldly. Everything about him is shades of glacial: iceberg-blue eyes, square-jutting shoulders, shiny silver-gray suit.

Nadia Walter has sharp-bladed cheekbones, endless legs, and impressive cleavage.

"Consul General Chung is conducting a training at our mission in Samoa. I'll be your liaison during your stay. I'm very sorry for your loss."

"Thank you." Nadia's eyes are puffy and red from crying. "This all seems like a nightmare."

"Damn right it's a nightmare. People are treating our son as if he's a criminal," Glen says.

"What do you mean?" I ask, taken aback.

"We've just been interrogated at our hotel by a rude detective who insinuated that Bruce might have something to do with Bowie Bishop disappearing. He barely knew her! Now they want to keep his body for more testing." His nose flares, and his voice crescendos. "It's fucking outrageous."

A harried-looking nurse in light blue scrubs approaches. "Mr. Walter, as I explained, no one is accusing anyone of anything. We're merely following the protocols requested by the police and—"

"I don't give a good goddamn about your protocols."

"We'll do what the police tell us to do." The nurse stands her ground, but she's clearly unaccustomed to aggressive, blustering Americans. Her shoulders shake with fear or fury, or both.

"I want to speak to the director of the hospital. If he's not out here in three minutes flat, I'm calling Ambassador Hunt and he'll contact every member of your board of directors."

"The director of this hospital is a woman, Mr. Walter, and she's not here on a Sunday."

An imposing, bearded man wearing a long black trench coat strides into the room and whispers in Mr. Walter's ear. I catch the words *perimeter* and *police*. He has the self-important, intense expression of a Secret Service agent.

"Thanks, Colgan," Glen replies.

"We haven't been introduced," I say, holding out my hand toward the man.

"Ryan Colgan. Mr. Walter's chief of security." His handshake is nearly bruising, his gaze calculating. His eyes tell me he finds me lacking—in stature, status, beauty—in everything that matters to the wealthy.

Dr. Grayson enters the reception area wearing a crisp white lab coat, her auburn hair falling in a long braid down her back. "Mr. and Mrs. Walter, I'm Dr. Charlotte Grayson. I was the medical examiner at the scene of your son's death. I'm extremely sorry for your loss."

"Take us to Bruce," Mr. Walter says through clenched teeth.

"I'd like to prepare you for what you're going to see. You'll be viewing your son's body in the mortuary from behind a large glass window. You may have an unexpected reaction—"

"We don't need any speeches. We're ready."

"I'm not." Nadia's face crumples, and tears slide down her cheeks.

"Pull yourself together, Nadia." Glen takes her by the elbow. "We're going to get to the bottom of this."

What does he think he's going to get to the bottom of? The worst has already happened; they've reached hell. Their only child is dead.

"Please follow me then, Mr. and Mrs. Walter."

Dr. Grayson leads us through a set of swinging doors and down a hallway toward an elevator. No one speaks as we ride to the fourth floor, pass through a corridor, and then take another lift down two floors to the mortuary. I glimpse shiny metal gurneys through high windows. The bleach-coated scent of suffering hovers in the air. I never visited a hospital until after we left The Fold. They believed only in faith healing.

My collarbone twinges, and I wrench my right shoulder higher, correcting the bad posture I developed as a compensation for my injury.

Inside the mortuary, Dr. Grayson leads us to a viewing room. She indicates that Glen and Nadia should move closer to the large window. There's no way to escape the main attraction. A body covered by a white sheet, lying on a shiny metal mortuary slab.

A mortuary technician pulls down the sheet. Bruce's skin is tinged with a grayish pallor now, like thick-cut bacon that's been in the fridge too long.

Nadia's shoulders heave as she sobs. "Bruce." She sways and Dr. Grayson steps toward her but Glen catches her instead, steadying her with an arm locked around her waist.

"It's my son," he says gruffly. "My father took him to get that tattoo. Son of a bitch. It's Bruce."

Waves of rage roll off him and charge the air with barely restrained violence. He looks like he wants to punch his fist through the glass. He's accustomed to bullying the world into submission with limitless money and power. He can't change this outcome, and it's killing him.

"I'm sorry, Mr. Walter." Dr. Grayson studies him with softly sympathetic eyes. "I performed a postmortem and confirmed that he died of inhalation of vomit into the lungs, causing asphyxiation. I've prepared a provisional report, but we're waiting on the additional testing. He was taking prescription pain medication, hydrocodone. Traces of ketorolac tromethamine were found as well. I assume the medications were for the meniscus injury."

"All football players take pain meds. Hell, I was on so many pills during my career. We had to have a quick fix to get us back out on the field."

"He was injured during a preseason game," Nadia says shakily. "I don't understand why he's here. Why did he travel to Wellington without telling us?" Her voice catches, and more tears stream down her cheeks. I hand her a pack of tissues. I always keep them on hand for the family members I meet with.

"Do you want a moment of privacy?" Dr. Grayson asks.

"We've seen enough," Glen says. "When can we take him home?"

"We're still waiting on the results of several tests."

Glen takes a menacing step toward her. "What tests?"

"Blood, samples from under his fingernails."

"There's no need for any of that. We want to take him home as quickly as possible for the funeral."

Time for my most soothing, professional voice. "Mr. Walter, you'll be allowed to transport your son home, but as the information I sent you detailed, the CDC has guidelines for the repatriation of remains. There will be paperwork to sign and protocols to follow. That's what I'm here to assist you with."

"What I'm hearing is that you're here to make my life even more difficult during this painful time. Does that about sum it up?" He reverses course and stalks toward me instead of the doctor.

I plant my feet and stand my ground even though my first instinct is to run for safety. "I know this is a very difficult time for you. I understand that you're grieving. I'm only doing my job. There are rules to follow."

He's so close now that I can smell breath mints covering tobacco and a whiff of strong spirits.

"Your boss is going to hear about this. Believe me."

"Ambassador Hunt is well aware of the necessity of following international protocols."

He sneers. "I think Lyndon is also well aware of the necessity of keeping major donors happy."

"Glen." Nadia places a hand on his arm. "I don't feel well. I want to go back to the hotel."

There's a tense moment as he stares me down. I clasp my hands behind my back so he won't see them shaking.

"You'll be hearing from me, Ms. Harlowe," Glen says, and spins on his heel, dragging his wife toward the door.

14

LAKE

"Still no leads on Bowie Bishop?" my supervisor, Consul General Samantha Chung, asks early on Monday morning. She's positioned precisely at the center of the screen, looking elegant and composed as always in a black suit and a turquoise statement necklace.

She's not one for preamble. She always gets right to the point and makes every word count. She doesn't have time for anything else—not with the avalanche of paperwork and the oversized egos she deals with every day.

"No leads. She's simply vanished. They haven't found her on any CCTV footage after Wednesday afternoon when she and her host sister, Isla, were seen in a coffee shop together. She hasn't used any credit cards. Her cell phone rings to voicemail and wasn't found in her room." A device location search came up empty. The police are requesting cell phone records.

"And the death case—Bruce Walter—they could be related?"

"Bowie Bishop's mother, Suzie, works as a bar manager for Glen Walter in Las Vegas. There could be a connection between his visit to Wellington and Bowie's disappearance. We're waiting for the autopsy test results."

"I read your notes from the mortuary visit yesterday. Is Glen Walter causing problems?"

"He expresses grief through anger. He feels powerless, so he's lashing out at everyone—the New Zealand police detective, the medical examiner, me. The test results should be back soon. He won't be delayed much longer."

"And how are you holding up, Lake?"

"I'm fine."

"I have confidence in you. I heard great things about you from CG Bakersfield."

"That's nice to hear. Phnom Penh was a challenging tour." I smile ruefully. "I was hoping for a mellow tour in Wellington."

Samantha's a highly effective consul general, one of those career diplomats who takes pride in her work and encourages those around her to reach their full potential. She somehow manages to make everyone feel seen and supported, even while staying laser-focused on the outcome she desires.

"You never know in our profession. I was a young officer serving in Bangkok during the 2004 tsunami."

"I didn't know that."

"More than five thousand confirmed deaths, including over thirty Americans. It was devastating. I remember a few weeks later I wanted to call one of the contacts I'd been working with, and then I remembered—his entire coastal town had been wiped away. No one survived."

She stares at a spot over my head. "The only thing that kept me going during that horrific time was the knowledge that I was making a real, quantifiable difference. I couldn't bring back beloved sons, daughters, brothers, sisters . . . but I could be there for the families. I could help them navigate the nightmare. Be a calm, steady, sympathetic listener, guide, and support."

I nod. "I know we make a difference. I know we do. It's the inconclusive cases, though, isn't it? You had so many missing, presumed dead during that tsunami. I remember reading about it. It's almost worse when there's no body. When the family members cling to hope for years and years."

If Bowie had been riding her bike home at night and been hit by a car, thrown from her bike, and left for dead, if she'd died slowly, painfully, with blood filling her lungs, at least Suzie would know what happened.

"I'm meeting Suzie Bishop at the airport at noon," I continue. "We have a public appeal and press conference scheduled for this afternoon."

"I'll be back Wednesday morning. I had a call with Rob this morning. Sounds like RSO is working around the clock with New Zealand police on this. Rob has his hands full and so does Public Affairs. Rob gave me a heads-up that Suzie Bishop might be a little difficult. What's your impression?"

I think of ice clinking against glass. The way she talked about Bowie's music career as if it was her own second act. Her desperate request that I stay on the phone with her until she fell asleep. "I have the feeling that she's . . . unpredictable."

"That's kinder than what Rob said. He said she's a loose cannon. She'll need a handler, and she already knows you. I think it's best if you delegate some of your workload this week and stick with Suzie. Keep her occupied. And anything you find out, anything she says that could help the case, make sure to report it back to Rob."

"Of course."

There's a knock on the door of the conference room. "Samantha, someone's knocking at the door."

"I was about to sign off anyway. Take care."

"See you soon."

"I'm so sorry to interrupt, Lake," the ambassador's executive assistant, Judith Conolly, a former air force cadet who wears her silver hair in a severe bob, says when I open the conference room door. "Ambassador Hunt wants to see you right away."

"Do you know what it's about?"

"He's on the warpath. Something to do with his friend Mr. Walter?"

Glen must have followed through on his threat to report me to Ambassador Hunt. My pulse speeds as we walk to his office. I've had only brief interactions with the ambassador, none of them particularly pleasant. He thinks he's an irresistible lady's man, even pushing sixty-five, and with his much younger Southern belle wife in tow.

Ambassadors, especially new political appointees who purchased their appointment with funds or fealty, are prone to becoming drunk on all that power and protocol: the "yes, sirs" and everyone having to stand when they enter a room.

Ambassador Hunt is one of those. He swaggers around the embassy making inappropriate jokes and demanding that photos of himself be hung in every office and hallway. He bullies people in staff meetings and expects everyone to listen to rambling irrelevant stories and laugh at his bad jokes.

The deputy chief of mission, a mild-mannered, milquetoast career diplomat named Harvey Canter, called me into his office last week. "Lake, I've noticed something at Country Team meeting. You seem to be grimacing when Ambassador Hunt tells stories." I must have snorted disbelievingly because he frowned sternly, told me that he wasn't the only one who had noticed, and reminded me blandly that he was my employee evaluation rater. I wanted to ask him if he had ever reprimanded a male officer for not smiling sweetly at someone's stories.

I leave my cell phone in a locked cubby and follow Judith into the Front Office reception area. I hear Ambassador Hunt bellowing at someone as we approach his closed office door.

"Good luck," Judith whispers, before knocking on the door and opening it.

The ambassador makes an impatient gesture, and I take a seat on a low chair positioned in front of the enormous ambassadorial desk, feeling like I've been called to the principal's office. His brown alligator cowboy boots are propped up on the desk, directly in front of my face. He's yelling into a landline telephone.

"I told you we should have bought more! Now it's a runner. You were all 'Be cautious,' and look where that got us. A day late and five hundred G's short. What do I even employ you for?" The skin showing above the collar of his crisp white shirt is red and stippled with razor burn. His salt-and-pepper hair is coiffed into a feathered style best left in the eighties.

"Call me back when you pull your head out of your ass," he barks into the phone and hangs up with a bang. He takes his feet off the desk. "My trader needs to grow a pair."

I clear my throat, biting back a comment. It's a clear violation of State Department policy to conduct personal business on embassy equipment, and we both know it.

"Good morning, sir. Judith said you wanted to see me?"

"Lake, is it?" His gaze slides over me, pausing at chest level for an appraisal before oozing back up to my face. "What kind of name is that?"

"I'm from Alaska, sir. My brother's name is Heron."

"Hippies," he mutters. "I do want to see you. I just received a call from my good golf buddy Glen Walter, who's here to pick up his dead son, which is a fucking travesty because Bruce was going to win a Super Bowl, just like his grandaddy, and he said that you and some mouthy Kiwi female detective have been making false accusations about Bruce." He places both of his hands on the desk and leans toward me. "Well? What's going on here?"

"I accompanied the Walters to the mortuary. I wasn't present when he was interviewed by the New Zealand police. I believe what he's referring to is the fact that they questioned him about any connection between his son and the missing American exchange student you were briefed on. I'm sure there were no accusations made."

"That's not how Glen tells it. He says that the detective thinks that maybe Bruce murdered this girl, hid her body, and then drank himself to death."

The way he says *this girl*, as if she's interchangeable with all the other girls who inconvenience powerful, rich men, makes my shoulders tense. He wants to intimidate me. Put me in my place. I've known too many men like him. He wants me off-balance, on edge, and sputtering with anger.

I take a deep breath. I won't rise to the bait. "*This girl* is Bowie Bishop, sir. She's housed with Myra and Stuart Shepherd. She performed at an embassy-sponsored arts festival that you attended."

"I don't care if she's won ten Grammys. Bruce Walter didn't murder anyone, and I'll vouch for him personally. What about the host parents? I've met Stuart Shepherd several times. He's a greenie," he says scornfully. "A real tree hugger. You can't trust guys like him."

"I'm sure the police are looking into every suspect."

"Well, they should stop harassing Glen pronto. They don't know who they're dealing with."

"I'll relay the message, sir." Not a chance. He seems to think he's living in a Hollywood Western, throwing his weight around, making threats. "The police are simply exploring all plausible theories for her disappearance. Again, I doubt very much that any accusations have been made. Bowie's mother, Suzie, works for Mr. Walter in Las Vegas."

"Be careful with Suzie Bishop. She's a real piece of work. Totally unstable."

"You know her?"

"I've heard all about her from Glen. He says she's a washed-up former musician with a drinking problem. He only keeps her employed because he feels sorry for her. You don't want to put those two in the same room together. You don't want to mess with Glen. Stick to your wheelhouse. The RSO will find the missing girl. You go back to whatever it is you do. Issuing visas or whatever."

I'm seething by now, crawling out of my skin. I want to call him out, but I can't play his game. He's not going to manipulate me into losing my temper. That only makes men like him feel more powerful.

"Respectfully, sir, this is my job. I'm helping the Walters repatriate their son's remains and assisting with the investigation into a missing American citizen."

"You know what Glen thinks? He thinks the daughter is as unstable as the mom. She's probably a runaway. Or she offed herself. Whatever happened to her, I can guarantee you that Bruce Walter had nothing to do with it. I'll be monitoring this situation very closely."

"Understood, sir. Was there anything else?" I struggle to keep my voice calm and my expression neutral.

"That's it. Close the door on your way out."

Gladly.

"How'd it go?" Judith asks when I'm back at her desk.

"Not so hot."

"I heard about the missing exchange student at the morning briefing. So scary. I saw Bowie perform at the arts festival. She's very talented. And now this dead football player. It's all over the news. I hope they find her soon."

"Thanks. Hey," I lower my voice. "I was wondering if you know anything about why Jordan Singer curtailed? Was it his choice?" Based on the confrontational meeting I just had with the ambassador, he could have chosen to leave.

Judith glances around. We're alone in the reception area. The DCM's executive assistant isn't at his desk. "Here's the weird thing," she whispers. "I heard a rumor that Jordan curtailed because of something to do with Bowie Bishop. He was the ambo's control officer at the reception after the arts festival. Something happened that night."

"But you don't know what?"

"I'm afraid I don't."

"If you hear anything else, can you let me know?"

"I will." She sits up straighter and her voice grows louder. "Thanks for stopping by, Lake."

I glance behind her and see that the ambassador's door is cracked open now.

I leave swiftly, avoiding further contact with Ambassador Hunt.

He's friends with Glen Walter. Glen Walter's son may have some tie to Bowie's disappearance. Jordan Singer was possibly curtailed because of something that happened with Bowie.

It's all interwoven. It must be.

There had been a threat running through the conversation with the ambassador like a vicious undertow. Do my job and leave the detective stuff to law enforcement. Don't mess with Glen Walter. Or with Ambassador Hunt. Ignore the warning, and I'll be sucked under the waves, demoted, disgraced.

But how can I stop searching for answers now? An eighteen-year-old girl is missing without a trace. Every second that ticks by makes it less likely she'll be found alive.

I have to know why Jordan left and what it had to do with Bowie.

15
LAKE

I'm standing in front of the metal ACS classified safe. It's standard issue, built like a tank, painted a color trapped in the cold dead space between gray and green.

I'm not doing anything wrong. I have a right to look in this safe, but I still feel furtive, like I'm being watched, reported up the chain. The ambo will know if I'm directly disobeying his orders.

I searched Jordan's electronic ACS files for any mention of Bowie Bishop and found nothing. If it was something highly sensitive, he would have kept it in here, with the other classified and personally identifiable information.

I have the combo written on a piece of paper that I'll shred later.

Twist the dial, hit the white marks in sequence. I practiced opening safes during training. If the embassy was under attack, the prerecorded message would blast through the loudspeakers: SECURE ALL CLASSIFIED. SECURE ALL CLASSIFIED. In the pecking order of the State Department, secrets sometimes feel like they rank higher than personnel.

I wrestle with the handle, and the drawer makes a high-pitched screeching noise as it opens, releasing a smell like an old gym locker, but with the scent of stale secrets instead of socks. A sharp tang of metal and the faintly sugared pulp of decades-old paper. Paper clips wedged beneath metal corners. The metal dividers are rusted into lopsided angles.

The files are thin because this is New Zealand, not Southeast Asia, where Amcits get up to all kinds of trouble—a whole drawer for each year; a phalanx of safes along a wall.

There's a file for Bowie Bishop, but it contains only two pieces of paper. One is a photocopy of her passport; the other is typed-up notes by Jordan about Bowie. It includes the fact that she performed at the arts festival in May, and goes on to detail a meeting that took place between Bowie and Jordan, in which Bowie asked him to pass along some information. Frustratingly, there's no mention of the nature of the information she gave Jordan, or to whom she asked him to pass it.

I search through the adjacent files. Nothing. I'm no closer to discovering why Jordan left. I'm about to close the drawer when I notice a piece of ruled notepaper stuck beneath the divider. I pull it out gingerly, wrangling it free from the lopsided drawer carefully so that it doesn't tear. It's a handwritten list of names.

S. Shepherd
AMBO
A. Gil
G. Walter
B. Walter
Florica "Lo" Baciu

Are these notes from Jordan's meeting with Bowie? I take the paper and close the drawer, spin the dial, check to make sure it's locked.

Back in my office, I search the department's Global Address

List and learn that Jordan's posted to Guadalajara, back on the visa line like a first tour officer. Quite the demotion. It's early evening there. I might still catch him. I open a chat window.

> Hey, Jordan. It's Lake Harlowe, TDY ACS in Wellington.
> Would you be available for a quick chat or call?

I give him my desk line. The phone rings ten minutes later.
"Lake?"
"Yes. Hi, Jordan, thanks for calling me so quickly."
"How's the embassy remodel coming along?"
"It looks nice. Modern with wood accents."
"At the beginning of my tour there it was hellish. There was water coming through the ceilings, jackhammers going all the time. Gritty dust all over our computers. One of the local staff was injured by a falling ladder."
"Glad that was before my time."
"I miss it there, though. I loved the mountain biking. And how safe it was."
"Security measures must be a little different in Guadalajara."
He snorts. "Just a little. So how can I help you? If it's winery or bike trail recommendations, I'm your man."
"It's about an American exchange student named Bowie Bishop."
"What about her?" His tone changes, becomes terse and wary.
"She's gone missing."
"What do you mean, missing?"
"Her host family went on a camping trip, and she arranged to stay in Wellington with a friend, but she never showed up at the friend's house. She's been missing nearly four days now."
Silence. "Jordan? Are you still there?"
"Yeah, I'm still here."
"There's more. Bruce Walter was here in Wellington, and he was found dead in his Airbnb on Friday morning."

"Bruce Walter . . . as in Glen Walter's son?"

"That's right. I found this piece of paper in the safe that—"

"I can't really chat anymore. I'm too busy. Sorry, Lake."

"I'm sure you must be busy. I only have a few quick questions. What happened at the arts festival? And what was the information Bowie wanted to pass to you?"

"Gotta go. I'll miss the shuttle."

"Wait—Jordan, don't hang up. What's this about? Does it have something to do with why you curtailed? I found a list of names I think you wrote that includes Stuart Shepherd, Ambassador Hunt, Glen Walter—"

"Lake." His voice drops to a low murmur. I strain to hear what he says next. "You don't know who you're dealing with. I can't say anything more. You could be in danger if you pursue this. Leave it alone."

The call goes dead.

You don't know who you're dealing with. The same words used by Ambassador Hunt. A chill chases between my shoulder blades.

Something is very wrong here. I have a few hours before I pick up Suzie Bishop at the airport. I also have a list of names. And Stuart Shepherd is at the top.

———

"How's it going?" I ask as I poke my head through Sara Kashani's office door. She's a Public Affairs officer, and our tours overlapped for one year in Shanghai.

"I'm a little hungover, to tell the truth. I had too much fun over the weekend with this new guy I'm seeing. You're here for the press conference remarks for Suzie Bishop. Perfect timing, because I printed them five minutes ago. I emailed them as well."

She hands me the remarks on notecards. "You're picking Suzie up from the airport?"

"In a few hours. I'll go over these with her before her briefing with you."

"Thanks. This is all really upsetting. I introduced Bowie

onstage at the arts festival. She's super talented. I really hope she's okay."

"Me, too. I can't think about anything else. My regular work's piling up."

"I know how that goes." Sara nods at her inbox. "I have literally a thousand unread emails."

"I won't bother you long. Did Bowie's host father attend her performance?"

"Stuart Shepherd? Yes, with his wife and kids. He seems like a good guy. Rides his bike to work. Wants to install solar energy at all the government buildings. He's old money, old New Zealand politics."

"I read his bio. Nothing too salacious. Ancestral connections to New Zealand politics. One of his relatives was briefly governor-general of New Zealand in the 1920s before he was forced out of office by a marital scandal."

"You don't have such a long line of politicians without a few skeletons in the closet," Sara remarks.

"Did you get any strange vibe from him?"

"Not strange. Intense, for sure. He's genuinely committed to green policies and uses that ancestral fortune for environmental causes. He's ambitious. Some even think he might try for prime minister. All this press about Bowie being missing on his watch can't be good for his public image."

The office door of the Public Affairs chief opens, and Sara jumps. "Talk later," she whispers. "I'm up for promotion this year. Gotta keep the boss happy."

I used to be ambitious, too, I think as I leave her office. I wanted to climb the ranks swiftly, maybe even try for consul general.

Now I'm like the classified safe. Hiding in a corner. Pieces of me rusted into lopsided angles with memories wedged in tight for safekeeping.

But I have a new ambition now.

I'm going to find Bowie Bishop.

16

BOWIE

"Are you ready?" Sara Kashani asks, smiling at Bowie as they wait behind the red velvet stage curtains.

Bowie nods, adjusting the fit of her guitar strap. This is the first time she's performed onstage since she spontaneously joined Dean at the Cat's Meow. It's a bigger venue, a historic theater in downtown Wellington, with antique velvet seats and faded murals on the faraway domed plaster ceiling.

Suzie contacted the embassy and bragged about her daughter, as she did constantly, and they invited Bowie to play a showcase at the Wellington Arts Festival, along with a U.S. jazz band they flew in from New Orleans. She'll be playing for the U.S. ambassador and other dignitaries, including Stuart, who's seated in the third row back with Myra, Isla, and the twins.

Sara takes the stage. Bowie does breathing exercises as she's introduced, trying to quiet her churning stomach. Dean's in the audience, too. He and Isla aren't sitting together, even though Bowie's fairly sure they're still secretly dating.

"And now the U.S. Embassy is proud to present a talented young singer-songwriter from Las Vegas, who is an exchange student here in Wellington. Please welcome to the stage Bowie Bishop!"

Terror freezes her to the wooden floorboards for a few excruciating seconds. There's still time to escape. Run out the back door and keep running. Never play her guitar for anyone again.

Then she hears Suzie's voice in her head: *Believe in yourself. You're my shining star.* Suzie's been pushing Bowie onstage her whole life. Her training kicks in. She walks confidently through the curtain, head held high and spine straight, finding her spotlight.

The audience is a dim blur, the stage lights hot on her face as she launches into a cover of Wilco's "Casino Queen" that she's given her own vibe.

People clap along and some even know the words, singing along with the chorus. She plays a few more Suzie-chosen songs. Then deviates from the set list her mom prepared.

"This last one is a new song I wrote yesterday, called 'The Other Side.'"

She wrote it for Lo, as she sat in the graveyard behind the Shepherds' house. There are miles and miles of old gravestones, some of them crumbling to dust while others are kept shiny and new, with fresh flowers weekly. Her favorite grave has an angel standing on top of a once-white marble mausoleum, with columns in front and a locked door painted green but turning to black with moss around the edges. The mausoleum a grieving family built for Dulcie Morris, their beloved daughter, only seventeen when she died. It's where Bowie feels closest to Lo.

Emotion clogs her voice, making the low notes thrum and buzz.

> *When you turn out all the lights*
> *Do you feel alone?*
> *Or is the darkness home?*
> *When you turn out all the lights*
> *Where does your mind reside*
> *On the other side.*

SHE FELL AWAY

I'm entranced by you, the other side
Intoxicated by your view
The electric fence is shocking but
A stronger urge pulls me through

I keep you with me always
You're the toll I'll have to pay
Without you I'll be stranded
I'll never find the way
To the other side.

With fading voice, I call to you
Until the music dies
In the heart of the night, I'll come to you
On the other side

When they turned out all the lights
Did you feel alone?
Or was the darkness home?
When they turned out all the lights
You became the night
On the other side

Eerie quiet descends after she finishes. Lo is standing there beside her. She's the only one Bowie cares about impressing. Her eyes are shiny with tears. *Love you forever, Bo,* she mouths, then fades into the velvet curtain.

Bowie becomes aware that the audience is cheering loudly. Myra leaps to her feet, clapping and whistling like a madwoman. Bowie blows her a kiss and takes a bow.

There's a reception afterward in the bar and outdoor patio.

"You were amazing," Myra gushes. "Wasn't she, Isla?"

"You sounded good." Isla still keeps her distance. She's friendly enough at home in front of her parents, but at school it's like she's pretending Bowie doesn't exist. Bowie's been living with her for five months now, and she still hasn't figured out how to maintain the peace. Isla always finds something to be mad about. It hurts more than Bowie wants to admit.

Myra and Stuart go off to shake hands and do the politician thing. Bowie stands alone for a moment, watching Isla talking to Dean. It's not really a secret if you stare at each other like that, she wants to tell them.

Bowie's friend Alejandro, a fellow ILA exchange student from Spain, and another exchange student from the U.S., Clementine, join her.

"You were amazing!" enthuses Alejandro.

"You're such a star," Clementine agrees, but her gaze roams the room. "I wonder if we'll have a chance to talk to Ambassador Hunt. I've never met an ambassador before."

"Are you hungry?" Alejandro asks. "Have a pastry."

Bowie accepts a mini pastry stuffed with spinach and feta.

"He's over there!" Clementine points to a short man wearing a cowboy hat and talking to a woman in a low-cut evening gown. "His wife is on a trip to the U.S. to visit their sons. I hear he likes to drink when she's gone."

There's a thin, worried-looking guy trailing his boss around the room, taking photos for him and fetching drinks.

Ambassador Hunt turns toward a light, and Bowie catches a good look at his face. She almost chokes on the pastry.

Alejandro pounds her on the back. "Are you all right?"

"S-swallowed wrong." With growing dread, Bowie recognizes him. The old dude with the feathered hair and the white fringed cowboy shirt who was there in the VIP room the night Lo died. Glen had introduced him as Mr. Palmer, a high roller from Texas. Bowie remembers thinking that he wore those heeled cowboy boots to push himself over Tom Cruise height. She remembers his intrusive stare, the asshole *I own you* energy.

Is there time to run before he sees her?

Fuck. He's making a beeline for her. Maybe he won't recognize her. He was drunk that night, nose red and eyes bleary.

"Well, well, what do we have here?" He winks at Bowie, plucking a flask from his breast pocket. He recognizes her. She has nowhere to run. "That was quite a performance, young lady."

"Thank you," she says stiffly. Memories crowd her mind. The last time she'd seen this man she'd been making out with Travis McCray, high on her performance, while Lo disappeared with Bruce Walter.

The guilt and shame of that night eat her from the inside. Every day fresh acid poured on her heart. She'd brought Lo to the casino that night. She'd stood there while she was introduced to a handsome predator. And then she hadn't been there to shield her, defend her, stop her from making a decision that cost her her life.

And Ambassador Hunt had been there. Under a false name. What the fuck?

"Isn't Bowie amazing?" Alejandro steps in, sensing her discomfort. "We're having a great time, sir. This is a wonderful event."

"You're having a great time because you're here with the two prettiest girls, am I right?" Ambassador Hunt winks at Alejandro.

"Ha ha," the skinny guy laughs nervously, moving forward so he's standing beside, instead of behind, the ambassador. "Just a little joke."

"Are you saying they're not pretty, Jordan?"

"No, sir."

"Bowie, you could be a model or a movie star, you know that?"

He's toying with her. She wants to sink down, hide underneath the rows of red theater seats.

"And what's your name, sweetheart?"

"Clementine."

He's practically drooling down the deep V of her gown. "Where are you from, Clementine? Do I detect a Southern accent?"

"Georgia, sir."

Jordan never takes his eyes off the ambassador. He has a worried furrow between his brows. His bow tie is askew, his hands flailing slightly as if he wants to physically pull his boss away from them.

"A Georgia peach right here in Wellington. You must drive all the boys crazy."

She giggles, eating it up. "Can I get a selfie with you, Ambassador?"

"Why, of course, darling. How about over by the flags?" He places his hand on the small of her back, a little too low, as they walk away.

Bowie witnessed this kind of thing all the time in Las Vegas. Old dudes groping young girls. Didn't matter which country she moved to, it was the same story.

Jordan takes a photo of Clementine and Ambassador Hunt in front of the U.S. and New Zealand flags, and then Alejandro takes his turn.

Bowie edges away until her back hits the wall. She stands in the shadows near the emergency exit, wondering how she can escape before the ambassador returns.

A man approaches her. "Hiding at your own event?" She shrinks backward into the shadows, but then she recognizes him—Mark Edison, the music producer Dean introduced her to at the Cat's Meow.

"Hi, Mr. Edison. Guess I'm not feeling it."

"Call me Mark." He takes a sip from his glass of wine. "This is the second time I've seen you perform. You're very talented. I liked the song you sang at the club. Tonight, those first three songs were a little predictable, but the last one . . . that intrigued me. I wonder who you wrote it about? It had the ring of authenticity, of true emotion. The best art comes from pain. Helps us make sense of this sad world."

Bowie glances behind him. The ambassador is talking to another group of people, ignoring her. Maybe he didn't recognize her, after all? "Thanks. Yeah, I wrote that about my best friend who died. It's very personal to me."

He inclines his head. "There's more to you than social media suggests, Bowie Bishop. I'd like to hear more from you like that last song."

"My mom doesn't want me to write depressing songs. She says they won't sell."

"She's wrong. It's the intersection of authenticity and art where the magic happens. If you can tap into that . . . live there. That's when the money will come to you. If you're selling an image, or a person who isn't really you, it's hollow, and your audience will sense the emptiness."

"Huh. I don't think she'd buy that argument. She says the market has strict parameters. People want to escape from their lives. They want sass, smiles, and sexy."

"Ah . . . Suzie's 'Three S' philosophy. Is that what you think?"

"I don't know. I want to write songs that matter, but I guess making people happy matters?"

"I'm working with Dean on another album. You should come with him someday. Check out my studio."

Dean is walking toward them, but then Isla grabs his arm. He changes course.

Bowie is suddenly deeply sick of the drama. All she wants to do is hide. "It was nice talking to you, Mr. Edison—Mark. Maybe I'll come with Dean someday."

"I hope you do."

Bowie leaves the theater and retreats to the back patio. There's a path leading into a dimly lit garden. She sinks down and leans her back against a tree, brushing her fingers over the lawn. It's easier to breathe, to think, with her fingers threaded through the cool, fragrant grass.

She misses Lo so much. How they used to stay up all night talking. Lo was going to change the world. Bowie feels the weight of the necklace she wears.

Someone's coming down the garden path. Bowie scoots around the tree, staying hidden. She hears a deep voice and a high-pitched giggle. Through a leafy branch she sees Ambassador Hunt maneuver Clementine into a shadowy corner. "Let's get to know each other a little better, darlin'."

What a sleaze.

Clementine's long, waxed legs gleam in the lamplight.

He trails a hand along the bottom of her miniskirt. Is he really going to feel up a young woman in the garden at an embassy party?

The bigger the risk of discovery, the more men like him want it. They get off on power, on control, and danger.

He lifts his hand and puts it around her neck. He's literally about to kiss her. Where's his minder when his boss is groping a young guest right outside the theater?

She pulls her phone out of her pocket and zooms in on them. She takes several flashless photos. It will be moody, like a film noir, the furtive couple in the alleyway, before it all goes wrong and ends in murder, ends with a body in a pool of blood. A hard-boiled detective will do a voice-over about men in positions of power brought down by their bad deeds.

"You're bad," Clementine giggles.

"And you like it, don't you, sweetheart?"

Bowie's had enough. She rounds the tree and clears her throat.

"Jesus H. Christ. I didn't know anyone was there." Ambassador Hunt jumps away from Clementine.

"Clearly," Bowie says bitingly.

"You didn't see anything."

"Didn't I?"

"Go back inside," he says to Clementine. She glances at Bowie, shrugs her shoulders, and leaves.

Ambassador Hunt stalks toward her, not stopping until he's almost on top of her. She stands firm. She's not going to back away. Not from him. Not from any man.

"Your wife might want to know you're harassing students in your garden while she's gone."

"That wasn't harassment. There was . . . something in her eye. I was helping her get it out."

"Seriously?"

"I know who you are, Bowie Bishop. I know what you're willing to do for fame."

"You don't know anything about me."

"I was there. I saw you. At Glen's casino. He told me all about you and your mother."

Bile rises in her throat. She should go back inside. She smells alcohol on his breath. Clementine's floral perfume clings to his collar. She'll scream for Jordan. He's probably frantically searching for his boss.

He whispers something in her ear, low and guttural.

At first she thinks maybe she didn't hear him right. Then he repeats it.

Her stomach heaves.

He smiles nastily. "See you later, Bowie."

She's left shaking. Glen and Ambassador Hunt gloating over the power they hold over girls like her. How they collect them like trophies. Move them like pawns on a chessboard. She feels like she's coated in filth, like a seal trapped in an oil spill.

That last thing he whispered. It wasn't true, was it?

It couldn't be true.

She'd thought she could leave her past behind. She'd had the ridiculous notion that she could start again. There was no escaping her past. It followed her, marked her, like a permanent jet trail smeared across the expanse of her short life. Pollution marring what was once blue-sky innocence.

New Zealand wasn't far enough away.

She doesn't care what time it is in Vegas. She's calling Suzie. Now.

17

LAKE

The next name on the list is A. Gil. It takes me a little while to realize the initials refer to Alejandro Gil, an ILA exchange student from Spain who's also hosted in Wellington.

When I call, he says he's already been interviewed by the New Zealand police and couldn't tell them much, but he agrees to meet me urgently at Te Papa, the New Zealand national museum where he has an internship.

I meet him in the first-floor café near the gift shop. He's wearing a chunky asymmetrical sweater in vivid shades of indigo and teal. His eyes are shadowed with concern. "Any news about Bowie?"

"Nothing new, I'm afraid."

"I'm freaking out a little bit, I'll be honest. It's not like Bowie to just disappear. She lives her life online, and she hasn't posted anything since Thursday."

"Were you two close?"

"We were friends but not that close. We bonded during ILA orientation in Auckland before we were sent to our families around New Zealand. I only see her occasionally."

"When was the last time you saw her?"

"Weeks ago. We met here for coffee. She loves Te Papa. I've

seen her spend hours in Toi Art—that's the National Art Collection. She would sit and stare at one painting for twenty minutes, scribbling lyrics in one of her notebooks. I've been busy with this internship. I should have called her more often, asked her how she was doing. She's been distant lately. Kind of checked out from the exchange student community. I assumed she was busy with school or dating someone new."

"Did she tell you she was dating someone?"

"The police asked me the same question. I honestly don't know. I think she had a few casual hookups, but she never mentioned anyone more serious."

"Do you think she was on any dating apps?"

"No. She didn't need any apps. She attracted more than enough attention just being in the world."

"Did Bowie ever talk about Bruce Walter, the son of the casino owner her mom works for?"

"She never mentioned him to me. Did Bruce . . . do they think he hurt her? Is that why he drank himself to death?"

"It's one theory the police are pursuing." The savory beef pastry I ordered sits heavy in my stomach. The memory of Bruce lying motionless on the bathroom floor won't leave me alone. "How would you describe Bowie?"

"Hot but dangerous, like her cheekbones might cut you. Like she could play an alien on *Star Trek* without much makeup. I'm gay, but plenty of the other exchange students fancied her. Talking to her, you felt like you were talking to a movie star, someone larger than life. And the stories she'd tell . . . she'd seen so many bands and even hung out backstage with them because her mom used to be in the music industry. She had a funny way of talking. English is my second language and I studied it intensively before I became an exchange student. Bowie uses old-fashioned idioms. Maybe she talks more like someone her mother's age? She's an old soul—I think that's the expression."

"You're not the first person to describe her that way."

"She was always handwriting lyrics with a fountain pen in

leather journals. She loved vintage guitars more than almost anything else. She was all over social media, but you wouldn't know it to talk to her. Most people who are that engaged, have that many followers, you see them taking selfies, you see them posting, studying their numbers, but she was private about it. It was almost like . . . almost like she was ashamed of posting? Like she didn't want to flaunt it, or that it was her job, something she had to do, but it didn't give her that rush. Influencers, and I've known a few, they all get that high from posting the most flattering photos and collecting gushing comments. I think maybe her mother runs her social media and she's the one who gets off on it?"

Every conversation about Bowie always came back to Suzie. The two were inextricable. Suzie is a stage mom, and Bowie her creation. "Did Bowie ever mention having a difficult relationship with her mother?"

"She did say something once about her mother using her to reclaim her lost chance at fame."

"That makes sense. I've had a few conversations with Suzie Bishop, and I got the same impression. I'm meeting Suzie at the airport after this. We're holding a press conference this afternoon. Please tell the other exchange students to watch it and call in any tips."

"I'll put the word out."

"One more thing. I'm interested in the arts festival where Bowie performed—I think you were there?"

"Bowie was a real star that night. She performed some of the standard hits from her social media and then she did this melancholy song called 'The Other Side' that made everyone sit up and pay attention."

"Did you meet Ambassador Hunt that night?"

Alejandro chuckles. "Couldn't miss him. He was wearing this ridiculous cowboy hat and everyone was taking selfies with him, me included. Wanna see?" He reaches for his phone, swiping through the photos until he finds the one he's looking for. "Here he is with Clementine. And here we are."

I hold the phone and zoom in. "Who's that skinny guy hovering nearby?"

"I think his name was Jordan? He was the ambassador's assistant or something."

"Jordan Singer."

"That's right. It was kind of funny. His boss kept going off the rails, drinking out of a flask, making inappropriate comments to women, and Jordan was doing his best on damage control, but you could tell it was making him crazy."

"Did Ambassador Hunt make any of those comments to Bowie?"

"Not that I know of. She was acting strangely, though. She looked at the ambassador as if she'd seen a ghost. After she met him she faded away. Left the reception early. Never even said goodbye, which wasn't like her."

"Huh. Interesting."

"Lake." He lays his palm flat on the table, looking into my eyes. "Find her, okay? She's too bright of a light to be gone forever."

"We'll do our very best." I gather my purse and jacket. "I really appreciate you dropping everything to talk to me. If you think of anything else, even something that you might consider trivial, please don't hesitate to call me, day or night."

"I will. Absolutely. Anything to find Bowie."

I call Sara's desk phone after I arrive at the airport. Suzie's plane doesn't land for twenty minutes.

"Hi, Sara."

"Hey, Lake. How's it going?"

"I'm at the airport waiting for Suzie to arrive. I just talked to one of Bowie's fellow exchange students about the night she performed at the arts festival. He said a certain someone was getting drunk in public and being inappropriate?"

"Welcome to my world."

"Do you have any video footage from that night?"

"We were filming, but mostly the performances. Let me check with the AV folks."

"That would be awesome. But Sara, please be careful. Maybe find the footage yourself and don't involve anyone else?"

"Um . . . okay. It's not unusual to review event footage."

"Yes, but this is different. Bowie is missing." I lower my voice instinctively, as if that would make any difference to someone monitoring the call. "There could be a link between that night and her disappearance. I don't know what yet. I'm exploring all possibilities."

"Should I call you Detective Harlowe now?"

"I know, I know. It's not really my job. It's just that this is personal for me now. I took the duty call. I feel like I know Bowie. I want to find her."

"I get it. She's charismatic. Her performance that night was electric. You could feel it after she stopped singing. The audience was entranced. I'll do whatever I can to help."

"Review the footage on the down-low. Tell me if she talks to anyone, does anything out of the ordinary. Keep it to yourself. The Front Office doesn't need to know." I'm purposefully not saying Ambassador Hunt's name. It feels risky to name him. The warning he gave me was explicit. He told me to drop it. Let law enforcement do their job. Or else . . .

"Got it. Will do. Good luck with Suzie Bishop. I'll see you at the press conference."

I call the IT section next. "Robin? How's it going?"

"Oh, you know, a paper shredder overheated and set off the fire alarm. Just returned to my desk."

"I don't want to add more work to your plate."

"No, it's fine. How can I help? Is it about the missing exchange student?"

"I'm at the airport waiting for her mom to arrive from the U.S. I have a favor to ask. You know Jordan Singer, how he left so suddenly?"

"Yeah."

"I talked to him this morning. He said he met with Bowie Bishop, but I can't find anything about it in his online files, and he clammed up when I asked him about the meeting. When you have a chance, could you recover his deleted work files? Maybe there's something there."

"I'll see what I can do."

"I'd really appreciate it. Like I said, next happy hour is my treat." Even though a world where carefree happy hours exist doesn't seem real right now. "Oops, gotta go, the mom's plane landed early."

I hang up and hurry toward the woman who could only be Suzie Bishop.

Even after her seventeen-hour journey to Auckland and short flight to Wellington, her heavy makeup is flawless, eyes rimmed with black and at least four layers of mascara, bleached-blond hair perfectly straight. She's wearing shiny black leggings and an off-the-shoulder black sweatshirt.

"The customs lady took away my dried baby alligator head keychain. Can you believe it? She didn't even search the grungy kids in front of me with all the camping gear."

No "Hi, Lake, I'm Suzie." She's full on.

"I warned you about that. No animal products through customs. They're serious about keeping invasive species out of this country."

"They treated me like I was an invasive species."

In a way, she is. So very American, marching through the airport like the rules don't apply to her.

"Have there been any developments?"

"I'm afraid not."

"How can there be no news? Eighteen-year-old girls don't vanish off the face of the earth without a trace. Where's Bowie?"

It's the question I've been asking myself on a punishing loop, as if I'm a lab rat and finding Bowie will earn me a double portion of food.

"The search is in full swing," I tell her as we wait by the luggage carousel. "The police have organized a door-to-door search of every neighborhood in Wellington. RSO Rob Smith is heading up a task force with FBI and Coast Guard Search and Rescue."

"And the surveillance camera footage? Why don't they have Bowie leaving the house on camera? Why don't they know who searched her room?"

"The angle of the Shepherds' security camera is positioned toward the front gate. It's only there to monitor incoming traffic. It's unusual that they have a security system at all. But there's a back entrance that's not monitored."

"What about all the street cameras? I mean, we're being watched twenty-four-seven by the eyes in the sky."

"Not so much in New Zealand. There are about four hundred thousand privately owned CCTV cameras in public outdoor spaces. Number goes way down for publicly owned cameras. The Privacy Act here is pretty strict in regard to their usage. Wellington only has about seven hundred cameras that can be accessed by the CCTV safety team. It's hardly Las Vegas."

"Which should make it safer. So why is my baby missing?" She suddenly turns and digs her long, black-lacquered nails into my arm. "Lake. I'm so scared."

"So am I."

"It's been too long. She's been missing since Thursday and it's Monday. I've read all the statistics. Every day that goes by . . ." She gulps back tears. Adjusts her black sunglasses.

Her battered guitar case and a matched set of leopard print luggage arrive, and I help her load everything onto a cart. She barely glances at her surroundings as we head to my car. I can't blame her. She's only thinking about Bowie.

"I thought the embassy would send an armored vehicle for me with a chauffeur."

"That's only at larger posts with a motor pool for security reasons. Only the ambassador has a car and driver here."

"Great. So I get to squeeze into your Mini Cooper? Just kidding. I'm glad to have the chance to talk to you privately before I meet with Rob. Mind if I smoke?"

She doesn't wait for a response before rolling the window down and lighting up.

"What's his deal? He's very curt on the phone. A tough guy with a gun. Single, from what I gather. What does he know about teenage girls?"

"Rob has made finding Bowie his number one priority. His deputy is taking care of all the other embassy security concerns. Rob's formidable, and so is Deputy Senior Sergeant Jill Sutherland."

"That Jill woman has blinkers on—she's convinced Bruce Walter is the reason Bowie's missing. I want you to investigate other possibilities; will you do that for me?"

"I told you that I'm not a detective."

"But you get me, Lake. You're empathetic. You stayed on the phone with me until I fell asleep. It's that kind of dedication I need right now."

Something I shouldn't have done. I'm not a grief counselor, either. "I'll do my very best."

"I'm hiring a private investigator. God knows I don't have the money, but I'll go into more debt, whatever it takes. I'd sell my soul to find Bowie. I'll come up with the money somehow and bring the best of the best to Wellington."

"And in the meantime we're all one united team searching for Bowie. I know you told me she would never run away . . . but we can't discount that theory."

"Absolutely not." Her face closes down. "She'd never run away. She wouldn't do that to me. She has too much going for her."

Wouldn't do that to *her*. Like Bowie being missing is all about Suzie.

"Then maybe DSS Sutherland has it right. Something bad could have happened with Bruce Walter. I met with his parents yesterday."

"Are they still in Wellington?" There's something about the way she asks the question, as if the prospect scares her.

"They'll be leaving today with Bruce's remains."

She shudders. "What a horrible word. **Remains**. Whoever thought of calling a person that? Some priest or funeral director who was tiptoeing around the word *death*. God, poor Nadia. I never really liked her but I wouldn't wish this on my worst enemy. Bruce was her whole world. Poor woman."

"Are you friends with Glen?" I'm thinking of the comment the ambassador made about Glen calling Suzie a washed-up alcoholic.

She stares out the window. "I wouldn't say friends. He's a paycheck. I've been working at the casino for fifteen years. We've had our ups and downs. But he's never been a real problem. I know how to manage guys like him. Use my looks, play dumb, and get whatever I want from them without them being any the wiser."

The traffic is light. We reach her hotel swiftly. I help her up to her room. She opens the minibar immediately and pours herself a shot of vodka.

"Stay for a drink?"

"I need to go back to the embassy. Maybe you should have a rest. This afternoon you have briefings and then the public appeal."

"I want you there for the briefings. I want you to be my primary contact. I don't want to talk to this Rob guy."

"I'll be there. Don't judge Rob until you've met him."

She flops onto a chair and slings one slim leg over the chair arm. "For the public appeal I'm going to play one of Bowie's songs. Lately she's been writing these odd, sad songs. I told her they're never going to sell or go over as a demo, but this one's perfect for the press conference. It's called 'Fly Home' and it has this line: *Fly home, lost and lonely. Fly home, my one and only.* There won't be a dry eye in the studio, or at home. Want me to play it for you?"

She jumps up and opens her guitar case.

"I'll hear it in a few hours. It does sound perfect. Public Affairs wants you to make the appeal as personal as possible. Here are the remarks they prepared." I hold out the script. "You can put your own personal spin on it. I emailed these to you as well. You can make track changes and send them back."

"Ugh. Track changes. Gives me the willies." She opens another airplane bottle. "Say what you mean the first time. None of this endless dithering about nuances and shit. When I write lyrics, they come to me all in a rush. I never edit a word. I wrote "Hurt So Happy" in fifteen minutes, high as a kite and sitting on a fire escape at the Chelsea Hotel. And that went on to hit number three. Not that I ever see more than the paltriest of royalties. Those fuckers stole my work. The only people making money off my mega hit are rich old men."

As she steamrolls on about being wronged by her former bandmates and manager, about how all Bowie needs is that one big break and then Suzie will be there to make damn sure she holds on to her rights, the thought flashes that maybe Bowie did run away.

Suzie Bishop is a lot. I remember wanting to run away from Ruth and her mood swings—aloof one moment and clinging to me the next. But where would I have gone? There was only one road leading out of our town, and it went straight to Canada, where I would have required a passport and an adult accompanying me.

It's not that Suzie reminds me of Ruth. They couldn't be further apart. Vegas glam and Alaska granola. The way she lives through Bowie, though. The way Ruth lived through me, and how I still feel her tentacles, invisible suction cups wrapped around my mind.

"I'll pick you up at three," I tell Suzie, breaking into her monologue.

I hope she doesn't open too many more bottles from the minibar before the press conference.

18
LAKE

The briefing with Rob went better than expected—possibly because he looks a little like a young Patrick Swayze. Afterward, I deliver Suzie to the greenroom of the local TV station, where Sara and her team are waiting for her.

"I love Bowie's song, Suzie," Sara says. "It brought tears to my eyes. The fact that you're playing it live is really going to make this appeal special and effective."

"She's so talented, my Bowie. Such a star. I want the world to know her, to worship her like I do. Is the film crew experienced here? I mean, they'll film me from my best angles, right?"

"Absolutely," Sara assures her. "I've been interviewed on the show before and they are pros."

"You're in good hands with Sara," I tell Suzie, making my escape. I noticed Myra and Stuart Shepherd in the audience holding room, and I want the chance to talk to them.

Myra's a natural beauty who doesn't wear makeup and has allowed silver to generously streak her brown hair. She's wearing flowing off-white linen trousers and a mauve linen tunic. Stuart has blond hair with gray streaks and deep grooves around faded blue eyes. He's dressed in a tan business suit over a plain white T-shirt, and he's wearing a large greenstone *pounamu* necklace.

They're the New Zealand version of a power couple, the politician and the grief counselor. Committed to environmental causes, social justice, and green energy.

Their young twin sons, Byron and Oliver, sit in chairs against the wall playing games on tablets.

"We're gutted. Simply gutted," Myra Shepherd tells me when I introduce myself, her light green eyes swimming with tears. "Bowie disappeared on our watch. She's a part of our family. If Isla was the one missing . . ." She shakes her head. "We could be the ones making this heartbreaking public plea."

"We do believe that the appeal will have more impact coming from Suzie alone, though," Stuart is quick to add. "We don't want to muddy the message. A desperate mother's entreaty to find her only daughter will reach the most hearts."

I read between the lines. He wants to be associated with Bowie as little as possible. As Sara pointed out, this can only hurt his reelection campaign.

"Is Isla here?" I ask.

"She wanted to be," Stuart replies, "but it's the first day of Term Four and she has to attend school and swim practice."

Myra sighs. "She's gutted, as well. She and Bowie were like real sisters, with all the good and bad that goes along with that."

"The bad?"

"They had their little tiffs, though they always sorted it out."

One of the twins lifts his head. "Are you going to find Bowie soon?" he asks, hazel eyes cloudy.

"She's doing everything she can, Oliver," Myra says, going to kneel between her sons. "We're all praying she comes home soon."

I make a mental note that Oliver is the one wearing the Wētā Workshop T-shirt that says "Be creative and make cool stuff."

"I like your T-shirt," I tell him. "I've been meaning to visit Wētā." The special effects workshop that produced the sets, costumes, and creatures for *The Lord of the Rings* trilogy, and other projects, is one of the most highly recommended tourist sites in Wellington.

"The tour is really fun!" Oliver replies. "We saw actual mithril."

Byron looks up from his tablet to add, "Yeah, it was the mithril shirt that Aragorn wears in the Battle of the Morannon."

I smile. "That does sound exciting."

"Are you going to bring Bowie home?" Byron asks. "We miss her. She's always writing songs for us, about the *Lord of the Rings*, or about Marsh, that's our fluffy tabby cat. My mum named her after Ngaio Marsh."

"The famous New Zealand crime writer. I've read most of her books."

"As have I," Myra says.

"I have a literary cat, too," I tell the boys. "His name is Edgar Allan Three Paws."

Byron cocks his head. "Does he really only have three paws?"

"I'm afraid so. One of them had to be amputated when he was a tiny kitten."

"Can he run?" Oliver asks.

"Can he hop?"

"Can he catch a mouse?"

Their questions tumble out, making me laugh. "You'd be surprised. He races around the house and only falls over every now and then."

"Bowie would definitely write a song about Edgar Allan Three Paws," Byron says with a decisive nod.

"Want to hear Marsh's song?" Oliver stands up and makes a gesture as if his hands were cat paws. "Listen, you can never ever make Marsh do something that she just doesn't want to do," he sings.

"I'm gonna tell you true," Byron joins his brother. "You just need to show a little bit of patience and wait for Marsh to come give her love to you."

"And then there's the verse about the litter box." Byron giggles. "I'm not gonna lie, that litter box gets smelly," he sings. "You gotta scoop out the—"

"It's quite a long song, really, isn't it?" Myra smiles, putting her arm around Oliver's shoulders. "I'm sure Lake has other things to do."

Oliver tugs at Myra's hand. "I want Bowie to come home. The song's not finished yet. She promised to write us more verses."

Myra places a hand on each boy's head. "We all miss Bowie very much, don't we?"

The boys nod solemnly. Stuart is checking his phone. When his wife glares at him, he stuffs the phone into a pocket. "Sorry. Work emergency."

I'm about to ask more questions when Sara hurries over. "Lake, I need you."

"If you'll excuse me, Stuart, Myra. It was nice to meet you. And Byron and Oliver, you as well."

"Lovely to meet you, Lake," Myra replies with a warm smile.

"What's going on?" I ask as Sara steers me out of the waiting room.

"Suzie keeps asking for you, says she doesn't trust, and won't work with, anyone else," Sara says, exasperation written all over her face. "She sent my staff away. She's sitting in the greenroom holding a silence strike until you come."

"Sorry, I was greeting the Shepherds."

"We're live in a little over thirty minutes. Here's what I want drilled through her head. Keep it simple. Keep it short. Humanize Bowie, build empathy. The more people she reaches, the more people will join the search."

"Got it."

"She's refusing to use the script I wrote."

"I'll convince her."

"Best of luck with that."

Suzie is sitting at a table with a bottle of Evian and an obstinate look on her face. "Lake, there you are. Finally."

"Sorry, I was talking to Stuart and Myra Shepherd."

"I thought they weren't going to take part in the press conference."

"They'll be in the audience. They're here to support you. What's this I hear about you not liking the prepared remarks?"

Sara leaves and closes the door behind her.

"I'm too rock-'n-roll for those stuffy remarks. No one will believe me if I sound like a government talking head. I want to speak from the heart. Off the cuff. The right words will come to me in the moment."

"This isn't a song, Suzie. This is Bowie's life on the line. Sara has a lot of experience with public appeals. Her remarks are sensitive, eloquent, and designed to cast a wide net."

"All right. Whatever. I'll use them. But I can't promise to stay totally on script."

"That's fine. Why don't we practice a few times? Sometimes cameras have a way of muddling our minds."

"Not mine. I'm used to cameras. Have you seen my video for 'Hurt So Happy'? I sent you the link."

"Loved it. You look gorgeous. Quite the menacing bass line."

"It's not about looking gorgeous, although that helps; it's about connection. Channeling your emotions to reach the audience. Tapping into something larger than yourself. There's an energy at a concert, when so many people are so ecstatic and transformed by music. And there'll be an energy today, with the reporters, the law enforcement, all the people watching at home. I'll feel it, and I'll know what to do."

Not good enough. I want her promise to keep things simple.

I drop to one knee beside her chair. Look into her eyes. "Suzie, this is simple, though, isn't it? This is about finding Bowie. You don't want to do, or say, anything that distracts from the message."

She bites her lip. "I understand that."

"Good. So keep it simple. Keep the message direct. Share a few details about Bowie, humanize her."

"Because if some sick man has abducted her and he watches this, we want him to think of her as human, not just some . . . some piece of meat to chew up and spit out."

"Exactly. Can you do this, Suzie? Do you believe you can reach out to the person who needs to hear this message and speak directly to them?" Whether that's Bowie herself, or an abductor.

She clutches both chair arms, knuckles turning white with the strain. "I believe it with all my heart, Lake. I'll say the right words. I'll use the remarks that your officials gave me, but I'll personalize them. I believe this will work."

I wait a beat. She's sincere.

"Excellent. I know you can do it. After you perform Bowie's song, you'll take some questions from the press. Remember, if you don't like a question, you can simply pass to the next person, or hand it back over to DSS Sutherland. For example, if they ask you about a connection to Bruce Walter's death, what will you say?"

"No comment. I leave that to the police."

"Perfect. The press here should only throw softball questions. They've been hand selected, so don't worry."

She crosses her long, leather-clad legs. "Scared of a few reporters? Hardly. In my day I had paparazzi following me everywhere, even into the bathroom. Especially into the bathroom. I was doing a lot of coke in those days. LOL." She laughs. And then tears well up in her eyes. "Lake . . ." Her voice trembles. "Where's my baby?"

"We're going to find her." Suddenly parched, I open a bottle of water. "When you or Bowie perform, do you have any rituals before you go onstage? Any breathing exercises?"

"I do alternate nostril breathing. You know, in through one nostril, hold it, out through the other nostril."

"Let's do that together now."

The door opens. "You're on in fifteen minutes, Ms. Bishop. They want you on set to meet the hosts."

"Give us three minutes," I tell the studio assistant.

Suzie leads us in the breathing exercises. When we're finished, she looks as calm as I've seen her. She reaches for my hand and gives it a squeeze. "Let's do this."

SHE FELL AWAY

I give Sara a thumbs-up as I accompany Suzie to the set. As they're miking her and chitchatting, I slip into the wings.

The press conference is going well. Suzie is self-assured, calm, and effective. She's mostly stuck to the prepared remarks, and I see Sara's shoulders relaxing.

She makes a personal appeal, speaking directly into the camera. "Bowie isn't a victim. She's a fighter. My shining star. She'll set the world ablaze someday, and I can't imagine her light being extinguished too soon. Please." Her voice quivers. "Please, if you've seen Bowie, or you know anything about where she might be, please call the number listed on your screen. Bowie needs you. I need you. And now I'd like to play you one of Bowie's original songs. Listen to her words. I'm singing them for her. To her. Bowie, wherever you are, sweetheart, fly home now."

When you're sure nobody's watching
In the middle of the night
Stretch your wings out on your pillow
Get ready to take flight

Fly home, lost and lonely
Fly home, my one and only
Fly on home

You've been waiting for this moment
You've been searching for the signs
Now the window is wide open
Now the path is yours to find

The cars out on the highway
The ships upon the sea
Nobody sees you soaring
Nobody knows but me

I'll keep my doorway open and the
Light above it lit
Don't fly too close to the bright stars
You might lose track of it

Fly home, lost and lonely
Fly home, my one and only
Fly on home

She's playing this perfectly. The more attention focused on Bowie, the more likely she is to be found. I have no doubt this will be picked up by news outlets in the U.S.

The TV host wipes a tear from her eye, thanks her, and announces that it's time for a few questions from the press before a statement from the police.

"Ms. Bishop, do you think Bowie is a runaway?" a reporter who looks only a few years older than Bowie asks.

"Absolutely not. She wouldn't do that. We're very close. She tells me everything."

"But did she have mental health struggles? I have some of her lyrics here . . . a song called 'The Other Side.' It says, and I quote, '*In the heart of the night, I'll come to you . . . On the other side.*' That sounds, well, it sounds like it could point to self-harm."

I hold my breath, but Suzie handles it like a pro.

"It's artistic license. She sings about the struggles we all face in a way that lightens everyone's load."

A man in a wrinkled linen suit raises his hand. "Ms. Bishop, I understand that American football star Bruce Walter died in Wellington and that there may be evidence linking him to Bowie's disappearance?"

"I have no comment on that. I leave that to the police investigation."

I relax back against the wall. I should have had a little more faith. She may be chaotic, but Suzie Bishop knows how to turn it on for the cameras.

"But do you think there's a chance that Bruce Walter killed Bowie and hid her body somewhere?" the man persists. I stiffen. Who let him in?

"Ms. Bishop can't and won't speculate on any—" DSS Sutherland begins, stepping forward, but Suzie cuts her off.

"Bruce and Bowie barely knew each other. They'd only met once, to my knowledge. It's all a tragic coincidence. I'm very sorry for Greg and Nadia Walter's loss."

"If you say she didn't run away or harm herself," the same reporter asks, "then who took Bowie, Ms. Bishop?"

"I'm sure you've read the statistics. If someone took Bowie, kidnapped her, it was highly likely that it was someone she knew." She found Stuart Shepherd in the audience and stared straight at him. "Someone she knew very well."

Fuck. I squeeze my eyes shut. This is bad. Beyond bad. An American making sordid insinuations against a Kiwi politician on live television.

Reporters start talking over each other.

"Are you accusing MP Shepherd of a crime, Ms. Bishop?"

"What's the angle? Why take Bowie?"

Sara gestures wildly from the wings, telling the TV producers to shut it down.

"I'm not accusing anyone," Suzie says loudly. "I'm only saying that Bowie has an attraction for rich, older men who want to own her or who want to control her."

Which is basically another accusation.

"No more questions at this time, ladies and gentlemen. That will be all. The hotline number is on your screens. Please report all tips there. Further press inquiries may be directed through the Public Affairs department of the U.S. Embassy."

Reporters still shouting questions. Suzie with a half smile on her face, never breaking her stare down with Stuart Shepherd.

After the cameras stop rolling I pull Suzie backstage and into the greenroom and shut the door. "Suzie, that wasn't what we rehearsed. You were supposed to follow the script."

"I improvised."

"You accused Stuart Shepherd of harming Bowie."

"I'm sorry, Lake." She tucks a lock of hair behind her ear. "I don't want to make your life more difficult. But I always speak truth to power. I told you I'm too rock-'n-roll for a script. And he was giving me this creepy look. I know he's hiding something."

"If you're going to cast suspicion on someone, why not on Bruce Walter?"

"Oh, he had nothing to do with it."

"How can you be so sure of that?"

"Why would he want to screw up his precious football career?"

She's protecting Glen Walter. Is that what this is? What's his hold over her, other than being her employer? It's more than that. There's something rotten here, I can feel it. It's time to burrow to the core of it, find the worms squirming at the heart of the apple.

"You were supposed to say no comment, and instead you make accusations about a prominent Kiwi politician who has a rock-solid alibi and absolutely no reason to be under suspicion."

"Is his alibi rock solid, though? I mean, they say they left without Bowie. But what if she was in the van with them? What if she did go on the camping trip and then there was an accident or something, and she died, and they're covering it up? The whole family took a pact of silence. Or what if Stuart decided that he wanted her. Living together day after day. Maybe he's keeping her in an apartment in the city. Hiding her there. He could be a total sicko."

"Suzie," I groan. "The front-entrance security camera caught everyone except Bowie entering the camper van. You know that. I wish you had voiced these suspicions to me before the press conference. We could have talked it all through. You could have talked to the police, instead of to the entire world."

"Myra Shepherd is always judging me. Did you read what she

said to that reporter for the *New Zealand Herald?* She said that Bowie had led an undisciplined life before she came to live under her roof. Undisciplined. Like I was letting her run wild or something. Like I was a bad mother."

"That comment may have been taken out of context."

"And Bowie told me that Isla was jealous of her and refused to talk to her sometimes. Why wasn't Isla here today? Huh? I tell you, that family is hiding something. They mess with my daughter and they're going to feel the consequences."

"This isn't a war, Suzie. This is Bowie's life we're talking about. You turned the conversation away from finding her. Now everyone will be talking about the feud between you and the Shepherds."

"Maybe this will be good for Stuart's reelection. Loud, crass American bitch accuses him of crime. He'll get the sympathy vote."

"Suzie, we both want the same thing. We want to find Bowie. We have to work together. You can't undermine the investigation like this."

My words finally sink in. "Shit, Lake. I wasn't thinking. I got carried away. I'm sorry."

"Yeah. So am I."

"Let me buy you a drink?"

"I have to get back to work." Where I'm going to be called back to the ambassador's office. Maybe he'll fire me. Or maybe I'll be forced to curtail like Jordan did. Why did he curtail? I still have no idea.

"Did you see the response to the song, though?" Suzie asks with relish. "I'm going to release it as a single. I'll have a producer I know clean it up first. It'll go viral. The more people that know she's missing, the better."

"Just please, *please* promise me you won't make any more accusations. Let the police do their job. Let the investigators and other authorities work; don't make it harder for them. Now they're putting out the fire you started instead of focusing on finding Bowie."

"I promise," she says contritely. "Now, if you don't want a drink, I do."

My phone rings. "Hi, Mason."

"Lake, are you with Suzie Bishop right now?"

"I am. Did you watch the press conference?"

"I did. That was . . . interesting. But that's not why I'm calling."

"What is it?" Suzie clutches my arm. "Have they found her?"

"We haven't found her." Mason answers her question. I shake my head, and Suzie's shoulders slump. "But there's a new development. Can you bring Ms. Bishop to the station? DSS Sutherland and Rob Smith are already on the way. We want to gauge Ms. Bishop's reaction to the news."

"I'll bring her in right away."

"I'll send you a location pin."

"See you soon."

Suzie tugs at my arm. "What? What is it?"

"I'm not sure. Rob is on his way to the police station. They want me to bring you there as well. They wouldn't tell me what it was about."

"How fast can that Mini Cooper go?"

"There'll be some rush-hour traffic, but it shouldn't take more than twenty minutes."

"Make it fifteen." She grabs her guitar and her leather jacket. "If they've found something, anything, I want to know *now*. Don't you have diplomatic immunity? Put on some speed!"

19
BOWIE

"Suzie, I need to talk to you. Call me back, okay?"

Her mom will still be on the night shift. She's not supposed to take personal calls, but Bowie knows she'll call back on her smoke break.

Myra knocks before opening Bowie's bedroom door. "Could I talk to you for a moment, Bowie?"

"I just left a message for my mom to call me."

"It won't take long." She enters the room. "I noticed some tension between you and Isla tonight at the arts festival. I don't know what it's about. I only want to say that the issues may seem large now, but later in life you'll find that what seemed to have life-and-death importance to you right now was much smaller and more easily resolved than you thought. Life is filled with these little aches. Avoiding them only turns them into bigger injuries."

Suzie tells Bowie stuff like this all the time. She says what Bowie feels right now won't matter when she's older. *You don't even know how perfect you are. All shiny and new. Toned body and skinny ass. When you're my age, you'll look back and realize that you were absolutely fucking perfect. Stop moping and start living.*

She says things she shouldn't say when she's had a few drinks.

That she's jealous of Bowie. That she wishes they were in one of those movies where they swapped bodies and she could be Bowie for a few weeks and really live it up. She says that Bowie will never amount to anything without her guidance. She builds a cage with words to keep Bowie under her control.

Myra sits beside her on the bed. "I'm not saying that your problems are small."

"Isla hates me."

"Oh, Bowie." Myra takes her hands, forces her to make eye contact. "That's simply not true. She cares about you and this conflict is quite difficult for her. She won't be at peace until you clear the air."

"She says I take up too much space. She doesn't like seeing me perform. Music is in my DNA. I can't stop to please her."

"And you shouldn't have to stop. Never make yourself smaller for someone else's benefit. It's one of the things I most admire about you—the big, bold energy you bring to a stage, to your life. You shouldn't have to change yourself to fit her, though it does help sometimes to see things from others' perspectives. Why do you think she feels that way?"

"I don't know." Bowie shifts away from Myra, putting space between them.

"I think you do."

"She's jealous. She's your only daughter, but now I'm here taking up your attention."

"That's probably part of it. I sense there's something else, though. Is it about a boy? Perhaps it's about Dean Hira?"

Not Bowie's secret to tell. "You made her promise not to date him anymore."

Myra tilts her head, regarding Bowie thoughtfully. "We didn't make you promise anything, though. If you and he—"

"I think he's extremely talented and I appreciate his musical vibe, but I'm not dating him. I swear."

Myra lets out a sigh. "Right. That's good then. Dean's a party boy—playing at clubs, drinking until all hours. We just want what's best for Isla. She's my good girl who makes top marks and still brings home sports trophies."

"And I'll be gone in six months."

"Oh, sweetheart, I didn't mean to make you feel belittled. You're very special to me. You've had a different upbringing than Isla, haven't you?"

Thrifted clothes and sour milk in the fridge. Hours by herself while Suzie worked at the casino. Dodging Suzie's boyfriends in the hallway. She hadn't written any of that in her application to become an exchange student.

"I want to put you two in a room together and talk it all out. Should we go for a girls' spa day soon?"

"I'd like that. And honestly, Dean's pretty wholesome for a bad boy."

"Have you known really bad boys?"

And there it was. The searching question, the one that led to dangerous, forbidden places. "Yeah."

"Tell me about him."

"I don't want to think about him."

"What's his name? You can at least tell me that."

"Bruce."

"And this Bruce hurt you?"

"He hurt my best friend."

Myra turns toward the collage of photos and mementos Bowie carefully arranged on the wall beside her bed. "Florica—wasn't that her name? She was very beautiful."

Bowie had taken a photography class and learned how to use an old-school Nikon camera with real film. They'd done this epic Goth photo shoot at an abandoned amusement park out in the desert. Lo and Bowie with their arms thrown around each other's shoulders, laughing as if they had all the time in the world to be silly on ghostly, rotting Ferris wheels.

"The most beautiful. I miss her every day."

"You correspond with her mother. I've seen the letters you receive from Livia Baciu in Las Vegas."

"Livia and I will always keep in touch. I'm a link to her daughter."

"You think this Bruce harmed Florica?"

"I know he did."

For a few seconds Bowie considers telling Myra about that night. How she thinks Bruce murdered Lo. How Bowie played a role by introducing them. How can she ever forgive herself?

But then she remembers that Myra, Isla, even Stuart, who's a politician and therefore has sold his soul to the devil, can't comprehend her life. They simply don't know what it was like to be raised in Vegas by a mother who chases fame like a drug.

"You hate him?" Myra asks.

"I want to kill him." It slips out, and she immediately wishes she could take it back. "I don't mean that literally."

"Of course not. This is a safe space. I want you to feel comfortable voicing your darkest thoughts. That's what they are—thoughts. They don't define us. They're not who we are. Thoughts come and go. Even thoughts of harming other people . . . or ourselves. The lyrics of the last song you sang tonight were, perhaps, pointing in that direction."

"I'm not suicidal, if that's what you're thinking."

"There's no topic that's off-limits, Bowie. You can tell me your worst thoughts, your most frightening memories, and I won't judge you. Having a friend and a confidante makes our burdens easier to bear."

Despite the dread clinging to her mind from the encounter with Ambassador Hunt, Bowie feels comforted. There's something about Myra that disarms her, makes her want to trust. She uncrosses her arms. Maybe if she gives Myra something, a little taste of the darkness, it will be enough to stop these questions. "There is something I've been wanting to tell you."

Myra goes still. "I'm here. Take a few deep breaths and let it out."

"I'm worried that my mom owes money to her boss. I'm

worried that he's going to use the debt to manipulate her . . . and me when I return to Vegas."

"What's this man's name?"

"Glen." The name like a lump of coal in her mouth.

"Glen Walter, the owner of the casino where your mother works. Bruce's father."

Bowie sits up fully. Has Myra been researching her past? "They're greedy, entitled, and they think they can have whatever they want."

"I'm going to call your mother. I don't like you being frightened of this family. She's not keeping you safe."

"No!" Bowie shakes her head violently. "Don't call her. I told you this in confidence, okay? You said you wouldn't tell anyone." Actually, she hadn't said that. Bowie had volunteered the information. Myra's tactics work.

"All right, I won't call her, though if I thought you were truly in danger, I would want to do something about it, to protect you." She says this fiercely, and a warm glow spreads through Bowie, as if she's had a few shots of tequila.

Myra truly cares about her. Or she wants to protect Isla from being tainted by association.

"Thank you for confiding in me, Bowie. I'm here for you."

"You won't call my mom?"

She crosses her heart. "I promise."

Bowie's phone starts playing "Hurt So Happy."

"And there's your mum now." Myra strokes a lock of hair away from Bowie's forehead. "You're stronger than you know, my darling." She leaves, closing the door softly.

Bowie accepts the video call.

"What's that shapeless thing you're wearing?" Suzie's leaning against a wall in the service alley outside of the casino, smoking a cigarette.

"A wool jumper. Myra gave it to me."

"Oh my God, you sound like one of them. A jumper? Seriously? And wool? You can't wear wool in Vegas—you'll get a heat rash."

"I still have six months here."

"Just don't forget your roots, honey, that's all I'm saying. And don't lose your style. They may wear lumpy wool sweaters in New Zealand, but you're gonna be rocking the tight black leather when you come home. So how did the arts festival go? Hobnobbing with ambassadors and dignitaries. My glamorous rock star."

"That's why I called you. Something really disturbing happened. I recognized Ambassador Hunt. He was in the VIP suite the night Lo died. Glen introduced him as Mr. Palmer."

"Was he there when I arrived?"

"Yeah. He was still there. The short one in the shiny white fringed cowboy shirt."

"Oh yeah. That one. He was a real piece of work. Those oil barons think of women as just another well to be sucked dry."

"Why was he there under a false name?"

"I don't know. You think he'd want to be throwing his title around, make us all call him 'sir.'"

"So you didn't know who he was?"

"I didn't have a clue."

"I caught him in the garden after the concert hitting on one of the exchange students, even though he's married, and he kind of threatened me. He said . . ." She doesn't even want to repeat it. *I remember you in your short skirt, sitting on a record scout's lap . . . and your model friend falling out of that tight dress . . .* "He said he knows the desperate things we're willing to do to become famous. He asked me what I did for Glen to make him pay for my exchange program. That's not true, is it? Glen didn't pay for my program."

The alley is dimly lit. Suzie is a shadowy blur. Every time she takes a drag from her cigarette, there's an orange glowing ember. Even though her image isn't sharp, Bowie knows she's about to tell a lie by the way she turns her face away from the camera slightly.

"It's not exactly—"

"Mom." Bowie cuts in sharply. "Don't lie to me."

Suzie finishes her cigarette and stubs it out against the wall. "All right. It's fucking true. There. Now you know."

"But you told me you made a private donation fund with your friends and those high rollers who tip you so well. You said that—"

"I'm sorry, baby, I knew you wouldn't approve, but you wanted to go so badly. You were so excited. And after the year you had, mourning Florica's death, I was worried about you. I wanted to make you feel better. It was the only way I could find to raise the funds."

"Fuck, Mom." Bowie burrows her head back against the pillow and closes her eyes. "What did you do for him in return?"

"Nothing. Jesus. Get your mind out of the gutter. He wanted to help you. You're an investment for him. He'll take a cut of your first album profits because he made the introduction to the record scout."

"And you were willing to agree to that? Aren't you the one who's always telling me not to give any of my recording rights away?"

"It's a small cut. He's smart enough to know it will add up, though. You're gonna be such a big star, baby. You're going to light up the world. Believe it and it will come true."

"He owns me now. That's why he did it, don't you see? You're the one who comes home drunk and tells me that all men are liars. That I can't trust anyone. That they're all looking for an angle, a way to use me."

"One hundred percent true. Best advice ever. But we're going into this with eyes wide open. I don't trust Glen, but I know him better than you do. I know how to twist him around my finger. I'm in control."

"No you're not. You think you are, but you're not."

Just like that night in the VIP room. She'd thought she was in control, but it had all been a lie. She'd slept with Travis McCray, not to land a record deal, but because she'd thought he was hot and she'd been flying from the high of commanding the room during her performance. She hadn't heard her phone ringing when Lo had called her.

Bowie was the reason Lo was there that night. She'd let her leave with Bruce Walter. She'd abandoned her when she needed her the most.

It was her fault that Lo died that night. Bruce gave her sweet, innocent friend those drugs. Who knows what else he did?

"We'll use Glen to launch your career, and then we'll leave him in the dust. I promise, baby. This little loan will mean nothing. You're going to take over the world."

The speech she's heard a million times. The fairy tale her mom's been telling her since before she learned how to read. You're a star. Your destiny is to be famous.

"I don't like you lying to me."

"We all tell little lies sometimes. We couldn't get through life otherwise. And what I really want to talk about is this Ambassador Hunt hitting on a girl during an official event. Wears alligator boots and has short-man syndrome. You should report him to the embassy. Better yet, contact a tabloid and tell them about it."

"I'm not going to report him. I don't want to get in trouble. Reporting it won't stop him from hitting on the next girl at the next party."

"At least isn't there someone you can talk to at the embassy? He can't get away with that kind of behavior. Someone should challenge him."

"He had an assistant following him around all night trying to keep him in line. I could talk to him off the record, tell him to keep a closer watch."

"What's his name? I'll call and talk to him."

"I can do this myself, okay? I'll handle it my way."

"What's his name?"

"Don't worry about it. I'm sorry I told you."

"Let's not fight, okay, baby? My smoke break is almost over, but I need a smile from my shining star."

Bowie sighs. "I don't really feel like smiling."

"So what else is new in Wellington?"

She considers telling her mom about meeting Mark Edison for the second time, how he loved her song about Lo and asked her to come to his recording studio, but something stops her. She wants to keep this to herself—Suzie is her mom and her manager. If she tells her, she'll immediately start researching Mark and pestering him and probably stop Bowie from visiting his recording studio because she's already picked out a studio and a producer in Vegas.

"Not much. I was thinking about Lo tonight. How she was the one who really wanted to be here."

"Oh, honey, I know you miss her. We all do. Livia walks around the halls like a zombie. I'm really worried about her. I know you're in New Zealand to honor your friend and you've been there almost six months. Isn't that enough? It's time to live your own life. Leave early. Come back home and record those demos. I've been working on cover concepts for your first album."

"Um . . . I don't have a record contract yet."

"You will, baby, you will. It's gonna be classy. You and your Gibson. I'm thinking you'll wear a black leather bodysuit."

Suzie wanted her to play their game. Wear the skimpy clothes and sing the songs they want her to sing. A slow overdose of powerlessness. "You did things your way with Bitter Pill. You were antiestablishment and wore whatever you wanted to wear."

"And look where that got me." Her voice drips with vinegar. "Absolutely freaking nowhere. You're not going to make the same mistakes I did. You have me guiding you. We play the game for one album, get that big hit on constant rotation, and then you reinvent yourself any which way you want to."

"I don't want to have to reinvent myself. I want to be me right out of the gate."

"That's my little iconoclast," Suzie says fondly. "Do you know why I named you Bowie?"

"For David Bowie. Duh."

"Yeah, but I could've named you Jagger, or Joplin, but I chose Bowie because he was the king of reinvention. He was a chameleon; his music never sounded the same from album to album. And the fans stuck with him. Iconoclasts have that power. The fans follow them no matter what. Crap. Break's over. Are we good?"

"Yeah. I know you did it for me."

"Everything's for you, baby. Everything." Suzie blows her a kiss, and the screen goes dark.

Bowie's jaw clenches. It's not all right. They're not good.

She's felt this divide between her and her mom for a while now. A discord. The harmony didn't work anymore. Suzie was singing the same old part and Bowie had learned a whole new song.

Bowie had taken photos of Suzie while she was sleeping after a long shift one night. When she developed the photos at the darkroom at school, her mother's face had appeared on the paper. Her *real* face. No makeup. No fake smile. This face wasn't trying to get as many likes and new followers as possible. To Bowie, it had seemed that she was meeting her mother for the first time. She'd seen a vulnerability, a softness, and she'd felt a rush of love for her mother.

She'd been excited for Suzie to see the photos, but when she showed her that night after school, Suzie ripped them up and told Bowie to never print more. She hated them because her mouth was hanging open and she didn't have any makeup on and she said Bowie was fucking weird even to have taken the photos.

If Bowie allowed Suzie to see how she really felt about New Zealand—how she's tumbled into love with this new life—Suzie would have the same reaction. She'd destroy Bowie's fledgling freedom, her longing for a new kind of life. She'd find a way to pull the strings that tie them together, yank her back to Vegas.

She doesn't want to be her puppet anymore. She's not going to be the fulfillment of all Suzie's dead hopes and dreams. Suzie 2.0.

She loves her mom despite their messy life, the partying, the brutal ambition. But allowing Glen to pay for her exchange program had been a huge mistake.

He'd been spreading rumors about her to his asshole friends. Spreading poison across oceans, invading what she'd thought was a haven, temporary but safe.

Bowie isn't going to allow the poison to spread. She'll reinvent herself right here. Right now.

20

LAKE

Rob meets us at the entrance to the police station. "Hi, thanks for getting here so quickly."

"What's this about?" Suzie asks impatiently.

"The New Zealand police have made a discovery, and they want to ask you some questions."

Mason holds the door to an inner hallway open for us.

"This is Sergeant Mason Yates," Rob says. "He'll take us to DSS Sutherland."

Mason falls into step beside me. "Good to see you again, Ms. Harlowe."

"Sergeant Yates."

"Been hunting any moose lately with your big sharp knife?"

Rob glances back with a perplexed look.

I elbow Mason in the chest, and he grunts and gives me a private smile.

DSS Sutherland sits behind a desk piled high with paperwork. She's a petite woman with curly ash-blond hair and a button nose, but her expression says: *Don't fuck with me and I won't have to fuck you up.*

Being a senior detective must be a draining job. My infrequent brushes with death take a heavy toll. I can't imagine investigating violent crimes for a living. How each case, each crime scene photo, permanently stains your mind.

Mason stands beside her desk, an intimidating wall of muscle. He's built like a heavyweight boxer, but there's a genuine warmth in his smile that's like a sunbeam on this gray, rainy day.

"You've made a break in the case?" Suzie asks.

"Ms. Bishop, please have a seat."

"I'll stand." In her platform boots, Suzie is all of five feet three, but she projects an air of owning the room.

The two women size each other up. DSS Sutherland would win in a fistfight, but my money would be on Suzie in a match of wills.

"I'll get right to the point, then. We did an analysis of the bloody fingerprints on the shirt Bruce Walter was wearing when he died. We have biometric data on Bowie from her student visa application. Fingerprints on fabric are difficult to verify due to the surface being porous and stretchy. However, since this is an urgent missing persons case, we were able to also request rapid DNA testing. It was Bowie's blood on Bruce Walter's shirt."

Suzie's face registers genuine shock. "I don't understand. Why would her blood be on his shirt? I think I will sit, after all."

Mason helps Suzie to a chair.

"Would Bruce Walter have had any motive to harm your daughter, Ms. Bishop?" DSS Sutherland asks.

Suzie grips the arms of the chair. She's silent for a few moments, her face registering a struggle, lips set in a firm line. Finally, she takes a sharp breath. "Bowie made accusations about Bruce."

I'd specifically asked Suzie if there was a connection between Bowie and Bruce, and she'd lied to my face. What else was she lying about?

"What kind of accusations?" the detective probes.

"She thought he murdered her best friend, Florica Baciu, by giving her drugs. She even went to the police and made these crazy accusations."

DSS Sutherland's sparse eyebrows shoot up. "And did he?"

"The police don't think so. Florica died of a drug overdose, alone in her house, with every door and window locked."

"Then why would your daughter accuse Bruce?"

"Bruce was the last person Florica was seen with. He took her dancing at a club and then called her an Uber. Bowie swears that Florica never would have taken drugs. She was looking for someone to blame."

"I've met Bruce's father, Glen Walter," DSS Sutherland says with obvious distaste. "He insisted on leaving before we had these test results back, and so he won't be immediately available for questioning. Perhaps you'd better walk us through what happened that night, and the accusations Bowie made."

"I was supposed to be the bartender in the VIP room the night Bowie was performing for a record scout, and she brought Florica with her. I was called in to cover for another waitress, and it was late by the time I arrived. Florica had already left with Bruce Walter and Bowie was . . . with the record scout. Bruce maintains that he took Florica to a club, then put her in an Uber back to her house. She must have scored drugs at the club. She did them later, at home, and she overdosed and died."

"Did anyone see Bruce give Florica the drugs?"

"No witnesses came forward. Bowie insisted that Florica never would have done drugs unless they were slipped to her, or she was forced to take them."

"And what do you think?"

"I think temptation comes in many forms. I think that young girls make mistakes. One wrong decision, one screwup can kill a career, or a girl."

"Then you don't believe Bruce had anything to do with Florica's death?" DSS Sutherland asks.

"Bruce was an elite athlete with the potential to become a star quarterback like his grandfather—I honestly don't believe he would have done anything reckless to endanger his career."

Mason meets my gaze. We're thinking the same thing.

"This gives Bruce a motive to harm Bowie," Rob says, voicing everyone's thoughts. "Maybe Bowie had found a witness who saw Bruce give Florica the drugs, or maybe she was about to make new accusations against him. He found out, traveled to Wellington."

"He talked to Bowie. Things went wrong. He searches Bowie's room, goes back to his Airbnb," Mason continues.

"But Bowie would have told me if she was going to accuse him again." Suzie tugs on the end of her ponytail. "She tells me everything. She never hides anything from me."

"Maybe she didn't have a chance to tell you," I say gently. "Maybe it all happened too quickly."

DSS Sutherland nods. "Bruce arrived on a flight into Wellington on Wednesday evening. We have CCTV footage of him driving a rental car from the airport to the street next to his Airbnb. Unfortunately, we have no cameras on the house itself. We catch his car again on Thursday at eleven a.m. He returns at two p.m. We don't know what happens in the interim; we're still searching cameras. Bowie's mobile and internet records don't show any communication between them. We do know that Bowie's blood is on his clothing. He must have met with her at some point."

"Ms. Bishop," Mason says. "I know it's not something you want to consider, but the evidence points to Bruce Walter harming your daughter. Her blood on his shirt. We also found traces of calcium carbonate under his fingernails. We believe this could be from the skeletal fragments of marine organisms like coral or shells that make up limestone."

Suzie lifts her head. "Can you speak English?"

"Limestone." I think of the crumbling, weathered mausoleum. "Gravestones."

"Precisely, Ms. Harlowe." DSS Sutherland folds her hands on the desk. "Karori Cemetery is at the Shepherds' back gate."

"Oh God," Suzie moans. "What if my baby is lying in that graveyard, too injured to crawl to safety. She could still be alive!"

She jumps up from the chair, takes a wobbly step. Mason is there instantly with a steady arm under her elbow.

"We're mobilizing a massive search-and-rescue effort with hundreds of volunteers and dogs to sweep the entire site starting at first light." DSS Sutherland stands up from her desk. "If she's out there, Ms. Bishop, we'll find her."

What she doesn't say: If we find her, she'll most likely be dead.

Rob took Suzie back to her hotel for some sleep before the search starts tomorrow morning. She'd wanted to go directly to the cemetery, but Rob had explained how enormous it was, how a coordinated search effort with volunteers was the best way to cover the most ground. I'm grateful for the breathing space after what she pulled at the press conference.

Mason walks me out of the police station. "Want to grab a coffee?"

I should go back to the embassy, but I don't want to face the fallout from the press conference yet. This new information has me buzzing with questions. I want to talk it through with Mason. Maybe even seek his opinion on Jordan Singer's list and how it might be connected to the case. And, if I'm being truthful, I just want to be near Mason. The solid bulwark of his shoulders. The teasing light in his eyes.

"How about a beer?" I counter.

"Thought you'd never ask. My favorite pub's nearby. They know me well."

Mason leads me to a corner table on a covered outdoor patio with a lovely view of the harbor.

The local stout he orders is exactly what I need.

"I watched the press conference." Mason quirks one eyebrow. "So how much trouble are you going to be in tomorrow?"

"Ugh. I'm drinking to forget about tomorrow. I don't want to see the headlines."

"You weren't kidding. Suzie's a—"

"Loose cannon?"

"I was going to say badass bitch but same thing. She's not going to let anyone tell her what to do. You'll have your hands more than full keeping the lid on her."

"She prides herself on never doing anything by the book. She swore to me before the press conference that she'd keep it focused on Bowie."

"And then she attacks one of our illustrious politicians. Why did she do that?"

"Something about settling a score with Myra. She thinks Myra judges her for being a bad mother. Nothing justifies what Suzie did, though."

"Unless there's some truth in it . . . but I don't really see the Shepherds as capable of violent crime, do you?"

"Suzie said she thought that Isla was jealous of Bowie. What if . . ." I take a swig of beer, mind racing. "What if Isla accidentally or deliberately harmed Bowie, and the Shepherds are covering it up? It could have happened before they left on the camping trip. Isla wasn't at the press conference. Myra could be protecting her daughter."

Mason taps his fingers to the beat of the John Cougar Mellencamp song playing on the classic internet radio station. "I might buy that. My sister has five kids, and yeah, I completely believe she would be capable both of murder and covering it up if it meant protecting them. I don't have any young ones myself—not married and currently single."

He pauses for a moment.

"Same," I say, wishing the circumstances were better, and my heart wasn't so heavy.

"It's almost insane how much she loves her kids. I've seen her go ballistic when her boy was bullied at school. I thought she would rip the other kid's head off." He flags down the waiter. "We'll have another round."

"Easy as, Mason," the mullet-rocking waiter replies.

"Chur, mate," Mason calls. "Like I said, they know me here."

"It's a nice spot." Golden light plays over Mason's strong features, highlighting the dark stubble defining his angular jaw.

Even though my mind is troubled by the police bombshell, I can't help acknowledging the buzz of attraction between us. I don't want to imagine Bowie buried in a shallow grave in Karori Cemetery. So I distract myself with thinking about how rough Mason's stubble would feel under my lips. I notice the enticing way his woodsy aftershave mingles with the molasses finish on the stout we're drinking.

I wonder what it would be like to have all that heavyweight muscle pinning me against a mattress. One of his large hands trapping both of mine above my head, taking control. That high-wattage smile gone teasing and seductive as he inches his way down my body and . . .

"Lake?" He lifts the new beer, expecting me to clink my glass against his.

"Sorry. I was just thinking about . . . something. Cheers."

I know my face has turned red. The amused light in his brown eyes says he knows what I was thinking about. And maybe he's thinking along the same lines.

"Care to elaborate?" His voice is low and husky.

I clear my throat. Take another gulp of beer. "I found a list of names," I blurt, because he's a police officer and this is a case of mutual interest and we're absolutely not hooking up tonight. Or ever.

"A list of names . . . ?"

I do a swift sweep of the area. No one within earshot. "It could be a list of suspects. Bruce is on there, and so is Glen Walter. And then there's Ambassador Hunt and Stuart Shepherd."

"Where did the list come from?"

"Jordan Singer's notes. When you worked with him, did he ever mention anything strange happening at an arts festival where Bowie performed?"

"We only worked that one case together."

"I think something happened at the festival. It could be tied to the reason Jordan curtailed so suddenly. Bowie asked to meet with him. That's when he wrote the list of names in his notes."

"Can you ask him?"

"I tried to. He shut me down. Said I didn't know who I was dealing with and I could be in danger if I pursued it."

Mason narrows his eyes. "I don't like that. Maybe I should have a little chat with him. Give me his number."

"He's not going to tell us anything. He wants to keep his job. He's already been demoted once. He must have witnessed something or done something to anger the ambassador. Maybe you could do a little digging from your side? Anything about the arts festival. I'll give you the date and a list of attendees. Any rumors or insinuations about our ambassador."

"Are you asking me to investigate your top guy?" He laughs softly. "Aren't you worried the spooks are listening to us right now?"

"Kind of, but I'm getting desperate. She's been missing too long."

"It's not looking good, Lake. I'll be honest."

"All I want is to find Bowie. I'm not suggesting Ambassador Hunt had anything to do with it—the Bruce angle seems most likely—but I want to know what happened at the festival and how Jordan was mixed up in it. Until we find her I'm going to keep searching, crossing names off his list. Someone knows something. Someone's hiding something. Suzie lied to me about Bowie and Bruce not even knowing each other. Maybe she's lying to me about other things as well. She's so intimately involved in Bowie's life. I wouldn't be surprised if she was writing some of Bowie's social media posts."

"Stage mum, much?"

"That's what I was thinking. She's her manager. She's pushing her to record an album, become famous, make all the money that Suzie never saw from her hit song. I can't rule out Bowie running away to escape her mom's ambition and control."

Mason finishes his beer in one gulp and wipes the foam from

his lips with his sleeve. "Definitely. But why the bloody prints, then?"

"I don't know. Maybe Bruce was here to force Bowie to go back to Vegas for some reason? She panicked and lashed out. There was an altercation. She's on the run still, worried that people will blame her for his death?"

"Yeah . . . naw. That doesn't hold up. Why would he want her back in Vegas if she'd been accusing him of murder?"

"I don't know. Nothing adds up, Mason. There are so many pieces, but none of them fit together."

"We find more motives. We look for patterns. We find Bowie."

"Alive," I whisper, the word a heartfelt prayer.

"DSS Sutherland believes Bruce Walter killed her and buried her body in the cemetery. There's a lot of ground to cover, some of it severely overgrown with thick underbrush. We'll have drones, and dogs, and your forces to help. I'll see you bright and early?"

"Absolutely."

When he smiles, a deep dimple appears in one cheek. "How about we agree to meet here another night, when this is all over? They have an excellent steak night on Fridays."

My mouth waters thinking about it. I love steak nights in Wellington pubs. Twenty dollars for a spicy unlabeled house pinot noir, curry-infused gravy on thin-cut fries, and a perfectly medium-rare beef fillet.

"It's a deal. Although I might get fired tomorrow?"

"It's not your fault she went off script."

"That's not how certain people will see it."

He goes to the counter to settle the bill, and I make the mistake of scrolling the news.

"Mother of Missing American Student Bowie Bishop Accuses MP Shepherd of Hiding Secrets."

Fuck. I really might get fired tomorrow.

21

BOWIE

Mark Edison's house is a sprawling estate set into a cliff overlooking the ocean in a small seaside town near the train tracks twenty-five miles northeast of central Wellington.

The last time Bowie played at the Cat's Meow, Dean convinced her to come with him to the recording studio. She's heard some of the recordings for Dean's new album, and they're acoustically stunning. She can't help wondering what her voice would sound like with that expert level of sound engineering. They have an agreement not to tell Isla about the visit. She wouldn't want them spending time together offstage. She's at swim practice for the next two hours.

Mark greets them wearing an unbuttoned pale blue linen shirt, tan chinos, and leather flip-flops. He's trying hard to be casual, but his decor is straight out of *Downton Abbey*—crown moldings, velvet couches, and fussy stained-glass windows.

Bowie researched him before she agreed to Dean's invitation. There isn't much online. He cultivates an air of mystery, preferring only to post photos from his twenties and thirties, when he made a name for himself producing Lance Booker's five solo albums after he left the nineties pop band Bliss Patrol.

He moved to New Zealand because he fell in love with a

Kiwi singer-songwriter named Veronica. They got married but divorced less than a year later. Veronica doesn't perform anymore. Bowie couldn't find anything else about her.

Mark grew up working class on a farm in Iowa, but he obviously wishes he'd been born into the British aristocracy.

Gold-framed photographs of him with celebrities line the walls. There he is with his arm thrown around Prince Harry at a horse race. In one he's standing beside a glossy white piano with a grinning Sir Elton John.

There's a huge portrait of Mark standing on the beach with his house in the background. His hair is windswept; he's wearing a black T-shirt, jeans, and strips of black leather tied around his neck and wrists. Who hangs a portrait this large in their own house?

Narcissist much? Bowie thinks. Yet another old music industry dude who thinks he knows what's best for her career. She's only here to watch Dean record; she'll interact with Mark Edison as little as possible.

"I was working on the new single this morning, Dean. I think you're really going to dig this version."

Mark leads them down a hallway and a long flight of stairs into what must be the basement of the house. The cavernous open-plan space is paneled in pale birch wood, illuminated by glowing panels of recessed lighting. It's all very clean and modern—stainless steel kitchen appliances, furniture that looks like it was handmade by the designer IKEA is copying. Everything melts away, though, when Bowie sees the wall of guitars.

She stares, awestruck. "Oh my God. Your guitar collection!"

Every high-end, custom-made, outrageously expensive guitar she's ever fantasized about owning is here. Some are hung on the walls while others rest on stands. Her fingers itch to hold them, stroke their strings, hear their voices.

"It's my weakness. I can't resist a rare or custom guitar at auction."

"Do you play?"

"No, but my artists are welcome to use them for recording."

He laughs. "You should see the look on your face. Go ahead, take a closer look."

"It's heaven, am I right?" Dean asks.

He's right. She can't decide which guitar she wants to hold the most. There are so many beauties. And then she sees it—a mint-condition Gibson J-160E acoustic-electric. It's almost too precious to touch. Lightly, with reverence, she rests the tips of her fingers on the amber-colored wood.

"Excellent choice. That's the one John Lennon played in 1964. I'm not going to tell you how much I paid for it." Mark lifts it down from the wall. Holds it toward her. "Want to try it out?"

"I couldn't."

"Why not? Here. Take it. Noodle around. Fridge is stocked with whatever you want." He waves toward the kitchen. "I'll be ready for you in fifteen, Dean." He disappears behind a door set into one of the walls.

Bowie sits on a leather couch and gently fits the guitar against her chest. It's already in an open tuning. Does he hire someone to come down here and tune the guitars every week?

Dean opens the fridge. "Want a beer?"

"I'm good." She has all the intoxicant she needs. This is the guitar of her dreams. She strums a simple melody and almost feels like crying—the sound is so true and sweet.

It warms to her touch, whispering to her. *Cradle me. Make me yours.*

"Glad I brought you? He'll probably let you play that if you do any recording with him. He has all the best instruments and gadgets."

"What kind of a cut is he taking from you?"

"Standard industry rate. It's worth it. He makes me sound good. I have a session booked with the band next week. You're welcome to come along and sing some backing vocals."

Mark sticks his head out of the door of the recording studio. "I'm ready for you."

Bowie takes a back seat as Mark and Dean listen to the single. It's a love song about a girl with hair streaming in the water, tangling around the lovers like seaweed, leaving strands around his wrists, around his heart. It's ominous, sexy, and obviously about Isla.

"What do you think?" Dean asks.

"Love it. The strings wrap around your voice like the strands of her hair. Love the synth-pop vibe."

"Yeah—we used Mark's Yamaha DX7. Oldie but goodie."

"Would you like to record a line or two, Bowie? See if you like my RCA 44?"

"I've used one before. So silky smooth. I think I'll just watch."

"Suit yourself. Dean, how about laying down some vocals and guitar for 'I'm All Yours'?"

Mark's a stern taskmaster. Bowie thinks the song sounds perfect by the fifth take, but Mark makes Dean play and sing ten more until he's satisfied.

She can't help picturing herself in the booth, working on the songs she's been writing for Lo. Mark had liked "The Other Side." It was only one of many she'd been writing, keeping them a secret from Suzie, because she knows exactly what her mom will say: *Too sad, not commercial enough, where's the sexy? Sexy sells.*

When they're finished, Dean flops down on a couch in the main room. "Phew! I deserve something stronger than beer after that marathon, don't you think?"

Mark pulls a bottle from a shelf. "Right you are. Here's the good stuff." He tosses the bottle to Dean, who catches it, unscrews the top, and takes a swig. "Damn. That is smooth. Aged longer than I've been alive."

"What have you been working on, Bowie?" Mark asks. "Any new songs?"

"I'm writing songs for the demos I'll record when I go back to Las Vegas. I have a first-look deal with Stratus Records."

"Hope you'll include the song you performed at the arts

fest. I can't stop thinking about it." He hums the melody. "I'm entranced by you, the other side. Intoxicated by your view . . ."

"My mom won't like that one."

"She only wants you to record stuff like this . . ." He flicks a switch on a console hidden in the arm of the couch and one whole wall becomes a screen, leaping to colorful life. A sound system starts pounding and suddenly Bowie's voice and heavily made-up face fill the room. Shot from above, she is splayed seductively on the vivid green felt poker table, wearing a tiny, shiny croupier's vest and matching hot pants. Unseen hands pour a shower of poker chips on her body as she writhes and mouths the words.

You know how to hold me, baby.
Know how to fold me.
I'm addicted to your touch, baby.
Need someone to show me.
Wanna learn to play the game, baby.
Wanna learn to play it right—

"Turn it off," Bowie shouts. "Make it stop!"

"Oh, sorry." Mark hits pause and giant-screen Bowie freezes midcrawl, lips glossy and beach-wavy hair cascading over her shoulders.

"Why would you have that cued up?" she asks, her heart still pounding. "I hate that video. I hate that song."

"You hate a video that's been viewed millions of times?" Mark scoffs.

Dean sips from the bottle of Scotch, watching them with a bemused expression.

"I wish I'd never recorded that song."

"Who chose your outfit for the shoot?"

"Suzie."

"Who choreographed it?"

"Suzie."

"Why didn't you push back if you hated it so much?"

"At the time I thought I was being sexy. Now it's just cringey. It makes me feel queasy. Please turn it off."

The screen goes dark. Mark leans forward, resting his elbows on his knees. "You should never have to record anything that goes against who you truly are. I think the real Bowie was the one singing that luminous, mysterious acoustic song, holding the audience in thrall. Am I wrong?"

Bowie closes her eyes. He sees her too clearly. "I don't want to be a pop star," she whispers. "It's like that Sinéad O'Connor quote, 'Being a pop star is like being in a type of prison,' or something like that."

"I get that."

"I don't want to have to act sexy for the cameras. All I want is to write and perform songs that matter."

"You already have, only you're not being allowed to develop them. Your mother doesn't own you, your music, your talent. There's no law that says she has carte blanche to mold you in her own image. You have everything you require inside you already. I wish someone had told me that when I was your age. Listen to yourself. Be still. Tune out all the other voices. Stop comparing yourself to everyone else. You're an innovator, not an imitator. There's a big difference."

Dean says, "Hear, hear," and raises the bottle.

"Suzie is my manager. Fame is a business she knows from the inside."

Mark shakes his head sadly. "You were meant to be famous, Bowie. But on your own terms. Think about it. I'll be here if you want to try recording a song your way, not hers."

Bowie shakes her head. "It's not that simple."

"It really is."

"We should probably get back, Dean. Isla's almost finished with swim practice."

On the ride home Bowie stares at the endless blue-green

ocean and the faraway cliffs. "Suzie would never let me work with Mark."

Dean shrugs. "Then don't tell her."

"And then there's Myra. She'd insist on being my chaperone. She has this thing about older men."

"You don't have to tell me. I'm not that much older than Isla but I'm forbidden. She's overprotective."

"I know you're still together."

"Could be."

"Don't worry, I know how to keep a secret."

"Ta."

If she worked with Mark, she could keep it a secret from Suzie. The idea is seductive, but she shakes it off. Suzie's already lined up a producer, someone she's worked with before. And yet . . . a dangerous little thrill rumbles through her belly. It's about risk-taking, cutting Suzie and her boundless ambition out of the equation.

It's about survival. Escape routes.

Digging a tunnel with a spoon under the walls of the prison Glen Walter wants to build around her. He holds all the power, and that's unacceptable. There must be a way to break his hold over her. To make him and his entitled murderer son pay for what they did.

22

LAKE

We receive our marching orders from a stone-faced senior sergeant. "Look for anything out of place. A hair clip. A cell phone. An article of clothing. Anything that doesn't belong in a cemetery. You've been assigned a search mate. Do not wander off on your own. Always wear your nitrile gloves. If you find anything, don't touch more than necessary; immediately alert one of the authorities. We will process any evidence."

An article of clothing, stiff with blood. Bowie's body, buried in a hasty, shallow grave over other, older bones.

"I lost my young son, Barry, in a drowning accident five years ago," my search mate, a Kiwi named Candace, tells me, her face expressionless, blue eyes opaque as a frozen pond. "His body was never recovered."

"I'm so sorry."

"Now I volunteer every chance I get to help find the missing. That poor woman." She glances ahead, nodding at Suzie's forlorn figure. She's clutching a megaphone, into which she occasionally shouts encouragements and sings fragments from Bowie's songs. It's a counterproductive touch that she must have insisted on, against the better judgment of the organizers. Makes it harder to hear the yelled directives from people on the perimeter marking progress. But it keeps Suzie and her grief center stage. "I know the agonies she's going through."

The air carries the scent of last night's torrential rain. We're lucky it cleared up today, but everyone knows that the rain was bad. It could have washed away footprints, bloodstains, other evidence, making this search that much less likely to unearth anything.

We're focusing on the overgrown areas, the inaccessible areas away from the main footpaths. The graves in these unkempt areas have been swallowed by greedy tree limbs, the lettering worn away by rain and wind.

The cadaver dogs were given Bowie's clothing, her hair scrunchies. They are a blur of purposeful motion, noses and ears busily assessing every root, every mound of vegetation. Their handlers follow silently. I find myself holding my breath, straining to hear barks of detection over the tinny bleat of Suzie's megaphone and the persistent, far-off whine of drones. The human daisy chain of people in rubber boots advances, grim faces trained on the uneven ground.

I catch glimpses of Mason's broad shoulders up ahead, leading a group through the more difficult terrain. He's using a machete to clear a path in places. They're searching the underbrush, anywhere a body could be hidden.

The smell of the woods closes in on me. The wet leaves in clumps along the path. I can't avoid stepping on graves, decomposing leaves. We're walking over ghosts.

I keep my gaze down, searching for evidence. Out of the corner of my eye I see a flash of something behind one of the trees. Neon-yellow fabric. Charity's hand-me-down parka. It was too big for her. The sleeves hung below her mittens. I glimpse her face for a brief second; she's laughing, running away from me. We're playing hide-and-seek.

Come out, come out, wherever you are.

I stop walking and Candace stops beside me.

"Did you see something?"

I blink rapidly. "No." I didn't see anything. Charity is still in Alaska, at least I think so. I've tried to contact her, but there's no internet allowed at The Fold. I hope she's still alive.

"Let's keep going then."

I stumble over tree roots, submerged headstones, memories. There are old bones everywhere under our boots. They're stirring, disturbed by our incessant slog. Aware. Angry.

I'm losing it. Seeing ghosts from my past. Imagining angry bones. I shut my mind down and tramp along beside Candace. One foot in front of the other.

Hours later. No one's found anything exciting; some vape canisters, crumpled beer cans, one gray tennis shoe several sizes too large for Bowie.

"I'm going to take a break, grab a coffee," I tell Candace. I saw a coffee shop down the road as I was arriving.

She puts a hand on her lower back. "My sciatica is acting up. I'm going home."

I'm waiting in line for coffee when I notice Dean Hira in front of me.

"Dean!" The young woman behind the counter lights up like a Christmas tree. "Long black and a toastie?"

He flashes her a lethal grin. "Just the long black, lovely."

"Let me buy it?" I ask, moving to stand beside him.

"Ta," he replies.

I order a flat white and pay for both coffees. Dean's out on the deck smoking a hand-rolled cigarette and slouching against the wall.

I do a quick sweep with my tongue over my front teeth to make sure my freshly applied lipstick hasn't smudged. I'm not exactly looking, or feeling, my best. I've been tramping through the woods for hours.

"I didn't find anything; did you?" He's playing it nonchalant, but there's an intensity in his eyes, a wariness. He has large hands with long, elegant fingers that are covered in scratches.

"Nothing except a used vape pen. Are the Shepherds here? I didn't see them."

"Not that I know of. I think they didn't want any more scenes with Suzie Bishop."

"You watched the press conference?"

"That was crazy. Isla is . . ." He stops. "I'm sure Isla was quite upset by the accusations. Ridiculous, if you ask me. Everyone knows it was Bruce Walter, eh? He shows up and suddenly Bowie's missing."

"It's damning, for sure."

"The police questioned me for hours. I didn't have anything to tell them. I was working at my uncle's garage all day Thursday. Then I had band rehearsal. The police tried to get me to admit that Bowie and I had a fling, but we didn't."

"You're still dating Isla, though, right?"

"No, that's all over. Her father forbade us to be together."

With a brand-new lie there's always a moment of hesitation, the mind churning, maybe even stumbling over the words. Older lies are more practiced, glib, harder to detect.

He's been telling this lie for some time. It rolls easily off his lips. He shoots me a hard look. "Why does that even matter?"

Because he's not telling the truth about Isla. He might be lying about other things, too. "I'm trying to make sense of everything. Isla and Bowie arguing about you. The video of you and Bowie performing—the obvious chemistry there."

He shrugs, drinking his coffee between drags on his cigarette. "Like I said, it was all for the cameras."

"What about these new songs Bowie's been writing? Her mother says they were really depressing and wouldn't be commercial."

"Suzie Bishop wants Bowie to follow in her footsteps as a pop star. Bowie's more complex than that. She's thoughtful. She cares about being true to herself, not selling out."

"Like you."

"Yeah, like me. Although selling out begins to look attractive when you can't pay your rent. Interview's over, Lake, love. Gotta get to work. Busted carburetors wait for no man. Gigging doesn't exactly pave the streets with gold, now does it?"

"You're very talented. I hope you keep going with your music."

"Life gets in the way of dreams sometimes." His eyes narrow. "I suppose you popped out of your mum's womb crying, 'I want to be a bureaucrat.'"

"Well, there are people like that."

"But you aren't one of them."

"Maybe not."

He stares down at his empty coffee cup. Stubs out his cigarette. "What was the dream you abandoned, Lake?"

I think about the unfinished manuscript on my laptop. I haven't even opened it in years. "During university I wanted to write Victorian detective novels."

I'd been taking a Victorian lit class at Evergreen, and I was steeped in Virginia Woolf, Wilkie Collins, and the Brontë sisters.

I haunted coffee shops in a black Audrey Hepburn turtleneck, imagining Anaïs Nin sitting beside me, smoking a thin cigarette and dispensing advice.

We write to taste life twice!

"There you have it," Dean says. "That's why you're interrogating innocent mechanics. You're pretending you're a character in one of your books. You're playing detective."

His words strike too close to the heart. This case is dredging up my past. I'm having nightmares every time I close my eyes. I'm too involved, too invested.

"We all want to find Bowie. If you think of anything else, even if it's only a gut feeling about something, let me know."

"I told everything I could think of to the police."

He blinks, breaking eye contact for a few seconds. "Thanks for the coffee."

"Sure."

I watch him lope away, striding confidently.

He won't call.

I toss down the last of my coffee. It's lost its heat and does nothing to fortify me for my return to the cemetery.

Fatigue settles back in once I reach the gates. The remaining volunteers struggle forward, barely visible through the trees. Faces weary, as long as the shadows streaking the grave plots. Suzie leans against an obelisk, megaphone at her side, tear-wetted face glistening in the afternoon sun.

If nothing else, my unsatisfactory conversation with Dean has quelled the clamor of ghosts. The old bones have quieted. I'm more unsettled by now, by the present.

What does Dean know that he won't say?

23

LAKE

"I hear the search party didn't find anything?" Sara asks the next day when I visit her in her office.

"Nothing. It was disheartening." I hadn't returned home until eight p.m. I'd left Suzie in her hotel room. She'd wanted to keep searching, but she'd been physically exhausted, shoulders slumped and face a crumpled mess from sobbing.

"Did you look through the arts festival footage?"

"Sorry, I didn't have time yesterday; we were preparing the ambassador for his trip to Napier. He left this morning, so if you want we can look at the footage now?"

"That'd be great." I close her office door, then pull up a rolling chair next to hers. She opens a video file, and suddenly there's Bowie onstage.

"I'm entranced by you, the other side, I'm intoxicated by your view," she sings, and her voice, low and throaty, gives me the tingles.

"The police have heard this song, right?" Sara asks. "It could be interpreted as a longing to die."

"A lot of her lyrics are melancholy like this. We can't rule out that possibility. But the whole thing with Bruce Walter and the blood on his shirt . . ."

"Suspect number one."

"Exactly."

"So what are we looking for?" Sara fast-forwards through a few other performances.

"I'm not sure. I'm trying to figure out what happened between Bowie and the ambo at the reception. Her friend Alejandro said when she met him, it looked as if she'd seen a ghost."

The footage of their meeting is brief. They exchange a few words. Bowie looks uncomfortable. She avoids the ambassador, turning away from him. Alejandro and the other exchange student, Clementine, take selfies with him, but Bowie fades away.

Jordan Singer is there, nervously shadowing Ambassador Hunt.

"He's leering at Clementine openly," I note, pointing at the ambassador and the exchange student.

"Sadly, I have multiple instances of his misbehavior caught on video over the last years. He doesn't make much of an effort to hide his misdeeds. Whenever his wife leaves town, out come the flask and the inappropriate comments to women."

"Ugh."

"I know, right?"

"Wait," I say, "go back a few frames." Behind the ambassador and Clementine, Bowie is standing against the wall next to a fire escape door.

Sara zooms in. "Why is Bowie standing all alone like that?"

"Looks like she's hiding."

"Trying to blend into the wall."

We watch as conversation eddies around her and she shrinks farther back into the shadows. A man approaches her. It's difficult to see his features because this is all happening in the background. The videographer is filming the ambassador talking to the jazz band from New Orleans.

"Who's that man?" I ask.

"I don't know. I don't recognize him. He's not one of the performers and he's too old to be an exchange student. He must be an invitee. I have a guest list for the event I can pull up."

"Try to zoom in."

She does, but we can't see the man's face, only his legs and hands. He's wearing a black leather bracelet on one wrist.

"Damn. Wish we could see his face. Send me the guest list. We can try to weed people out, figure out who she's talking to."

There's a knock on Sara's office door. We both startle. She minimizes the video. "Come in."

I breathe a sigh of relief. "Hi, Robin."

"Hey, you two. You look guilty. What are you doing?"

"Some sleuthing," I reply.

"Do you recognize this man?" Sara rewinds to the blurry view of the man walking toward Bowie.

Robin walks around the desk and peers at the screen. "Nope. Sorry. But I was able to recover Jordan Singer's deleted files. This is a printout of a photo he deleted." She sets a piece of paper on the desk. Sara and I bend our heads to look at it.

The photo is grainy, but it appears to be a man wearing a cowboy hat with his hand up a woman's skirt and his head bent as if he's kissing her neck.

"Is that who I think it is?" whispers Sara.

"Yep." Robin taps the photo. "And when I zoom in, the person he's kissing is wearing a nose ring, so unless his wife just got a piercing, then this is some straight-up cheating."

I glance around the room. Robin closed the door when she entered, but that doesn't mean this entire conversation isn't being listened to. We have no expectation of privacy at our workplace.

"When was this photo taken?"

"Time stamp says May of this year."

"The arts festival." Sara studies the photo. "This could be the garden outside of the theater. And yeah." She rewinds the video. "Look who has a nose ring."

Clementine. "How old is she?"

"Eighteen, like Bowie," Sara says.

It's one thing to hit on someone in public, surrounded by witnesses. This is something else entirely. The ambassador kissing an eighteen-year-old exchange student in private, in a dark garden. "This photo could have been taken by Jordan Singer the night of the arts festival."

"Maybe," says Robin. "That was my first thought. It's seriously blurry, though. I don't think anyone would be able to prove anything from it. The faces are in profile. There's that big shadow from the cowboy hat."

"Or someone else took the photo and sent it to Jordan."

We exchange glances. "Jordan's notes say that he met with Bowie and she gave him something. Then he curtails suddenly."

Robin folds the printed photo and puts it in her pocket. "I'm going to shred this now. Send me that video, Sara. I can run some recognition software and check it against the guest list to uncover the identity of your mystery man."

Robin comes to my office a few hours later. "The man Bowie's talking to at the arts festival is Mark Edison. He's an American music producer who moved to New Zealand ten years ago. He's been producing Dean Hira's music. I did some background research on him. He had a nasty divorce from a much younger Kiwi wife who wanted to be a pop star. She's not posting anything online these days, but I read some comments on her earlier posts and her fans claim that Edison was extremely controlling and that he killed her career after she left him."

"Okay, so he has a thing for young aspiring pop stars? I ran into Dean Hira at a coffee shop yesterday. He was helping search for Bowie. Wish I'd seen the video before I talked to him. I could have asked him about any connection between Bowie and Edison."

"Lake." She lays a hand on my shoulder. "I'm worried about how involved you're becoming in this case and how far you've gone off the rails of your job description. Maybe you'd better run all of this by RSO before you do any more investigating on your own. Rob is the one working with the New Zealand police and the Feds. I'm happy to do my part to help find Bowie, but I want to make sure you're reporting this up the chain."

I take a calming breath. "Finding Bowie has taken a stranglehold over my life. Nothing else matters to me right now. But you're right, of course. I know it's not my job to investigate. I'll go talk to Rob right now."

Rob's not in his office. The Regional Security Office admin assistant tells me he's in a meeting. I ask her to have him call me when he's free.

Dean doesn't answer his phone, and when I call the garage where he works, they tell me he's not there.

Who else might know about a connection between Bowie and Mark Edison?

Isla Shepherd. Surely Bowie's host sister would have known if Bowie had befriended the music producer. Isla will still be at school. I should stay here and work on the case backlog. But this connection to Mark Edison, his history with another young singer. It feels like something could be there.

One quick trip down the hill to Isla and Bowie's school, and then I'll come right back.

24

BOWIE

Bowie and Mark are sitting on the beach. It's a chilly afternoon, but the sun is bright on her face. She ditched music theory and took the train to his house instead. She's been working on new lyrics, letting him see them. They haven't recorded anything yet, though.

"I love New Zealand. Maybe I'll come back after my exchange program."

"I wouldn't blame you one bit. You don't see me living in L.A. anymore. It's so much more peaceful here. Want to take a dip? I always swim before sunset."

"It's a little chilly."

"People swim year-round here. I see them down the beach plunging into the waves even in winter."

"I'm used to deserts and swimming pools."

"Come on, it'll do you good. Get your blood pounding."

"I don't have a swimsuit."

"No prob. Down the hallway, past the recording studio, and up the stairs. Big wooden door with a black metal lamp hanging over it. My ex-wife left some clothes and swimsuits. I'll be out in the water!"

The ceilings are even higher in the basement bedroom. There's a loft bed with luxurious-looking bedding in shades of pale gray. One side of the room is floor-to-ceiling windows. This must be the room that's directly over the cliff, the windows you can see from the beach. She walks to the window. Mark is stripping out of his clothes on the beach. As if he can feel her gaze, he turns and waves.

She shrinks back into the room, warning bells sounding in her mind. Is this going to be where Mark turns out to be a creep, after all? Lure her down to the beach and hit on her in the water?

This isn't Las Vegas. She doesn't have to be wary of everyone. He's been nothing but respectful and encouraging. She doesn't get a creepy vibe from him. He's genuinely excited about her music. He's a little self-obsessed, definitely egotistical. That doesn't make him a predator. She'll keep her guard up, of course. He'll have to earn her trust.

The closet is filled with frilly, feminine clothes and designer jeans, but there's one drawer that contains a selection of one-piece suits and bikinis. Bowie finds the most modest one—a purple, high-cut one-piece, and changes quickly in the bathroom. Slipping her baggy button-up shirt back on, she heads for the beach.

At first it was freezing, but now that she's out in the water and the sun is warming her face, it's exhilarating. Floating with her feet raised, pointing to an island. Floating, letting the ocean cradle her, the waves sway her.

Far away from Las Vegas. No concrete walls bounding this pool.

A rare moment when she shakes off the darkness, like water from her hair, and it slides away. The perfect slant of light on her face. Sunshine soaking through her. Finding the veins beneath her skin. Sea-foam froth of hope in her belly.

SHE FELL AWAY

She's inside her body in this moment. She left her phone back on the towel. She left her necklace. It will be waiting for her when she swims back to shore.

Mark is swimming so far out she's almost afraid he'll be swept out to sea.

He's leaving her alone, and she appreciates that. It's okay to be alone. She doesn't always have to be constantly surrounded by people, or constantly scrolling through comments, refreshing her feed.

There's nothing refreshing about it. The duty to post every moment of her life online is a heavy chain around her neck. It requires constant care and attention. Floating here, she has the insane thought that the world wouldn't end if she just stopped posting. She could choose to step off the nightmare social media carousel.

A spike of adrenaline. Like the warm rush of tequila hitting her bloodstream. Separate notes finding each other to form a chord.

Beauty emerging where there was only blankness.

Suddenly, Mark rises out of the water at her elbow, and she screams and thrashes for a minute. He splashes her, standing on the sandy ocean floor. "Got you."

She splashes him back. "Jesus. I thought you were a shark."

"No sharks here. At least not this close to shore. Usually."

"You're not making me feel better."

"What are you thinking about with such a dreamy expression?"

"I was just thinking that maybe I'll never post on social media ever again."

He snorts. "Yeah, right."

"I mean it. I'm sick of it." She swims until she reaches a place where her feet touch the bottom. She turns to face him. "Maybe I don't want to be famous."

"Okay. But you'll still write lyrics. It's who you are. If you didn't write and play music, you'd feel like an amputee."

How does he see inside her like that?

"I'm not talking about giving up music. Just the online stuff. The constant sales push. Building my brand."

"You can do anything you want to, Bowie. Go to Juilliard. Stay in New Zealand. Whatever you do, live your own life, not Suzie's version."

"What's your mom like?"

"Dead." He ducks his head beneath the water and reemerges, pushing hair out of his face. She sees something in his eyes she's never noticed before. A cold emptiness.

"I'm sorry."

"Don't be. I never knew her. I was raised by my dad. He was a real hard-ass. Wanted me to have a better life than him because he worked so hard on the farm. Scraped enough money together to send me to a military academy but I refused to go. He said I broke his heart. Now he's dead, too."

Awkward. Bowie changes the subject. "So I'm wearing your ex-wife's swimsuit? What was her name?"

"Veronica."

Bowie already knows this from the search she did before she and Dean visited that first time. Veronica Edison. She'd sung with a local band but had dropped out of the music scene after the divorce. "She was Kiwi, right?"

"Yeah. She's the reason I moved here. After we divorced I decided to stay."

"Why isn't she performing anymore?"

He shrugs. "I have no idea. We don't talk. It wasn't a friendly split. She tried to take me to the cleaners. She was talented but not like you. The lyrics she wrote were dreamy, languid." He skims his palm over a wave. "She floated on the surface of her emotions. She didn't have enough edge. She couldn't access her pain, her anger, the way you do."

"You think my songs are angry?"

"That one you sang at the Cat's Meow was intense. That's

the Bowie you should unleash. Don't keep her hidden away to please Suzie."

Bowie shivers.

"Are you cold? Let's get you dry and warm."

Mark swims beside her back to shore. She wraps her towel around her hips and sits on the sand, knees hunched up.

"Do you really think I could break free from my mom?"

"I think you can do anything you set your mind to, Bowie. Absolutely anything." He flops back on his towel, shading his eyes with his arm. He has a dad bod. A soft belly but strong legs and arms. He's powerful, and not unattractive.

He rolls onto his side, propping himself up on one elbow. "Want to stay for dinner?"

Was this where things got weird? Here's where he hits on her and she has to add him to the long list of older men who only pretend to like her art, her words, her mind, but really they only want to sleep with her. She's suddenly aware that they're all alone. No one would hear her if she screamed. She doesn't even have any mace or a rape whistle.

"I have to go home."

He rolls onto his back. "Myra can wait a few more minutes. You've been working on a new song. I heard you humming it earlier. Sing it for me."

"I don't have a guitar."

"I'll be able to imagine the instrumentation."

She clears her throat. He isn't looking at her. No reason for stage fright. The beach is deserted. Some kids shriek and laugh, but they're far away.

She sings to the ocean, to the seagulls. Her voice gathering strength with each line.

One foot and then the other
We've got some ground to cover
Before we stop tonight

LENORE NASH

Oh baby, don't you know
You shouldn't let it hurt you
You've got to let it go

One battle then another
You never will recover
If you fight them all
No, you must be like water
And always find your level
Or your waterfall

Oh baby, don't you know
You shouldn't let them hurt you
You've got to let it go

Something's weighing on your mind
You've got something on your mind
You can't let it go
You can't let it go in circles
'Round it goes, and what does it expose?
A plastic rose that doesn't know it's fake
A beating heart that doesn't know its fate

The more you push and pull
The harder to control
The more you scratch and claw
The tighter it grows
The more you squeeze and grasp
The more it slips on past
You've got to let it go

Oh baby, don't you know
You shouldn't let them hurt you
You've got to let it go

He rolls onto his side again. "Bowie. I heard it all. Two guitars, a snare drum played with brushes only. A cello, low and soft, arrives right before the chorus, builds to a crescendo in tandem with your voice."

She hears it, too. It's perfect.

"Did you write that for Suzie, by any chance?"

She loves that he realizes it right away. "She's living her life in the past. She's still so angry about being cheated out of her royalties for 'Hurt So Happy.' It's like I'm her revenge plan. If I'm ultra-successful, then she can say 'fuck you' to all the industry people who hurt her. Also . . ."

His eyes search her face. "She's smothering you. She has to let you go." He sits up. Turns toward her. His eyes are intense, serious. "Record a few demos with me. The songs that matter the most to you. The right song can change the world, Bowie. All you need is that one breakout hit. The one that everyone can't stop singing. The one that makes everyone cry. Emotional and heartbreaking."

"Yes." It's not a difficult decision. "Let's do it." The words were already there. She knows how many people would kill for this chance. She's not going to turn it down because Suzie already has a producer lined up. One she can control.

"I always say jump first, ask forgiveness later. Your mom will forgive you when we come up with a massive hit."

"We'll have to keep our collaboration secret for now."

"No problem. Invent an after-school activity and come here instead."

"It's not that simple. Myra would never allow me to come here alone."

"Then bring her along."

"She's too busy."

"Then come here at night."

"You mean sneak out?"

"I'm a night owl. I do my best work in the studio at three a.m.

And don't worry about the train schedule. Take one of my cars. There are five in the garage. Do you have a license?"

"In the States. I could get in trouble here."

"Don't worry about that. The police don't make many traffic stops here. Only if they think someone's drunk. Drive one of my cars home tonight. Leave it a few blocks away from the Shepherds' house. They don't need to know you have it."

Has he said similar things to other female artists? Had all of those bikinis really belonged to his ex-wife?

She's right to be wary. Music producers can be notoriously shady. But she senses that he truly believes in her music. He wants her to have creative freedom.

"Take the Volkswagen Beetle; it's yours for the duration of our collaboration. My ex refused to drive a Jaguar or a Benz, and the car I bought for her to use has just been sitting there gathering dust."

He thinks this is all going to be so easy. It's difficult to evade Myra's searching questions, her constant vigilant attention. And then there's Suzie, jumping in to post as Bowie if she misses even one day. Her mom is constantly monitoring her, even from the other side of the world.

And that's why the idea of going off their grid, slipping away from their grasp, carries such a strong allure.

"I'm not talking about signing you to a contract, Bowie. I don't want a cut of any future profits. I only want to see you reach your potential. Record one or two songs with me. Just vocals and guitar. If you like the songs enough to show your mother, she can negotiate a contract with me for producing more, adding a backing band."

It makes sense. There's no way to make her mother realize the potential of her new music until it's packaged in a way that she can hear, until she calculates the profit margins.

"I won't be able to come often. You'll never know what night I'll show up."

He shrugs. "Like I said, I'm a night owl. Text me an hour

before you leave Welly. If you're really worried about Myra finding out, use a burner phone. I have several I can lend you. If I'm busy, I'll let you know. We have all the time in the world. Until your exchange program ends, at least."

She doesn't want to think about returning to Vegas. Life is so much slower here. The scenery is saturated, old-timey, like she's living inside one of Myra and Stuart's family slideshows.

Click.

The next slide is Bowie on a solo journey, face turned toward the setting sun, hope rising in her heart. Freedom around the corner.

25

LAKE

I park in the lot of Bowie and Isla's girls' school. I called ahead and made an appointment with the principal. If Isla is here, I'll try to find a way to talk to her.

Girls roam the halls in packs, chattering and laughing. The noise is nearly deafening. They wear the school uniforms I saw on Bowie's Instagram—some of the skirts shorter than others.

The principal, Mrs. Bonham, says she has only a few minutes to spare. She has a permanent frown line between her eyes and round glasses that make her look like an owl. She's in her mid-forties, dressed like a Middleton sister in a yellow linen sheath dress, pearls, and tasteful low heels. I can imagine her dispensing etiquette advice to her students.

"As I mentioned, I'm a consular officer at the U.S. embassy and I wanted to ask a few questions about Bowie Bishop."

"I've already spoken to your Mr. Rob Smith, and with DSS Jill Sutherland at length."

"It must be very stressful with everything going on."

"One of our girls is missing. The media is swarming. Our students are understandably distressed."

"I won't take more than a few minutes of your time. May I ask your opinion of Bowie?"

"A very bright girl and, obviously, very talented. Come to think of it, bright is precisely the wrong adjective. There's a darkness behind her eyes. A haunted look. I believe her mother pushes her daughter to become famous when it might not be what Bowie would have chosen for her life. In my conversations with Myra Shepherd we both agreed that this time in New Zealand is good for Bowie, a welcome break from the pressure to perform. An emphasis on more wholesome goals, such as scholastic performance, forging friendship bonds, and spending time with family."

"Mrs. Shepherd talks to you about Bowie?"

"Of course. I consult with every one of our parents. I keep them informed of any behavioral or scholastic issues, and they, in turn, confide their expectations or concerns for the young people in their care."

"Were you, or Mrs. Shepherd, ever concerned about Bowie's mental health?"

"As I informed the police, she did sink into depressions from time to time. She would retreat from the other students. Spend hours by herself in the music room practicing her guitar. Myra Shepherd is a well-respected counselor, and Bowie was lucky to have been placed in her capable hands."

"And what about Bowie's relationship with her host sister, Isla?"

"It seems quite normal to me. Girls will have their petty rivalries, but they were part of the same groups, and I never witnessed any tension between the two of them. They gave me far less trouble than some of the girls, I can assure you. Managing this many young ladies is a bit like trying to harness a cyclone."

"Could I speak with Isla Shepherd?"

"I'm afraid that won't be possible without permission from her mother. Now, if you'll excuse me, I'm afraid I'm late for a meeting. I'll have a student escort you out."

"Thanks for your time."

Mrs. Bonham flags down a tall girl with her hair in long plaits. "Beatrice, please escort Ms. Harlowe back to her vehicle."

"Do you like going to school here?" I ask Beatrice.

"'Course. It's empowering. All female students, mostly female teachers. The boys' college down the way gets all the funding because it's a rugby school. You should see their gymnasium! But I don't mind. I like our shabby old sports center."

"Do you know Bowie Bishop?"

"Not well. She's gone missing, we all know that. Everyone's talking about it. There's a shrine where we all put flowers and candles and notes. When she returns she'll know we cared about her."

"Will you show me the shrine?"

She chews on the end of one of her braids. "I suppose I could, though I'll have to run soon. I don't want to be late for biology."

The shrine is a heap of flowers, notes, candles, and artwork piled against a wall in a covered area near the parking lot. I notice a large paper heart decorated with guitar picks. *Come back and sing me that Taylor Swift song.* It's signed Isla.

"Is Isla Shepherd here today?"

"I saw her earlier on the sports field." She points. "Sitting under the bleachers."

"Thanks, Beatrice. You've been so helpful."

"Please find Bowie, Ms. Harlowe. We're all praying she'll come back and finish the term with us."

I sit in my car but I don't turn the key. When Beatrice is out of sight, I keep off the main path as I make my way to the field. I'm acutely aware that I'm trespassing now. I've been told to leave the premises, but I can't leave without at least trying to talk to Isla. She might know something about Bowie and Mark Edison.

I duck under the bleachers and there she is, a few yards away with her back to me, wearing headphones, thumbs flying over her phone. My footfalls are muffled by grass as I move closer, but she probably wouldn't hear me anyway with the headphones.

I see Dean's name on her phone. Then I see my name. I clear my throat.

"Christ!" She jumps, pushing the headphones off her ears. "You frightened me."

Her curly hair is piled into a bun. She has wide-set green eyes and a generous mouth.

"Hi, Isla. I'm Lake Harlowe, a consular officer with the U.S. Embassy."

She regards me suspiciously. "My mum said she'd met you at the press conference. She also said that I shouldn't talk to any officials without consulting her."

"That's right," I say quietly. "You don't have to talk to me. But I very much hope you will. We both want the same thing. We want Bowie to come home."

"How did you even find me?"

"One of your schoolmates told me where to look."

"I could sound an alarm. You'd be thrown out for trespassing."

"I only want to ask you a few quick questions." I drop to the ground across from her. "What were your first impressions of Bowie when she arrived from the U.S.?"

She takes a moment, and her eyes focus somewhere in the distance. "At first she seemed so different. The way she talked, cramming everything in so quickly, speaking loudly. And she's so forthright and direct. She says what's on her mind. But after she'd been here a few months she started to kind of, I don't know, slow down a little. She became more like one of us. My friends thought she was special because she has so many followers and she hangs out with famous musicians, but then the stories she'd tell . . . honestly, it made me think that maybe fame isn't everything it's cracked up to be."

"She's been living with you for ten months now. She must be like a real sister to you. How are you holding up under all of this stress?"

"No, thanks. My mum psychoanalyzes me more than enough."

There's a toughness to her. The broad swimmer's shoulders. The careless smile.

"It must be difficult. Your family on edge. The other students whispering about you."

I think she's going to remain silent, but then she meets my gaze. "You have no idea, Lake. I was sitting in class and these detectives practically pulled me out of my chair and marched me away. Like I was a suspect or something. It was humiliating. Everyone's talking about me, whispering about my family, saying horrid things, accusing my dad of disgusting crimes."

"Which is why you're hiding out here when you should be in class."

She nods.

"Why do you think the detectives were treating you as a suspect in Bowie's disappearance?"

"They think I'm jealous of her or something."

"Are you?"

"Maybe I was, but we worked it out."

"A neighbor, Martha Tilbury, said she overheard you and Bowie arguing about Dean."

"Oh, that." She shrugs. "All a misunderstanding. I thought she was trying to steal him from me. It's all water under the bridge. Dean and I aren't together anymore. We're just friends."

"You were just messaging with him."

"That's not a crime." Wide eyes, an honest expression, and one forefinger tapping her phone, like she's sending a message in Morse code. "Have there been any developments? Have you found anything new?"

"I'm afraid not."

She slumps back against a post. "This is a nightmare. Make it end. Hordes of people searching the cemetery. Dogs barking and drones flying over our house. Bowie's mum pointing fingers at my dad. You know she tried to come here and talk to me? My mum shut that down. Guess Suzie Bishop's not as sneaky as you. Are you a spy?"

The abrupt shift from interviewee to interrogator catches me off guard. "I'm not a spy. It's my job to help American citizens overseas. Suzie called me when she hadn't heard from Bowie in forty-eight hours. At first we thought she was on the camping trip with you."

"Nope. She wanted to stay and play a show with Dean."

"And that didn't bother you?"

"Like I said, we're just friends. But to Bowie he can open doors for her. She's always looking for an excuse to perform, to be idolized."

"Did she ever mention a music producer named Mark Edison to you?"

Her finger taps harder on her cell phone. "I was there when Dean introduced him to Bowie."

"Was it at the arts festival?"

"Months before that. At the Cat's Meow."

"Did Bowie and Mark Edison hang out a lot?"

"I never heard about it if they did."

I glance at her. Measuring her. I believe her answer. "Did Bowie hide things from you?"

"I wouldn't be surprised."

"What type of things?"

"I get the feeling that bad things happened to her in Las Vegas. Like maybe New Zealand was her way of escaping. She told me her best friend died, and that's why she chose to come here."

"If you think of anything else Bowie might have been hiding from you, will you call me?" I hand her one of my business cards. "Or call the police?"

"I've already promised to tell my mum if I think of anything new, and she'll contact the police."

"Do you miss Bowie, Isla?"

There's no mistaking the truth and the hurt in her eyes as she answers steadily and without hesitation. "Every second of every day."

26

LAKE

I'm on my way back to the embassy when my personal cell rings with a number I don't recognize. "Hello?"

"Lake, this is Myra Shepherd. You just paid an unauthorized visit to my daughter at her school."

My heart sinks. "I'm sorry, Mrs. Shepherd, I should have cleared the visit with—"

"I'm not angry, Lake. Far from it. I'm only glad you're out there urgently searching for Bowie, pursuing all avenues instead of focusing solely on Bruce Walter. Where are you right now? I'd like to invite you over to my home, to see the collage on Bowie's bedroom wall. The police were very interested in it. I thought perhaps you might find something they missed."

"I'm in my car. Not far from you. I'll be there in ten minutes."

"Perfect. I'll put the kettle on."

Fifteen minutes later I'm holding a mug of steaming manuka honey and chamomile tea, and Myra is showing me Bowie's room.

"It could use a tidying, but I've left everything exactly the way it was. The police searched thoroughly, although I will say this for them—they put everything nicely back. Bowie is a chaos magnet, dear thing. She has this ability to whirl through a room leaving disorder in her wake. I'm always finding scribbled lyrics, guitar picks, or hair clips in the oddest of places."

The room is spacious, with at least ten-foot ceilings and crown moldings. I would have loved a room like this at Bowie's age. Her walk-in closet is an explosion of black clothing and colorful platform boots and shoes.

"This is what I wanted you to see." Myra's eyes mist over as she draws my attention to the eclectic collage spread over one whole wall. "I said she could paint her walls any color she liked, but instead she did this." She trails her fingers over the collage. "Concert and movie tickets. Dried ferns and flowers. Stickers. Photos of her and her friends. Drink coasters. Boys she thinks are hot. Notes her friends wrote her. It's all here. The record of a young life."

"I've seen this before . . . on her Instagram? A selfie in front of the collage where she's sticking out her tongue."

"The young ones do try to make themselves look unattractive and silly in photos these days. Difficult, in Bowie's case."

I study the collage. I don't know what I'm searching for. I'll know it when I see it. Most of the coasters are from pubs and bars in the central business district. She went to see the film *Heathers* at a film festival. Most of the photos have a Polaroid filter applied. They've been printed on glossy paper and carefully cut out. Bowie and Isla in front of the school. A group shot from a theater class hamming it up onstage.

"The police focused on this, understandably." Myra touches a newspaper clipping about Bruce Walter being drafted into the NFL. Bowie, presumably, crossed out his eyes with a black Sharpie.

"There's Florica." A photo from the abandoned-amusement-park shoot I saw on her Instagram. "What a tragic thing. She died so young. If you look closely, this whole section in the middle is a shrine to her."

Instead of Kiwi memorabilia, it's all from Las Vegas. Ticket stubs to big-name bands. A photo of Florica blowing out sixteen birthday candles. An open-mic set list with Bowie's name first.

"Florica was stunning."

"Wasn't she? Bowie still misses her every day. I think most of the songs she writes are for her friend. She calls her Lo."

There's a handwritten sheet of song titles on the far right of the collage, maybe the last thing Bowie hung before she disappeared.

The Other Side
Graveyard Rose
Murder Ballad
In Circles
Drops of Rain
Fly Home
I'll Never Fall
Shooting Star
Never Grow Old
Shadows Long for the Night
Slip Away

"Shadows Long for the Night" is underlined three times, and something is scrawled next to it. I move closer, trying to decipher the words. It looks like it says, *album title??* but it's nearly illegible.

"She posted 'Graveyard Rose' on her socials and performed 'The Other Side' at the arts festival. Do you recognize any of these other titles?" I ask Myra.

"Maybe. Bowie was always writing lyrics. Sometimes she wouldn't finish dinner because a song came to her. A dreamy look would invade her eyes and she'd drift away, mid-conversation. Nothing could make her come back to earth until she'd written everything down. She had notebooks full of songs. I gave them all to the police."

"This one"—I point to "I'll Never Fall"—"there's a line I read of hers, some lyrics she wrote down at the Cat's Meow: *Tell me I'll shine brightly, tell me I'll never fall.*"

"You're welcome to take photos of the collage."

I take photos to study more closely later.

"If you're finished here, let's drink our tea in the conservatory," Myra suggests.

It's a sunny enclosed porch that's been converted into a sitting room at the back of the house, bordering the cemetery. It's filled with potted ferns. The chairs are inviting and overstuffed, covered with a rose print. The walls are painted a soft yellow.

"I've tried to give Bowie a safe, normal homelife. Show her the simpler ways of enjoying life. We went tramping and she became a different person in the woods. She became a young girl again. Her laugh is so rare, her smile so fleeting. I was always trying to coax her to smile. I was worried about her. I don't think she has a healthy relationship with her mother."

"Do you think Suzie is too controlling?"

"It's something deeper than the usual chafing against rules that every teenager goes through. I think Suzie is attempting to reclaim her fame through Bowie. I think Bowie felt smothered."

"I've been meaning to apologize for what happened at the press conference with Suzie."

"Oh, that. Stuart took it badly but I saw it for what it really was—a grieving, frightened woman's attempt to take some control over her narrative."

"That's magnanimous of you."

"I believe that Bowie was sent to me for a reason. I've tried my best to give her stability, to give her love that doesn't make unreasonable demands. I've given her a healthy and happy home. I worry about her. I don't worry so much about Oliver and Byron. They fight a lot, but that's normal. And Isla's never given me any trouble. She brings home top marks, always captain of every sports team. She's driven and ambitious, like her father. I see so much of him in her. She's my shiny, happy girl."

She didn't seem all that shiny or happy when I questioned her. She'd been on edge, tapping her fingers, glancing compulsively at her phone.

"I so wanted Isla and Bowie to be friends. I have a dear older sister who is my best friend. But it's not a guarantee, is it? She's a stranger living in our house, transplanted into our lives, and I'm afraid it's been a little difficult for Isla. Bowie takes up a lot of space. Not in the fame-hungry way that Suzie does—in a more organic way. It's her talent. She can't hide her light. She could no more stop writing lyrics and singing songs than she could stop breathing."

"And Isla had some natural envy."

"I think they found their own path through the difficulty. I was proud of them. I love Bowie. Not in the same way that I love Isla—it could never be like that, but Bowie is special. She has so much life in her, and she's had such a difficult past—I want to make things easy for her. Sometimes I fantasize that she could stay here with us. That we could adopt her as our own. I could be her real mother. But I can't. I know I can't be that."

"Bowie has less than two months left on her exchange program, is that correct?"

"Yes." Myra closes her eyes for a moment. "Thank you, Lake. Thank you for talking about her in the present tense. I make a point of it. Those detectives . . . the security officer from your embassy, they all asked me questions as if she's already dead."

"Why did you invite me here, Myra? I'm not a detective."

"You're American, and you had a troubled past, similar to Bowie."

"What makes you think that?"

"It's written all over you. The shoulder injury that perhaps never healed properly, for one. Don't look so surprised. I'm a therapist. I notice the small things. The tells. You hold yourself stiffly on your right side. You touch your shoulder sometimes when you don't want to talk about something."

I'm supposed to be the observant one, the one looking for tells. I don't like having the tables flipped on me. I'm seated across from her, as if this was a therapy session.

"It's a childhood injury. I broke my collarbone, dislocated my shoulder. You're right, it never healed correctly."

"Because you didn't receive proper medical care. Do you want to talk about it?"

Myra's skilled at disarming people. She's a professional therapist. A therapist is someone who manipulates you into telling them secrets. She won't pry any secrets out of me.

"This isn't about me."

"But maybe it is. Maybe Bowie is alive, and this whole thing with Bruce is just a coincidence or only part of the equation. Maybe you're meant to solve this, Lake. Because you're closer in age to Bowie than the detectives, because of your troubled past, your difficult relationship with your own mother."

I haven't told her any of this.

"You're making a lot of assumptions about me."

"Not assumptions. Deductions. I read your past in your eyes. The way you hunch your shoulders. You scan every room for threats. Position yourself to face the door. When you speak of Suzie, I hear unspoken echoes of your mother."

A chill chases up my spine. "I should be getting home. I have to feed my cat."

"Have you ever tried therapy, Lake? I sense that you're a trauma survivor. You could benefit from therapy."

After the dead sex offender in the hotel room in Phnom Penh, they'd sent a psychiatrist to evaluate me. "Your emotions could be very complicated," the doctor had said. "You might be relieved that he's dead and you could feel guilt around that."

Damn right I was relieved he was dead. I'd read the list of his heinous crimes. His death had been mob justice. A young girl's father had shot him in the forehead. Tortured him first. I'd imagined myself pulling the trigger. I would have happily killed him.

I didn't say any of that to the good doctor. I expressed an appropriate amount of confusion. Exactly what he wanted to hear. I'm good at telling people what they want to hear.

"I did try therapy once. It was very helpful," I say blandly, but I can't meet her gaze. Instead, I stare out the large window. The sill is old, pockmarked wood. There's something small and plastic caught between the window and the sill.

I reach over and pry it free. It's a black guitar pick branded with a red B in a gold circle.

"Bowie's always leaving guitar picks everywhere. She liked to come to this room and play her guitar in front of the window."

"Can I keep it?"

"Of course. I have dozens." She leans closer. "I could hypnotize you if that's something you're interested in. It sometimes opens locked rooms in our minds that are holding us back."

"No, thank you." I don't remember rising from my chair, setting down my mug, but here I am, standing by the door, pulling out my car keys. The idea of hypnosis terrifies me. It's been suggested to me before.

It's impossible to uncover the layers of Bowie's story without disturbing the carefully arranged layers covering my own dark secrets. Diving into her world is sending ripples of shock through mine. I'm risking everything. If I remember my past, it could be something so bad that I couldn't live with it.

"Thanks for inviting me."

She stands. "I didn't mean to make you uncomfortable."

"You didn't."

"Old wounds are the deepest. I know too well. I'm a trauma survivor, myself. If you change your mind, you know where to find me."

"That list of song titles for an album. Do you think Bowie was maybe keeping these new songs secret from Suzie?"

"Why don't you ask her yourself? She's been sitting out in the cemetery for hours."

"What? You mean she's out there right now?"

"Right beyond the view of this window. She's in the spot that Bowie loved so well."

"Dulcie Morris's grave."

"That's the one. She refuses to come in and talk to me. She

just sits there like she's turning into one of the stone statues. I think she's trying to intimidate us."

"I'll go and talk to her."

"Would you? I'd appreciate her leaving before Stuart arrives home. I understand, of course, that Suzie is at her wit's end. We all are. She needs to keep her strength up, not sit in the cold for hours on end."

I say a hasty goodbye and leave to go find Suzie.

27

LAKE

"What are you doing out here, Suzie? Aren't you chilly?"

"Lake." Her shoulders sag. "I'm searching for Bowie. Who cares if I'm cold?" She lights a cigarette and takes a deep drag. "Nothing matters until I find her." She's reeling, her voice plaintive. "Everyone left. They all left the cemetery last night, even though we didn't find anything. There's something here. I know it. My baby's trying to tell me something."

I sit next to her on the cold stone steps of the mausoleum. Wrap my silk scarf around her neck. "Myra thinks you're trying to intimidate her."

"I'm really not. At first I suspected them; now I don't know. I don't know what happened." She swipes the back of her hand over her cheek angrily. "All I know is that she's been gone too long."

"Why don't we find you some food—you must be hungry."

"How could I eat?"

"It's going to start raining soon."

"Appropriate." She glances at the gray clouds gathering above the broken-winged angel. "I'll leave soon. Sit with me for a sec."

SHE FELL AWAY

I angle away from the acrid cigarette smoke. "I saw the list of song titles on Bowie's bedroom wall. Have you listened to those songs?"

"A few. I told her they weren't very commercial."

"Do you help Bowie with her social media?"

She glances at me intently. "What's wrong with that? It's a lot to post every day. I was helping her out."

"I'm not saying there's anything wrong with it. Just wondering." Suzie's defensive for a reason. She was too intimately involved with Bowie's life, the lines blurring between mother and daughter. At least online.

"I found this on the windowsill in the Shepherds' house. Did you give Bowie this guitar pick?"

She studies it, a frown furrowing her brow. "No. She has branded BB leopard print guitar picks." She flips it over. "This looks older. It's jogging something in my memory . . . I think it's from a club where we all used to hang out in L.A. The Balladeer. This is their logo, the B in a gold circle. They were piled in bowls at the entrance. Wonder where she got this?"

"You told me to investigate all possibilities."

"I know, and you're very persistent. The truth is that it's time to face the facts. It was Bruce. The blood on his sweatshirt, the limestone under his nails. He flew to Wellington, hurt Bowie, and then drank himself to death out of remorse. Glen is ghosting me. Won't answer my calls. My coworker told me he cleaned out my locker. I obviously don't have a job anymore. I don't know what I'll do. My savings are gone. I can't find a private investigator who's willing to work on credit and a promise. I owe money to people. I'm fucked, Lake."

"Do you owe money to Glen?"

She sucks on her cigarette. "Bowie had her heart set on coming to New Zealand to honor her friend Florica's memory. Florica's parents divorced, and her father moved to Auckland with his new family. It was her dream to be an exchange student here, to be closer to him. I couldn't find a way to scrape together the money for the program, and Bowie was devastated. I told Glen, and he transferred me the money then and there. Said he'd take it back out of the profits Bowie made on her first album."

"Wait. Glen Walter paid for Bowie's exchange program?"

"It was a business investment for him."

"Did Bowie know he paid?"

She hangs her head. "I kept it a secret. I didn't want Bowie to know that Glen fronted the money. Anyway, she called me one night after she played a set at an arts festival sponsored by the embassy. She was freaked out because Ambassador Hunt told her about Glen paying for her program. The bastard."

I remember the conversation I had with the ambassador. How he'd called Glen Walter his golf buddy. And how he never mentioned having any contact with Bowie at the arts festival.

"Bowie was livid when I told her the truth. Now I wish I'd never taken his money. I wish she'd never come to New Zealand. I should have kept her in Vegas with me."

I pat her shoulder. The hard stone of the grave is getting uncomfortable. "Why don't we go back to your hotel? We can talk about this more. Maybe we can have Rob Smith come over. He should know this."

"How is it relevant? It's about Glen, not about Bruce."

"And Ambassador Hunt."

"She told me she caught him kissing an exchange student in the garden that night."

"Did she take a photo of it?"

"Maybe. She said she was going to deal with it. Talk to the ambassador's assistant or something. But how can that night have anything to do with Bowie being missing? I mean, your ambassador is a world-class douche, but there's no way he could abduct my daughter when he lives in the public eye."

She says abduct, not murder. She believes fiercely that Bowie is still alive. I want to share her conviction. I want it with all my heart. Sitting in this graveyard doesn't help. Too many people die far too young.

"You said it at the press conference: Bowie attracts attention from older men. Did she ever mention a music producer named Mark Edison? I saw video footage of her talking to him at the arts reception. He was producing Dean Hira's new album."

"She never mentioned him. Mark Edison . . ." Suzie taps her cigarette pack against her hand. Realizes it's empty. Crumples it up and shoves it into her pocket. "Didn't he produce Lance Booker's albums? Oh man, I go way back with Lance. Bitter Pill opened for Bliss Patrol at this big stadium show in L.A. That was a crazy night. We made the rounds of all the cool clubs. The Balladeer, of course. I ended up in Lance's king-sized waterbed . . . I want Bowie to have epic nights like that, where she's the brightest star in the sky . . ."

She buries her face in her hands. Her shoulders shake.

"Did you drive here, Suzie?" I ask softly.

"I Ubered."

"I know a comfort-food pub nearby." I help her stand up. She turns her face away so I won't see her ugly crying.

As we're leaving, Suzie stumbles over a tree root in her high-heeled boots. I grab her leather jacket and lose my footing. We tumble together into dense, overgrown laurels. I'm surrounded by the smell of decaying leaves.

A hand reaches up from the ground to clutch my ankle. My pulse pounds. My mind jars back to Alaska. A memory buried in rotting leaves.

It's only tree roots. Not a clawed hand. Only Suzie, grabbing my hand.

I take a few deep breaths. Fat drops of rain begin to pelt the leaves above our heads.

"Are you all right?"

"I'm okay." She laughs shakily. "Maybe I should eat some food after all."

And that's when the glint of silver and glass draws my gaze. There's something caught in the branches next to my head. I reach my hand out, branches scratching my wrists.

My fingers close around smooth glass. I tug it loose. Hold it up. A small glass vial filled with something dull gray.

"Oh my God." Suzie digs her fingernails into my arm. "You found Bowie's necklace."

28

BOWIE

Bowie's been secretly visiting Mark's recording studio at night, when the Shepherds are asleep.

It's a thrill to sneak out of the house. She creeps down the stairs and exits out the window in the back sun porch where Myra sees patients sometimes. The wood of the window is rotting, and she found a way to prop the latch open with guitar picks that's not visible from inside the house. There's no security camera in the back of the house. The Shepherds have one of those stickers from an alarm company, but they never actually set the alarm.

She always parks Mark's car in a small dead-end alleyway a few blocks from the Shepherds' house. She takes the back path up the hill behind the house. There's a hole in the gate hidden by brambles. She wears jeans and thick sweatshirts, so the sharp brambles don't scrape her too much.

Sneaking through the graveyard at night isn't frightening. She loves this graveyard, knows it intimately. She's spent so much time there sitting on Dulcie's grave, playing her guitar and writing lyrics for Lo. What started as one or two songs with Mark has quickly become a whole album's worth of new material that feels so much more authentic.

Suzie would hate it, though. Too depressing. Not enough sex appeal.

Earlier tonight, they laid down the final track of "In Circles" and started working on "Drops of Rain," the song she'd begun writing on that first camping trip with the Shepherds.

Suzie asks her why she's so distracted, why she's not posting every day. Bowie wants to tell her the truth, but she keeps delaying. Suzie set up all the passwords for her accounts anyway. She posts as if she's Bowie. The fame-hungry version. She highlights other artists. Gushes about the fans.

> You guys, I'm working on new songs! I'll share them here soon. They're all for you. My amazing fans. Because you keep me going. It's all about you. Remember that. #SoBlessed #SoGrateful #BestFansEver

And on and on. Thirty freaking hashtags.

Suzie never got the memo that hashtags are over. Just say what's on your mind. Don't worry about making sure everyone likes it. Don't try to link it to the entire world. Fuck discoverability. Let them find her because she's saying something they need to hear.

She's almost back to the Shepherds' house. It's getting late. She'd better sneak back into her bed before Myra's up and about, making them breakfast. She's passing Dulcie's mausoleum when something shoots out of the bushes and grabs her wrist.

Bowie screams, but a hand clamps over her mouth, muffling her cries.

"Quiet! Do you want my mum to hear us? We'd be in so much trouble."

Bowie stops struggling, and Isla releases her. "Isla? What are you doing out here?"

"What are *you* doing out here? Have you been out all night? I know you haven't been with Dean."

"Because *you've* been with Dean tonight."

Isla grunts. "So what if I have?"

"I'm not judging you. Sometimes our parents don't know what's best for us."

"They can't stop me from being with Dean. We love each other. Actually . . . can you keep a secret?"

"I'll take it to my grave."

"He asked me to marry him."

"What the fuck? You're only eighteen."

"Hey, I thought you weren't judging me."

"Sorry. It's a little young."

"My parents married at twenty."

"What's the rush?"

"He wants to go on tour. He says he wants me to come with him. He's going to be a rock star. You know that. I can't let him go off by himself."

"Oh, Isla." How can Bowie tell her that going on tour with a charismatic star like Dean is most likely a recipe for a quick divorce? "Sit with me for a minute."

They sit on the mausoleum steps together, far enough away from the house not to wake anyone, but close enough to see the windows.

"Did I ever tell you what happened to my mom's career?"

"I googled her. They had that hit song and then she got pregnant?"

"My big sister. She lost the baby. But the guys in the band . . . when they found out she was pregnant, they replaced her. Threw her out like garbage. You haven't really been in that rock-'n-roll world. I've seen too much of it. Dean's not a bad guy, but fame changes people."

"It won't change him. We're meant to be together."

"If you're meant to be together, then you can wait a little while. Let him go on tour. If he comes back and he still wants to marry you, then you can think about it. But go to university first."

"God, you sound like my mum."

"Myra's only trying to protect you. She wants to keep you innocent and shielded from growing up too fast."

"She wants me to stay a child forever, never leave her."

"Suzie always says that if she tries to stop me from doing something, I'll only rebel. She says the drugs today are way more lethal than the ones she did. I can't even accept a joint from anyone at a party because it might be laced with fentanyl. She educates me about the dangers and then urges me to experiment safely with anything I want to try. She wants to be the cool mom. The big sis."

"Sounds good to me."

"Don't you see? It's two sides of the same coin. We're both under a lot of pressure. You're expected to be the honors student, the champion swimmer, like your dad was. You can't screw up because Daddy wants to become prime minister one day. Your life is under scrutiny because he's under a magnifying glass."

"That's exactly it."

"Suzie doesn't care about my grades or whether I even apply to universities. She's focused on making me a star. I'm expected to collect more followers, more likes, write that hit song, score that record deal, fulfill her hopes, her dreams . . . not my own."

Isla stays silent for a few minutes. Bowie can't see her eyes in the darkness, but she feels her warmth through the fabric of her sweatshirt.

"I never thought about it like that," she says finally. "About us being so different but similar in the way that we're both under pressure from our parents. So . . . where were you tonight?"

"I can't tell you yet."

"Come on. I just told you my big secret." Isla stiffens. "You're not doing anything illegal, are you? You were just talking about drugs."

"No, nothing like that."

"Then I bet you're seeing someone. Someone my mum wouldn't approve of. An older man? Or maybe a woman?"

"Not necessarily seeing someone . . . but yeah, I'm doing

something that neither one of our mothers would be happy about."

"Come on, tell me."

"I'll tell you soon. Actually, I'm going to have to tell everyone soon; I won't be able to keep it a secret." She feels as though she's living more inside the new album than in the real world. Everything that isn't lyrics, chords, tunings is somehow unsubstantial, irrelevant. This album is bigger than anything Suzie's ever imagined for her. Mark's subtle guidance, the way he pushes her to go deeper with the lyrics, but gently, not like Suzie's bullying, is helping her feel free to discover who she truly is as an artist. Not who Suzie wants her to be.

"Just be careful, okay?" Isla says.

"What, like you care what happens to me?"

"Bowie . . . I know I've been difficult to live with. I do care about you."

"And I care about you. If I thought Dean was a bad guy, I wouldn't stop until you dumped him. You're using protection, though, right?"

"Duh."

"Because that would be bad for your father's campaign . . . unwed teenage mum."

"I'm so sick of his campaign. He can't stop me from being with Dean. When I listen to him sing, his voice is a scalpel slicing through my chest and exposing my heart. I'm in love. There's nothing else to call this pain, this *wanting*. When he touches me, it's like the feeling when I dive into the pool and start swimming. Powerful pleasure. The only drug I'll ever need."

"Isla, that was poetic." Bowie's never heard her talk like this before. She's usually so matter-of-fact and down-to-earth.

Isla bumps her with her shoulder. "Maybe you're rubbing off on me. I've never been this happy before. I don't trust it. Do you ever feel like that? Like you're too happy, you're floating around on fluffy clouds and your life is a rom-com and you can't trust it—something bad will happen soon to ruin it all?"

"All the time." It's surprising to hear Isla voicing the thoughts in Bowie's head. "Maybe you should take a stand. Tell your parents about Dean. It's not like they'll kick you out or anything. They love you. Tell them what you told me. That you love him. You want to marry him."

"Not yet. We need to figure out a few logistics first. I don't want to hurt my parents until I have everything worked out."

"There's no way to avoid hurting people sometimes, Isla. It's just the way things are. We can't go along our whole lives never causing any pain. People love us more than we love them. Someone tears us down, makes us feel small. A boy you hero-worship turns out to be evil. You should see the street I live on in Vegas. The house a few doors down is a flophouse for junkies. There are underage prostitutes on the corner. Girls our age. Younger. I mean, the evidence of pain and hurt is all around us."

"It's here, too. Maybe just buried a little deeper. My mum's an abuse survivor. I don't know the details, but I think it was when she was very young and it was a family friend. I think that's why she became a counselor. She's a survivor."

"I didn't know."

"Maybe I shouldn't have told you."

"I'm glad you did. It makes more sense now why she's so protective of you."

"And of you. Can you imagine what she'd say if she knew we were both sneaking out at night?"

"We'd be so grounded."

"It's our little secret, okay?"

Bowie nods. It's the first time she's felt like they could really be sisters. "Our little secret."

29

LAKE

I drove Suzie to the police station, and we turned over the necklace to the police. Mason wasn't there and I felt his absence like it was winter in Alaska and I hadn't seen the sun in weeks. I left Suzie at her hotel room, then had a long meeting with Rob.

I told him about Jordan's list. How I'd been investigating the names. He told me that the police had already interviewed Mark Edison because he was Dean Hira's record producer and had been introduced to Bowie. Edison was out of town around the time Bowie disappeared. And he has no motive. They didn't consider him a person of interest.

Now that Bowie's necklace had been found in the cemetery, they were doubling down on the search there. He told me the same thing Ambassador Hunt had told me: leave the investigation to trained law enforcement. Only he was much kinder about it. He said that my role as liaison with Suzie was invaluable to them. It was good for her to have someone she trusted and connected with in Wellington.

He promised to have someone call me after they analyzed the contents of the vial Bowie had worn around her neck.

My mom calls, but I don't answer. I can't face her resentment about my not visiting. Not right now. My mind churns like an overflowing gutter during a tropical rainstorm. Some thoughts are too murky to wade through.

It's ten p.m., but there's no possibility of sleep. I pace my apartment, gathering everything I've collected about Bowie's case and sticking it to my bedroom wall with museum putty.

Soon my bare walls are covered with Bowie—bloody fingerprints, lyrics, photos of her, the guitar pick with the logo from the Balladeer. Post-it notes connecting everything in chaotic spirals.

Edgar sleeps in the middle of my bed, a puddle of black like an oil slick on my blush-pink vintage satin bedspread. When I start singing along with one of Bowie's songs on my phone, he covers his eyes with one paw, as if he can't bear to witness my off-key performance.

I'd do anything
To feel your satin petal skin
I'd give anything
To see you bloom again
My graveyard rose

What if she's gone forever and these songs are never properly recorded? A life's work lost. A dream abandoned.

What was the dream you abandoned? Dean had asked me in the coffee shop.

That's easy. I open my laptop. Pull up a file I haven't opened in years. The Victorian detective novel I was writing during college and never finished to my satisfaction. The writing pulls me in as if it was written by a stranger. Maybe it was. I wrote this before I joined the Foreign Service. Before I chose a career that means I never settle in one place, never put down roots.

My name is Florence Atherton. Last month my husband, Reginald, fell from a cliff and was drowned. I was there. He stood too close to the edge, you see. He was berating me, as he was wont to do, his face blotched with rage, and he grabbed my shoulders and shook me until my teeth chattered, as he had done so many times before.

I twisted free from his grip. In his haste to catch me again, he slipped and lost his footing.

I watched him fall. Awkwardly flapping, he fell. And fell.

His head hit an outcropping of rock halfway down and burst open like a rotten tomato.

When he hit the turbulent waters far, far below, his body was sucked under the frothing white waves and carried away. The last I saw of him was his outstretched hand. The glint of a gold wedding band. The symbol of my captivity.

No. That's not true. The last I saw of him was his brain-splatter on the jagged rocks. A smear of scarlet. Like something in a pot you might dab upon your lips, or smooth over your cheeks.

At the inquest, I told my story to the police inspector. I had marks upon my arms. The imprint of all ten of my husband's fingers where he'd gripped me so violently. I wept. I wailed. I swooned.

I was young and not unattractive, and every one of our friends and acquaintances had known me as a devoted, compliant, and pious wife. A silently suffering spouse, one who would never lift a finger in retaliation, no matter how provoked, how abused.

There were no witnesses to his fall save I. None to cast blame upon me. I had no motive of greed. I was left propertyless and nearly destitute. My brother-in-law and his odious wife inherited the house, the carriage, and the estate. Because of this, my story was believed. I was set free.

My widow's portion was barely enough to let a small hovel in a down-at-the-heels neighborhood. And yet I was not friendless. A benefactor, or benefactress, offered me a small fortune on condition of anonymity, and with the directive that I use the funds to open a detective agency.

The note said that I was uniquely qualified to help women in similar circumstances.

I wondered what that could mean until my first client walked through the door, sent by my anonymous patron. Miss Adele Harrison was a young woman soon to be accused of a heinous crime and hanged by the neck. She had no one else to turn to. And I was a woman who knew all too well the cruel blows dealt by men, the cages they build to keep us servile, to clip our wings.

Who else would feel compelled to take her hopeless case if not I? The only female detective in London. Perhaps the world.

Miss Harrison was innocent. I was determined to prove it.

But I was not innocent.

My name is Florence Atherton. Last month my husband, Reginald, fell from a cliff and was drowned. I was there.

I pushed him.

My detective got away with murdering her abusive husband, and she set out to help other desperate and wronged women. The first short chapter came to me nearly whole after a night of drinking in college. My head spinning from cheap wine, fingertips flying over my keyboard.

I remember making my detective deliberately flawed, not in the opium-addicted way, but in a self-doubting way. Male detectives in novels rarely second-guess their every move. They act on instinct, moving forward with confidence. I've made second-guessing into an art form. I reject things about myself first so that if or when someone else rejects me, I've beat them to it.

I never sent my book out to agents because I could picture the rejection so vividly. NOT GOOD ENOUGH. Big bold Sharpie letters across my forehead.

Maybe I was being too hard on myself. I read so many detective novels and I knew the basic tenets: Trust no one, believe nothing anyone tells you until it's proven to be true or false. I was thinking like a detective. I remember planting the clues in my novel very deliberately. I had Ronald Knox's Ten Commandments of Detective Fiction taped to the wall above my computer. *No more than one secret room or passage is allowable . . . The detective must not himself commit the crime.*

What am I missing about Bowie's case? Her short life had been troubled. None of what I'd discovered about her past in Las Vegas was good. Her best friend dying of a drug overdose after partying with Bruce. Glen secretly paying for her exchange program, possibly as a kind of underhanded leverage over her.

If I really was a detective, how would I organize the clues? I begin rearranging everything in order, making a timeline from Florica Baciu's death up to Bowie's disappearance, filling in everything I have thus far. Bowie and Isla fighting about Dean. Bowie performing at the arts festival, taking the photo of Ambassador Hunt, meeting with Jordan Singer. Talking to Mark Edison.

Edgar watches me balefully, wondering when I'm finally going to settle down in bed so that he can curl up next to his human heater.

If I tap the right vein of inquiry, the solution will bleed out. Like tapping a maple tree. Truth flowing, blood-sticky, and sweet.

Bowie's lyrics wrench me back to my childhood. The barnacle-encrusted anchor we pulled out of the mud. My rebellious teenage years. Wanting to be a writer.

Images and notes splayed across my wall. Bowie in a thin red camisole, those haunting eyes of hers staring directly at the viewer. *You can't ignore me.*

A stone mausoleum consumed by moss, sheltered by trees, breathless and silent.

An aging playboy in a cowboy hat. *The daughter is just as unstable as the mom.*

A glint of glass hung on a tree branch.

A vial filled with something gray and grainy.

I keep you with me always, you're the toll I'll have to pay. I'd pegged it as a reference to paying the ferryman's fee on the River Styx. It was also literal.

I catch sight of myself in the vanity mirror. My hair is wild, my eyes shadowy.

Florica's ashes. Bowie had brought her friend to New Zealand with her.

30

LAKE

"I have the results of the contents of Bowie's necklace. You were right, Lake." Mason's deep, gruff voice never fails to give me butterflies. "It's ashes. Human remains."

"She brought her friend Florica to New Zealand with her. It fits with the lyrics from her songs." I'm walking back to my apartment after work. It's nearly impossible to focus on my other work with Bowie still missing, but the State Department machinery continues to grind, dragging me along with it.

"Wearing human remains around your neck is taking goth a little too far, if you ask me."

"You heard Suzie at the police station; Bowie made accusations but no one believed her. How lonely that must have been. And how frightening. She had to leave Las Vegas. She applies for the exchange program because it's what Florica wanted to do. She brings her friend's ashes with her in a vial she wears around her neck."

"Pretty macabre."

"Young girls are dramatic, Mason."

"You don't have to tell me. I have plenty of nieces."

"I remember when I was eighteen. Everything was outlined in bright bulbs, like a musical sign on Broadway with a big red arrow pointing to my chest: *High drama here*. I walked so many tightropes where one step could have sent me careening into an early grave."

"I've been busy redoubling our search efforts in the area of the cemetery where you found the necklace. Haven't found anything else yet."

"I asked Suzie about Bowie meeting music producer Mark Edison at the arts festival. She said Bowie never mentioned it. Rob said he's not a person of interest."

"DSS Sutherland and I interviewed him. He said that Dean brought Bowie to his house once to listen to a recording session."

"The evidence points to Bruce, but Alejandro Gil told me that Bowie seemed distant, checked out, in the weeks before she disappeared. He thought she might be seeing someone new. Keeping it a secret. Could it have been Edison?"

"He's what, fifty?"

"I know. I keep going back to the video of Bowie and Dean singing together. There was a palpable attraction there. You said Dean brought Bowie to Edison's recording studio. Maybe Edison saw something happen between them."

"That's an interesting thought. Have you ever considered becoming a detective? I think you'd make a damn fine one."

"This case is personal to me now. I'm invested in finding Bowie."

"You feel a connection with her. Understandable. You've been living and breathing nothing but Bowie this week."

"She's out there somewhere, Mason. She's in a shallow grave already beginning to decompose. Or there's that slim, shimmering hope that she's still alive. Either way, she's waiting for us to find her."

"Do you want to pay Edison a visit with me this evening?"

"Just show up at his house at dinnertime?"

"Why not?"

"Will he let us in?"

"If he has nothing to hide. His house is a half hour's drive away. We'll stop for a meal at a proper fish-and-chips place on the way there. I'll pick you up at the embassy gate in twenty."

"I'm walking home right now." I give him my address. I'll have time to feed Edgar and change out of my vintage frilled-neck shirt and pencil skirt into something more comfortable. Maybe show a little cleavage?

Simmer down. This isn't a date.

Though he was the one who suggested the meal in that adorable Kiwi accent: *fush* and *chups*. Milk sounds more like *mulk*. His growly voice and that accent do something flip-floppy to my stomach. I realize how hungry I am. For a greasy, salty meal. For a rough-edged detective who doesn't laugh at my outlandish theories and instead offers to help me investigate.

Nope. There's no longing for Mason. No pining, either. He's a colleague. A damn sexy one who made a point of telling me that he was single, but a professional contact, nothing more. Longings lead only to heartache, and I haven't recovered from the last disaster.

The accusations like arrows piercing through chain mail.

You never loved me. You're incapable of love. You're too damaged.

I still feel the touch of Lucas's hand on the small of my back. It lingers like the imprint of rocks after I walk barefoot across a beach.

He said we'd grown apart. It hadn't felt like a growing, it had been the sharp shock of an axe splintering me down the middle, like a block of firewood.

I was so blind. He cheated on me, and I never suspected a thing. I was too wrapped up in my job. Too stressed. My defense mechanisms on high alert given the predators, addicts, and criminals I dealt with daily in Phnom Penh. I'd relaxed my defenses at home. Assumed the person I'd chosen as a partner wouldn't betray my trust.

The day after he left me, there had been a frenzied hatching of flying ants in the bathroom of the apartment. They were feeble things, fluttering against the window, their wings an opaque amber like dried flakes of shellac. I sprayed Windex on them and they crumpled in soggy heaps on the windowsill. The next day there were only a few survivors weaving across the white tiles, desperately clinging to life.

That's how I feel. Like someone tried to wipe me out. Erase my existence.

I'm still here, but it's precarious. Extreme caution advised.

Armor repaired and in place.

31

BOWIE

Bowie's in the recording booth. Not for the first time, she thinks that Mark's basement recording studio is like living in a casino. No windows. She can't tell what time it is.

She's lost inside the music, and she wants to live here forever.

This will be the take. She feels it. The lyrics and music have fallen in love with each other. Now she'll allow them to have their way, use her voice.

The expensive microphone gives her voice a warm, silky finish, like the polished rosewood beneath her fingertips.

She closes her eyes and begins to strum.

You caught the light like a windowpane
You baptized me like falling rain
When the embers died, you were firelight
When nightmares came you held me tight

But this isn't a love song
This is a murder ballad
Because now you're gone
And love's lost to me
Down in the deep dark ground

A place that will never be found
Bury it deep and word won't get around

We've all got our cross to bear
Pretty eyes and long brown hair
Wherever I go I know you're not there

But this isn't a love song
This is a murder ballad
Because now you're gone
And love's lost to me

Down in the deep dark ground
A place that will never be found
Bury it deep and word won't get around

She holds her breath for a few seconds after the last note fades away.

Mark's voice in her headphones. "You nailed it."

"You sure I don't need to do ten more takes?"

"Normally, yes. I drill my musicians hard. You're a natural. I wouldn't want to change the rawness, the edge. It's dark, yes, but gripping."

"I've been working on something new, something slightly more hopeful."

"Brilliant. Let's hear it."

She changes tuning. This one is more complicated. The key modulates with each new verse, and the rhythm changes.

"Take one, Shadows Long for the Night," she says into the microphone.

Summer breeze makes you sing
Casts a glow on everything
Mountain stream cools you down
Erases all the other sound

SHE FELL AWAY

True, you can stand in the light
But also true, shadows long for the night

Winter wind makes you bow and bend
But in the end spring uncoils again
Frost makes the ground buckle and heave
But underneath the seed waits for its leaf

True, you can't see in the dark
But also true, it only takes one spark
True, you can stand in the light
But also true, shadows long for the night

Autumn leaves will journey down
Join their sisters on the ground
The pebbles crashing on the beach
A perfect circle out of reach

True, you can stand in the light
But also true, shadows long for the night
True, you can't see in the dark
But also true, it only takes one spark

Mark is silent for so long that Bowie begins to think he's trying to find a way to tell her he thinks the song is crap. "You still there?"

"I'm here. You're the real deal, Bowie. You know that?"

"Thanks." His praise gives her goose bumps, sets off sparklers in her mind. She's in an airplane, flying over Vegas on the Fourth of July, watching fireworks bloom and fade from above. This is her without Suzie. Her true voice. Mark doesn't care that the lyrics are melancholic, or that there's no dance hook.

While Mark works with the raw recording, Bowie sits by the window that overlooks the ocean in his basement guest bedroom. She wants to tell someone about this album. She wants to call Suzie. But not yet. Not until the songs are perfect.

Instead, she calls Livia, Lo's mom. She hasn't talked to her in too long, not since she started recording the album. She can trust her to keep the secret.

"Livia, hello!"

"Bowie, how are you, sweet girl?"

"I'm doing great. How are you?"

"Not so good. But you don't worry about me. Tell me about your life." Her accent is strong, but Bowie had years of practice understanding her. She even learned a few Romanian words and sentences.

"I'm working on an album of songs I wrote for Lo. It's a tribute album. I'm going to make sure she lives forever."

"That's so beautiful, Bowie." She chokes up. "You loved her so much."

"I still love her. I think about her every day, Livia. Every single day. She's here with me right now."

"I see her everywhere, too. I saw her at church on Sunday. She sat beside me on the pew. She looked so beautiful. She asked me about you. I told her you were safe in New Zealand with the sheep and the Hobbit houses."

Bowie smiles through tears. "I still have the necklace. I can't . . . I can't let her go. It's the last piece of her I have."

"I understand. And now you have these songs. Your mother will be so proud of you."

Bowie straightens. "You can't tell her about the album, okay? She doesn't know yet."

"Why not?"

"It's a . . . surprise. For her . . . birthday."

"All right. I won't tell her. But I don't see her much. I'm working the late shift. She's leaving as I'm arriving. I don't like this schedule."

"Then you should talk to management. Do you want me to have Suzie talk to Glen?"

"No! Bowie, no. Don't talk to Glen." She sounds weird, her voice strangled.

"Livia, is something wrong?"

"I . . . I can't tell you, sweetheart."

"You can tell me anything. You know that."

"I wish I could. I want to tell someone. It's too much for me to bear."

"Are you crying, Livia?"

"Sorry. I should go. Goodbye, Bowie."

"Wait! Don't hang up. Tell me what's wrong. Please. I'll be worrying about you if you don't tell me." The line goes silent. "Livia, are you still there?"

Her voice is a whisper. Bowie concentrates on deciphering the soft, heavily accented words. "I was cleaning the office and I heard Glen on the phone."

Bowie strains to catch her words. "He says he needs another girl like . . . like my Florica." Her voice cracks. "And then he says . . . what a fucking waste that had been. This time be more careful."

The bottom drops out from Bowie's stomach. She's suddenly sick. "You're sure that's what he said?"

"Yes. I get out of the room. He doesn't see me. I'm lucky."

"Who was he talking to?"

"I don't know."

"Bruce." It must have been Bruce. That fucking murderer.

"Maybe. Bowie, I don't want to tell you this. It's so bad. So, so bad. The next day I was cleaning a guest's suite, and I saw something on his laptop. A video of a girl. She was drugged. Something bad was happening to her."

"A porn site."

"I don't think so. It was happening in a room in The Trophy. One of the VIP suites. I was so angry. I wasn't thinking right. I went to the store and bought a . . . what do you call it? A thumb stick."

"A thumb drive. A USB flash drive."

"That's right. A little plastic thing to stick in a computer. I went back to the guest's room and I copied the video. You can hear Glen's voice on the video. He's directing everything. I . . . I don't know why I did it."

"Fuck, Livia. This is bad."

"She was a pretty girl, like my Florica. They drugged her, Bowie. Maybe it could be they drugged my Florica, too."

"You have to give the video to the police."

"How could I? You know Glen owns the police here. It's useless, Bowie. And he owns me, too. I'm still here on a work visa. I can't say anything, or he could have me deported. I shouldn't be telling you this. I want you to be happy. I don't want you to know about ugly evil things like this."

"No, Livia. I'm glad you told me. Glen and Bruce can't get away with this. They could harm more girls."

"I don't know what to do."

Bowie makes a quick decision. "Mail the USB drive to me, Livia. I know what to do. I know someone who works at the U.S. embassy here." Jordan Singer, the skinny guy who had been minding the ambassador. He'd given her his business card at the reception. "He can help me set up a meeting with an FBI agent."

"It's too dangerous."

"Not so dangerous for me. I'm over here in New Zealand. I'm safe. My host father is a powerful man. We'll make sure they can't trace the video to you. I'll wipe away your fingerprints."

"I don't know . . . I can't ask you to do this."

"Please, I want to help. Let me do this for you. For Lo. For the other girls in danger."

"Yes. My Bowie. You are a strong girl. I will mail it to you tomorrow. I had already written a letter to you that I was going to mail. But be very careful. Promise me, Bowie."

"I promise."

"Good." Her voice cracks. "Bowie, Florica is watching you from heaven. She will keep you safe. Goodbye, sweetheart, I must go now."

Bowie's grabbing her guitar and backpack from the recording studio when Mark comes up behind her. "Is something wrong?"

"My mom is having a crisis. I'll see you later."

"I made us a snack and opened a bottle of good wine." He holds up a charcuterie plate. "We should celebrate these new songs."

"Sorry. Gotta go."

A flash of something—annoyance—in his eyes. Then his face goes bland again. "Sure. See you soon."

32

LAKE

The road sheers off into cliffs so close to the wheels of Mason's car that I grip the door handle like a life preserver. Evening sun flames over the ocean, splashing the waves with red and gold.

I'm pleasantly stuffed full of grease and salt after a delicious meal in a quaint wood-paneled pub where none of the waiters were under sixty.

A scenic drive out of Wellington hugging the stunning Kapiti coast with its breathtaking cliffs and endless sandy beaches. If it was a date, and not a missing persons investigation, maybe next he'd take me on a boat, an excursion to Kapiti Island, the famous bird sanctuary, where, I've read, if you're lucky, you'll hear the eerie call of the endangered blue-wattled kōkako bird.

Then a winding walk along a deserted beach. Laughing and collecting shells. Wine at sunset overlooking the ocean. Then back to his place, because mine is an unholy mess. Edgar never did like Lucas. He thinks he's the only creature allowed in my bed. He wouldn't be happy if I brought a gruff detective home with me. But my mom would be ecstatic.

Life will pass you by if you're not careful.

"What are you thinking about?" Mason asks.

Nothing I can tell him. "I was thinking about how I visited

Queen Elizabeth Park for an event a few days after I arrived. I had no idea there were over fifteen thousand U.S. troops stationed here during World War II."

"It has a long history before that. There were Māori pā sites, fortified settlements, on the beaches here for hundreds of years. My auntie owns a cottage in Paekākāriki. We used to come here as kids and play on the beach. Here we are." He takes a hard left over the train tracks and slows down along a short main street lined with cafés and shops. He parks on a side street. "We'll walk from here."

He points out Edison's house, a stately white edifice with a high black iron gate. We give our names and credentials to the guard. He radios into the house. A few minutes later the gate swings open.

We walk down a wide pathway bordered by trees with branches arcing overhead, creating a false twilight.

"The front of the house looks imposing, but if you view it from the beach below, you see the truth—it's clinging to the cliff, in constant threat from erosion and from the ocean. It's all bolted on securely, but if a tsunami hit . . . I'd want to be on higher ground."

We're being watched. Two security cameras are prominently displayed on either side of the wide veranda. I point upward.

Mason nods. "If Bowie was coming and going, we would be able to see her on security camera footage. There's the tall wall around the entire perimeter of the front, and the cliff at the back."

"Sergeant Yates. Ms. Harlowe." Mark Edison is wearing chinos and a white button-down shirt, open at the neck. He's barefoot, and his curly hair is messy, as if he just woke from a nap. "To what do I owe the honor?"

Mason has his tough police face on, and I love it. "Same as last time. We're here about Bowie Bishop. Ms. Harlowe took the initial missing persons call from Suzie Bishop."

"I thought I answered every one of your questions most

thoroughly, but please, do come in. I have a half hour before I leave for an engagement."

He acts like a man with nothing to hide. He's the relaxed, jovial host.

"Ms. Harlowe, would you like a little tour? This is the day parlor." He ushers us into a spacious room with windows overlooking the ocean. Gleaming wood floors, gold velvet curtains, walls painted a light celadon green with cream trim. There's a fireplace to the right of the windows with an eighteenth-century portrait of a woman hung over it. Dainty plasterwork garlands frame the walls and continue on the high ceilings. A crystal chandelier drips from a medallion crisscrossed by lines like spiderwebbing.

He leads us into a dining room and then a living room punctuated by blown-up, framed photographs of himself with royalty and celebrities. I pause in front of a solo portrait of him standing on the beach with his house in the background. He's younger, with fewer wrinkles around his eyes and a fuller head of hair. He's dressed like an indie rocker in a black T-shirt and jeans, with multiple leather bracelets. The honey glow of a sunset kisses his face, and his arms are outstretched, palms flat, like he's some kind of rock-'n-roll saint giving a benediction.

"Where's your recording studio?" I ask.

"In the basement."

Mason joins us by the portrait. "Could we take a look?"

"By all means. Follow me."

Down a hallway and a long, steep flight of stairs. The narrow stairwell opens up into a cavernous room with light wood covering the walls and polished concrete floors. There's a large collection of guitars adorning one wall. It's intimate and welcoming, a far cry from the pomp and circumstance upstairs.

"The recording studio is through here." He leads us to the back wall and opens a door to a windowless room with recording equipment and a large glass pane through which there's a view of the sound booth.

I trail one hand over the thick, metal door of the booth. "May I?"

I step inside and close the door. It's still and silent. There's a stool, a microphone stand with an impressive professional mic. An empty guitar stand. A drum kit and a gleaming upright piano.

I close my eyes. I hear Bowie singing. *When they turned out all the lights. Did you feel alone? Or was the darkness home?*

Why had Dean brought Bowie here? To impress her? This basement recording studio probably looked like heaven to a singer-songwriter with a love for vintage guitars. When I open my eyes, Edison is watching me through the window. Something about his intent stare gives me an uneasy feeling. Had he stared at Bowie like that? Had she come here more than once?

"Impressive," I say with a smile as I exit the booth. "Is this where Bowie recorded her new songs?"

The tiniest facial tic on the side of his mouth. "You must mean Dean Hira. This is where I record Dean and other artists."

"Never Bowie."

"She only visited the once, with Dean."

"And your security camera footage would back that up?"

"Of course."

"Did you see any evidence that Bowie and Dean were a couple?" Mason asks.

"They weren't. And I didn't."

I meet his gaze, alert for any sign that he's lying. "Did Bowie bring her guitar with her when she visited you?"

"Why would she? I told you that she only visited the once."

"Can we see the rest of the basement?"

"There's only a guest bedroom down the hall and some wine storage rooms."

"We'd like to see the bedroom," says Mason.

"Be my guest." He leads us out of the recording studio, down a hallway, and up a few stairs. The bedroom is the first room down here I've seen with a window. It has an expansive view of the ocean.

"Beautiful view."

"Isn't it?"

The room is tastefully furnished with light-colored wood and sheepskin rugs. Mason riffles through the pink, frilly clothing in the closet. He turns to Mark with a questioning expression.

"My ex-wife left some of her things," he explains.

Nothing Bowie would ever be caught dead wearing. "Her name was Veronica, right?"

He's about to answer when my phone rings. It's Suzie. "Sorry, I have to take this."

"Lake, it's S-suzie. A boy came to my hotel. He had her clothes. There's a note. I can't . . . I can't read it. Please. You have to come." She's sobbing heavily. I can barely make out her words.

"I'm sorry, I can't hear you very well."

"Lake," she wails. "It's from Bowie . . . it's a . . ."

My reception cuts out for a moment.

"Suzie, I'm losing you. I'm in a basement. Let me go outside."

"Just come to the hotel right away. Please. I need you."

"I'm on my way."

33

BOWIE

Bowie arranges to meet Jordan Singer in the French bakery eight blocks from the embassy. She's already seated when he arrives. She chose a corner table with a view out the window and of the whole room. She already has a croissant and a flat white. He comes over and smiles at her, a shy smile; he's kind of nerdy and cute. No more than twenty-three, she guesses.

"Hi, Jordan."

"Hi, Bowie. I was surprised to hear from you."

"You gave me your card at the arts festival."

"Just in case you had any issues during your time here."

"You helped my friend Melissa when she lost her passport."

"If it's something like a missing passport, you can make an appointment during regular consular hours—"

"It's nothing like that. I want to ask you a favor."

"Okay." The waitress brings his order of a ham and cheese croissant and an espresso. "What's the favor?"

"I was going to ask Stuart, my host dad, to help me contact the authorities, but he would never want to be involved with a scandal."

"What kind of scandal?"

"You have FBI agents at the embassy, right?"

"Maybe. What's this about?"

"It's about my best friend, Florica Baciu. She died of a drug overdose in Las Vegas. Her mom called me. She's a housekeeper at The Trophy casino and hotel, where my mom also works."

"Okay . . ." He takes a bite of his croissant. "I'm sorry about your friend. But I'm not understanding exactly why you're telling me this."

"Because you're the only person I know at the embassy. I may need to meet with an FBI agent. I may have evidence of crimes committed by Glen Walter, the owner of The Trophy, and his son, Bruce." She can't keep the hatred out of her voice. Off her face. "And maybe your ambassador was involved. He was there in the casino the night Florica died."

He sits up straighter. Swallows hard. Glances around the room like maybe someone's here listening to us. "What kind of crimes?"

"Drugging girls. Selling them to high rollers. I'm not sure exactly yet."

"You said you have evidence?"

"Not yet. It should be here soon."

"Florica's mom is sending it to you?"

Shit. She hadn't meant for him to put that together. "No. I'm gathering it from . . . other sources. Could you arrange the meeting for me?"

"You can call up the embassy yourself. Say you're an American citizen with information about a crime to pass on to the Feds."

"I could do that. Or you could help me set up a more personal meeting, where I don't get dismissed as a crazy person."

"Look, Bowie. This isn't really my wheelhouse, okay? I'm just a consular officer."

"You were following Ambassador Hunt around at the arts festival. You know the kind of things he's capable of."

His eyes narrow. "What do you mean?"

"Oh, come on. You saw the way he was hitting on me and Clementine."

He sighs. "Yeah, it's not a good look for the USG."

"No, it's really not. It's not your fault, but that dude needs to learn a lesson."

"He's been disciplined by Washington before. It didn't stop his behavior."

"The night of the arts festival I took a photo of him kissing Clementine in the gardens."

"What?" His jaw drops. Now he's really nervous. He keeps checking out the tables nearby to see if anyone's eavesdropping.

"I was out there minding my own business getting some fresh air when I hear her giggling and him being all sleazy. He had his hand up her skirt. He was kissing her neck. I don't know why I snapped a pic—I think because I wanted to document yet another instance of an old guy being a creep. I put a stop to it, of course. Clementine ran off, and the ambassador wasn't very happy about that."

"Jesus, Bowie." He lowers his voice when a woman at the next table looks over at us. Drops of sweat form on his brow. "What are you going to do with that photo?"

"I could send it to a reporter in the U.S. They might be interested in a story about ambassadors behaving badly."

Jordan's fingers clench around his coffee cup. "Yeah, they might be."

"He's a ticking time bomb. You know that."

"I know. Shit. Maybe you should turn the photo over to me and I'll send it to the OIG."

"OIG?"

"Office of Inspector General."

"You would do that?"

"I have a whole file I've been keeping. He's breaking so many rules it's not even funny. Although he's a political appointee, not a career diplomat. So it's not like he won't just go back to his life in the private sector and do the same stuff."

Bowie's impressed. She'd expected Jordan to be less cooperative. She'd been planning to use the photo as blackmail if he didn't agree to help her.

"So we're on the same page here. I'll send you the photo. You help me make the meeting with the FBI once I have the evidence gathered."

"I could possibly help you set up a meeting, but I'd need to know what we're talking about here. What kind of evidence you think you have."

"Okay. I'll let you know when I know."

"But let's not meet so close to the embassy, okay?"

"Got it. There's something else I wanted to ask you. Let's say I was looking to stay in New Zealand, and I had my own income source. Would they give me an extension on my visa if I had enough money to rent my own apartment?"

"It's tricky. New Zealand doesn't make it easy to overstay your visa, and applying for a new one at your age would take parental approval. Would your mom help you apply?"

"She wants me to come home to Las Vegas."

"For good reason. You're too young to stay here alone."

"At least I could stay a few more months, right?"

"Maybe. I'll send you the visa regulations to review. Even though you're eighteen, it would help if your mom was on board."

"Okay, thanks. I appreciate it."

"I have to get back to work. Take care of yourself, Bowie."

He leaves, and she sits there for another hour, Googling visa extensions and apartment rentals. It's scary and exhilarating. Escaping everyone's control.

Striking out on her own.

Does she have the courage? She's not sure. All she knows is that she can't go back to Vegas. Not until Bruce and anyone else involved in this sick, twisted scheme is brought to justice.

Not until he pays for what he did.

34

LAKE

Suzie's been crying so hard a blood vessel has burst in her left eye, spreading crimson branches against the white.

"Lake." She collapses into my arms, burrowing her face into my shirt.

"What's happened, Ms. Bishop?" Mason asks.

She points a shaking finger at a bundle of clothing sitting on a hotel chair. "That's Bowie's. Her black Cure sweatshirt. Her high-tops. There's a . . . suicide . . . note."

I pat her back soothingly as Mason pulls a pair of latex gloves out of a vest pocket before unfolding the piece of paper. He reads it and then looks up, eyes clouded. "Who gave this to you, Suzie?"

"This tall Dutch kid named Remy. A tourist. He said he was taking a walk at Mākara Beach and he found the clothes and the note stuffed under a rock."

"Why didn't he go to the police?"

"I don't know. He said he searched the hashtag on the note and saw my posts about Bowie. I think I said I was at this hotel. I asked people to give me tips. He came here. He said he didn't want to talk to the police. He just dumped the stuff and ran."

"Well, he's going to have to talk to us," Mason says grimly. "How long ago did he leave?"

"Right before I called you. Twenty minutes ago? Oh God." She clutches my arm. "I think I'm going to be sick."

I help her into the bathroom, holding her hair back as she retches into the toilet. "Fuck." She rests her head against the toilet bowl. "Why? Why would my baby kill herself? She had everything to live for. Everything." She collapses onto the bathroom floor, sobbing uncontrollably.

"I'm calling this in," Mason says. "We'll track down this Remy. Take an official statement. Are you all right staying here?"

"I'll be fine." I wish I had some sedatives to give Suzie. She's scratching at her wrists as if there were ants crawling across her arms.

"I'll be back quickly. Don't touch the clothing or the note until my team arrives." Mason leaves, and I'm alone with Suzie.

"He said it was a remote beach . . . really rocky and turbulent. He said the water would have carried her away. There'd be no trace." She laughs—a desperate, heartbreaking sound. "Maybe she was still alive on the day I arrived. Why didn't she come to me? The note says she blames herself for Bruce's death. She must have been in such a dark, lonely place. My baby. If only she'd come to me. I would have kept her safe."

"We don't know the timeline, Suzie."

"It doesn't matter. She's gone. She'll never record her debut album. Never have a child of her own. My Bowie. My shining star."

"I'm so sorry, Suzie." I haven't read the note yet. I'm doing triage, trying to keep Suzie from harming herself.

She raises her tearstained face. "I did the best I could. A single mom trying to make it in the entertainment industry. Cocktail waitresses make good money when they're young. I'm too old now. The tips aren't as good. I think the big mistake was allowing her to come here. I should have kept her with me, where I could watch over her. I love her more than anything in this world, more than myself."

"I know."

"I only wanted the best and the shiniest life for her. Was I harming her? Oh God."

I don't say anything.

"I took some pills, Lake." She forms each word carefully, as though she has a mouthful of marbles. "Before you came."

"What kind of pills, Suzie?"

Her head flops onto the toilet. "Lots of pills."

Damn it. I should have thought of that possibility. At least she just threw up. That should help. I soak a washcloth with cold water and place it on her neck. "Don't fall asleep. Suzie."

"What?"

"Suzie. Don't fall asleep." I slap her cheek lightly.

She bats my hand away. "All right, all right."

I help her sit up, leaning her against the wall. I call 1-1-1 emergency services and request an ambulance. I tell them I don't know what type of pills she took or how many.

I continue sponging her down with cold water and keeping her awake while we wait for the ambulance. I don't want to try moving her downstairs by myself. I wish Mason was still here. He could have easily lifted her.

The suicide note is lying face up on top of the pile of clothing. I take a quick photo and return to the bathroom. Suzie's head lolls against my shoulder as I surreptitiously read the note.

If you're reading this, I'm gone. I don't want to live without my Lo anymore. My graveyard rose. I tricked Bruce into coming here. I wanted revenge. I couldn't go through with it. He died anyway. Blood for blood. Love you, Lo. I'll be there with you soon. On the other side. #BoLoForever

35

BOWIE

Today is the day.
    She's going to call Suzie. Tell her about the album.

It's nearly finished now. It's mostly acoustic. Just Bowie and her guitar, layered vocals, the occasional drumbeat or synth line added by Mark. They're going to record the final two songs with a band. Mark suggested asking Dean's band to play, but they're planning to go on tour soon.

Before they start asking local musicians to play on her album, Suzie needs to know about the project. It'll be harder to keep it under wraps when it's not just Bowie and Mark.

It's a perfect spring day. Cool and shadowy on the porch of the mausoleum, but the sun is shining and birds are singing and grass is pushing up between the graves into the world.

Inside her it's the same. Half in shadow and half in sun. A padlocked door separating the two Bowies. The dead and alive. The fear and the hope. Mark says it's a big album. He says she should be making big plans.

Her mom, her best friend, her enemy, won't own her anymore. She won't be able to live through her. How many years will it take for Suzie to forgive her? When Bowie makes it big, when the money comes in, and Bowie gives her half . . . then she'll be fine with it, won't she?

These songs have become Bowie's church, her religion. They're where she goes to worship, to feel connected to Lo, and to her newfound desire to live life on her own terms.

"Help me find the right words, Dulcie," she whispers. She knows Suzie isn't going to understand. She'll be angry. Hurt that Bowie didn't confide in her.

Once she listens to the music she'll understand. Won't she? Maybe . . . or maybe not. This could all go really wrong.

She can't wait any longer. Just rip off the bandage. Call her and deal with the consequences. She unlocks her phone.

A call lights up the screen before she has a chance to call Suzie.

"Livia?"

"Bowie? Where are you. Are you safe?"

"I'm fine. Everything's fine. I'm sitting outside of my host family's house."

"You got my package, right?"

"Yeah. Sorry. It took weeks to arrive. I haven't called you yet because I haven't been able to set up that meeting with the FBI. This guy I asked to help me left New Zealand suddenly. I was worried that maybe him leaving had something to do with the meeting I had with him. I've been waiting to contact the embassy until the ambassador is out of Wellington on a trip."

"Oh, thank God. I would never forgive myself if anything happened to you because of what I sent you. He came here just now, he visited my apartment, Bowie."

"Who did? What are you talking about?"

"Bruce Walter. He was just here."

Bowie gasps. "Did he threaten you? Do you think he knows about what you did? What you sent me?"

"Maybe. He tried to get me to admit that I knew something. I didn't tell him anything, Bowie. Nothing. I promise. You're safe."

"But you're not. Livia, I'm scared. Can you leave town for a little while? Don't you have a friend who lives in Colorado?"

"I can't leave. You know that. I'm barely making enough money to pay my rent."

"Okay. Maybe I can send you some money. You can call in sick for a while. Just until after I visit the embassy."

"Where will you get this money, sweetheart?"

Mark's loaded. He's always trying to give her expensive gifts—guitars, watches, jewelry he says his ex-wife left and he doesn't want. She's refused everything, but this is different. It's to keep Livia safe. "I'll find a way. You hold tight, okay? I'll call you again soon."

She shivers, wrapping her arms around her chest. Bruce at Livia's apartment, sniffing around. Asking her what she knows. This is bad.

The USB drive Livia mailed her is safely tucked away. The video on it was stomach-churning. A girl she didn't recognize on a hotel bed. Unresponsive but alive. Several male voices in the background. They were watching what happened on the bed.

Laughing.

Bowie couldn't finish watching. She'd gone to the bathroom and thrown up. When she called Jordan's number, someone had told her that he no longer worked at the embassy, had left New Zealand.

She'd been scared then. Maybe she'd gotten him fired with the photo she sent him, the allegations she'd made. She'd decided to wait awhile. Wait until the ambassador was out of town. She should have taken the video to the embassy immediately, not waited until it seemed safe.

She'll tell Suzie about the album later. This is more important.

The Shepherds are leaving on a camping trip tomorrow. She's staying in town to play at the Cat's Meow with Dean. She'll have four whole days alone, without Myra's searching questions. Plenty of time to go to the embassy. Call Suzie. Perform one of her new songs on stage for the first time.

SHE FELL AWAY

That's it! She can have Suzie watch the performance live. That would be the best way to give her the news. Let her see the song first, feel its power.

She won't give her name when she calls the embassy. She'll say she has information to hand over, like Jordan told her to. Then she'll go in person. Tell her story. Hand over the video.

She does a search for the embassy phone number.

Takes a deep breath before she calls.

36

LAKE

It's over. Bowie is gone.

I've been repeating those words to myself endlessly. Tossing in my bed, sheets soaked with sweat. Staring at my face in the mirror and seeing her standing beside me, dripping wet, skin tinged with green. Plastic bottle cap eyes.

Flotsam washed up on a beach someday.

Or lost at sea forever.

I can't hold food down. I'm existing on tea and dry toast. Even Edgar is being nice to me, sensing that I'm not myself. He rubbed up against my legs this morning while I was getting ready for work and stared up at me with a worried look in his yellow eyes.

I'm drowning. My computer looks alien. What is the text cursor trying to tell me? Who made that symbol? It looks like it's growing leaves, dark tendrils starting inside the processor, tapping at my screen, curling inside my head.

She hid for days and then threw herself off a cliff. Left that strange, terse note behind.

BoLoForever. She gave her death a hashtag.

The tendrils of family and friends weren't enough to hold her to this world.

SHE FELL AWAY

Symbols coalesce into words on my screen: **Come and see me when you have a moment.**

It's Samantha. I respond. Wait on the couch outside her office.

She opens the door. "Come in, Lake."

She closes the door, indicates that I should sit on the black leather sofa. She sits in a chair across from me. "How are you feeling?"

I'm losing it. "I'm sad. I still can't believe she's gone."

"How is Suzie Bishop holding up?"

"She's devastated. I'm writing up my report. Bowie can't be declared dead yet, of course. Suzie wants to leave tomorrow. I'll drive her to the airport."

"I know this has been a difficult case for you. I sense you were taking it personally. Maybe it reminded you of something from your past?"

Am I going to be psychoanalyzed again?

"When you become close to a case like this, sometimes it helps to speak to a mental health professional afterward. Our regional psychiatrist will be visiting next week. I strongly urge you to consider scheduling an appointment."

"Thanks. I'm doing okay. I just don't want to accept that she's gone. There's no body for me to repatriate. No death certificate yet."

No physical evidence except a sweatshirt and a very short suicide note. Wouldn't a lyricist have written a song for her own funeral? It was so tense and strange. But it had been her handwriting, the experts had agreed on that.

"Sometimes I think those are the hardest cases. After the tsunami I had recurring nightmares that I was drowning. Underneath the waves I saw them. The lost ones. I knew their faces intimately. I'd returned their personal possessions to their families. A traveling journal with dried flowers between the pages. A linen scarf. Cell phones heavy with happy memories. I'm not saying that I know exactly what you're feeling. I can only tell you my story. I started seeing a therapist and it helped. Eventually, I stopped having the nightmares. There's no shame in seeking help."

"I know. I'll consider it. I just need a few days." I've trained my whole life for this. I'm an Olympic-level survivalist. Shove it all into the back of my mind, lock the door. Don't let anyone in. I'll go back to being the Lake I was before I took that call from Suzie. I've done it before.

"Is there anything else you want to tell me about the case? Maybe something you didn't put in your official notes?" Samantha probes.

"We still don't know where she was hiding out between the time Bruce died and when she jumped off the cliff."

"Maybe she was camping out at the beach. It's an isolated spot."

"When I can't sleep at night I come up with scenarios where she faked her own suicide. She had so much to live for."

"And she had a demanding stage mom who turned her life into a pressure cooker. This wasn't a spur-of-the-moment decision. The confrontation with Bruce pushed her over the knife's edge she'd been balancing on for years. She was conflicted; it took her days to decide, but ultimately, she jumped. You want her to still be alive, but you can't let that take you away from the urgent, important, and meaningful work that we do. Trust me, the work will save you. Keep you moving forward."

"I let this case under my skin." I square my shoulders. "I'll get my head back in the game. I promise."

Samantha smiles. "Why don't you take a few days off after the weekend? Take a trip to the South Island. You haven't visited Milford Sound yet, right?"

"Not yet. Robin Garcia invited me to travel to Martinborough with her and her girlfriend."

"It's lovely there. We'll call it sick leave."

"I'm not going to leave you high and dry. Didn't you just tell me to keep working?"

"That approach worked for me, but maybe it's not for you. At least take a day or two to think things over and decide what's best for you. What you need right now."

"Thanks, Samantha."

"You know my door is always open."

37

BOWIE

The Shepherds left an hour ago for the South Island.
Bowie's supposed to go and stay at Daphne's, but she decided not to. The album is nearly finished. This will give Mark and her time to work without all the sneaking around. She can even stay at his house for a few days. She trusts him now. He's never once made a move on her, even if she does catch him staring at her sometimes.

She can ask him about sending money to Livia.

When she called the embassy yesterday, she kept getting stuck in an automated loop, until finally a U.S. Marine answered the phone. He told her to just come to the embassy gates. They would send someone out to meet with her. They wouldn't turn her away.

She'll do that before she goes to Mark's house. She sits on Dulcie's grave. Calls Daphne and tells her that she decided to go on the camping trip after all.

Freedom. She's nervous about going to the embassy but excited about completing the album, performing with Dean.

She's about to walk to her car when someone pushes aside her leafy covering and invades her sanctuary.

At first she doesn't recognize the tall man with the shaggy hair and purple shadows under his eyes. "Excuse me!"

"Bowie." His voice breaks. He jams his hands inside the pocket of his white hoodie, hunches his shoulders.

"Bruce?"

She scoots backward and hits hard marble. There's nowhere to run.

She's trapped.

38

LAKE

"Lake, can I talk to you for a minute?"

Judith's eyes are troubled, her hands twisting in the pleats of her navy-blue skirt.

"Of course." I motion her toward the chair in front of my desk. "You heard the news?"

"Yes. Poor Bowie. It's so devastating. I wish she'd reached out for help. Her host mother was a grief counselor, after all. Why didn't she talk to her?"

I slump in my chair. "I know. She was hiding while we were searching for her. That's the thing I can't get past. That she must have known her mother was here, desperate to find her. The weight of her grief about her best friend's death in Las Vegas, the guilt she felt after Bruce Walter died, it must have been too heavy, too much to bear. I feel like . . ." The words stick in my throat. "I feel like we failed her. I failed her. Samantha said I should take some time off work."

"I've always thought it must be difficult to be an ACS officer. Especially if things go wrong for one of your Amcits."

"I've had proud moments in my career, when I really felt like I was helping people. But this . . . this just feels so wrong. Such a young, talented soul snuffed out."

"That's what I came to talk to you about." She glances at my open office door. "In private."

"Is Ambassador Hunt back from his Napier trip?"

She nods. "He's at a reception this afternoon. Lake, I don't know if I should tell you this, or not. It won't change anything. It's just I couldn't believe what I was hearing. I don't know if I can work for that man anymore." Her lip trembles. "I love this job. I don't want to lose it. But I have to live with myself, don't I?"

I get up and close my office door. "What's going on?"

"I put a call through to Glen Walter for the ambassador this morning." She's whispering, leaning forward, her gaze intent. "As I was delivering some paperwork, I overheard the ambassador talking about Bowie. He said . . . he said she'd stay quiet now. There was nothing to worry about. What happened in Vegas stayed in Vegas."

My stomach heaves. "What the hell does that mean?"

Judith holds my gaze. "The ambassador attended a conference in Las Vegas a little under two years ago. He had me make two separate schedules. One for him, and one for his wife, who stayed in Wellington to host a charity event. He paid for rooms in two separate hotels. One at the Marriott, on his official schedule that I gave to his wife, and one at The Trophy. I saw his credit card statement when I processed his reimbursement voucher."

"Does he always have two schedules when he travels?"

"Only that time and another time when he attended a military event in Bangkok. Jordan was his control officer for the Bangkok trip. I assumed he wanted two separate schedules, two hotel rooms, so that his wife didn't know what he was up to. The trip to Vegas is troubling to me now because of this whole thing with Bowie's best friend dying after a night at The Trophy. I don't know if there's anything there . . . and obviously Bowie is gone either way, but I wanted to tell someone."

I drum my fingers on my desk, my mind marching to the staccato beat. The ambassador at The Trophy. Florica's death.

Bowie luring Bruce to New Zealand. The incriminating photo in Jordan Singer's deleted files.

"I'm glad you told me."

"It might be nothing . . . obviously I have no evidence of wrongdoing. I want to keep my job, so please don't let this get back to him."

"Of course. I completely understand."

She stands. "I'd better go back."

"I promised to drive Suzie Bishop to the airport, to see her off."

"That's kind of you."

I walk Judith to the elevators.

My mind whirs, slotting back into investigative mode. The shock on Bowie's face in the Public Affairs footage when she met the ambassador.

As if she'd seen a ghost, Alejandro had said. I'd assumed it was disgust at the way he was flirting with Clementine. Was it more than that? Could she have met him before?

The conversation Judith overheard. *What happened in Vegas stayed in Vegas.*

So what had happened in Vegas? Had Ambassador Hunt somehow been involved in Florica's death? Judith obviously suspected something like that. It had been a huge risk for her to relay the conversation to me. She'd been here when Jordan Singer was curtailed. She doesn't want to be next.

This case won't leave me alone. I'm a hunting dog who cornered a porcupine. Barbed, stinging questions left embedded in my mind.

39

BOWIE

"Bowie. Please don't run away. I just need to talk to you."

"Are you going to murder me, too?"

He tears at his hair. "I didn't murder Florica, Bowie. I want answers about that night just as much as you do. That's why I'm here."

"What was she to you? A one-night stand that went wrong. Almost got you in trouble until Daddy bought off the police."

He doesn't look like the Bruce she's met before. The golden boy sports god. His eyes are rimmed with red. There's stubble on his chin. "My father is a monster." He clenches his fists.

He has her hemmed in with the stone mausoleum at her back. She'll have to make a break for it. Maybe try to lure him closer and then knee him in the balls? Then run like hell to her car and hope he doesn't follow.

He's a professional athlete with swift reflexes, but he's injured. How much has he recovered from his season-ending knee injury? She should probably try to kick him in the left knee.

"Yeah. Glen's a monster. So are you."

He takes a deep breath, like he's gearing up to run a sprint across a football field. "I could never live with myself if I let my dad and Colgan and the other assholes get away with what they've done. I didn't know. Bowie." He takes a step toward her. Sees the look on her face. Steps backward. "I swear I didn't know."

"Know what?"

"That my dad caters to high-roller assholes. He has Colgan procure them anything they want. Drugs. Girls. Drugged girls."

A pulse hammers in Bowie's ears. He's describing the video Livia sent her. "Drugged girls?"

"Florica. They drugged her. Jesus. It makes me sick."

"So you're sweet and innocent, is that it?"

"Fuck." He clenches his jaw, kicks a pile of leaves. "I knew you wouldn't believe me. But I had to try. I was complicit; they used me to get to Florica. The guilt is eating me up. I can't sleep. I can't bring her back."

"You visited Livia. You threatened her."

"I didn't threaten her!" He's trying to stay calm but there's violence in his voice, his clenched fists. "We're on the same side, Bowie. I don't know how to make you believe me. I visited Livia because I heard Colgan say that she was acting strange, that she might know something. I waited outside her door after our conversation, to see if she contacted anyone. I heard her ask you if you'd received her package."

An intense cramp of nausea hits Bowie's stomach. She hates Bruce Walter. He murdered Lo. He's saying that he's innocent but how can she trust him?

"Bowie." He swipes his fist over his eyes like maybe he's about to cry. "My night with Florica was a dream. You saw us. She was so smart, so gorgeous. I fell so damn hard. We danced, drank, we were having a blast. She said she had to go home, that her mom had a strict curfew. I took her down to the valet and called her an Uber. I was too drunk to drive. If only I'd been sober. I could have made sure she made it safely inside her house."

She hates him, but she's beginning to believe him. He's a football player, not an actor. His words, the anguish on his face, it all rings true. It's like she's outside of herself right now, looking

SHE FELL AWAY

down at this scene from the vantage point of the angel with the broken wing. She's writing a song about love at first sight. A son who discovers his father is a killer. A broken man who can't bring his love back.

"So what do you think happened to Lo?" she asks quietly.

"I don't have any proof but I think maybe Colgan was waiting for her at her house. He brought her back to the hotel to serve her up to a VIP who requested her for the night. My guess is she had a bad reaction to the drugs they used and ended up dead. Colgan covered it up. Brought her back. He had her key so there was no forced entry. He gave her the fentanyl-laced pills. Made it look like she was alone when she overdosed. My dad paid off the medical examiner and the police. Case closed. Like I said, my dad is a monster. I think he always felt like a failure because his football career went up in flames. Controlling the casino, catering to influential men, is a sick power trip."

His breath releases in a shuddering sound that breaks her heart. "I ditched training camp; I was sidelined anyway. I flew here to find you. To ask you about the package Livia mailed. Was it evidence, Bowie? Proof we can use to bring my dad down?" He rips some ivy off a marble column. "Because I'm going to get him, Bowie. He's my dad but I'm going to put that fucker in prison for what he's done."

This could be a trap. Glen sends Bruce here to track down the evidence. Once she tells him about it, he'll silence her, like he silenced Lo.

"Don't do this for me. Do it for Florica. For the other girls who will be drugged and harmed if we don't stop them. Tell me what Livia sent you."

"Yes, Bowie." The voice sounds nearby, low and mocking. "Tell us what she mailed you."

Bowie gasps. It's Ryan Colgan. He has one hand at his waist, pulling back his black trench coat. She catches a glimpse of a pistol handle.

"I knew I couldn't trust you," she spits.

Bruce rounds on Colgan, fists raised in a boxer's stance. "We're not together. He must have followed me here."

"You're not exactly stealthy. Why couldn't you just leave it alone? Guess I should thank you, though. I wasn't sure Livia had any proof until you figured it out."

"It's not proof," Bowie says, her mind scrambling for an angle. "She mailed me a flash drive but the video was too grainy."

"I don't believe you."

"If I had proof why haven't I done anything with it?"

"I'll need to see that video," Colgan says icily.

"There's more proof out there," says Bruce. "You can't keep something this bad hidden forever. Why don't you turn witness against him? Save yourself."

Colgan's eyes blaze. "You're a fucking traitor. His own son. This is gonna break his heart."

"You're tied to him. If he goes down, so do you."

"I'll never let that happen. Glen employed me when no one else would. He paid for my daughter's heart transplant. I owe him my life. And my loyalty." He shakes his head. "Now what the fuck am I going to do with you two?"

Bowie's wondering if she can lunge for the gun at his waist. Colgan's so tall and solid. She's afraid she'd bounce off him like a Ping-Pong ball hitting a brick wall.

Bruce catches her staring at Colgan and shakes his head at her. "Let's make a bargain. You allow Bowie to walk away from here, and I'll go home with you. I'll promise not to pursue this any further."

Colgan laughs. "Really? After what I just heard? I don't think so. I need that flash drive, and Bowie's laptop so I can wipe it, and then I'll decide what I'm going to do about you two."

A coldness sweeps over Bowie, as though she's turned into a stone angel.

As though she's already dead.

Colgan has a weapon, but it's two against one. Bowie catches Bruce's eye. He gives her a slight nod. They need to stall for time. Find a way to disarm him. Her mind hits a blank wall when she tries to think past that. They'll do what they have to do.

"I'll bring you the flash drive," she says, injecting a quaver into her voice. "I'll keep quiet. We can pretend none of this ever happened."

"Oh, I know you'll keep quiet, Bowie. I have enough dirt on your mom to ensure that."

"I'm sure you do. She isn't exactly the poster child for clean living. You said you have a daughter. I didn't know that."

"I keep my private life private."

"But doesn't it make you sick? Would you want your daughter to be one of Glen's victims?"

"These are girls no one cares about."

"I loved Lo," Bowie says harshly. "And you took her from me."

"Regrettable. She was beautiful. We just wanted her passive. Must have been a bad batch."

Bowie doesn't think; she lunges toward him, fists raised. He smacks her across the cheek with the butt of the gun, hard. Her cheek and nose explode with pain. She holds her nose, blood streaming down her hands. It might be broken. The pain is like nothing she's ever felt before. So intense she might faint.

"Just let her go, okay?" Bruce pleads. "Let her go, and I'll come with you. I'll swear to keep my mouth shut. I won't take this any further."

"I can't let her go, not until I get my hands on what Livia sent."

"And then you'll kill us both."

"Maybe." He shoves Bowie against Bruce, who catches her in his arms. She rests her bloody hands against his chest, finding her balance.

"Start walking." Colgan marches them deeper into a wooded area. A branch snags at her necklace, snaps it from her neck.

They're going to die.

When they're hidden enough to his liking, Colgan points the

gun on them. "Start talking, Bowie. Tell me where to find the flash drive. Tell me what's on it."

Bruce tenses his thigh muscles. She knows what it means. He's going to make a move.

Her job is to keep Colgan distracted. Keep him talking.

"Okay. I'll tell you everything. Livia recorded a video off one of the high roller's laptops. It shows a young woman on a bed. She's been drugged. You can hear Glen's voice in the background. Several other men, too." Her voice begins to shake. "I couldn't keep watching it."

She infuses her voice with loathing, spitting the words. Willing him to keep his attention on her and ignore the way Bruce is inching closer to him. "You and your boss are sick, disgusting monsters. You're going to prison. I made copies of the video. It's in the Cloud. You can't make it go away. I already met with the FBI at the embassy. They have the video."

She hadn't made any copies. She'd been planning to hand the drive over to the Feds. She hadn't wanted its evil to taint her laptop, taint her.

"You're lying. You said earlier you hadn't done anything with it."

"Or I'm telling the truth. I gave the video to the embassy. Maybe Glen's friend Ambassador Hunt turned on him. Maybe he turned on you. To save himself."

Colgan hesitates for a second. She's finally managed to shake him.

Bruce rushes Colgan. Even though he's injured, he's an athlete in the prime of his life. He knocks the gun from Colgan's hand and wrestles him to the ground. They grapple wildly, both attempting to recapture the gun.

Colgan reaches it first.

He presses the barrel against Bruce's temple. "Don't make another move or you die."

Bruce freezes.

Bowie grabs a rock and heaves it at Colgan. It hits the back of his head. He only laughs. "You'll need something a little bigger than that."

She doesn't have any other weapons. He has a gun. He holds all the cards.

Bruce's gaze finds Bowie. His eyes are desperate. She sees one of his hands ball into a fist. He gives her a tiny nod. He's going to make another move.

He's going to get shot.

"Bowie," Bruce shouts as he twists his body to the right and grabs Colgan's collar. "Run!"

40

LAKE

Suzie smells like stale tobacco and grief.

We're sitting in my car in the airport parking lot. It's cramped, airless. She's bent over, with one hand on the door handle and the other clutching Bowie's Cure sweatshirt like a child with a favorite blanket.

"Suzie," I say gently. "Your flight's leaving soon."

She stares vacantly at me, mascara running in black rivulets down her cheeks. "I can't leave her here. I have nothing. Nothing without her. I have this." Her fingers convulse around the sweatshirt. "I have this." Her other hand wraps around the glass vial hung around her neck. "I have a gaping chest wound instead of a heart."

What can I say to her? "I'm sorry, Suzie. So very sorry."

"After Florica died, Bowie was lost to me for months. She stayed in her room crying and playing her guitar, writing sad songs. She loved that damn guitar more than she loved me, I think. I tried to make her see a therapist. She went to one session and refused to go to another. What could I do? The therapist told me that it was healthy for her to process her pain through lyrics. But the things she wrote scared me. After a while, she emerged from her room. She wasn't the same Bowie, but she was back in the land of the living. That's when she became fixated on applying for Florica's exchange program. Coming here. And I wanted so badly to make her smile, to hear her sing a light, happy song again."

Her hand drops to her lap. "When I want something, I make it happen. I made this happen. I sent her to the other side of the world. So far away from me. Did she hate me? Did I push her too hard? She must have known I was here in Wellington; it was all over the news. And yet she remained silent. And then she . . . and then she died. She left me all alone."

I've been here before, I think. Desolation. Isolation. Guilt. "In the note, Bowie said she tricked Bruce into coming to New Zealand. Whatever she told him brought him here. She wanted revenge badly enough to engineer a plot to kill him."

"My baby, a murderer. Jesus Christ. What was going through her mind?"

"We can't know that. Something happened in the cemetery. Maybe he discovered her plan and lashed out, injuring her. She ran. He got drunk. When he ended up dying, Bowie was . . . in a dark place. It's not your fault."

"Isn't it? All those songs in her notebooks, scribbled fury, lashing out at me. She hated me. I know she did."

"She was eighteen, Suzie. You can't take everything she wrote literally. You said she was using those notebooks as therapy, allowing the bad thoughts to tumble onto the page so they didn't fester inside her mind. When she wrote that final note, she was only thinking about Florica. She wanted to follow her to the other side."

I've been here before.

A memory clamors, backlit by harsh hospital lights. Flimsy cotton nightgown tied with knots. Chemical taste in my mouth. Cramping stomach.

She's coming around.

Before the lights . . . a small room with cold white tile. Cramming acrid pills into my mouth with no thought but deep, blank despair.

Face bloated and unrecognizable.

Think of the pain as a tiger, crouching just behind your eyes. It's separate from you, fully distinct. It can be hunted down. Eliminated.

When? *When.*

"Lake? Are you okay?" Suzie's holding my hand. Her black nail polish is chipped away, the ends of her nails ragged.

"Sorry." When these memories surface, they don't care where I am, what I'm doing. They pound my skull from the inside. Bowie's death is making it worse. I've been taking sleeping pills, but they don't work. I haven't slept more than a few hours at a time since I heard the news.

I can't trust you, memories.

Suzie was the one who crammed pills down her mouth, her head resting on a porcelain toilet seat. She's the one who had her stomach pumped. I visited her in the hospital. That was her gown, tied in knots.

What kind of pills, Suzie?

Lots of pills.

Her face is puffy, and her eyes swim with tears. "You loved her, too, didn't you? Even though you never met her. That was her superpower. Everyone who heard her sing fell in love with her. You should have seen all the sick comments from dirty old men. That's why I was so worried that someone had abducted her."

"I imagine that fame takes its toll."

"But it's worth the price. That's what I told her. She was my shining star. What does all that star power matter now? I don't care that her songs and videos are trending. I don't care that every reporter wants to interview me. Fucking Lance Booker called me last night. Said he'd written a duet for us to record about Bowie. Said he'd revive my career. Jesus. What a leech. A month ago I would have jumped at that chance."

I'm glad to hear that she doesn't want to capitalize on Bowie's death. "Too many brilliant artists die young."

"Why did Bowie have to die to make me famous again? Why is the world so fucked up? Why do we dwell in the darkness? Why does it call to us? Why did Bowie listen to it . . . and not to me . . ." She breaks down into wrenching sobs, her forehead braced against the car door, face turned away from me.

I rub her back lightly. There's nothing else I can do or say. Her flight leaves in forty-five minutes. She may miss it, but flights can be rebooked.

Lives can't.

She sits up with the jerky movements of a marionette, rips the necklace from her throat, holds it out to me. "I want you to have this. Scatter Florica's ashes in the sea. It's what Bowie would have wanted."

I nod. My eyes burn, and I can't speak around the wad of steel wool crammed down my throat.

"Will you keep in touch, Lake?"

I nod again. I mean it. I've come to care for this messy, complicated woman who reminds me of my mother. Flawed heroines. The only ones allowed in my book.

She rummages through her purse and finds a pack of tissue. Blows her nose. Uses the visor mirror to wipe away mascara from under her eyes.

"What will you do now?" My voice an unfamiliar croak.

"I don't know."

"I'll be here for you, if you need to talk."

"You've been wonderful this whole time. You've been my rock. I'll be following your career. When you become an ambassador, you can invite me to come and play a set at your Fourth of July party."

Small chance of that. But it's good to hear her talking about the future. I'm afraid for her.

"You're strong, Suzie."

"I'm hashtag rock-'n-roll." She makes the metal sign of the

horns with both hands. Puts on a pair of aviator sunglasses. "And rock-'n-roll it will survive."

At home, with Edgar curled on my lap, I finally call my mom back.

"Took you long enough."

"Sorry. It's been insane here."

"I saw on the news about that dead NFL player in Wellington. And the missing teenager."

"She committed suicide."

"Do you ever think that maybe this job is just too difficult?"

"It's not like I'm a first responder or something. Death cases don't happen every day."

"I worry about your mental health."

"You know what this job gives me? A new home every few years. I don't have to see the same people day after day. I'm anonymous."

"Oh, Lake," her voice breaks. "I'm the reason you want to keep running, aren't I?"

I've blamed her for a long time. For the shame instilled by The Fold. For refusing to tell me why she decided to leave so abruptly. I was bruised, broken, hurting from wounds that no one could see.

"It's more complicated than that. Mom, do you ever hear anything about Charity? Is she still living at The Fold?"

"I don't know. I hear most of the young people have left. You remember Sister Laura? She left with nothing, like we did. She's in California now. She writes to me sometimes. She gave me the contact for an online support group for former members. Maybe I should forward it to you?"

"Okay." Maybe Charity made it out. Maybe she's a member of the support group. I'd like to think she's alive and healing.

"Come home for Heron's wedding. I don't like talking about

this on the phone. I want to see you, Lake. We all do. We miss you so much."

"I don't know how long I'll be here. I can't buy my ticket until I know where I'm buying it from."

"Fine." I can hear the guilt trip she's biting back. I appreciate the effort. "I read some articles about Bowie Bishop. Clicked over to her Instagram. She was such a beautiful girl, with so much to live for. Just like you, Lake. You don't post anything online for me to read."

"I keep things private."

"This Bowie girl lived online. Posting every day. It's strange that she took her own life. Right before she disappeared, her posts were more uplifting. She was excited about writing new songs. Thanking her fans for being there for her. It was all very cheerful. But I suppose that's the dual-edged sword of social media, isn't it? We post one thing and live another."

Uplifting. Cheerful. Hardly the adjectives I would use to describe Bowie's online presence. "You really think her posts were cheerful?"

"Well, she had more good days than sad ones lately."

"What did you say about new songs?"

"There was a post about how she was writing new songs for her fans and she would share them soon."

My heart starts beating faster. Good days and sad days. It makes sense. "Mom, can I call you back later?"

"We haven't even talked that long."

"I know, but you just gave me an idea."

"Okay, but Lake—"

"Mom, I have to go." I end the call. Why didn't I see it before?

I study the printout of the suicide note I stuck on the wall.

#BoLoForever

My breathing quickens. I pull up her Instagram account, scroll back through the posts. There's a pattern I didn't see before. Some of the posts have hashtags, dozens of them, and some have none.

The selfies of Bowie, the ones clearly taken in Wellington—I can assume those were her actual posts—don't use hashtags. The ones that sound more generic, less Bowie-like, have twenty, sometimes thirty.

Suzie in my car. *I'm hashtag rock-'n-roll.*

The suicide note has a hashtag.

Bowie didn't write it.

41

BOWIE

Bowie runs to the car she has hiding in the dead-end alleyway, her breath coming in gasps, nose throbbing, the gash on her cheek bleeding.

Her nose isn't broken, at least she doesn't think so.

Think. Pull yourself together. Bruce won't be able to hold Colgan long.

She needs someplace safe to hide. Someone she can trust. She smashes her regular cell phone with a rock so that Colgan can't track her and throws it into a nearby garbage can. She still has the burner phone that Mark gave her to use, but no one else has that number. She turns the key in the ignition, and the distinctive sound of the motor tells her where to go, whom to trust.

Her mind is dull on the drive. She's careful not to speed, careful not to attract any attention. She prays that Bruce was able to overpower Colgan. Maybe everything will be okay. They'll do this together. Gather evidence against Glen and Colgan. Do whatever it takes to stop them.

All this time she'd thought Bruce had harmed Lo when he was a good guy. He was willing to testify against his own father. He'd sacrificed himself to give Bowie a chance to escape, when he could have made a deal with Colgan, her instead of him.

Before, when she visited Mark at night, she'd parked on this quiet, abandoned side street. She usually walks down to the beach using her cell phone as a flashlight. The stairs leading up to the back of his house from the beach are steep and rickety. She'd enjoyed the danger of it, the illicit thrill.

Afternoon shadows drag long fingers across the car. She's waiting until it's dark. No one can witness her here.

Thankfully, she has some granola bars in the glove compartment and a bottle of water. She cleans herself up as best she can. Her nose is swollen and bruised, but the bleeding has stopped. Maybe she should go to the police. Would they believe her? Protect her? Or should she go to the embassy? Colgan could be waiting for her. She can't do anything predictable. Wait him out. Hide for one night. Then reassess her options in the morning.

The one house on this street is boarded up and half consumed by blackberries gone thorny and suffocating. A jogger appears in the distance. Bowie ducks down, heart pounding, until they pass the car and disappear into the overgrown ghost of a path that leads down to the beach.

Mark will hide her tonight. Then tomorrow, if they can find out who won the fight, she'll plan her next move. If Colgan hurt Bruce, she'll have to stay hidden. He'll come after her next. He won't stop until he has the flash drive. If only she'd gone to the embassy gates earlier, demanded to see the FBI. Maybe they would have given her asylum, like in the movies. But Ambassador Hunt is there. Wouldn't he have the power to shut her up? Make her accusations go away?

It's all a tangled mess. At least Colgan won't have any idea where to find her. No one knows about the album she's recording with Mark except Livia, and she hadn't given Livia any details.

But Colgan's a professional; he'll track her down eventually.

Fear and hunger tie her stomach into knots. She has a blinding headache. Wild, disordered thoughts on a loop. Her fingers reach for the vial around her neck, and it's gone. Lo's ashes stayed behind in the cemetery. She's just another dead girl. Another name on a headstone.

Finally, night falls. On the walk down to the beach, she trips over a stone and falls to one knee. Another bruise for her collection. She walks along the sandy beach, waves pounding the shore beside her. The moon is sullen tonight, wrapped in clouds, sulking.

She creeps up the winding wooden staircase that scales the cliff, watching for any movement above her. She reaches the wall safely. Slides the hidden panel open. Punches in the code. Everything is silent. Mark always stays up late; he's probably in the recording studio. She texts him but he doesn't respond.

"Bowie? What the fuck?" he says when she opens the inner door to the recording studio. "I didn't know you were coming tonight."

"I . . . didn't either."

"What's wrong with your face?" He rips off his headset and rushes toward her, placing his hands on her shoulders. "What happened?"

"I need help."

"I'll drive you to a hospital."

"I won't be safe there."

"A police station?"

"I'm not safe anywhere. Can you hide me tonight?" The tears come then.

He puts his arms around her. She rests her head on his chest.

"Shhh." He strokes her hair, the back of her neck. "It's okay. I got you."

"Have your staff left?"

"They're long gone. You're safe now. Tell me what's going on."

The story pours out. Something stops her from telling him about where she stashed the package Livia sent her, or what was on the video. "If Colgan killed Bruce, he'll be hunting for me next. After he realizes that I lied about backing up the video."

"What's on the video, exactly?"

"It's better you don't know."

"Okay. I'll use my imagination. It's something about your best friend, Lo, the one you wrote the album for."

"Yes. It's about Lo."

"Don't worry, Bowie. I'll keep you safe. I won't let anything happen to you. You can hide here tonight. We'll figure out what to do in the morning."

"I'm sorry. I didn't know who else to turn to. I wasn't thinking clearly. He'd probably assume I'd go to the police, or the embassy. I couldn't risk doing anything predictable. I don't think there's any way he could track me here. I smashed my regular phone and threw it away, and no one has my other number except you. I haven't told anyone about our recording sessions. I don't want to put you in danger, too."

"You did the right thing. Don't worry about me. I can defend myself. You'll stay here as long as you need to, Bowie. Do you hear me? I'm not going to let him hurt you. I have an excellent security system. You're the only one who knows how to bypass it."

"If he finds a way to track me here tonight, you need to be able to deny that I'm here. Can you hide me somewhere?"

He nods. "Yeah, I get that. Okay. I have somewhere for you to hide. But what about your injuries? Are any of them serious? I don't want you to bleed to death or anything."

"I don't think my nose is broken. It looks worse than it is. I have a headache."

"Are you sure it's nothing worse?"

"Yeah. Oh, wait. Mark, I have another favor to ask you."

"Anything."

"Could I borrow like a thousand bucks? It's not for me. It's for Lo's mom, Livia. I'm worried about her. I think she should leave Vegas for a few weeks."

"No problem at all. Consider it done. I'll have my assistant send her the money. Come on." He takes her by the hand and leads her down the hall and up the stairs to the basement bedroom. "No one knows about this, not even my household staff or my security guards."

He walks to the center of the room. Pulls back the sheepskin rug. He shows her the outline of a hidden door. She never would have seen it. He pulls on a thin piece of wire, and the door raises from the floor. A stepladder leads down into darkness.

"Climb down the ladder. There's a small chamber—an old bomb shelter that was here when I bought the property. It's totally secure. There's plumbing and a kitchenette stocked with food. First-aid supplies. I'll come back as soon as I hear word about Bruce or Ryan Colgan. Oh, here." He walks to the bathroom and returns with a plastic pill bottle. "For your headache."

"Do you have a spare phone charger? My battery is almost dead."

"There's no cell reception in the room. It's very basic. But it will keep you hidden."

"How will I know it's you tomorrow?"

"I'll knock six times before I open the door."

She takes a shaky breath and lets it out. "Thank you."

"Of course. I'd do anything for you. The album's not quite finished, right? Maybe you can write some lyrics tonight. Here." He hands her a notebook and pen off his desk with a lopsided smile. "Use the darkness, Bowie. Use your fear. Transform it into art."

He hands her down into the gaping hole in his floor. "You'll be safe here." He presses a button on the ceiling and faint lighting illuminates the steps leading down. "Don't forget, I'll knock six times before I open the door again."

She climbs down the stepladder carefully, wincing from the pain in her nose.

The room is small. The walls are granite. There's a metal toilet, a small sink with no mirror above it. She finds a cabinet filled with dry and canned goods. She rips open a tin of beans and eats it cold. For a rich guy his bomb shelter is surprisingly bare bones.

She would have expected him to have a memory foam mattress and expensive cotton sheets, not this creaky old metal cot with a lumpy mattress.

She can't help thinking it looks like a prison cell.

Hopefully, she'll have to endure it for only one night. Bruce is young and strong. Maybe he punched Colgan, knocked him out. Maybe the police are already searching for her.

Everything will be fine tomorrow.

She'll go back to the cemetery and find Lo. This time she'll do what she's been meaning to do. Find a beautiful beach, sprinkle her ashes into the water. She'll find her resting place in the restless waves of the country she longed to visit.

42

BOWIE

Bowie's been waiting for Mark all day.

Why hasn't he come yet?

She paces around the small room, imagining all kinds of scenarios. Colgan tracked her here somehow. He's up there, searching for her. It's only a matter of time before he finds her hiding place. The trapdoor under the rug.

She strains her ears, searching for sounds.

She thinks she hears faint footsteps. Wind howling outside.

No one comes.

She doesn't have a watch and her cell phone is dead. There's no clock in here. No windows to judge the passage of time.

She eats more canned food. Drinks a bottle of water and uses the metal toilet.

Where the fuck is Mark?

Finally, she falls asleep on the lumpy mattress.

She's awoken by knocking. Where is she? Disoriented, she rubs her eyes. Fuck. That hurts. Her nose is tender and swollen.

Six knocks. *Mark*. The door in the ceiling opens, and Mark climbs down the ladder.

Bowie throws off the covers and gets out of bed. She's still wearing the leggings and sweatshirt she wore yesterday. Her mouth is gummy and dry. "What time is it?"

"Sorry. I forgot I had a meeting scheduled in Featherston all day yesterday. I just got home."

"Well? Any news about Bruce?"

He scrubs a hand through his hair. "It's bad, Bowie."

"How bad?"

"He's dead. The news is saying it's most likely accidental. He died in his Airbnb from inhaling vomit."

"Yeah, I don't think so. Colgan killed him. He must have made it look like it was accidental." She collapses to a seat on the bed. Tears flood her eyes. "Poor Bruce."

"So this Colgan guy, he's capable of anything."

"He'll be hunting for me right now. He wants the video Livia mailed to me."

"So maybe we should give it to him?"

"What?" Bowie shakes her head. "We can't do that. It's the . . ." She'd been about to tell him it was the only copy. Something stops her. "We can't trust him. If I give him the video, he's still going to want me out of the way. I'm a liability for him and Glen now. I'm a loose end."

Mark sits beside her on the cot. "You honestly think he would kill you?"

"I have zero doubt about it."

"Then Bowie, you have to hide here longer." He strokes a strand of hair off her cheek.

She freezes at his touch. He drops his hand.

"Hide just until he leaves New Zealand. Then you can go to the authorities."

"Okay. Yes. I'll stay here for one more night." It's not so bad. It's better than being dead. "But everyone will be worried about me. They'll search for me."

"And you'll be safe and sound. Waiting to reappear. Think of it as a writing retreat. I'll bring you your guitar and more notebooks. Those fountain pens you like. These walls are thick, so no one will hear you playing or singing."

"Can you bring me some fresh clothes?"

"Of course. Are you craving any food? I'll bring you whatever you want. I'll monitor the news for you. You can rework the lyrics on 'Drops of Rain' and write the final song. The album closer must be perfect. Always leave them wanting more. If we have to wait a little while to record the last songs, so be it. Keeping you safe, that's priority number one. Then breaking you into the charts. Then world superstardom."

"I don't think I want to be a superstar."

"Sure you do. And it will be on your terms, not your mom's." He smiles reassuringly. Squeezes her hand. "Don't worry about anything."

"Bruce is dead." Her jaw clenches. "It's my fault."

"Not your fault. He was the one who came after you. No one would blame you."

"My mom's going to be so worried about me. I wish there was a way to send a message to her. Let her know I'm okay."

"Absolutely not." His eyes go hard. "There can be no links between us yet. Not until you're safe from Colgan. That's the only way this will work. You told me you never told anyone about the album, about collaborating with me. That's true, right?"

"Yes. I mentioned the album to Livia, but I never mentioned you."

His shoulders drop. "Excellent. Then you'll be safe from Colgan here. Think about if there's anything you want. I mean, besides your Gibson. I'll send it down in a few minutes."

He climbs back up the ladder.

"Mark?"

He stops. Angles his head down.

"Thanks for hiding me."

"Anything for you, superstar."

43

LAKE

Jordan Singer has consistently refused my calls—so this time I use subterfuge.

One of the officers who was in my A-100 orientation class is posted to Guadalajara. She told me Jordan is on holiday at a beach resort and gave me the name of the hotel. I call, tell them that it's an emergency, that I have to WhatsApp video with Jordan on urgent government business and he's not answering.

An accommodating staff member hands him the phone.

"Jordan, hi."

"Lake. What the fuck? I told you not to contact me again." He squints. "You're a redhead."

"And you're wearing a Hawaiian shirt with too many buttons undone."

"I'm on vacation." He lifts what looks like a margarita. "Isla Holbox. You can't drive a car on this island, but there's all these golf carts running around . . . kind of defeats the purpose."

"I won't take more than a few minutes of your time. Did you hear about Bowie Bishop?"

"Yeah." He sucks down more of his drink. "Suicide. What a tragedy. Another death case for you."

"But no body."

"New Zealand waters are known for a high rate of unrecovered casualties. The case is closed. Why are you calling?"

"There are a few things still bothering me."

"Just let it go, Lake. Let's bond over Welly for a few minutes, slap each other a virtual high five, and you go back to living in paradise and I'll order two more of these margaritas. Deal?"

"No deal. I'm in too deep now. I want answers."

"You have your answer."

"I'm not convinced she wrote the suicide note. I think someone else did. They're either covering up a murder or an abduction. She could still be out there, Jordan. She could still be alive. Help me figure this out. Put the pieces together."

"You're grasping at straws, Lake."

"Please tell me what you know. Or how about this. I'll tell you what I think, and you nod if I'm on the right track?"

"Shoot. I shouldn't have gotten so drunk that I didn't hang up on you." He wipes his brow with the back of his hand. "Five minutes. My wife will be back from her massage soon. You talk. I listen."

"The ambassador was staying at The Trophy casino around the same time Florica Baciu died. Maybe Bowie met him there. She meets him again at the arts festival and takes a photo of him making out with an exchange student in the garden. Maybe she thought he had something to do with Florica's alleged murder. Maybe she met with you, showed you the incriminating photo, and said she'd use it as blackmail if you didn't help her investigate your boss. He got wind of it and had you curtailed."

He doesn't have to nod. I see it in the widening of his eyes. The gulp he takes from his drink to cover it. "You've been busy."

"Am I on the right track?"

"Here's the deal." He puts the phone right in front of his face. I can see his pores, the sweat on his brow, grains of sand stuck to his hair. "I met with Bowie and she told me about the photo, but she wasn't going to blackmail me with it. She wanted me to set up a meeting with an FBI agent. She said she might have knowledge of crimes committed against Florica, and other young girls, by Glen Walter and his son, Bruce, at the casino. She said maybe the ambassador was involved, but she had no proof of anything yet. I think she was waiting for it to be mailed to her by Florica's mother."

"Did you set up the meeting?"

"She was going to contact me when she had hard evidence. I never heard back from her. She emailed me the photo of the ambassador and Clementine. I have no idea how the ambassador found the photo, but he did. He assumed I was going to use it against him, report him to Washington. I hadn't decided what to do yet. Next thing I know, there's some bullshit story about sexual harassment complaints against me from locally employed staff and I'm on a plane out of Wellington."

"We recovered the photo from your deleted files. This is a clear case of retaliation. Why didn't you go to the OIG? Retaliation is easier to prove than the mishap itself."

"Because Glen Walter, and by extension Ambassador Hunt, is not someone you want to fuck with. Seriously, Lake. You need to forget I ever told you any of this. Glen has friends at all levels of this administration. He's the one who had my name smeared. I want to keep my job."

"The story they tell at the embassy is that you chose to curtail for family reasons, although some people didn't buy it."

"I did choose to accept my curtailment and stay quiet about the photo because of family reasons. I have a wife and now a child on the way. I'm not going to do anything to jeopardize my career. And you should leave it alone for the same reason."

He's sweating even more now; it's dripping off his face and hitting the screen. "I shouldn't have taken this call. Someone could be listening."

"Jordan, wait!"

The screen goes blank. My mind lights up like a slot machine. This is bigger than any of us previously thought. Bowie wasn't just making accusations about Bruce. She'd believed she had evidence of criminal activity involving other vulnerable young women at The Trophy. The kind of evidence that might have gotten her killed.

Had her death been a suicide, or was the suicide a cover-up? Were there more people involved than just Bruce?

If her suicide was faked . . . she could still be alive.

Bowie could still be out there. And I'm the only one who's still trying to find her.

44

BOWIE

How long has she been down here? The days blend together like separate vocals on an album track. The pills Mark gave her for the pain of her injuries make her jittery. She's been writing letters to Suzie, disjointed lyrics, her memories of the conversation with Bruce.

Mark keeps her informed. Says there's a massive search for her. Shows her the press conference. Suzie singing her *Fly Home* song. It made her weep. She'd wanted to leave then, to go to Suzie, seek police protection, but Mark had convinced her it wasn't safe yet. That leaving now would put her mom in danger, too.

She hears footsteps overhead, voices. It's not the maid. She never talks, only vacuums the rug over Bowie's head. Mark is with someone. Talking to someone.

Colgan.

She crouches on the floor, searching the room for a weapon. The jagged edge of the lid of a tin can is all she comes up with. She holds it in the palm of her hand. Not daring to breathe. Sure that Colgan will outsmart Mark. Make him reveal her hiding place.

More voices. Footsteps over her head.

Then everything fades away. Whoever was up there is gone.

Hours later, she hears six knocks. Mark descends the ladder and holds his phone up. She winces in the sudden, harsh light of the screen.

MISSING AMERICAN EXCHANGE STUDENT BOWIE BISHOP TAKES OWN LIFE

Tears sting her eyes. "What's this?"

"Ryan Colgan must have faked your suicide. He even forged your handwriting on the note. Convincingly, it would seem."

Something scratches at her mind. "Wait. Why does your cell phone work down here? I thought you said there was no service?"

He shoves his phone back into his jeans pocket. "There might be a weak signal, but it's spotty, at best."

"The note doesn't sound like me. I'd never use a hashtag in a suicide note."

"Well, maybe it means the case is closed. The media frenzy will end. Colgan will go back to Vegas. You can start over, rise from the dead. We can say the suicide note was a publicity stunt. Maybe there's a way to tie all of this into your album launch. How are the final songs coming along?"

She stares at him. "Are you being serious right now?"

He blinks. "What?"

"Colgan's not just going to go away. Not until I'm no longer a threat. Don't you get it? He faked my suicide because he's confident he'll find and kill me and this gives him the perfect cover."

"Wow. That's cold-blooded."

"I told you he was a murderer. He's Glen's fixer. He specializes in making problems like me go away."

"Okay. Okay." Mark paces to the wall and back. "Let's think this through. It's getting too complicated. What if I make a deal with Colgan. I can bargain for your life. You give him whatever Livia mailed you and I give him an insane amount of cash."

"You can't trust Colgan. If he knows where I am, I'm as good as dead."

"All right." The cot creaks as he sits beside her. "This is a bad situation but we'll find a solution. I have a private yacht. I own property on an island off the coast of American Samoa. We sneak you away. You hide there instead."

"Maybe. It would be more comfortable than this tiny cell. I'm going crazy down here. And my mom is suffering so much. She needs to know that I'm alive. It's time for me to go to her."

"Why aren't you playing your guitar?" He'd brought her the Gibson she'd left here the last time they had a recording session. "Music is the only way out. I want you to write that last song for the album knowing that your mom thinks you're dead. Knowing the powerful men who killed your best friend are going free. Feel the rage and darkness. Harness it. Own it. Make it intensely personal and you'll reach a universal audience."

"I can't focus. I'm too scared. I want to talk to my mother, but I don't want to put her in danger." She starts to cry.

He puts an arm around her shoulders. "Hey, Bowie. Everything's going to work out. I'll think of something. I hired some people to research Colgan. If we find something objectionable enough to be used as leverage, we may be able to buy your freedom."

"Maybe." But this isn't how it works in Vegas. Colgan won't stop until she's not a threat to Glen anymore. He'll do anything for his boss. The man who saved his daughter's life.

She shivers.

"Are you cold? I'll bring you extra blankets."

"I don't think I can stay down here much longer."

"I know. We'll get you out of here soon. I promise. Trust me."

"I want to leave now. This has gone too far."

He climbs the stairs and hoists himself into the upper bedroom. She's about to follow when the trapdoor closes.

"Mark," she yells. She tries to open the door but it won't budge. "Fucking let me out!"

There's no response. She bangs her shoulders against the door until she has bruises. She's locked in here while her mom is out there grieving for her, probably mixing a bunch of pills and alcohol. What if something bad happens to Suzie? Fuck. She has to get out of this room. The next time he comes, she'll rush the door, fight her way out.

She closes her eyes. Opens them again.

The next slide in the carousel.

Click.

She's still here in this prison of a room.

45

LAKE

"Slow down," Mason says when I call him. "You're not making sense. You think your ambassador killed Florica?"

"No, he was staying at the casino; he may have been involved. Jordan told me that Bowie met with him and said she had evidence of girls being harmed at The Trophy casino. She wanted Jordan to set up a meeting with an FBI agent. Jordan didn't have a chance to before he was curtailed. He thinks someone was monitoring his computer. They saw the blackmail photo Bowie gave him."

"What type of evidence did Bowie have?"

"Jordan didn't know. She told him she'd contact him when everything was in place, but she never called before he left. He thinks Glen owns someone high up in the department. That's why he told me it was dangerous to ask too many questions about Bowie."

"He should have gone to the FBI, fuck the consequences."

"He didn't have any evidence. He was waiting for Bowie to contact him. Think about it, though—if someone found out that Bowie was asking for a meeting with an FBI agent, they could have extrapolated that she had evidence. Maybe Bruce was sent to silence her. Maybe he wasn't alone. The suicide could have been faked. It could be a cover-up for murder."

"As far as DSS Sutherland is concerned, the case is closed. None of what you're telling me would be enough to reopen it."

"I know. It's all conjecture."

Bowie's necklace is on my bedstand. The glass glints coldly. Florica is dead, but if there's the smallest chance Bowie still lives, I'll pursue every lead.

"The suicide note could be a fake. It uses a hashtag and Bowie never used hashtags in her social media posts. It was my mom who gave me the idea. I was asking her about a girl I used to know, when we lived in this creepy religious agricultural society called The Fold. We escaped but my friend was still there. Charity. I wonder if she's still alive."

"Have you tried to contact her?"

"They don't allow cell phones or computers."

"I was wondering about your past in Alaska. I noticed you hold your shoulder as though you have an injury that never properly healed."

"I broke my collarbone and my shoulder was dislocated. They believed in faith healing." I shudder. "We were living in a rural community. I was never taken to a hospital."

Fractured memories. A sickening feeling of something giving way, shifting, breaking. I knew I'd broken something right away. I was far from the tabernacle, and I was alone. I lay in the dark and cold with rain pouring on my face and I screamed for help. No one could hear me. I inched my way across the ground, the pain excruciating. A tidal wave of pain, a torrent, white-water rapids pounding my body.

"I only remember what happened after the accident. The elders tried to heal me with prayer. There were no pain meds. I think the trauma of that blocked out the memory of how I broke the bone in the first place. Maybe it had something to do with climbing a tree?"

I remember a tall, strong tree in the woods with the perfect crooked branch for sitting and reading books. I hid up there, reading and watching the forest floor below. Porcupines wandered by and once a brown bear lumbered underneath the tree. I held my breath, knowing that bears actually do know how to climb trees and I wasn't safe up there.

I knew how to hide. To observe. I witnessed things, and my mind decided it would be better not to remember.

"When we left The Fold I was lost. I was a good girl who followed all the rules, and suddenly those rules had evaporated like smoke, like a bad dream. I started partying. Hung out with the dangerous crowd. I was a small-town bad girl. Only medium bad. Like, I wasn't doing lines of coke but I was chasing my whiskey shots with hard seltzers."

Why am I telling him all of this?

"Lake . . . it's okay. You can talk to me."

"You don't want to hear my entire history."

"You're not the only one with a checkered past. I was in and out of court during my misspent youth. My wake-up call was a car crash. We'd been drinking. My mate Johnny was driving. He hit a tree and it saved us from going over a cliff. Johnny died. I survived. After that it was like my head cleared. Like the sky after a squall blows through. Clear and bright. I didn't want to be the twisted, broken mess anymore. I wanted to be that tall, strong tree. I wanted to save other people from crashing off cliffs. I guess . . . in this instance, I wasn't successful. Bowie leaped to her death. We didn't find her in time to stop her."

"Or someone faked the suicide. Maybe even Bowie herself? Although then I'd be wrong about the hashtag thing."

"I want to believe she's still alive."

"Clear your mind of the idea that she committed suicide. Think about this: Bowie knows something. She's going to tell. Testify. Bruce and Glen find out. Bruce comes here to threaten her. They struggle. She's hurt. She pushes him away with bloody hands. He beats her. Leaves her for dead. But she's not dead. She wakes up and finds the strength to crawl away. She leaves her necklace behind. She flags someone down, or steals a car, or whatever. She finds someplace to hide."

"Okay," he says skeptically. "I guess that's within the realm of possibility."

"When she hears the news that Bruce is dead, she thinks about going to the police, asking for protection. But no one believed her when she made accusations about Bruce before. Maybe she doesn't trust police. Glen Walter is still a threat. She thinks her only choice is to disappear. She hides out for a while, then fakes her own suicide. Plants the note, leaves her clothing for a tourist to find. Then she takes off."

"With no money. No passport. With her photo plastered everywhere, on every telephone pole, every station, every news outlet."

"Bowie is strong. Smart. She's a survivor. She found a way."

Mason sighs. "I want what you're saying to be true. The problem is that it's a fantasy. It's because you identify with Bowie. You survived trauma. You want her to survive, too. I'm sorry, I don't buy it. Bowie wrote that note and then jumped off a cliff in a moment of severe depression. It happens all too often, I'm afraid. That first day I met you, I saw darkness in your eyes. Suffering. Life doesn't always reward the virtuous. Good doesn't always triumph over evil. You know that, Lake."

"Damn it, Mason." He's right. I've seen it too many times. Innocent tourists killed by accidents. Sex offenders never brought to justice. Domestic violence spanning decades. Men manipulating young girls to make themselves feel powerful. The rotten cycle of secrets and lies.

Jezebel. Unclean. You've fallen from the path of righteousness.

"I'm sorry, Lake. I wish it wasn't true. I put in for some leave the next few days. Gonna go camping. Clear my head in the forest. Maybe hunt some wild boar. I could take you along for safety reasons."

"When are you leaving?"

"Tonight. I'll drive all night and watch the sun rise over the lake with a morning beer in my hand." She hears him open a door. "Want to come with me?" There's hesitation in his voice. Hope.

"I do, I really do, but this case has taken me away from my regular work, and everything's been piling up." And I can't let Bowie go. I have to keep searching.

"Right. Duty calls."

"Maybe another time?"

"Maybe. Goodbye, Lake."

"Goodbye, Mason." I have a nearly overwhelming urge to call him back, say I made a mistake, that I'll ditch work and jump in his car tonight. Keep him up by singing songs and telling jokes as he drives to his favorite campsite.

Sit beside him as the sun rises in the quiet of a forest overlooking a lake.

After we set up the tent we'd crawl inside, close the zipper, and shut the world out.

It's a seductive fantasy. Better than resuming my life. Anesthetize myself with lonely nights in front of TV shows. Drift through this country and on to the next.

I've lost myself somewhere along the way like a pair of sunglasses left on a park bench. It's been gradual. One week, one year, ten years later here I am wondering, what happened to . . . me? The wild, poetic girl who carried signs at political rallies and took spur-of-the-moment trips to new cities, navigating them from thrift store to thrift store. The girl who sat in cafés scribbling her detective novel.

I ended up in this government job where fitting in, being homogeneous, keeping your head down, and looking the other way is in the job description. Am I just like Jordan? I don't want to rock the boat. I'm hiding my true self.

Could I regrow myself like a fingernail or a plant? Maybe the seed of me is still there somewhere. I'm living half a life. I walk around every day protecting a shadowy secret that can never come to light. Something I've hidden even from myself.

I can't go camping with Mason. My heart is too bruised.

The secrets I carry are too heavy. They weigh me down. They could drown us both.

I'm attempting to fall asleep when my personal cell rings.

"Hello?" I say groggily, the sleeping pill already kicking in.

"Lake?"

"Yes, who's this?"

"Isla Shepherd."

I push myself up until I'm propped against the headboard. "Isla, hi."

"Sorry to call so late."

"No worries. What's up?"

"I didn't tell you something when you visited me. Dean and I agreed not to tell anyone."

My heart beats faster. "You can tell me anything, I told you that."

"It doesn't really matter now, does it? Bowie killed herself. My mum is gutted; she hasn't left the house for days. I can't believe it's true. I want it to all be a mistake. I want her to come home."

"We all do. What did you want to tell me?"

"I know you think I was jealous of Bowie, and maybe I was. But I genuinely cared about her. It's been weighing on my mind that I didn't tell you when you came to my school. You gave me the perfect opportunity to do the right thing, and I didn't. I sometimes think, maybe if I'd told you . . . maybe they would have found Bowie before she jumped. She was missing for almost a week before she died. She must have been hiding out somewhere."

"Do you know where?" I ask eagerly, fully alert now.

"Not exactly. All I know is that one night I was sneaking home at three a.m., and I ran into Bowie in the cemetery. She'd snuck out, too. She wouldn't tell me where. I asked her if she was doing anything illegal, like drugs, and she said no. Then I asked if she was seeing an older man, and she said 'not necessarily seeing someone' but that she was doing something neither one of our mums would like."

"Isla, why didn't you tell this to the police?"

"Because then I would have had to reveal my secret. Dean and I are still together. We're planning to get married soon. When Bowie went missing, there was so much attention on my family, my parents were so unhappy. If I told the police that I was sneaking out behind my parents' backs, it would have been even worse. Besides, I didn't know where Bowie was going; that's how I justified staying silent. Do you think if I'd told the police about our conversation it would have made a difference?"

"It's useful information, but I understand you did it out of self-preservation."

I'd known Dean and Isla were hiding something. I should have pressed harder.

"We're in love, Lake. We're getting married before he goes on tour. I haven't worked up the courage to tell my parents yet. Lake, I have to go," she whispers. "My mum's coming down the hall." She hangs up.

Does this change anything? Alejandro told me he assumed she was seeing someone in the weeks before she disappeared. And now Isla says she caught her sneaking back after a night away. Where had she gone that night?

I throw off my covers. The evidence I gathered is still stuck to my wall. I pry the guitar pick off and cradle it in my palm. Who gave this to her? Suzie had said she met Mark Edison in L.A. She'd also said she and Lance Booker hung out at The Balladeer club.

Could Edison have given Bowie this guitar pick?

And then there were the songs she'd been writing. The track list for a phantom album. Maybe not phantom, after all?

When I'd visited Mark Edison, I'd asked him where Bowie

had been recording her songs, as if I knew she'd been there. I'd wanted to see his reaction. His expression had remained neutral, but there'd been that small facial tic.

And then later, in the bedroom. The look on Edison's face when Mason and I rushed away to find Suzie at the hotel.

He'd looked relieved.

46

BOWIE

Sometimes Bowie wakes up and he's up there, looking down through the door. Just staring at her. Watching her sleep.

He says he's keeping her safe. He says he'll let her out after Colgan leaves New Zealand and she finishes the last song on the album to his satisfaction. But he never likes the versions she sings for him. He never comes down the ladder anymore, just talks to her from the room upstairs. When she tries to run up the ladder he slams the door in her face. He tells her that if she escapes, he'll only put her back in again. He says it's for her protection, and her creative process.

She longs to feel sun on her face. Sand beneath her toes. She longs for Suzie. What she wouldn't give to see her mom flick cigarette ash and make snarky comments about tourists.

Colgan must have left New Zealand by now. Maybe she can risk going to the police. Maybe they will protect her. She makes the argument, but Mark doesn't agree. He says to wait. He's so close to finding the dirt on Colgan. He'll end his hold over her for good. She'll never have to feel scared again.

He pushes her to write more songs but the words won't come. She's too exhausted. Too frightened.

If she doesn't leave this room soon, she's going to go insane.

She waits for her chance. It finally arrives when Mark tells her he'll be at a conference in Auckland all day and won't be able to visit her that night.

She climbs the ladder. This time she'll find a way to open the door.

She tries to remember how he opened it that day when he first brought her here. It feels like a million years ago. He lifted the sheepskin rug and did he press a button? Pull a latch?

A latch. There'd been a thin metal thread sticking up through the bamboo floorboards. He'd tugged on it and a mechanism opened the trapdoor. If she can wiggle something through the crack, maybe she can trip the mechanism?

She rips off one of the steel guitar strings and climbs the ladder again. She manages to push the stiff bronze up into the crack around the trapdoor. She shakes the string, hoping to trigger the door.

Nothing.

She keeps trying, over and over. Finally, when she's exhausted and heartsick, she hears a click. Holding her breath, she shoves at the door with her shoulder. It swings upwards a crack. She pushes harder, using all her weight. It opens inch by inch, enough for her to roll sideways through the gap. She blinks in the sudden light from the windows, even though it's evening and the light is fading fast.

She doesn't recognize herself in the mirror. Haunted eyes and faded bruises.

She searches through his desk. She remembers leaving the keys to the Beetle here. If she can find them, she'll go to his garage, take the car. She's done hiding from Colgan. Anything, even death, would be better than this.

She doesn't find the keys but she finds something else hidden deep in a drawer. A document with the name Veronica scratched out and her name added in. She's still reading through it when the door to the room opens and Mark strides toward her.

"Bowie, what are you doing up here? How did you get out?"

"What the hell is this?" She holds up the contract. "Are you fucking kidding me? You know I'll never sign this, right?"

"You'll sign it," Mark says calmly.

"No, I fucking won't. You can't keep me prisoner and you can't make me sign a contract for three new albums. No wonder Veronica divorced you! You wanted her to sign this and she must have refused."

"You have it all wrong. Veronica desperately wanted to sign a contract with me but her songs weren't powerful enough. I'm the one who dumped her."

"Give me a phone."

He regards her coolly, no emotion on his face. Had she thought he had a kind smile? There's not a trace of kindness left. "Sign the contract."

She rips it in half, her fingers shaking she's so furious. "No."

"You'll sign it eventually. Here's why. If you don't sign it, I'll turn you over to Ryan Colgan. If you do sign it, I'll protect you forever and have Colgan neutralized."

"What does that even mean—neutralized?"

"I hired a guy."

"And forever? Like . . . in perpetuity?"

"You're one of my artists now. It means until your songs stop making me money."

"This whole time you've been using me." She'd trusted him because he hadn't been pervy. He'd never made a move.

He hadn't wanted her body, she realizes now. He'd wanted to own her music.

Her future.

"I've been guiding you toward greatness. You need me to take you to the big time."

"Is that what you told Veronica, too?"

"Veronica wasn't talented enough. I've been searching for an artist like you, Bowie. A hitmaker. A raw, powerful, undeveloped talent."

"Just let me go. I won't tell anyone we were working together. I'll be out of your life for good."

He walks toward her, like he's going to touch her. She backs away. "Just finish the album. Accept my protection. Don't be a fool."

"You're fucked up. I'll never write another song for you ever again."

"You don't have a choice, Bowie. I'm keeping you here until you finish the album. Veronica could never tap into the darkness and feed it into her music. No matter what I did to her. I kept her down in that room for a week in the pitch-dark with only a recording device and it still wasn't enough. And she still loved me at the end of all her trials. It was pathetic. And unproductive. But I know you have it in you, Bowie. You're going to thank me for this one day."

"You're a psycho. I'll never thank you. There will be no more songs. No contract. It would be career suicide."

"You already committed suicide, remember?"

For a moment she'd forgotten. "How convenient for you."

"It is, though. Stop to think about it. You refuse to sign, I tell Colgan you're here. I take a holiday on my yacht."

"You find some other starlet to sing my songs."

"You catch on quickly."

"I told Suzie about the album. People will know I wrote the songs."

"You're lying. If you'd told her about it, the police would have been swarming all over this house. You kept it a secret from everyone. That was a mistake." He grabs her by the elbow.

He has the masters of the songs they recorded. He doesn't need her anymore. He can find someone else to sing her songs. She's disposable. She can be stripped of her creation, just like her mother was. Men owning their words. Their money. Their lives.

"So what will it be, Bowie?"

She searches his face for some sign of the patient, insightful, inspiring man she thought she knew. That man is gone. He never existed. This is the real Mark. He wants to own her like one of his guitars. Hang her on his wall, play her at his will, just like the song she'd written about Glen that night at the Cat's Meow.

How could she have been such an idiot? Her whole life her mom has been telling her to maintain the rights to her creative work. To not make the same mistakes that Suzie did.

"Our collaboration is over, Mark."

Anger twists his face into a stranger's mask.

He grabs her arm and drags her toward the trapdoor. "Then I have no further use for you, Bowie." She tries to fight, but she's weak from being locked away. She struggles as he opens the trapdoor. She nearly escapes but he holds on. He shoves her into the hole and she stumbles down the ladder, losing her footing and falling with a sickening thud onto her back.

Mark slams the door shut. She hears something heavy being scraped across the floor.

She's trapped down here in the darkness. The light switch doesn't work anymore. He must have cut the power. He said he'd kept Veronica down here for a week in the dark. What is he capable of?

She should have gone along with what he wanted, written the final song of his dreams, signed the contract for future albums. What if he gives her to Colgan? Could he be that cruel?

"Mark," she screams, trying to climb the ladder but slipping back down because of a shooting pain in her back. "Mark, I made a mistake. I'll sign the contract."

There's only silence.

47

LAKE

I carry Alaska inside of me. A mountain range bristling in my chest, making me wary. Don't open your mouth and let it out. Don't let the wilderness escape—the wildness—the line of spiky pine trees, the eagle talons grasping your heart.

Darkness inside my mind. The bleakness of a day of solid sleeting rain that melts all the snow away.

Relentless rain, gray sky, no mountaintops. Darkness that can't be dispersed with full-spectrum lamps or affirmations or blazing fireplaces. Darkness that is knitted around your bones, making them creak in their sockets and freeze. Cold that can never be warmed.

Glaciers are receding on this earth but not in my heart. I can't allow myself to feel, to be hurt, to be controlled. It's safer to stay locked inside.

Stay home. Stay in the dark.

My mind spinning, hurtling through the years, landing in a stately home built into a cliff.

Recessed lighting strategically illuminating blown-up portraits of Mark Edison, giving his head a halo. The portrait of him alone. Standing on the beach, his house visible in the distance. A beatific smile on his face. Sunlight in his hair. Hands at his sides, palms outward. Wrists wrapped in leather. A leather cord around his neck. A little rock-star edge. Portrait of an egotist.

Another portrait from my past.

Father Kincaid, larger than life, rendered in swirling oil paint.

He has one hand raised, and his eyes are lifted to the heavens. There's a halo of light around his head.

He's the anointed one. He will lead us to eternal life.

We had to kneel before his portrait in the mornings before we attended tabernacle.

I am the way. Give me your lives. I'll give you eternal salvation.

I'll give you fame. Fortune.

The two portraits blurring together in my mind.

Maybe Bowie had been visiting Edison's recording studio, working with him in secret. And if she was working with him, that means she trusted him.

She was alive the day Bruce died, on the run; with the Shepherds out of town, could she have turned to Edison for help?

Like my mother fleeing her grief, hoping to find solace and purpose at The Fold. Finding only lies, manipulation, danger.

"I have to go," I tell Edgar.

He stares meaningfully at his food bowl even though it's the middle of the night.

"I'll give you a double portion of crunchies when I get back."

He turns away. This is an unforgivable sin.

I dress swiftly in the most Alaskan things I can find: jeans, a black hoodie, hiking boots.

I slip my knife into a holster at my waist. Mason must have left for his camping trip already. His phone goes to voicemail, and I leave him a message telling him my theory and that I'm going to investigate.

I've been drifting through my life, skimming the surface,

SHE FELL AWAY

afraid to let anyone sink hooks into me, afraid to truly connect. Afraid of what might rise from the depths of my mind.

Find Bowie and I just might find myself.

No one else believes she's alive. It's up to me to find her now.

Maybe she did jump off that cliff. Or maybe she trusted the wrong man.

48

BOWIE

She should never have trusted Mark. She was so stupid. So incredibly stupid. She'd let her guard down. She knew not to trust anyone. She's from Vegas, a big-city girl in a small city. She knew that even the most innocent-looking person could be rotten to the core.

Mark was just another toxic Svengali. Thinking he could shape her, control her. He'd hurt her, and another woman before her, in a fucked-up attempt to make them bleed hit songs for him. Suzie had raised her on cautionary tales of men like him. The Phil Spectors of the music industry. Suzie's bandmates. The record execs who stole the rights to her music.

Maybe Bowie is here because she has a disease that was passed down from mother to daughter. She attracts the darkness because there's something wrong with her.

She's dead inside.

She's dead outside. The world thinks she killed herself.

She'll die down here. She hurt something in her back when she fell down the ladder.

She doesn't want to die. Maybe Mark already sold her out to Colgan. He hasn't visited her again. Her food is running out.

SHE FELL AWAY

She longs for her mother. She wants to hear that cigarette-roughened voice.

Do you believe you can do this?

No, Mom. I don't. I'm in pain. I'm scared.

The worst part of it is that she's here willingly. She'd trusted one of the men who kicked her back and forth like a soccer ball. She had been punctured. Deflated.

She feels so old. So weary. She'll never see nineteen.

She's back in the VIP room at The Trophy. If only she'd never performed that night. Never brought Lo with her. She'd thought she'd been in control of the situation, but like everything in Las Vegas, it had been only an illusion. Like the showgirls seen from a distance, perfect and shiny, and when you were up close you saw their pores, the black eyes covered up with grease paint.

As a child when her mother had brought her to the casino, left her with other children to play in a room, she'd caught glimpses of the world inside those walls and it had all seemed like a shiny carnival ride of joy, beauty, a frenetic spin out of the dull and ordinary and into a dream world of saturated colors, laughter, the trill and warble of slot machines, the excited shouts of patrons.

She'd wanted to be part of that world, a glittering singer onstage whom everyone adored, everyone clapped for. She hadn't questioned Suzie's dream because it was hers, too. Until that night. When the facade was peeled away and she'd seen the ugliness beneath it all. She wasn't a human being to Glen. She was a cashbox. Reach inside her, twist the right buttons, say the magic words, and she'd start spewing forth coins from her mouth; he'd capture them all in an armored safe, and she'd never have the combination.

That's how Mark sees her. Profit to be made. A hitmaker. A trophy.

She passes out from the pain of her fall. Wakes up again.

LENORE NASH

Her body aches, but her mind fills with lyrics. They don't rhyme or have any kind of flow. They just want to be heard.

Big dreams, bright heart, stars in her mind
Dollar signs in his eyes.
A hole in his chest instead of a heart.
Head in the papier-mâché clouds
Feet trapped by concrete contracts
Her heart has blackout blinds.
The sun is a memory stick she can't plug in.
Penniless girl. Pitiless city.
You're special, I'll make you a star.
You're one in a million and I like those odds.
Her lullaby the grinding of slot machines.
Scales to weigh the ingots. Scales to weigh the girls.
Her only worth her body.
Dead girl walking around in high heels.
You already have sand filling your mouth.
Crows picked out your eyes.
Your bones are bleached by desert sun.
You're already a grisly discovery.
You're only one of a million.
You never could beat those odds.

49

LAKE

The estate is shadowed and silent. No lights in any of the windows. The looming metal gate is locked, and there are no guards on duty. I rattle the gate to make sure.

"Edison," I yell. "Let me in."

There's no answer. No lights go on in the house. He wasn't exactly going to leave his front gate open for me, but I'd been counting on flashing my State Department badge, talking my way past the guard. Now what do I do? I don't even know for certain that Bowie's here. It's only this yearning I have for her to still be alive. This thin, tenuous thread of a theory that I've tied around the idea that she escaped from Bruce and ran here, instead of leaping off that cliff to her death.

She ran to this house thinking she'd find a sanctuary and found another predator instead. Mark Edison, reclusive music producer who purposefully stays mysterious. Never grants interviews. Only posts younger images of himself.

Did he see a way of recapturing his youth in Bowie? Her talent would make him relevant again. Give him a new hit record.

Or maybe I'm crazy. That's a distinct possibility. All I know is something has drawn me here. I couldn't save Charity, take her with me when we left The Fold. Maybe I can save Bowie.

I search the length of the gate. There's a high wall around the perimeter of the property with barbed wire on top. What am I doing here? Attempting to break into a private residence on a stitched-together theory. On a prayer.

I could turn around, go back to my warm bed and my sleepy cat. Come back in the morning with Mason. Did he get my message yet? I try his phone again. Still no answer. I leave another message, letting him know what I'm doing.

Or maybe I'll run away. My first idea. Every time. Run. Simple, clean. It's what I've been doing ever since I left Alaska. I've been running, avoiding my past, pushing away the buried memories. Safer to run, to hide.

Not tonight. Not if there's even the slimmest of chances I'm right.

I squeeze my eyes shut, attempting to recall the photo of Mark standing on the beach in front of his house. Zoom in on the background. I see it then, the narrow wooden staircase climbing the cliff from the beach to the house. Maybe there's a way inside his walls from the cliffside stairs.

I walk along the high wall until it ends, using my cell phone as a flashlight. There's an opening in the trees, and stairs leading down to the beach just past the property.

I climb down to the beach and walk along the shore. Wind bites my back; waves crash angrily. I slip on wet rocks but right myself and keep going. Finally, I see the rickety wooden stairs that wind up the side of the cliff. I can't see the top, or whether there's any hope of accessing Edison's property.

Wind lashes my hair to my face, and rain batters my cheeks as I climb. The narrow, moss-coated steps are slick with rain.

I hold on to the railing, pausing every ten steps to catch my breath. It's a steep climb. There's a landing halfway up with two high-backed wooden chairs set on an outcropping with a half railing. A tranquil resting place to watch the sun set over the waves. I'll rest there for a few minutes. Catch my breath.

Up above the landing I see the same forbidding metal and concrete gate that surrounds the front of the house, bristling with barbed wire. I'll never make it over. Dread surges in my chest. This is insane. I fight the urge to climb down, instead of up.

One foot in front of the other.

I'm climbing because I don't want to run away anymore. Climbing for the sake of that lost and lonely girl who learned to shove the bad things down beneath the surface.

I've reached the landing when a door opens in the gate above me. I stumble backward, nearly lose my footing. My wrist hits the jagged edge of the fence and my cell phone plunges off the side of the cliff. Fuck. I crouch against the fence, hiding behind one of the chairs.

A huge shape emerges. A man wearing a ball cap and black clothing. He's carrying something in his arms. He begins descending the wooden stairs. The thing in his arm flops with every step, head lolling and long dark brown hair streaming in the wind.

He's carrying a body.

Moonlight finds her face.

He's carrying Bowie.

Is she still alive? There's no way to tell. She's limp in his arms, a dead weight. He's headed straight toward my hiding place.

My cell phone is gone. I can't call for backup, and even if I could, it would take too long to get here. I pray that Mason received my message, that he's on his way.

It's up to me now. If she's still alive, I'm the only one who can save her.

The man drops her on the landing with a grunt and straightens up, pulling his phone out of his pocket. I hold my breath. He hasn't noticed me yet. I have the advantage of surprise.

I don't remember Mark Edison being such a large man. And then he turns his face, and I see that it's not Edison, it's Ryan Colgan, Glen Walter's chief of security.

I stifle a gasp. Colgan is all hard angles, neatly trimmed beard, and ice-cold eyes. He's a killer. It's written in the way he casually tossed her body onto the deck.

Bowie's face is bruised, hair matted. She looks dead. I'm too late.

But then her torso twitches and one eye opens. She moans.

"You lied to me," Colgan says, bending over her. "You said you made copies of the video. Backed it up to the Cloud, but there's nothing on your laptop or anywhere in your files. Now, for the last fucking time. Tell me where you hid the video, or I'll shoot you."

"It's . . ."

I strain to hear over the wind. I can't make out her words. She's telling him what he wants to know.

"You should have told me earlier and you wouldn't have suffered so much."

She wriggles weakly, attempting to sit up. He places his booted foot on her chest. Lifts his cell phone.

"I know where it is," I hear him say. "Just dealing with the other thing. Uh-huh. Yeah. No problem. I'll be back soon. Don't worry. I said no problem."

He kicks Bowie in the ribs, and she screams—a hoarse, animal sound that sets my teeth on edge.

Blood pounds in my ears. Or it's the surf below, battering the rocks.

In the mandatory Foreign Affairs Counter Threat training program, I had to triage a penetrating chest wound, use a tourniquet, ram a car into a parked car to move it out of the way, crawl on my hands and knees through a smoke-filled building, defend myself against a surprise attack.

Simulations. Dummies.

This is real. He's going to kill Bowie. Get rid of her body. It's up to me to stop him. Pure adrenaline guides me.

"Colgan," I shout. "It's all over. The police are on their way."

He starts, staring wildly. "Who's there?"

SHE FELL AWAY

I take a deep breath and stand up, sticking my hand in my purse and holding it like I have a gun. "Lake Harlowe. Remember me?"

"The little redhead." He sneers. "You better hope those cops get here fast because there's no way you could take me by yourself. Unless you have a really big gun in that purse."

I don't have a gun. But I do have my hunting knife. It's in a holster at the back of my waist. While I was crouched there I decided on a strategy. I'm going to distract him with the pretend gun, while I reach around with my left hand and pull out the knife. Then I'll rush him.

His eyes are flat. His hand rests over his jacket pocket, over his gun. "You don't stand a chance. You're a diplomat. Not a killer."

"I'm not afraid to shoot you."

Bowie lifts her head. "Help," she croaks.

In the split second that I turn to look at her, Colgan attacks. Of course he attacks. He's a trained killer. He punches me in the face, and I hit the railing; my purse goes flying. He picks it up, shakes it.

"No gun." He laughs nastily. "Red didn't come prepared."

I was taught that when defending myself I should retaliate with attacks to vulnerable areas. Gouge his eyes. His nose. A palm to his throat. A knee to his groin.

None of it works. He's too quick, too strong. His palm slams into my injured collarbone and then a huge fist rams into my stomach. I retch, doubling over in thick, suffocating pain. He's in a boxer stance, fists raised, a sneering smile on his face, as if he's enjoying this. Toying with me. Playing with me first.

Before he shoots me.

He punches me in the face, and my head whips backward, over the railing. I nearly fall. Everything goes throb-sick-blank. Then it all goes dark.

50

LAKE

Sounds around the bed but it's pitch-black, only the faraway flickering firelight. Murmuring coming closer. Shadowy figures gathering around me. Father Kincaid, Sister Mercy, all of the elders. I know them by their voices, their shapes.

I try to sit up, but the pain stops me. I gag.

She's awake.

Get a basin.

Lake, sweetheart. I'm here.

Ruth is here. She's holding my hand. Why is my hand so useless? I can't move my upper body. Heavy blankets weigh me down.

Hands on me. Faces looming over me. Mouths opening, speaking in tongues. Father Kincaid places a hand on my shoulder. I scream. I thought I knew pain, but this is so much more.

The collarbone's broken. The shoulder is dislocated.

She needs a doctor. Please. Let me take her into town. Ruth's voice.

Hush now. He will heal her.

Hold her down. Give her something to bite.

I scream again. It sounds unearthly. Like the keening of the husky puppy whose foot was caught in the bear trap. He sounded like this before they shot him. I don't want them to put me down. I stuff my good fist, my left fist, into my mouth to keep from screaming.

Ruth is crying as the voices rise. The pain a sickness now, a nausea, a hungry worm in my belly, a crouching demon on my chest.

Hands on me.

Holding me down. Tying my wrists together behind my back.

My wrists? Where's Ruth? That's not Father Kincaid.

Consciousness arrives with the slap of rain on my face, the heaving waves of pain in my belly. It's lancing agony, but I pry my eyes open. I'm lying near Bowie, my wrists secured with something thin, like a zip tie.

Colgan is pacing along the landing, muttering under his breath. "Fuck. Now I have two bodies. Dead fucking bodies. The worst part of my job."

I almost laugh out loud. It's the exact same thought I'd had what feels like a lifetime ago. Fear and pain are making me delirious. Bowie catches my eye. She's still alive.

I wriggle my back. He didn't find my knife holster. Didn't expect me to be armed. If I can maneuver my wrists, undo the sheath button, find the sharp edge, I could cut through the bindings around my wrists.

"Sorry we're such a bother, Colgan. Messing up your tidy plan. You wanted the link made between Bowie and Bruce. You wanted it to look like she tried to murder him and then committed suicide. Then you'd find her and kill her."

"Didn't know it would take so long to find her."

"What's the plan now?"

He eyes me coldly. "Dispose of you both."

Fear strangles my mind. He's going to kill us both. All I can do is keep him talking. Hope that Mason's on the way. Try to free my wrists.

"Do you know how I realized that Bowie might still be alive?" I ask him.

"I don't care."

"It was the suicide note. You used a hashtag. She never used hashtags in her social media posts anymore."

"What are you talking about? Of course she did."

"The posts with hashtags were written by Suzie. You thought you were being clever, but you left a glaring clue for me to find. Maybe you're not as good at your job as you think you are."

He snorts. "I'm a problem solver, and you're a big fucking problem. You know what I do with problems? I make them go away. Maybe I should cut you up while you're still alive. I did that once."

"You don't have time. I told you the police are on their way." Jesus, I hope that's true.

"Taking their time, aren't they?"

"Maybe they're already here. Just waiting for the right kill shot. Boom. Right between your eyes." I have the sheath unbuttoned now. I'm working my wrist tie over the sharp edge of the knife with tiny movements.

Bowie's been staring at me this whole time. I think she knows what I'm doing. She spits blood, lifts her head. "Where's Mark? He left you to do his dirty work? He should be helping you. This is partly his mess."

"He's a scared little boy. He doesn't want to know the gory details. I don't mind. I'm golden. I'm laughing all the way to the bank. Edison's on his yacht, sailing away. He told me about the album you recorded." The wind distorts his laughter. "He may be gutless but he's not stupid. He has the masters. He'll find another hot young thing to record your songs. You're replaceable."

"I told Livia about the album. She'll tell Suzie. And Suzie will sue Edison. Claim copyright for me."

"Glen will have Livia deported. And who would believe a drunk like Suzie?"

"Do you like killing, Colgan?" I'm almost free. I'll babble anything to keep him talking.

"Oh, I don't know, Red. It's a job. It pays well but it does get a little old, a little boring. Like when you girls want to keep me talking, because you think it will give you a chance to escape."

It's working. The knife is nearly through the zip tie. My hands will be free soon. I'm careful not to show any emotion other than terror. Fear. I hide the mad surge of hope, of hatred, that is going to carry me into this desperate last move.

Bowie props herself up on one elbow. "You murdered Bruce. Aren't you scared that Glen will find out and have you killed?"

He pauses. "Glen would understand that I did what I had to do to protect him."

"But you went to such lengths to make it look accidental. That doesn't seem to me like you're confident Glen would approve."

"It doesn't matter. It's done. Glen will never know. The only two people who know are right here."

My wrists are unbound. While Bowie talks, I wrap my fingers around the hilt of the knife, gathering strength.

"Or maybe he already knows and he put a hit out on you," Bowie continues with contempt dripping from her voice. "You'll be met at the airport in Vegas by tough guys with automatic weapons."

"This conversation is over. Time to die." He pulls the gun on Bowie.

I'm free. I'm also injured. I can barely see out of one eye. Every breath drives a sharp shard of glass deeper into my ribs.

I can do this.

I meet Bowie's gaze, willing her to understand what I need her to do. I pray she has the strength left to provide a distraction.

Colgan thinks I'm weak. Defenseless.

That's where he's wrong.

Here's the thing. The shivery, razor-sharp thought that keeps slicing through my mind. The half memory I've buried for so long.

I think I've used a knife before to protect someone I loved. The metallic heat of it feels familiar in my palm. This rage feels like an old friend.

He doesn't know me. He doesn't know my past.

I'm a hunter. And he's the prey.

Bowie makes her move. She lashes out with her foot, kicks his ankle as hard as she can. He stumbles, only slightly, but it's all I require.

I surge upright, knife raised. Hurtle toward him. I plunge the knife into his chest, sliding between his lower ribs. He glances down, then back at me, shock in his eyes. "Well, well. Red did come prepared."

I knock the gun out of his grip.

His hands move to the hilt of the hunting knife as if he'll try to yank it out. His gun lies on the ground nearby. He moves toward it, but I kick it off the cliff.

He wraps his hands around my neck and drops to his knees, taking me with him.

We wrestle. His hands wrapped around my throat. My fingers clutching the hilt of my knife, angling it higher, hoping to puncture a lung.

He's squeezing so hard I can't think, can't move. I'm going to die. He'll crush my windpipe. With a last, desperate motion I shove the knife higher.

He moans and his fingers loosen. I gasp and cough, bending over, fighting for air.

He lurches backward, fingers scrabbling at the knife. Crashes to the ground. Body twitching, eyes closed.

He's losing a lot of blood. I search his pockets, find another large zip tie. Fasten his wrists together. His eyes are unfocused. It's a deep chest wound, but I could stanch the bleeding. I know how.

I press down on either side of the knife. Welcome the warm blood on my hands. Revel in it. His blood. Not mine.

"We have to keep the blood loss under control."

Bowie stares at me blankly. She's in shock.

"If he goes to a hospital, he'll have a chance of surviving. I'm going to use his phone to call an ambulance. I need you to apply pressure to either side of the knife, not to the wound itself. Can you do that?"

"My ribs are broken," she whispers. "My nose. Something's wrong in my back. Maybe other things, too. But I'll try."

I search Colgan's pockets. Find his cell phone and a switchblade knife. I use the knife to cut Bowie's wrists free. I help her crawl toward Colgan.

He's still breathing faintly. There's no blood on his lips. I don't think I punctured a lung.

Bowie crouches over him.

"Place your hands on either side of the knife and press down."

She grabs hold of the knife hilt.

"Not the knife—next to it!"

She stares at me for a moment, her eyes as flat and cold as Colgan's. She uses both of her hands and jerks the knife out of his chest.

"What are you doing?" I rush toward her.

She brings the knife down with all her strength, stabbing him in the heart.

His body spasms. His face goes slack. He stops breathing.

Bowie lets go of the knife. Flops to her back. She coughs and blood trickles down her lips. She winces.

"We have to get you to a hospital."

She looks up at me bleakly. "But not Colgan."

"No," I say carefully. "Not Colgan."

I use his phone to call an ambulance. I tell the dispatcher to call the police. Ask for Sergeant Mason Yates. Give him this phone number.

Colgan's phone rings a few minutes later.

"Lake! I've been trying to call you, but you're not answering your cell phone. Why did you go by yourself? I'm on my way. With backup. Tell me you're all right!"

"I'm okay." I cough, wince with the tide of pain in my ribs. "Mason, I have Bowie."

"She's alive?"

"She is, but she has serious injuries. We're behind Edison's house on the stairs leading down to the beach. You won't be able to reach us from the front because the gates are locked."

"Tell her to hold on. We're on our way."

My throat is raw, every breath torture.

"The police are on their way. The ambulance, too," I tell Bowie.

She nods and struggles to a seat.

"You should lie still."

"I can't." She convulses, staring at Colgan. "I can't stay here next to him. I want to go down to the beach."

"You might have internal injuries."

"Help me down the steps, please. Or I'll crawl down by myself."

She's a fighter. Just like Suzie. I place my arm around her shoulders, help her to half rise. We hobble down the stairs slowly. Sink to the sand. Face the stormy sea.

Rain washing the blood off our hands.

51

BOWIE

The air is so cool, so wet, it's the most delicious thing she's ever tasted. She sucks in breath after breath; she can't get enough. She's been locked away too long.

She'd felt nothing but joy as she drove the knife into Colgan's chest. Was she evil? She'd done it for Lo. Because he'd taken her light away and hurt so many other girls.

She'd enjoyed ending him.

She feeds on the beauty of this night. Of this freedom. Gulps it down. Swallows the stars that are shining beyond the rain. They shine inside her. Pinpricks of light in her chest. Little bursts of hope.

Star light, star bright
First star I swallow tonight
Wish I may, wish I might
Live forever in your light

The woman who risked her life to save her is sitting on the beach next to her. There are furious red bruises around her neck. She's petite, with red hair plastered to a pretty, heart-shaped face, and a sweet smile.

"Who are you?" Bowie finally has breath enough to ask. "How did you know where to find me?"

"Lake Harlowe. I'm a consular officer with the U.S. embassy. I've been searching for you with my friend Mason, a New Zealand police sergeant."

"But what made you come here?"

"I saw the list of songs that you hung on your bedroom wall. It seemed strange to me that you hadn't posted many of them on social media or allowed Suzie to hear them. I began thinking that it was an album you were secretly recording. And then Isla confessed that she caught you sneaking back in the middle of the night. She didn't tell the police immediately because she didn't want her parents to find out she'd been secretly dating Dean. If you'd been hanging out with Mark Edison, it followed that you hid here between the time when Bruce's body was discovered and your suicide was faked."

"By Colgan. You figured out that I would never have used a hashtag for my own death."

"It took me too long. I'm so sorry. Where was Edison keeping you?"

"I came here willingly, to hide from Colgan. I thought I could trust him. He hid me in his bomb shelter. But then he wouldn't let me go. He had some sick idea that keeping me down there would help me produce more intensely personal hit songs. He said he'd done the same thing to his ex-wife. I told him I'd never work with him again and he left me down there to die. Left me with a killer."

"Florica's mother Livia mailed you something."

"A video of a drugged girl in the casino. A girl like Lo." Rage churns in her chest like the waves when they hit the shoreline. "I kept it safe, Lake."

"You can give it to my friend Mason. He'll help you make sure it goes to the right authorities. The ones Glen Walter has no control over. You can trust Mason."

She doesn't think she'll ever be able to trust anyone ever again, but she nods. "I'll tell him where it is, but he'll have to be careful. Glen won't go down without a fight." She watches a rivulet of sand and water slide away beneath her feet. "Bruce came to help me, not hurt me. He was turning on his father. He came to New Zealand because he needed evidence to stop his father."

"He died a hero, then."

Sirens sound in the distance.

"They're almost here," Lake says.

"Are you going to tell the police about . . . you know . . ." She can't say it. She feels the hard steel hilt of the knife against her palm. Sees the blood soaking his shirt. Her hands.

"It will be our secret."

"Truly?"

Lake touches her cheek. "Truly. He tried to kill us. We were defending ourselves. End of story."

"You risked your life for me."

"Because finding you became an obsession for me. I couldn't accept that your voice had been silenced. I risked my life and I'd do it all again," she says, her brown eyes glittering.

"I thought I was going to die—I was sure of it—and now here I am. It's like being born again. A life I didn't think I'd have."

"I have something of yours." Lake reaches into a pocket and pulls out Lo's ashes. The rain has subsided. Between shifting clouds, the glass vial catches the moonlight. She drops it into Bowie's palm.

"I found it when we were searching for you in Karori Cemetery. Suzie gave it to me before she left Wellington. She loves you so much, even if her love can sometimes be suffocating. And she loved Florica. She told me to spread her ashes in the ocean."

Bowie stares out at the turbulent water, fighting back tears. Then she doesn't fight anymore. She lets them fall.

It's time to say goodbye.

52

LAKE

Bowie struggles upright and I follow, supporting her as we walk toward the water. She slips, but I hold her steady.

She holds the necklace toward the ocean.

"She was my best friend. She was so beautiful. She was part of me. Part of my soul. We were always together. They called us BoLo. Bowie and Florica. I called her Lo, and it was the perfect name for her because she was sad so often. She always said that I was the only one who could make her really smile. It was because of me that she met Bruce. When she talked to him, she lit up. That was the last time I saw her smile. The last time I saw her alive."

Sobs steal her voice away. "Lo," she croaks. "I'm so sorry. I never should have brought you with me that night."

"You can't blame yourself. Glen would have found another way to lure her."

"But I made it so easy."

"Don't carry that guilt. Let it go. Throw her ashes into the ocean and when they scatter, release it."

"I've been carrying her with me. I haven't wanted to let her go."

"You can do this."

I help her uncap the vial. She walks into the swirling water. "Goodbye, Lo."

The wind takes the ashes. They melt into the frothing sea. I bend down, washing blood and ashes from my hands. The taste of salt spray and tears in my mouth.

I'm weeping for Lo. For Bowie.

For myself.

For all the girls with a core of darkness drilled into their souls. The girls who must relearn how to accept light as their birthright.

Bowie turns around. "She's gone."

"But you're here, Bowie. I'm so glad you're here."

They release me from the hospital after a few hours. I have bruised ribs, bruising around my neck, a laceration near my eye, but I'm alive. They're keeping Bowie for observation. I called Suzie, spoke with Rob and CG Chung, and gave my statement to the police.

Mason retrieved the USB stick while I was at the police station. Bowie had wrapped it in plastic. Hidden it inside Dulcie's mausoleum.

Mason insists on driving me home. And helping me up the stairs.

"How about I come in and make you a cup of tea?"

"My apartment's a disaster zone."

"I won't judge you."

"I feel like a train wreck."

"All the more reason to let someone take care of you."

The refusal is on the tip of my tongue. I haven't had anyone over to my apartment yet. Push him away. Don't let him in.

But instead, I turn the key in the lock and open the door.

When I twisted that knife into Colgan's flesh, I realized that I wanted to live. *Really* live. Not the half of a life I've been leading. Not this dry husk of a life.

Besides, I'm too bone weary and high on painkillers to refuse his offer. Mason making me a cup of tea sounds like heaven.

"Whoa." His eyes widen as he enters the apartment, surveying the mess of my life. "You weren't joking."

I lightly punch his arm. "You said you wouldn't judge me."

"You've had a lot going on. Hullo, little fellow." Edgar sniffs Mason's hand. "A tripod, eh?"

I wait for Edgar to pronounce his disdain by presenting Mason with a view of his backside and running away.

Mason scratches between Edgar's ears, and he purrs loudly. He actually purrs. What's going on here?

"Edgar is letting you pet him."

"'Course he is. I'm good with my hands." He winks at me.

That cheeky humor of his. The way he sprinted down the beach, scooping up Bowie in his arms and carrying her to safety. The way he's looking at me right now.

"That's seriously weird. Edgar's a misanthrope. He hates everyone. Including me, most days."

"You seem friendly enough to me, eh, little fellow?" Mason drops to a squat, and Edgar purrs even louder, rolling over onto his back and presenting his belly.

"Wow. Okay. Traitor."

"I'm charming, admit it, Lake."

I wince. "Don't make me laugh. It hurts too much."

"Right then." He stands up. "Let's get you into a hot shower."

And I swear if my ribs hadn't been bruised, my throat nearly crushed, and my face battered, I might have invited him to take that shower with me.

53

LAKE

The next day I visit Bowie in the hospital. There's an armed guard outside her room. Suzie is scheduled to arrive in a few hours, but I want the chance to speak with Bowie alone. Her wrist is in a splint, her ribs are wrapped with bandages, her face is bruised, and one eye is swollen shut.

"We make a fine pair," I say as I add the rose-and-herb arrangement I brought to the riot of flowers on every available surface. The world has heard about Bowie Bishop being alive, thanks to Suzie. It looks like the whole world sent her flowers and get-well cards.

I have a vintage silk scarf tied around my neck to hide Ryan Colgan's fingerprints, but there's no hiding the cuts and bruises on my face.

Her smile is lopsided. "Lake. I owe you my life. The doctors said that if I had lost much more blood, if I hadn't received treatment for my injuries, I would have died in a matter of hours. Thank you for never giving up on me."

"I don't know if I'll be able to really explain what finding you means to me. Ever since your mother called to say that you were missing, I felt connected to you. I think because I was lost, too.

And finding you meant a chance of finding myself? It's difficult to put into words."

"Suzie will be here soon." Complicated emotions chase across her face. "I told her about the album. About keeping it all a secret. She doesn't understand why I did it."

"It's a lot for her to process."

"I did it because I want to be my own person. Is there a way for me to make her understand that without hurting her?"

"I wish I could tell you that there is. When I was your age, I left my small town in Alaska with so much unspoken between my mother and me. I thought I could ignore the silence, forget the hurt and anger, pretend it had never existed. But pretending your demons don't exist only makes them more powerful. I realize now that I can't avoid talking to her forever. I'm thinking about going back to Alaska for the first time since I left. It's going to be painful, though."

"All right." Bowie plucks some petals from the pink chrysanthemums on her bedside table. "I'll tell Suzie I refuse to wear leather halter tops and sing sexy pop anthems if you go back to Alaska and talk to your mom."

"Deal." Easier said than done. It's not only pain I'll find in Alaska. It's buried memories. Ones that have been clamoring at my mind, knocking insistently.

The knife in my hand. The thought that I'd held it in a desperate situation before, and not while I was hunting.

"Mark Edison's army of lawyers are already insisting that you were hiding out at his house without his knowledge. They're saying Colgan tracked you down and tried to kill you while Edison was away on a previously scheduled sailing trip."

"And his staff?"

"They're keeping quiet. He's paid them off."

She tears the rest of the petals off in one clump. "How could I have been so stupid? How could I have trusted him? I knew better. Myra tried to warn me not to trust older men. Suzie warned me about music industry dudes wanting to own me, my music. If I'd told her about Mark, she would have shut it down. That's why I didn't tell her. I thought I was breaking free from her, controlling my own destiny, and all the while I was building another prison. I'll never be able to trust anyone again."

"Oh, Bowie, you weren't stupid." How can I reach her? It's a lesson I had to almost die to learn. "Don't close yourself off like I did. I was so scared to trust, to love, that I wasn't fully living. Trusting is an act of bravery. And you're one of the bravest people I've ever met."

"I'm not, though. I'm terrified. Even with that armed guard outside my door. But I'm not going to let Mark go free, Lake. I swear to God. When I'm out of this hospital, I'm going to find Veronica, his ex-wife. If he really pulled the same shit with her, maybe she'll join me in pressing charges against him. We can stop him from doing this again. He left me with Colgan, knowing full well what would happen."

"Glen's under investigation. You might not even have to testify at his trial. I hear more witnesses have come forward. There's even talk about Glen's father, Bruce Walter the first, testifying. He's gone on record saying that he wants to establish a scholarship fund in his grandson's name. And Colgan is gone."

"I know." That flat look again in her eyes. "I was the one who . . ."

"Defended yourself."

We're blood sisters now. Like the bond I had with Charity all those years ago. We faced the darkness together. We lived to never tell the tale.

Although I don't know whether Charity's alive or not. It's one of the reasons I have to go back to Alaska.

"I'm going to write a song about you, Lake." She holds up her splinted wrist. "When I can play a guitar again."

"That would be an honor."

"Suzie is thinking about recording an album with Lance

Booker. She's hoping to revive her career. She's ecstatic because her version of 'Fly Home' is number one on iTunes right now. She says I should record more singles right away."

I give her a searching look. "And how will you respond?"

Bowie takes a breath, pushes her shoulders back. "I'll say that I need time to heal. And that I want to do things my own way. Maybe I don't want to be a singer. Maybe I'll just write the lyrics and let other people sing them." Her smile is tentative, but there. "Actually, I'm thinking of trying to stay in New Zealand. Attend university here. I love it here so much. Even after . . . everything." Her face darkens. "But Suzie won't understand."

"It's not going to be easy. She's a force of nature. But then again, so are you."

There's a commotion at the door, and Oliver and Byron burst through, talking over each other. "Bowie! There's a man with a gun by your door. You must be really important. Like the prime minister."

"Byron, Oliver, slow down! And don't hug Bowie. She's injured." Myra sees me. "Lake, we didn't know you'd be here."

I'm sure Myra had the same idea as me—a moment alone with Bowie before Suzie arrives.

"I was on my way out."

"Hi, Lake. How's Edgar Allan Three Paws?" Oliver asks.

"Grumpy, per usual. Which means he's perfectly fine, thanks for asking."

"Did you write a song about him yet, Bowie?"

"I haven't had the pleasure of making Mr. Three Paws's acquaintance," Bowie says gravely.

"Lake, before you go, I want you to hear this." Myra sets the flowers she's carrying on the last available table space. "Stuart is working very hard on something right now. He's attempting to have Mark Edison's visa revoked, since he never did apply for citizenship. He was here on an investment visa, and it turns out he's violated the terms on several occasions. He won't be living here much longer if Stuart has anything to do with it."

I catch her eye and smile. "That's good news."

"I was just telling Lake that I want to try to find a way to stay in New Zealand," Bowie says. "Attend university here."

"Really?" Byron exclaims, bouncing up and down. "Stay, Bowie! Stay with us!"

"Well, maybe not in your house. But I'd like to try to stay in Wellington."

Myra wipes a tear from her cheek. "That would be so wonderful, Bowie."

"If you stay, do you promise to write more verses for Marsh's song?" Oliver asks.

Bowie nods her head solemnly. "I swear."

Trills of laughter follow me out as I leave.

Sara visits me later that evening with a big container of homemade chicken soup.

Edgar hisses at her and arches his back.

"Aren't you a friendly guy."

"He doesn't trust strangers. But if you give him some crunchies, he might make an exception." Although he'd certainly taken an immediate shine to Mason.

"I made this soup for you."

"That's so sweet. Thanks for coming to check up on me."

"Everyone is talking about you at the embassy. How you searched for Bowie even when everyone else gave up."

"I couldn't let her go. I felt tied to her."

"I can understand that. Her performance at the arts festival was special. She's special. But what made you realize she might still be alive?"

"The suicide note didn't sound like her."

"So what's the real story on Mark Edison? Everyone has different theories."

"He kept Bowie prisoner in his house and then turned her over to Ryan Colgan. Colgan was going to kill her. Then I . . .

killed him." The shock on his face, staring down at the knife handle protruding from his body. I'd gravely wounded him.

Bowie had done the rest.

Sara avoids my eyes. "You need soup." She bustles around the kitchen, heating up the soup in the microwave and arranging it on a tray with some saltine crackers.

"This is delicious." I realize that I'm ravenous as I inhale the rich, vegetable-heavy soup.

"Mind if I have a glass?" She holds out a bottle of pinot noir she found in the kitchen.

"Be my guest. And pour me one."

"What did the doc say about alcohol?"

"I'm supposed to avoid mixing it with the painkillers."

"One glass." Sara gives me a good pour. "And what about that hot Kiwi police officer I saw you with on the news?"

My mind immediately travels to Mason's stubble-rough jawline. The warmth in his smile. Those huge hands holding me while we waited for the paramedics.

The shower not taken . . . yet.

"Aha! I knew it. You have a crush."

"I might."

"Eat your soup." Sara winks. "You need to build up your strength. He looks like he could be a lot to handle."

54

LAKE

"How did you know she was still alive?" Samantha asks with a probing look.

"I didn't. I had a theory. And I had this blind hope. Like you said, I couldn't accept that she was gone. I talked to Jordan Singer and learned why he accepted his curtailment without question. He was afraid of retaliation."

"He really loved it here."

"So do I." Though it would be untenable to remain here serving under an ambassador I suspect was involved in some of Glen's wrongdoing.

I'd risked my life for the brave young woman who could be his downfall.

"I need to tell you something, Lake. It's about Ambassador Hunt. A photo has . . . surfaced. I think you might know something about it?"

"Maybe. It was taken after the arts festival?"

"That's the one. An anonymous whistleblower sent it to Washington. The photo is blurry but it's enough to be incriminating. The young woman in the photo has come forward with a statement about the ambassador. He's been recalled. He has a matter of days to pack and leave."

I let out my breath, trying to keep from smiling. "I'm . . . shocked."

It wasn't me who sent the photo, but I have a pretty good idea who did. I'll find a way to ask Robin about it sometime when we're not in the embassy, or near any cell phones.

Being recalled is a good start, but I'll never rest until his potential involvement in Florica's death is investigated.

"There's also been an inquiry into the circumstances of Jordan Singer's curtailment. The allegations against him will most likely be proven false. If so, we'll offer him his old job back."

Shit. I wasn't expecting that. I'd thought I could stay here longer. "I'm happy for him."

"Which means you'd be out of a job."

"It was always temporary duty."

"I just sent an email recommending you to Ambassador Jennifer Valens. She's been confirmed as ambassador to the United Nations in Geneva, Switzerland. She's assembling a team of powerhouse women. I think you'd fit right in."

Ambassador Valens is a legend in the State Department. A diminutive, feisty career diplomat who gets things done and has been known to make grown men cry at staff meetings with her sharp tongue and exacting standards.

"Switzerland. Wow. I don't know what to say. I'm honored that you would put your trust in me and recommend me to Ambassador Valens."

"We need creative, tenacious people like you in the State Department, Lake. I'm honored to serve with you."

"And it's been my great privilege to serve with you." I'm struggling to hold the tears back. "And don't worry, I won't leave you with a backlog of cases. Jordan will come back to a clean slate."

"Take care of yourself, Lake. Take the time you need to heal."

Heron answers on the first ring. "Lake? We've been so worried about you. Mom told me what happened. Did you really stab a bad guy?"

"With my old hunting knife."

"That's freaking badass. I mean, I know it must have been traumatic and all that, but seriously, Lake, you saved that girl's life. It's amazing. The whole town is talking about it. I can't go to the grocery store without ten people asking me if you're going to join the FBI now and start taking down global crime rings."

I laugh. "Not anytime soon. That's why I'm calling. I have news. I'm leaving New Zealand. I've accepted a job in Switzerland."

"Switzerland? Shit. We were hoping for someplace closer. We miss you, Lake."

"I miss you, too."

"Have you told Mom yet?"

"Not yet. Hang on, I haven't told you all my news. I have a message for Dana. Tell her to order one of those god-awful neon-tangerine bridesmaid dresses in my size."

"Wait." There's a long pause. "Are you saying what I think you're saying?"

"Yeah. I'm saying that yellowy orange makes me look like death, but I'm willing to wear it for Dana."

"Oh my God, Lake, this is the best news! Dana," he shouts. "Lake's coming to our wedding!"

There's an excited squeal.

"And she says to order her one of those neon-tangerine bridesmaid dresses."

There's a soft laugh, close this time. Dana must have grabbed the phone from Heron. "The color is called poppy, Lake. And you're going to look lovely in it."

Far be it from me to contradict the bride-to-be.

"Ruth and Ray are going to be thrilled. This is the best wedding present you could give us."

"Here's the catch, Dana. I want something in return. Can

you squeeze out a grandchild or two so Ruth will stop guilt-tripping me about freezing my eggs?"

She laughs. "I'll try. I'm so happy. I can't wait to see you."

"Love you, sis," Heron calls.

"Love you both. See you in July."

The thought of going back to Alaska still terrifies me, but there's no avoiding it any longer. No matter how many countries I live in, how many stamps I collect in my passport, I can't escape my past.

And I made a deal with Bowie.

55

LAKE

I meet Mason at the crumbling mausoleum in Karori Cemetery a few weeks later. I want to see the Pōhutukawa trees in bloom. And for some reason I want to say goodbye to Dulcie Morris. She'd been hiding dangerous secrets in the cool interior of her mausoleum.

The brilliant bright red blooms are tipped with gold flocking. No wonder they call it the New Zealand Christmas tree.

We sit on the steps of the mausoleum, shoulders touching. A week ago we had that Friday steak night. He'd asked me what I thought of Aotearoa now, specifically its ruggedly handsome police sergeants. I'd told him I hadn't tried one yet.

He'd suggested we remedy that.

I'm still glowing. That's why this conversation is so difficult.

"Switzerland, eh?" He says it with an offhand tone but I can see the hurt in his eyes.

"They gave Jordan his old job back. I have to leave."

"You're a rolling stone. I understand. Don't get me wrong. I'd be much happier if you stayed. I like your . . . cat. Edgar. He's a lovable little guy."

My lips curve into a smile. "He is, isn't he?"

Damn it. Am I going to cry again? "We could have been good together, Mason."

"Yeah." He kisses my forehead. I wait for him to move to my lips. He doesn't.

"I'm going to ask you one more time: Have you thought about becoming a detective, though, Lake? I think you'd make a damn fine one."

"I don't want to carry a gun."

"Then move to New Zealand. We don't carry firearms unless it's absolutely necessary."

Move to New Zealand. "It's not that simple."

"I know. I'm mostly joking. That knife, though, the one they pulled out of Ryan Colgan's chest. Bloody hell, Lake. Maybe you really are Alaskan. You gutted him good."

"In self-defense."

"Like he was a moose."

Sometimes the only way to live with painful memories is to laugh about them.

"Can I kiss you, Sergeant Yates? Even though I'm leaving?"

"It's Mason. We don't take ourselves too seriously around here."

I kiss him under the Pōhutukawa blooms, the world filtered through scarlet and gold.

Later, in his cozy bungalow filled with books and home-brewing equipment, I lay with my head cradled in the hollow of his neck. "Mason?"

"Yes, my lovely?"

"Have you ever wanted to visit Switzerland?"

"Honestly? Never. I live in paradise." He waits a beat. Kisses the top of my head. "But maybe if Edgar sends me a personal invitation, I might consider it."

56

LAKE

Aria has a light, deft touch with a tattoo gun. Tasha from the Cat's Meow gave me her phone number, and I booked an appointment at the end of November, one week before I'm due to leave.

I'm leaving New Zealand before Christmas, but I'm taking a spray of red and gold flocked Pōhutukawa flowers with me on my left shoulder blade. Aria's already outlined them with black ink and now she's beginning to fill in the green shading of the leaves.

As the layers of abrasion and ink start to sting more and more, I think about hiding. Hiding from painful memories. From my past. Hiding from myself.

I think about how I've mended and patched over my brokenness with tattoo needles, each new country, each new piece of art a complicated layer of remembering to forget.

Searching for Bowie ripped me wide open. I can't hide anymore. Her songs have marked me permanently.

When I see these red flowers in the mirror, I'll see blood on my hands. Seawater swirling that blood away. Salt water in my wounds. I'll taste salty tears on my lips.

I'll hear Bowie's voice singing: *True, you can't see in the dark, but also true, it only takes one spark.*

I'll see beauty blooming over a grave marker for a young girl who died far too soon.

And I'll see Bowie twisting a blood-spattered knife deeper. Taking a life. Claiming her life as her own.

We are forged by pain, tested and shaped by it.

The problem with hiding from your past is that you can't do it without hiding from your life. This isn't the easy or the safe way—opening your heart. The urge to stay closed is an ever-present tide, tugging at my mind. It's been with me so long. It's whispered in my ear, ordered me to retreat.

I'm through with running. I want to make mistakes, love again, have my heart broken.

I want to make vivid, Technicolor memories.

I'm ready to face my past.

I'm ready to live again.

ACKNOWLEDGMENTS

I'm forever indebted to my amazing agent, Alexandra Machinist, who believed in this book and helped shape it—I'm so excited for this new chapter together! I'm enormously lucky to work with a dream team at Creative Artists Agency, especially Xanthe Coffman and Sarah Harvey, who gave astute feedback that made the book stronger. I'm so thrilled that this story found the perfect editor in Emily Bestler. Thank you for taking a chance on a different kind of diplomatic thriller. I'm hugely grateful to the entire team at Emily Bestler Books/Atria for their hard work, dedication, and support, especially Hydia Scott-Riley, Annette Sweeney, and Wren Watkins.

To my critique partners and beta readers—Charis, Maire, Rachel, and Neile—you have my heartfelt thanks and devotion. Gratitude and love to my talented siblings, Carl and Amelia, for collaborating on some of the song lyrics. All my love to my partner, Brian, and my extended family in Alaska and Wisconsin.

I've been the recipient of so much support over the last decade from readers, reviewers, librarians, and booksellers around the world. Thank you. I appreciate everything you do to spread your love of books.

The idea for this book grabbed me and wouldn't let me go

ACKNOWLEDGMENTS

while I was living and working in Wellington. I left a huge piece of my heart in New Zealand. Thanks to our Kapiti crew: Jen, John, Anna, and Regan, for the beach time, karaoke parties, tattoos, and steak nights. Esme, let's meet for wine words in Martinborough soon!

This book was written from the perspective of an American living in New Zealand. For more information about excellent mystery, thriller, crime, and suspense writing from Aotearoa storytellers, the website of the New Zealand Society of Authors, www.authors.org.nz, is a great place to start, in particular the list of Ngaio Marsh Awards finalists.